COX'S LUNGS
WERE BURNING...

...despite the augmented, oxygen-rich mix his computer pack was feeding him as he sprinted; he was sweating like a pig—sweating worse than his cooling system could handle. And, overhead, he heard a subtle change in volume that wouldn't be subtle for long: the pursuit aircraft, laying down rivers of flame as it did a one-eighty, had sighted him. It was coming back.

With the bogey on his tail and nobody to answer to, Cox hit his jet-assist. It was a one-time-only, emergency move, but there was no way he could outrun that aircraft, not on foot.

The wrench at his shoulders was immediate, the grab in his crotch comforting. And then he was airborne himself, skimming across the ground...

■ ■ ■

"Action sequences that would make *any* writer proud. OUTPASSAGE is a wonderful book."

—DAVID DRAKE

OUTPASSAGE

JANET MORRIS & CHRIS MORRIS

PAGEANT BOOKS

𝆑

PAGEANT BOOKS
225 Park Avenue South
New York, New York 10003

Copyright © 1988 by Paradise Productions

Cover artwork by John Berkey

Printed in the U.S.A.

First Pageant Books printing: October, 1988

10 9 8 7 6 5 4 3 2 1

To Anna Durkin

OUTPASSAGE

PROLOGUE

Fourth World Nightmare

THE SKY WAS thin and the color of dirty motor oil, except where it exploded above their heads. Concussion was delayed in the thin air but the smell of roasting rangers got to you right away, even through your air filters. The terraformers hadn't done much of a job on this classified ball of rock before the corporation workforce moved in, the shit hit the fan, and a request for military assistance followed.

The request wasn't denied, exactly, but it was rerouted to InterSpace Tasking Corporation's security division, who sent out a deniable reconnaissance team—thirteen US Rangers sheep-dipped for hazardous duty under the command of Colonel "Mad Jack" Reynolds.

It was Reynolds whose charred flesh was sending up the stink that made Cox gag as he dove for cover. Long Recon meant long odds, long dis-

1

tances, and long hitches, but nobody ever wanted to think it meant dying a long way from home.

Overhead, even through his flash-and-blast suppressing helmet, Cox could see the enemy coming in for another strafing run. Nobody ever thought the enemy was going to come at you with airpower, either, because there wasn't supposed to be any hostile force out here that *had* airpower.

In Cox's ear, Locke was screaming over the comset: "...suggest you form up for extraction, sir, at the beacon."

Cox huddled under an overhead of silicate, his rifle cradled against his chest and his knees pulled up, shifted enough to turn his head. "Reynolds?" he said into his com-mike, just to be sure.

But there was no way the barbecued officer lying beside him, charred limbs askew, was going to answer. The airpower came over and Cox covered his head: his helmet's recon pack had sent plenty of pictures already; he didn't need to risk his life for one more shot of somebody shooting at him.

He needed to risk his life to get to the extraction point, and that was about all he could handle. "Hey Locke," he yelled into his mike because the airpower was strafing what was left of Reynolds, "Reynolds is past it. I'm here by my lonesome." Rock exploded near him. Reflexively, he ducked his head in the shelter of his arms, eyes closed, and said as clearly and calmly as he could, "But I'm real ready for an order to get the fuck out of here."

"Then give it," came Locke's voice, laconic over the static and hard to hear because the sniper aircraft was coming back for another pass. "You're the only friendly voice I'm hearing."

"Falling back," Cox heard his own voice say, and

his body followed suit. He knew he was calling the roll as he got to his knees, then his feet, crouched under the overhang, listening hard for even a groan or a grunt in response.

But nobody came back to him over his com-link. Thirteen guys, and of the twelve on his com-link, Cox couldn't raise a single one but Locke. He was poised, his thighs cramping as he waited for what felt like the right moment to sprint across the scree, a mapping screen already punched up that gave routing overlays to his target—the extraction site.

But through the electronics, he could see Reynolds. Behind the colored grid with its pulsing points and alphanumeric displays, Reynolds seemed to be moving.

Sliding along the ground, almost. Cox didn't want to leave anybody behind that had a breath of life. . . .

He scuttled toward Reynolds, his pack scraping the roof of the underhang—scrambled close enough to see that not only Reynolds' left arm and leg, but the left side of his skull, was burned away.

"Shit." The shock of it propelled the ranger out from cover, along the computer-suggested track on his visor-display, as fast as he'd ever moved in his life.

But in the confines of his helmet, he knew what he'd seen: something moving; Reynolds moving. And he knew he was running from that vision, as much as from anything else here.

Because there wasn't anything else here. There wasn't anything but some kind of deep-space double-cross having to do with mining rights and racial hatreds spread across the stars. It was the gang bosses against the cheap labor, was what it was. There wasn't any alien life here, despite the security classification level of the planet designated X-31A, due to artifactual evidence. There wasn't any alien life anywhere, not above the vegetable level—a century in space had proved that beyond a reasonable doubt.

Everything that seemed artifactual had, eventually, turned out to be natural, not intelligence-made. There wasn't any reason for these IST honchos to be afraid of the boondocks on X-31A but the way they treated the contract laborers they'd trucked in here.

If Cox said different, he'd be in psych evaluation for the rest of his life—if he got off this shitball to have one.

It hadn't been anything, not anything, that he'd seen out of the corner of his eye. It sure as hell hadn't been a white, human-looking, delicate hand pulling Reynolds toward a wall of solid rock—coming *out* of a wall of solid rock.

It hadn't. His lungs were burning despite the augmented, oxygen-rich mix his computer pack was feeding him as he sprinted; he was sweating like a pig—sweating worse than his cooling system could handle. And, overhead, he heard a subtle change in volume that wouldn't be subtle for long: the pursuit aircraft, laying down rivers of flame as it did a one-eighty, had sighted him. It was coming back.

With the bogey on his tail and nobody to answer to, Cox hit his jet-assist. It was a one-time-only, emergency move, but there was no way he could outrun that aircraft, not on foot.

The wrench at his shoulders was immediate, the grab in his crotch comforting. And then he was airborne himself, skimming across the ground toward the extraction point where Locke's bird was already a dark speck lowering out of the filthy clouds.

Have to touch down before the transport does; got to watch his wash; wind-shear could crash him. You weren't supposed to do this—it was against every rule in the book; not jet to an extraction point: gave heat tracking to the enemy; gave random bad luck more of a chance to scratch you from the game-card.

He could still see the charred half of Reynolds' face, the eye like a lamb's eye that had popped up in his soup once during a Saudi tour. He saw it so clearly that when the enemy screamed overhead, ignoring him and going after Locke in the pick-up craft, it didn't bother him any.

Not even when Locke's VTOL exploded in a gout of dirty orange flame, because he could still see Reynolds inching along the rock like he was alive, that hand clamped on him.

And then he couldn't see anything, not for a long time, because something shorted his helmet's system and the ground hit him, hard, in the face.

Cox was sure he was dreaming again because you didn't sweat in a slow-freeze tank, and anyway, he had this dream all the time. Next, the enemy ship would land, like it hadn't—after taking out Locke's VTOL, which it hadn't—and lots of pale white hands would start dragging him inside. But he was getting better at dealing with the dream. He could feel the tangle of sopping sheets around him and he could feel the air conditioner trying to dry the sweat on his face.

Rehab was going to be pissed that he'd had the dream again, but he was getting better at stopping it—at least not letting it run its course, and that was something. IST was so nervous about the story of X-31A getting out that you weren't even supposed to dream about it.

He sat up, shivering and ignoring the tremors, rubbing his eyes with the palms of his hands. He was in a half-trashed motel room near the base, north of Boston, on the planet Earth, costing lots of people lost sleep and probably rating points.

He wasn't exactly AWOL, but he wasn't punching in and out, either. IST couldn't force him to do more than satisfy their question-and-answer people; he was still a ranger, off the duty roster only until IST certified him finished with their business and fit to fight.

If it took much longer, Cox was going to go talk to somebody in the Space Command about hurrying things up. IST brass might think they were buying him off with groundtime, but Cox needed more than a semi-isolated motel room and a couple of professionally concerned therapists.

Thirteen men had gone down to the surface of X-31A and two men had left alive. Now what had happened hadn't happened, officially—not on X-31A, an in-process terraforming project that had no need for a recon team, let alone US rangers borrowed from a government that hadn't yet officially obtained jurisdiction over that ball of rock. All mention of aliens or possible aliens or rumors of aliens had been squelched by IST, because aliens would bring the mineral-rich X-31A under immediate government control: either the US would claim it unilaterally as a territory, or the UN would win a suit to prevent American annexation and X-31A would fall under United Nations jurisdiction.

The cover story was something about a violent work stoppage by the Asian contingent of construction workers that Reynolds' men had happened to get caught up in. It was thin, but thin didn't matter unless somebody wanted to punch a hole in it.

And nobody did—it was three years later, groundside time. Families had been pensioned, pacified, where there were any. Recon teams like Reynolds' spent more time in slow-freeze (suspended animation) than they did doing the job they were shipped out to do. Even with superforce, space travel took its toll: Cox was physically under thirty, but his date of birth was fifty-three years ago.

Coming back groundside, you always felt the dissociation. They shouldn't have brought him all the way back here; they should have left him out at a Jupiter station, or somewhere his own kind were. These groundsiders were the real aliens. He couldn't make any connections with contemporary Earth—this wasn't the America he remembered. He hadn't been home for five of his years and thirty of theirs. Nothing made sense—not the society, not its music or its culture or its fashions or its morality. Not its drinks or its women, which was worse. When you came groundside, you were supposed to be coming home.

Cox hadn't realized, before, why so few rangers ever did. But here he was, because whatever had happened out at X-31A during the last three years was important to somebody—important enough to make sure groundsiders saw Cox's reports without any satellited risk of leakage, important enough to make sure that the stories didn't get around any ranger bars on Io or out-system.

Here he was, with a technical furlough he couldn't seem to end, with a credit card somebody'd given him without telling him its limit, and with nothing to do every day after his three hours in therapy.

And it was way too early for therapy. He peeled the soaking sheets from his body, got out of the motel bed, and went to his window. Pulling back the blackout curtains, he watched the light-sprinkled night. He could call room service; he was still well within his per diem. He could get dressed and go out, if he wanted—nobody followed him around. At least he didn't think so.

He went to the closet and looked in at what hung there. The weird civvies made him too uncomfortable—brightly colored see-through shirts, body-hugging pants and coats with padded shoulders like armored vests. His therapists had bought them for him, telling him that wearing them would make him feel "like a part of society." Well, he wasn't, not of this society.

He resisted the urge to go back to the window, stare up at the black sky, and reach for a couple more tranks. They gave him all the tranks he wanted; custom drugs that made it okay that this was taking way too long and stopped him from worrying that it might never end.

He'd never wanted to live on Earth, in a city, in a motel room. When his tour was done, he'd figured to get something out-system, somewhere he'd see open skies and others like him. This was what he was protecting—Earth and the US in all its teeming complexity, but you didn't have to live here. You didn't even have to like it.

You had to serve it, and then it would take care of you. That was the bargain he'd made.

He sorted through his closet, thinking he needed a little flight time, and got out his flight gear. He'd go out to the field and get a plane—rent one, if he couldn't scrounge one. Cox needed to get a little closer to the stars.

Then, if he still wanted company, he could hit a base bar or something at Hanscom Field, where he could get away with wearing out-system gear, not feel like a freak. Once he'd zipped into his coveralls, he reached reflexively for his workbelt with its combat weapons.

His hand stopped. That was what they didn't want him to do, though no one had suggested taking his hardware away from him—not more than once.

Finally, he let it go at slipping a laser-guided pistol into the pocket of his loose all-weather coat and a force-knife into his boot. Never could tell when you might need a little edge.

But he didn't go out after all. He put his hand on the doorknob and his fingers began to shake. He stood there for a minute, head down, thinking about pushing himself out the door. But his hand looked too pale and too delicate and it didn't have the right amount of hair on it—in fact, it had none.

He went back to the bed, his coat still on, sat down and surveyed his room. He wondered, one more time, where Locke was and whether IST was doing the same thing to him. If he could find Locke, he'd feel better. He reached for the com-unit beside his bed, flipped up the screen, and began punching numbers.

But instead of the base liaison office, he got a computer dating service by mistake.

The pretty girl (despite the garish painted dragon on her face) said to him, "Thank you for calling Dream Date, sir. I'm Merry. If you'll give me your customer number—"

"I don't have one," he said, conscious that the woman had big blue eyes that weren't at all dismayed that he hadn't shaved or showered in thirty-six hours. "I'm sorry. I got the wrong—"

"Oh, wonderful, a new client!" She broke into a broad and welcoming smile. "Well if you'll just give me your credit card number, sir, we'll be able to get started right away by issuing you a temporary customer number."

She looked at him expectantly, with an eagerness that told Cox she'd get some extra money if he did what she said; and if he didn't, he'd have to disappoint the first person of the opposite sex who'd looked at him like that since he'd come groundside.

"Okay, yeah." He reached into his hip pocket, got out his card, and read her the number.

After she'd looked away to punch it in, she glanced up again with approval in her eyes. "That's fine, sir. Now, if you'll answer some questions as to what sort of man or woman you'd like to—"

"Woman," he interrupted.

She blushed. "Yes sir, Mr. Cox. Now, if you'll just give me the profile data on the sort of lady who's your dream date, we'll be able to give you an immediate read-out of possible candidates. Should you like any of them, a date can be arranged as soon as both parties find it convenient."

He didn't know why he was doing this, really, except that it seemed a shame to disappoint her, and maybe it would take his mind off things. Maybe it would stop his hands from shaking. Maybe a woman was what he needed.

Damn, he *knew* a woman was some of what he needed, but finding a hooker with a clean health certificate might be a better way to go about it.

Except that he'd had chances to do that, and passed. Or blown it.

He didn't have to go on any dates, he told himself as the woman named Merry with the dragon on her cheek asked him personal questions in a pert way that was somehow flattering, not offensive. They probably wouldn't have anybody in their banks who matched his "profile" data. He wasn't exactly Joe Normal.

But it was something to do, human contact of the non-crucial, non-pejorative sort. And it beat the hell out of looking for a fight to pick in some seedy bar to see if IST would bail him out one more time. Or if they'd finally admit that they couldn't handle him, no matter how badly they wanted to keep him on ice, and let him go back to the rangers, back out-system where he belonged.

CHAPTER 1

Computer Date

———◆———

IN THE IST tower on Route 128, Paige Barnett's boss was God. She profited to some degree by the reflections of his aura: she was the administrative assistant of one of the world's—the universe's—most powerful CEOs, Raymond Godfrey.

When God spoke, not only on Route 128, in Massachusetts, and up and down the Northeast Corridor, but as far away as Alpha Centauri, people listened. But God had a wife and children, a mistress, and a company he loved more than any human: InterSpace Tasking Incorporated.

God didn't see Paige as more than a finely tuned and valuable piece of equipment, although he did consider her that: "Invaluable," he was saying now.

In his corner office, overlooking the Silicon Necklace and the carefully preserved green areas bordering it, the tall once-athletic executive paced before his desk, hands in his hip pockets, his jacket off, his stylish tie discarded, his sleeves rolled up. His wide, high brow was wrinkled; his glasses had slipped down on his nose.

Paige knew all of these mannerisms to be signs of concern, and she crossed her legs primly where she sat in a chair before his desk. She'd thought she was here to give him background on the impending inspection trip off-planet; she'd prepared notes for him on what was hot and what was not throughout the solar system—and beyond, in case God decided to extend his itinerary. Working for Godfrey for six years had taught her everything about this man's nature except an acceptable way to express her feelings.

"Invaluable," God continued in his rumbling voice, "to the extent that anyone can be. But Paige, I can't take you with me. Not this time."

"I never assumed—" But her voice was so choked he paused in his circuit of the room to peer at her from under his old-fashioned glasses.

"I know you didn't." He smiled his most professionally encouraging smile. "I'm going to be gone for at least three months, however, and I want you to take some time off—a paid vacation until I get back."

"I can't do that!" She shot to her feet. "With both of us out of the—" And she stopped because she saw something under that paternal smile that was hard as nails and distinctly out of place with her: this was a direct order; she must not disobey it. "Yes, all right, Mr. Godfrey. I'll bring in a temp, train her for a week, and then go."

"Tomorrow," said Godfrey. "I'm leaving tomorrow. You'll leave too. What do you think we have senior vice-presidents for?"

She shrugged, realized she was standing, started to sit down, hesitated, and at last said miserably: "Do you still want me to go over these notes with you? For your trip?"

"Yes, please. And relax, my dear. This is a bonus, not a punishment." His southern drawl peeked through the northern intellectual gloss for a moment; a bit of Texas showed around his eyes.

"Yes Mr. Godfrey, I know."

"Come on, Paige." With an unpremeditated step forward, he caught her hand and squeezed it warmly. "You're the best person I've got here at headquarters. I don't want to lose you."

"Lose me? You couldn't. I mean—" He loosed his hold on her hand and she retrieved it, clutching her computer pad.

"Oh, I could. Somebody from Washington might grab you, or from one of our competitors. If that happens, no matter the perks or the raise, you come to me. I'll outbid anyone, hear?"

Paige nodded. She didn't understand why God was behaving like this. There was something else, some hidden agenda; she knew him too well not to know that.

And then it came, as he suggested she sit back down and she settled in her seat: "I've been working you too hard," he said. "Or else you wouldn't feel the need to do all this digging into the X-31A thing. I'm not going out that far, and the matter's closed. At least it's closed to you unless I can get you a security clearance. Do you understand, Paige? There's nothing out of the ordinary in the X-31A file; we're going for certification as a territory at the normal rate. You don't need to keep this office apprised of every glitch out there—in fact, I wish you wouldn't."

So that was it. She'd seen a memo from security

that they were putting together another paramilitary team for X-31A and so she'd pulled the whole file and queried some of what she'd found. Then she'd abstracted recommendations and put them on God's desk.

One of those recommendations was that he, under no circumstances, visit X-31A personally, since the unrest there was so unremitting. When she'd written it up, she'd enclosed a dissenting opinion from an analyst who suggested police forces would only exacerbate the situation: that the Asian workforce was so at odds with the technocratic Anglo elite on-planet that a full-scale uprising was imminent. Some sort of cult had grown up among the workers, a cult who believed that the planet had indigenous inhabitants and IST was violating holy—and alien—sanctuaries. It was, in short, a very expensive, very sensitive mess.

But she'd been trusted with data as crucial, with matters as sensitive, in the past. Her mind raced. It must have been her recommendation about the policing that had done it—made Godfrey wonder if she wasn't overstepping her authority.

Political errors in the corporate world can be deadly. She stuttered: "I...I...I didn't mean to push, sir. I just wasn't sure if you were completely informed. When we're working so closely with government interests...I needed to know that you knew what..." She was just making it worse. She found her knuckles near her lips and bit them.

Godfrey didn't move to rescue her. He simply watched, letting her realize how close to irremediable had been her error and how far out on a limb he was, protecting her—all without uttering a word.

"Let's forget it, shall we? If you want to transfer

to analysis, we'll have to run some clearance procedures." He smiled now, a life-preserving smile.

And she knew just what to say: "No sir, I don't. I'm perfectly happy where I am. Working on whatever is important to IST—and you." She hated herself, but she could kiss ass with the best of them. At least the ass she was kissing was the best around. And the thought of losing Godfrey—her job, her access to him, her IST perks—was truly terrifying. She didn't have a life, outside of the company. She identified totally with its mission: making new states for America among the stars.

"Good. You always know what I want to hear, Paige. Now, let's get on to regular business. Start teaching me what I need to know about Copernicus and Einstein bases, and about Io. Think we can get that much done before lunch?" He shot a look at his atomic watch.

It was a tall order; she riffled the computer pad's keys. "I think so, Mr. Godfrey, if we hold all your calls," she replied, feeling the courage come back into her as IST's CEO put himself, at least for the next hour, totally under her control.

When she left his office, his secretary shifted the gum in her mouth out of her cheek and said, "That was a long one, Paige. Can I send his calls through?"

"Sure. Yes," she said, and headed for her own office. In it, she put down the computer pad and stretched out in her chair, tilted back, arms danging, feeling the wetness no deodorant pill could dispel. That had been close.

Raising her arms, Paige laced her fingers behind her head and peered blankly at her memo screen. The cursor was blinking. Slowly, her eyes focused.

She giggled, then laughed out loud. Dream Date had left her a message. After two weeks, they'd found someone for her. She reached out to let the data play, then paused.

She hadn't been serious about the computer dating service; she'd been depressed, bored, and angry. She'd done it, in fact, on a dare.

She tapped a colored square set into her desktop. "Hey, smarty-pants, come on in here."

The person who'd dared her to call Dream Date answered, "Okay, two shakes."

Paige eyed the screen, then got out her compact and looked at herself: sensible, short hair, natural brown; no make-up but silver above her eyes and lip gloss; a reasonable pseudo-tan. The face didn't give her away, although her above-average height and muscle tone might have, as anything more than a personable young female executive on the move. Once she'd complained to IST's second vice-president that she couldn't find any interesting men to date, she'd made up outrageous qualifications when the VP had pressed her as to what was "interesting."

Then, she hadn't been facing a three-month vacation. Then, she'd just been protecting her hidden, torrid, and fervent devotion to God, whom she could never have. And squelching office-borne rumors of something more going on behind the kola-wood doors than dictation.

Now, Paige was tempted. Godfrey had let her know that she was expendable; he'd violated her loyalty by questioning it, by telling her there were places not only in his personal life, but his business life, where she couldn't go: where her input, her attention, her abilities weren't needed—or wanted.

"Jill," she said when IST's second vice-president waddled in, fat and motherly at forty. "Look at this. Guess you've found me my dream lover after all."

Jill Ekberg was VP in charge of project development, liasion—which meant she interfaced with the military and other branches of government. "Terrific, dear..."

Jill came around and peered at the screen. "But where's the read-out?"

"Oh," said Paige airily, on impulse and because, if Jill knew, Godfrey was bound to hear, "I already looked at it—I'm going out with him tonight, if he's able." Sitting upright, she typed in her acceptance, a proposed time for her date to pick her up, and sat back, eyeing Jill boldly.

"What's his name?" Jill asked curiously.

"It's my secret, for now. But he's perfect. Just perfect, if he's everything his printout says."

"'Handsome, dangerous, sensitive, intelligent, well-traveled, experienced, with great prospects and an active imagination; ready and willing to encounter the unusual'—right?" Jill quoted Paige's date requirements from memory.

They'd giggled together, making out the sheet. "That's right," Paige teased in return. "I crossed out 'dangerous,' though—too likely to get me a pen pal in prison."

"You never can tell. Well, I've got a lunch." Jill patted her on the shoulder. "Have a wonderful time, dear—and on your vacation too, if I don't see you before you leave. Ta-ta."

Speechless, her enthusiasm dashed, Paige watched the doors sigh closed behind Jill's wide, tweedy buttocks. News traveled so fast around here, it could make you nervous.

Then she remembered that she hadn't looked at

the profile of her date for this evening, and dialed Dream Date. By the time she got through, the other party had already confirmed and accepted her suggestion that he pick her up at eight at her place, "ready, willing, and able."

CHAPTER 2

Ready, Willing, and Able

———————◆———————

COX STOOD BETWEEN two sets of closed glass doors and let the security cameras look him over. An overhead monitor showed him what they saw: a ranger in a raincoat with crow's-feet around anxious eyes and tension lines around his mouth. His hands were in his pockets. He couldn't seem to smile for the camera.

He said into the grille, when it demanded ID in a woman's voice, "Cox. If this is Paige Barnett, I'm your eight o'clock, remember?" That was how she'd put it—eight o'clock, not twenty hours, and he noticed things like that. Like he'd noticed that she lived closer to Hanscom Field than to Boston, on the Silicon Necklace; like he'd noticed that in her datapull it said, under employment, *major interspacial corporation*. And under her preferences, *adventure*.

He shuffled his feet in the pause before the buzzer sounded, thinking that, if she liked his looks at all, he could certainly give her some. He'd planned for it, surprised at himself, as though it were a foray. Whatever interspacial corporation she worked for, he was willing to bet that her job had never taken her an inch off the ground. He was going to do a lot better than that.

The pause was too long, though; maybe she'd changed her mind. He ran his hand through his overlong brushcut, thinking she'd seen his picture, like he'd seen hers.

And then, with a crackle that clipped the first word, the grille told him: "—ome on up, I'll only be another minute or two—door's open." And the buzzer sounded, allowing him to push through.

Cox took a look back at the rented sportster he'd left at the curb and at the buzzer panel that listed her apartment. Then he headed for the elevator, hands still in his pockets, whistling. His therapists thought this was a great idea. If he got laid at the end of it, it would be. Even if he just had a good time with her—if she liked the flight plan he'd filed—he'd be winning.

So why was he so nervous? The computers had matched them up; she wasn't going to look at him and faint—she'd seen him, had his vital stats on tap. Maybe it was *because* some computer had decided they were compatible—computers screwed up all the time. Or maybe it was because his therapists were so goddamned happy about the date. Or maybe it was because the high-rise whose elevator he stepped into was so fancy, so high-security, so moneyed.

Whatever this Paige Barnett did for the corporation she worked for wasn't limited to making coffee. Cox leaned back in the swanky, wood-paneled elevator and let the cameras scan him, his right hand curled around the ten-millimeter belly gun in his pocket to mask any signature the surveillance gear might pick up otherwise.

When the elevator opened at her floor, he blinked. Before him was a glass-block alcove that had only one door opening off it, and that was ajar. Paige Barnett's apartment was the only one on this whole floor.

He stepped out of the elevator, through the alcove, and into a room the size of a small airport, full of eye-teasing effect lighting and post-modern furniture.

"Hello?" a woman called from somewhere down a pink hallway.

"Hello yourself," he said reluctantly, hearing the thickness in his voice, there whenever he had to raise it.

"I'm back here," she called again.

He knew that. He was fingering a rock sample on a presentation stand, one of several, and thinking there was still time to back out. The computer had made a mistake—this woman's idea of adventure was probably solar sailing with a bunch of her corporate buddies—or using chemicals as recreational drugs that Cox would have shot his way out of a security facility to avoid.

He turned to leave, hesitated, pausing before the display cabinet, the sample still in his hand. All he was risking was rejection. So he'd find out he didn't belong in groundsider society—so what? He knew that already. He conjured up the image of Paige Barnett that Dream Date had shown him; it wasn't as if she wore iridescent contact lenses or anything.

But he wasn't ready for this. He'd tell her he was sorry when she came out dressed for the Boston Symphony, and let it go at that. He didn't need encounter therapy. The only person he wanted to encounter was Locke, and he hadn't had shit for luck, trying to do that.

He was about to put the sample down on its stand beside the others on the fancy shelf when he heard her moving around and glanced down the hall.

She was smiling, striding toward him, one hand out in a practiced gesture. And she was just as advertised: nearly five-foot eight, slim and athletic, with a bright smile and hair almost as short as his. Not a hint of druggie or vamp about her, just a clean and sweet-smelling woman in a form-hugging purple dress that showed off her legs, waist and breasts enough that Cox felt a tremor of physical recognition run over him: a functional member of the opposite sex, all right.

She swept down on him like a gust of fresh air; by the time he'd taken her hand she'd come up on tiptoes and kissed him on the cheek.

Startled, he looked her over again and then realized she'd been talking to him for a while.

"... sorry, I tried not to be late, but today was my last day at work before vacation, so I had to clean off my desk. Are these clothes all right?" She stepped back, turned with unpremeditated concern. "I mean, for wherever we're going?"

"Fine, I guess." It was the first response he'd made and it came hard. He'd have preferred her without clothes, by then. "I filed a flight plan ... after I read your printout. Couple hours, up the coast ..." He shrugged.

She looked at him unblinkingly, waiting for him to finish. When he just watched her breathe, she said softly, "Well, maybe I should change, then? Into something more like your—"

"I'll get you coveralls at the base. You're fine for dinner ... Paige." She was standing close enough to touch and he wanted to take her arm, for starters, but didn't quite dare.

"Good," she smiled again, brightly. "Let me get my purse."

She threaded her way around the sectional, picking up her things. Cox turned away, looking again at the rock samples, hefting the one with a pale vein which he thought might be titanium-bearing. When, from behind him, she said, "Are you a rock hound too, Dennis?" he nearly dropped it.

"Me, no. But I run into this kind of thing sometimes." *No*body called him Dennis, but she'd gotten his data from a computer card; she wouldn't know that.

She slid her hand under his arm and it was resting in the crook of his elbow so smoothly he didn't know how it happened. "Sometimes when you're working? We gave almost the same job description, did you notice?"

Somehow they were moving toward the door. "Yeah, that's so. Look, I don't want to pry..." Cox didn't want *her* to pry.

She took her hand from his arm to lock her door and punch up the elevator. "You're not. I'm an administrative assistant at IST. That's where the rocks come from—terraforming projects."

The elevator door slid open; it must have been waiting there. He ushered her inside like he hadn't done since a high school dance. IST? He was supposed to return the confidence, obviously. Maybe she already knew. Maybe this was some kind of setup.

"Where's that rock from?" Cox asked quietly in a voice that Paige Barnett didn't know him well enough to take as a warning. "X-31A?"

"What?"

"Nothing. Sorry. Fishing. I work out-system, mostly. This is the first time I've been back in ... a long time."

But she'd heard what he'd said; there was a

shadow over her smile. "Out-system? Then do you work for us? We're the biggest—"

The elevator door opened to reveal people there. She changed conversational gears, saying, "It's going to be such fun, flying up the coast. When I logged on to the dating service, I was bored to tears. Everybody I know does the same thing I do; we just talk shop. And Dream Date didn't seem to have anyone for me. I mean, this is the first meeting they arranged for me. How about you?"

"First time for me too. I haven't been groundside long, remember?" Again he was wishing he hadn't gotten into this. Out the doors, and into the German sportster. He'd rented the fastest ground-effect machine he could find, but she wasn't impressed. Just took it for granted.

And she was so direct; she kept surprising him. She was too rich for his blood, that was certain. She crossed shapely legs in shiny hose and he cranked the car away from the curb, watching the rearview mirror. Even so, he nearly cut off the silver sedan pulling out behind him. He waved at the driver in apology but the man didn't respond.

She was asking him how he'd chosen Dream Date.

"I was calling a friend of mine and got a wrong number. Then it seemed like a harmless thing to do. Then I got your data, and..." Again, he shrugged. He wasn't used to this kind of small talk.

"You didn't tell me when I asked—about your affiliation. Some military, right? And then corporate? If you're from one of our competitors, a spy sent to pump me, let's get it on the table so it doesn't ruin our evening." This time her grin was disarming and yet challenging: this was the real Paige Barnett, some sort of executive female.

"Cox, 203rd Ranger Battalion, Space Command;

I've sheep-dipped for you people. You know what that means?"

"I...paramilitary, right?" Light splashed her face intermittently from the oncoming traffic.

"Sometimes."

"That's why you know about...rocks."

"That's why." He wheeled the fast little sportster up the on-ramp, punched up his destination pre-set, and watched as the map came up on his wind-screen. "That's us," he pointed to one blip, then another. "That's our destination. We've got a few minutes to change our minds. I'll take you home, no sweat. Call it a misfire. You said you didn't like shoptalk." Although the idea of fucking one of the people involved in getting his recon unit blown to bits was tempting, it was probably more trouble than it was worth.

"What's wrong?" she asked, honestly confused, hurt in her voice.

"What's wrong, lady, is that I really thought this wasn't part of any rehab or debrief program, and I'm pissed. I don't need my ashes hauled that bad. So—" He slapped at the control panel and the routing display disappeared. "I'll just take you back to your place and you can tell your people I wasn't amenable to coerc—"

"*Hold on*," she said in a voice accustomed to command. "I didn't know anything about you, if you'll recall. It's just an unhappy coincidence, I think...I'm sure."

"You don't sound sure." He had the car on manual now and it was risky to spend so much time looking at her face, but he did.

"I resent a number of those implications—more than whether you'll 'get your ashes hauled.' I just got aced today—a three-month vacation I didn't

ask for. My boss is Raymond Godfrey..." She
broke off and bit her lip.

He whistled. You didn't live in US space and not
know that name. "I'm sorry, I'm not used to it
down here. And that *was* a piece of X-31A in your
apartment, what with that much titanium in
the—"

"Look, I don't want to talk about X-31A. It's
what got me my vacation."

"It's what got me grounded, baby." He couldn't
help telling her. He'd never been close enough to
one of these bastards to get a chance to say what
he felt. "You people shipped us in there with no
fucking concern for what withholding that much
data was going to do to our survival rate. You
know that out of the thirteen of us, two came back
and I can't find the other one? You think hazard
pay and pensions make up for that sort of shit?
You think I appreciate being boxed by your medical people and treated like some kind of psycho
with delayed stress when there's nothing wrong
with me that going back to work won't fix?"

He got hold of himself, stopped talking, his
hands aching on the steering wheel. His therapists
would be proud of him, unless he strangled her
here in this car like he wanted to, cut the clothes
off her and taught IST something about the value
of human life.

"God did this," she whispered. "It's no kind of
coincidence. How could he do this to me?" She was
talking to herself, not to him, and her knuckles
were as white as his own. She looked at him then
with fear-pinned pupils. "What are you going to do
with me?"

"Me? I was going to take you to dinner and fly
you up the coast," he reminded her—and himself.

"Look, I'm sorry I got hot with you. You want, I'll take you home. Otherwise, I'm still game for the rest of this. You're right, it's probably no coincidence. But what if it is? And, if you're telling me IST's giving you a hard time too, maybe we can help each other—figure something out."

"Like what?"

"Like how come every move I make in this buggy, that silver sedan does the same?" He inclined his head toward her. "Want to eat? Or go home and see if he comes too?"

"Ah...eat," she said, her shoulders squared, leaning forward to look in his rearview mirror. Her breast brushed his arm as she did so. And this time the heat of her burned him like fire.

A civilian date was something scary; this, he could handle—whether she was here on IST's behalf, or the car behind was here because she wasn't, it was an opportunity to strike back at a target Cox had thought was out of his reach—if he wanted to take it.

And if he didn't, and she was just as advertised, she still knew people. If he asked her nice, maybe she could get his file closed and convince IST to return him to the military. At the price of dinner and three hours' worth of flight time, it was a cheap shot.

CHAPTER 3

Off-Base

———◆———

THE BAR SERVED food of a sort and the man across from Paige Barnett was trying his best. Dennis Cox was frighteningly intense, especially in this place right out of some adventure video, where men who'd never heard of salad forks staggered over a sawdust-covered floor to the flight simulator games and huge amounts of money changed hands over the outcome of silicon dogfights.

He hadn't said another word about X-31A or his problems with IST; it was as if the conversation in the car had never taken place. He'd waltzed her in here, obviously pleased at the stares and snickers and low comments her dress evoked. There were other women here, but of a very different sort.

The volatility of the place was palpable and Cox's confidence in his ability to handle anything that might come up made him seem very sexy. Among this crowd, he was right at home, known and respected, her ace in the hole. She had serious doubts that she'd get out of here unmolested without him; the way the waitress draped herself over him made Paige feel proprietary.

"I hadn't known there was anything like this near the Necklace," she remarked over her first drink, before she'd tasted it.

"I asked you at the door if you thought you could

handle it. I don't come here much, but the food's better than you'd think."

He didn't go anywhere much, she was beginning to think. And when he did, it was to places like this, where port workers caroused and off-duty pilots decompressed and the pictures on the wall were all taken off-planet.

When they'd parked under the neon solar system sign, Cox had helped her out like a gentleman. Then he'd leaned against the sportster's fender while it grumbled, cooling itself and venting hot air around her ankles. Finally she realized he wasn't waiting for the car to finish cycling—he'd already locked it—but was watching the parking lot entrance, his hand in his raincoat's pocket. A fine drizzle was falling and at last she'd said, "Acid rain's terrible for human hair. Can we go in? Unless you've changed your mind?"

He hadn't. And she'd thought, negotiating the slippery stairs and flinching in the face of the rank smells and the noise, that real adventure wasn't as much fun as she'd expected it to be. Then she'd chided herself for lying: she was excited; her pulse was beating fast; the man beside her was obviously comfortable in this element, one she'd never have dared explore alone.

Dennis Cox was exactly what she'd asked Dream Date to provide her: enough over six feet that she didn't feel tall; physically fit in a way the men she met never were, no matter how much squash they played; a pilot and Heaven-knew-what-else although she could guess; handsome in a weathered, severe way with large, intelligent gray eyes and a mouth that changed his whole face with its expressions. If she couldn't "handle it," now that she was outside the shelter of her corporate world, Paige ought to admit it to herself.

She could barely handle the drink he'd ordered
for her. Whatever it was, she'd never heard of
it—it was a military drink, or an antique drink,
and it spun her head in two sips so that she leaned
forward, elbows on the table, and nudged her glass
with a finger.

"You drink this all the time?" She tapped the
sweating glass.

"Nah. Don't drink most of time." His fingers
moved from his glass, half-empty, to hers, and one
of them ran along the back of her hand. "Right
now, I got nothin' better to do."

His voice was a little slurred, or her hearing was
affected. He picked up his glass and finished it,
then slapped it down on the table, his eyes taunt-
ing. "So? Want more?"

"I—we're going to fly after this?" But she lifted
her own glass and bolted the contents. By the time
she returned it to the table, she was seeing a
ghost-image and he'd signaled for two more from
the bar.

When the drinks came, they tried to order food.
She could barely read and it struck her funny that
she couldn't figure out what to have. He helped
her, the waitress left, and suddenly there was
somebody else there—*two* somebodies; men who
obviously knew Cox because they pulled up chairs
in a rush of jargon she couldn't follow.

Cox was slouched over his second drink and his
large eyes seemed to be swimming as he glanced
her way.

One of the men was saying, "...so if you want to
sign on, you gotta do it now. Tonight. We're counting on you, Det."

Her ears were really giving her trouble: it was
Dennis, not Det, across from her. Dennis Cox
leaned forward, elbows seeming to splay and,

looking at his glass, said, "Gonna need a lil' help. Gotta lady to fly..." He grinned but there was something wrong with his face.

Paige propped her chin carefully on her upraised fists, arms bolstered on the table, and tried to study the two men who'd joined them. One was big and uniformed; *what* uniform, her eyes wouldn't focus enough to tell her. The other was big and out of uniform, and this one was saying something to her: "...want to come along, you just sign this, honey. Wouldn't want to separate you two, not until you got what you came for."

She didn't know what he was talking about, this stranger, but she knew she was expected to sign the paper he held out with the pen the other man handed her. And thumbprint it. She did it, because she was supposed to and because Cox did it too and because she was desperately concerned that none of the three men realize how impossibly drunk she was—so drunk that, if she didn't know better, she'd think she'd been mixing alcohol and drugs.

She couldn't have stood up to save her life until one of the men told her to, and then her body obeyed as if it belonged to somebody else. Cox was standing too, and there were lots of arms to lean on, and she never did get her dinner.

But right outside, pulled up to the bar door, was a big silver sedan and its door was open.

CHAPTER 4

Fourth World Shanghai

———◆———

PASSAGE OUT-SYSTEM TO the Fourth World always felt the same, no matter if you were in a troop carrier debarking from an orbital station based around Io or on a commercial shuttle from groundside to low orbit. It felt cheap, it felt rough, it felt crowded, bumpy, uncomfortable and ominous.

And it felt real normal to Det Cox, even though he couldn't figure out why he was sleeping through everything but the correctional burns. He was skunked out of his mind was why, he decided finally when the transatmospheric vehicle around him shuddered hard enough to wake the dead during a docking maneuver. TAVs didn't space-dock like that, so he knew they were putting down on a surface somewhere.

Christ, where? He really must have crashed himself this time, wherever the hell he'd been decompressing. He couldn't remember anything since Earth . . .

He crooked an elbow over his eyes as a bright light came on, letting his other senses do the walking. He could smell body odor, leather, gun oil, and that acrid mix of must and mildew that always collected in troop holds like this, no matter the best efforts of air purification systems.

Guys stank when they were stacked three high

on yard-wide bunks for up to six months at a time; the smell got in the mattresses and in the blankets and in the lockers. And you couldn't get men out-system without transiting them from the inner planets the hard way: in hypersonic TAVs or Orbital Maneuvering Vehicles (OMVs), space trucks under chemical-burn and slingshot power.

Cox had no doubt that he was still in-system: he wasn't waking up cold as ice in a poly-cocoon with his throat raw from breathing the odorless, ultra-pure air of a slow-freeze tank. Therefore, the ride was just beginning. Ride...ride to where? He shifted the arm over his eyes and his chest began to rise and fall more rapidly: how come he couldn't remember where he was going or how he'd gotten here?

The last thing he recalled with any clarity was the off-base bar on Earth, where he'd taken his blind date from IST, Paige Barnett ...

No, that wasn't the last thing. It was just the last coherent thing he recalled. Then there'd been some guys with a venue to offer, the regular papers to sign, a car ride with them and the woman....

With the woman, Paige Barnett. Jesus Christ. He did remember bits and pieces: the silver sedan, some back hangar and an argument he wanted to give those guys about the woman but couldn't get out of his mouth because he was on some kind of drug-induced autopilot. Scopolamine? Pentathols? He thought it might have been something like that. Or designed obedience fixers. Tough stuff.

Not that he minded being sought out and signed on—somebody besides himself thought he was wasting his time on Earth. But it wasn't legal, or, if the paperwork was, the way they'd gotten him—and her—to sign it wasn't.

That couldn't be right. He *couldn't* be remembering that Paige Barnett had been helped up the same ramp he had, struggling with a pack she could barely hold, let alone understand. His lips quirked, behind the shelter of his arm. If it weren't so radically bad, it'd be funny: a woman like that shanghaied onto a troop carrier as a first timer.

Well, that part didn't have to be true: he'd had plenty of crazy dreams. She was probably back in her office making coffee, and his "memories" no more real than the white hand dragging Reynolds toward the solid rock wall on X-31A.

For his part, he was glad to be out here—wherever here was. Even if somebody'd bent the rules. He vaguely remembered that one of the two who'd collared him had known him well enough to call him Det, and had all the moves: the right uniform, the right mission parameters (if he could just remember what they were), and his heart in the right place.

Maybe the 203rd had decided they wanted him back, and screw IST. There were guys in military intelligence who wouldn't blink at pulling a scam like this—the "you want him; you got him" kind of guys that briefed you when all the briefing you were allowed was a verbal given fifty miles above your target of opportunity.

Still, it wasn't right—something wasn't. Maybe it was the way the TAV had docked so damned hard. This wasn't any scheduled commercial carrier on which ten or twenty like Cox were booked steerage; paying passengers wouldn't stand for this kind of bounce and jounce. And he could hear creaking and bitching as, around and above him, men slid off their bunks and grabbed their gear from lockers.

Cox stayed where he was, not moving a muscle, his face hidden under his arm, until all the noise of leaving men had ceased. Then he took his hand away, unbuckled his crash harness, and sat up.

He could put his feet on the floor, that was something: he had a first-level berth. There was a slot against the wall with his ticket in it. He pulled it out, then let it fall back. They had his name wrong. The serial number wasn't his. The destination wasn't given in anything more than high-security designators, and nobody had briefed him as to what or where X-66B might be. Beyond Jupiter, that was for sure. And "X" unigraphs always meant trouble.

Well, trouble was what he'd been trained for. He just wished he'd been sober enough to ask the right questions, or drug-free when he'd been recruited.

He really didn't want to get angry. There was probably a good explanation, even for doping his drinks, if that was what happened. He could already hear the one about name and serial number: if IST hadn't agreed to let loose of him, it was the only way he could have gotten off-planet, no matter who wanted him.

So he had somebody to thank for that part. And there were maybe eleven other guys in this shit-hole cabin who'd been glad enough to sign on to whatever mission Cox had joined—none of them were chained to their bunks or trying to chew their way through the decking—they'd gone to mess, or to a transfer tube.

He ought to too. He tried to stand but his legs were rubbery. His head spun. He sat back down, head in his hands, and breathed deeply. Hell of a hangover. Maybe the trip was just starting. He rubbed his jaw. Not more than a week's worth of beard, maybe less.

Come on, suss it out. And get off your butt. He took more deep breaths, lowered his head between

his knees, then raised it and did some quick iso-
metrics, forcing adrenaline into his system. When
he reached back to take his ticket out of its holder,
the room didn't twirl.

He stood up more cautiously and didn't fall over.
Needed to get his space legs back, was all. Gravity
was real light, part of why he felt funny. Maybe the
moon, then; or Lunar Orbital Station. If it was
LOS, he had plenty of time to bitch and there was
brass here to bitch to—if it seemed prudent.

He slapped his locker open and a regulation kit
was waiting for him there, weapons and all from
the heft of it. Before shouldering it, he slid his nail
under the vacuum seal and peeked in, hoping to
see his personal stuff—his workbelt, his custom
pieces.

They gleamed back at him dully and he
shrugged into the pack. Still in the locker were a
black jacket and combat helmet, and though the
name-tag matched his ticket, they'd got his sergeant's rank right. Somebody'd gone to a lot of
trouble and he told himself he ought to appreciate
that.

He also told himself, as he velcroed his boots on
and headed through the lock into an unfamiliar
corridor, that he'd better be quiet about how much
he didn't remember until he was sure that admitting the gaps in his memory didn't get him
grounded—sent back to the waiting arms of his
IST therapists, to his motel room ... to Earth. For
all he knew, somebody'd discussed this mission
with him at length and in detail.

Thinking about that possibility, he got goose-
flesh as he followed the red line amid the multicol-
ored ones on the corridor floor, helmet under his
arm: red lines always got you to the next mess or
the debarkation lounge.

Alone in the scantily-lit corridor, listening to his boot heels clank on the floor, he began to remember the uniformed man in the groundside bar saying, "So if you want to sign on, you gotta do it now. Tonight. We're counting on you, Det."

And there'd been something about Locke. Either the guy had been Locke, or had said something about Locke. He couldn't get it clear. But one of the two big guys had been a ranger captain from black projects, he was almost certain. At least, he'd been led to believe it.

So it was okay—it was his team, anyway. He was moving with more muscle in his stride, almost accustomed to the gravity change, when he came to the end of the red line and saw maybe thirty guys formed up for transfer. You didn't chatter in a transfer line; you put on your helmet, checked your pack oxygenator, hooked in your hose, and listened for orders.

It wasn't an exposed planetary or satellite surface they were debarking to, he was reasonably sure—nobody'd been issued pressure suits or armor. Not yet. Out of longtime habit, he reached back and slid his workbelt from the pocket in his pack, then settled it on his hip.

The worst thing he'd probably encounter in that tube was a pushy stranger or a rent in its pressure membrane, but you couldn't be too careful. By the time he could see the tube's insides over the shoulder of the man in front of him he had his gloves on, his jacket sleeves mated to them, and his radio up and running, in case there was anything on the air he ought to know.

What he heard was, "Welcome to Cerberus transit station. Please proceed immediately to Gate Nine. That's Gate Zero Niner."

"Shit," Cox muttered involuntarily in his helmet,

and the man in front of him gave him a visor-down stare. He'd been out of it longer than he thought, long enough to have missed the lunar stopover.

But somebody'd cleaned him up there, moved him, stowed his gear. Because he didn't have a month's beard, and because he realized now this was a ranger transport he was leaving: Cerberus was a ranger staging area, highly classified, in the asteroid belt. Which meant this was some sort of weird superforce jump mission, if it wasn't staging from Io.

Damn, he wished he could figure whether it was cool to admit he didn't remember a fucking thing about what was going on.

But if he asked, and it turned out that this was a "sealed orders" outfit—that nobody knew squat, yet—he was going to make a fool of himself. And, what was worse, he'd badly shake the confidence of the men around him, many of whom he outranked. And he might need their trust.

At least he wasn't going to have trouble with remembering the assumed name somebody had picked for him: on his helmet, and on the tape over his heart, the legend said *Det*.

CHAPTER 5

Rude Awakening

————◆————

WHEN PAIGE BARNETT was sure she wouldn't start screaming, she took her knuckles out of her mouth. The movement jostled the horrible, filthy black man squeezed next to her, and he bumped the Asian on his left. The disturbance ran down the whole bulkhead, eliciting a multilingual stream of invective that made Paige want to clap her palms over her ears.

But she'd learned in this endless interval of transit that one didn't move any more than was absolutely necessary. There were three hundred people packed into the hold of this ship and none of them was any more comfortable, or any happier, than she. The food was bad, the heat and stench intolerable, and the toilets a nightmare. Washing was out of the question.

And there was no one to complain to: no one, at least no one she could find, was in charge. The dark, cavernous hold was a Tower of Babel; Third Worlders from every impoverished nation Paige had ever heard of, and some she hadn't, made up her traveling companions, every one of them headed for a better—or different—life in the Fourth World, the out-system colonies.

Almost no one spoke English, and those who did spoke it so badly, or with such heavy accents and hostile attitudes that Paige had given up trying to make conversation. Early on, she'd attempted to slide her way through the crowd, to the big conveyor belt that wound through the center of the hold, a rubber, ever-moving strip on which bad food came and went.

But she'd nearly been raped; she'd been shoved and brutalized because places nearest the food were the most prized. She'd crawled back to her bulkhead and wept.

How long ago was that? She didn't know. She didn't have her Piaget watch anymore. She didn't have her purse. She didn't have her ID, her credit cards, her company card. She had a paper bag with a comb, toothbrush, and a punch card in it. On the punch card was plenty of information in binary, but only one notation in English, the printed information: Smith, f, 28, w; "cbh."

After days of wondering, she'd decided that "cbh" meant "clean bill of health."

She kept telling herself that eventually someone in authority would come within shouting distance and she could begin rectifying this gigantic error. She kept waiting for a well-groomed face to appear and solicitously peer down at her with profuse apologies and an outstretched hand. She was still waiting for that moment.

She'd run out of tears, she'd run out of energy. She'd lost weight and she knew her night-vision was going from lack of vitamin A, because the horrible tableau before her was getting dimmer every time they turned on the lights to simulate "day."

She wondered who "they" were, and fantasized about her revenge, once she found out.

A tremor ran through the horde—that was the only way she could think of these animals around her, living in each other's filth and jabbering in their polyglot tongue. The strongest men surged forward as bread began appearing on the conveyor belt.

Paige didn't try to join them. Usually, the black man beside her grabbed enough, eventually, for them both. She didn't thank him when he handed her a share—he merely had no wish to spend the rest of this interval next to a rotting corpse.

Three people had died that she knew of, but she'd never been awake to see the bodies removed. The lights would go out; you'd fall asleep—a heavy, sweet-smelling sleep—and when you woke, the corpse would be gone. An efficient system, but one that always ran late. By the time the corpse was removed, everyone was gagging on the smell. So they tried to keep each other alive, most of the time. Or the smart ones did.

The black man came back with bread, and handed her some. She'd given up trying to teach him English, too. She'd given up everything, in fact, except fantasies of what would happen to the culprits when she got out of here.

And thinking about Cox—she still thought about Cox: if he was involved, if he'd set her up for this intentionally. She thought about that night repeatedly, the last night she remembered clearly until she'd awakened here, soiled and worse.

She thought about Cox and she thought about Godfrey and she thought about Jill Ekberg and she wanted to kill them all.

She wolfed her dry bread and picked the crumbs from her smock. Not until she was finished with every one did she realize that the timbre of the sound in the hold had changed. There were vibrations coming up through the floor, shaking her very bones. There was a slow wave of stifled hysteria running through the mass of passengers.

And then, with a shudder that shook the bulkhead against which she leaned, the entire hull began reverberating with noise. It was so loud and so painful that Paige elbowed for room to clap her hands over her ears. People screamed. The noise got louder, the vibration more pronounced, more frightening.

People were beginning to panic, to lunge back and forth, to try to find somewhere to run. But there was nowhere to run. The black man beside her knew that. He put out a hand protectively, making a barrier between her and the people milling, now, before them.

She pressed herself back, away from his touch, away from theirs, into her filthy corner. She knew what was happening, and she knew that the most frightening part of it was that no one else here seemed to understand.

The cargo ship she was in was either making dock somewhere, or breaking apart. The former would be relief of one sort; the latter, of another. She'd rather die quickly in space than be trampled to death by the crazies around her, who couldn't adapt to anything or understand anything, or they wouldn't be here, failures from the Third World hoping to make a last-ditch stand in the Fourth.

She closed her eyes and prayed it would end quickly. End either way: dead was better than this, and space was indubitably cleaner than this metal coffin in which she'd been buried alive so long her hair had grown out. If she survived, there would be colonial officials who spoke English.

There had to be—InterSpatial Tasking was the largest single employer of manual laborers off-planet, in-system or out, she reminded herself.

Abruptly, where the conveyor usually emerged from the wall bearing food, a blinding light began to shine. An ear-splitting screech accompanied the expanding light as huge bulkhead doors drew back. A hull-to-hull dock!

An automated voice began telling the workers in the hold to "Proceed double-file through the door. Take the first empty cubicle you see and lie down flat. Do not be concerned. Robots will assist you," in first English, then Spanish, then another language Paige didn't recognize.

But she recognized what she was seeing and her heart sank: there wouldn't be anyone to complain to, no human in charge—at least not for a long time; not where Paige was going. She'd been present at the meetings that IST had held concerning "bulk slow-freeze of workforces" and she remembered how the new system worked.

She remembered, because one of the executives had remarked, "So what if we lose one out of ten of 'em? It's quicker, cheaper, more efficient to ship 'em fully automated—we can even charge them less, which means they owe us less. They never work any of it off, anyway. And what kind of casualties are we talking about, anyhow? Beaners, niggers, slants, wogs, and white trash."

She'd lowered her eyes that day demurely, feeling uncomfortable at having heard something she'd have to forget having heard. The automated slow-freeze system saved millions; allowed the transfer of workers more quickly and efficiently, and even with the human-assist systems, there was a risk of lost life, of people dying, unrevived or unrevivable, because of mechanical failure. Or human error.

At least there'd be no human error, she thought, trying to stand and finding her knees wouldn't hold her. On a cargo ship like the one to which her group was transferring, the only human life, besides cargo, stayed on the flight deck or in the few scientific mission suites. She wouldn't have to worry about someone purposely trying to monkey with her slow-freeze—to kill her.

There was no need for anyone to do that. Automated slow-freezing in bulk was available only on the new superforce jump ships that IST was experimenting with. And you didn't haul workforces by jump to close-in terraforming projects.

Again, Paige tried to get to her feet. This time, the big black man's hand closed around her elbow. She shot him a grateful look, having borrowed his strength. For the first time he smiled at her, showing small, yellow teeth. He wouldn't be smiling if he knew where they were going. Or perhaps he didn't care. But she did.

Superforce jumps were only necessary for distant, exploratory destinations—for out-system hellholes like X-31A. The pilots of the ship she was staggering into line to board were being paid quadruple their normal rate for flying jumpships because three out of the ten IST had launched had been lost in space.

And because, once you got a strong human contingent in a quadrant, you didn't have to boost from Earth's solar system: you got what you needed from neighboring mining or scientific or cultural colonies.

Stumbling into line with the black man's hand still on her arm and the computer's voice droning unintelligibly in her ears, Paige Barnett made her way toward the slow-freeze tank and the frontier beyond.

CHAPTER 6

Staging Through

———◆———

COMING UP OUT of the poly-cocoon when his alarm beeped, Cox felt almost normal. He checked his metering and hit his casing-lift button like always, when readouts told him there was air out there and power—that the ship around him wasn't derelict. They left that fallback for the slow-freeze transiters: if you happened to wake up in a ghost ship, you could use your cocoon like an ejection pod, hit the "homing" button that activated coordinate presets and started emergency beacons howling, and go back to sleep. Maybe somebody'd pick you up, or maybe you'd make an orbit on your own.

It happened that way sometimes, although it had never happened to Cox. There probably wasn't much of anything out here in the way of aid and comfort if it had happened this time—not on the far side of a superforce jump to an X-venue.

He knew little more about X-66B now, six months later by groundsider clock, than he'd known when he woke on Cerberus. But he knew who to ask. He'd bumped into the mission commander, a Captain Wiley, during embarkation, and been told to report to him after slow-freeze. Wiley had clapped him on the arm and given him a knowing look and somehow made Cox feel a whole lot better before he climbed into his cocoon and punched the canopy down for a long winter's rest.

Cox could see other guys up and dressing as his cover lifted, and the air that came rushing in was moist and warm. Reaching up with both arms, he grabbed the canopy assist bar and chinned himself up and out of his pod, bracing for the icy contact of bare feet to bulkhead. It came and went like a cold shower.

He dressed from the locker under his cocoon, zipping into sergeant's coveralls that said Det on them, took two stabilizer tablets from his pharma-kit because he still had some hangover, and punched up a wiring diagram of the ship so that he could find Wiley's stateroom. Commissioned officers usually had staterooms on higher decks, and Wiley was no exception.

Having absorbed the routing diagram, Cox slipped into his workbelt and boots and stood up, nearly bumping into the man standing there waiting to be noticed.

Wiley's aide was pale and freckled and he said, "If you'll come this way, Sergeant, they're waiting for you."

It really wasn't reason enough for everybody in the slow-freeze room to fall silent and stare, but it was a far cry from normal, so what could you do? His face impassive, Cox let his gaze sweep over the two dozen rangers watching and said casually, "As you were, girls," then followed Wiley's aide out through the hatch.

He didn't blame them for staring; he was new to them, had some rank, and they probably knew less than he did about the approaching mission. If that was possible.

Wiley's cabin was upper-tier all right, and Wiley

was sitting in it at a round table with three men out of uniform—that is, in quick-tab pressure coveralls without any service designators, nice black ones of the kind ranger battalions only issued for special service because they cost too much, even though they upped your survival quotient in a depressurization emergency, the most common kind in space.

Wiley, facing the door and Cox's perfunctory salute, nodded infinitesimally. "Sit down, Det." And returned his attention momentarily to the card game in progress and the other three men at the table. "Now that the sergeant's here, we can get on with this." He put down his cards and leaned back in his chair.

By then Cox had taken the only vacant seat, opposite Wiley, and was trying to keep his cool. One of the men in the pressure suits was Locke and Locke was watching him back, poker-faced.

"You know Lieutenant Locke, Det," said Wiley, who looked exactly like a balding beaver in fatigues.

"Sort of," Cox said. Locke had got to keep his name and wasn't in uniform, so what did Cox know about this guy, anyway? Locke was one hell of a pilot, that was what. He'd saved Cox's life on X-31A. Cox added, unstiffening, "I was wondering where you'd got to."

"I bet," said Locke, lounging bonelessly in his chair, a clean-cut, even-featured towhead who didn't seem one bit the worse for wear after X-31A. "We're going to do it all over again, I hear," Locke said with his pilot's knack for maximum articulation in a minimum of words.

About then Cox realized no one was going to introduce him to the other two, who had "spook" written all over them and who could have passed for brothers of the two guys who'd doped him and signed him on to this mission.

When Wiley said to the darker of the two big men, "Whenever you're ready, Captain," Cox was certain it was the same man who'd been in uniform at the Solar System Bar and Grille.

"Here we go, then," said the unnamed captain in the black pressure suit, pulling a memo card from his sleeve. He had that ultrawell-bred born-officer look and real pale eyes, startling against tanned skin and black hair. "Det, thanks for putting up with all this bullshit." A smile tweaked his thin mouth. "We'll bonus you for it, the best we can. You and Locke are the only guys we know—the only military personnel—who've seen the so-called aliens and lived to talk about it—"

"To talk sense about it," amended his counterpart, whom nobody'd named or spoken to, and yet seemed to Cox to be in charge. Maybe it was the way he sat, so relaxed, or the way he interrupted "the captain."

A room full of brass was always trouble, and Cox's eyes asked Locke if Locke thought the two of them had any business being up here. Locke's answer was to light a cigarette and stare at the flame.

"Right, sir," said the captain in black who wasn't Wiley. "To talk sense about it. We've got the same situation here on X-66B—or we think we will, if we're not careful."

"How's that?" Cox asked because that was what he was here for, unless he was here by mistake—to ask questions and get his mission definition clear. "On X-31A, we were attacked by workforce rebels with expropriated hardware, near as we could figure. You mean there's a revolt down there on . . . ?"

"X-66B, Ranger," said No-name, square-jawed

and clear-eyed and the end of everybody's reporting chain, Cox was now sure. "This is a policing
action; we're replacing the bulk of this workforce,
but what happened on X-31A can't happen here.
Understand?"

Locke shifted in his seat, turning his cigarette in
his fingers. Cox looked from him to the captain,
then to Wiley, and said, "No, I don't. What happened on X-31A's a mystery to me, at least what
happened after we left it. Remember where you
guys found me—nobody's briefed me but you."

There was a long pause in which Cox went
through hell: if these guys *had* briefed him back on
Earth, he'd just admitted he wasn't fit for anybody's mission—that he didn't remember squat.

The captain in black said, "That's right. My
error. Cox, after your team got smoked down there,
it got lots worse. Total revolt. Alien rumors became alien-worshipping cults. We scratched every
worker on the planet and brought in new ones. But
somehow this 'holy ground, alien sanctuary' crap
got started all over again on X-31A. And somehow
it seems to have spread to here—to X-66B."

Cox couldn't find anywhere to rest his eyes so he
closed them. Shock wasn't something he usually
felt. But scratch a whole population? Start over?
Because of hallucinatory white hands pulling
Reynolds into solid rock? He didn't know why, but
he said with his eyes still closed, "X-66B's got some
of the same geological structure, I guess—from the
unigraph and the designator similarities?"

"We don't think that's pertinent, Ranger," answered No-name and Cox opened his eyes.

Locke caught them in his and shook his head
"No."

"Sorry, sir," Cox replied to the unnamed briefing
officer. "But I saw something down on X-31A too.

You must know that—it's why IST wouldn't let ... This X-66B, is it an IST holding?"

Wiley entered the briefing: "It is, but IST doesn't know you as 'Det.' So they don't know you're a vet of X-31A and you don't tell them. And don't dig deeper than you need to, Sergeant."

"Just what I need, is all I want—to do my job."

"Your job," said the captain in black, "is to confirm or deny this alien presence business while you're supposedly part of the policing force on-planet. Can you handle that? We already know Locke can."

"Yeah, well, Locke just flies 'em," Cox said before he could stop himself. "With new guys? A green team on long recon? Undercover, yet? I don't know. What have I got for weapons, leeway, logistical support? What happens if I find something— aliens or crazy revolutionaries trying to promote a legend of aliens ...? That's two very different things."

"Very good, Det," said the nameless honcho. "You solve the problem, which I'm defining here and now as any element contraindicating a successful colonization effort. You'll be in at the beginning, almost—there's not much down there but techs, terraformers, and the beginnings of a workforce. We want this incipient problem solved before it becomes a real one. If there's some underground among the workforces running a game on us, we've got to make it too expensive for them. The US wants X-66B as a territory; IST wants it as corporate bastion, and the 203rd wants to even up the score for X-31A. Clear enough?"

Cox looked doubtful. "I just run recon teams."

"That's what you'll do, Det," said the captain in black. "We'll give you whatever we can. You and Locke are the only two men we've got who have any idea what we're fighting down there. As we said, we don't want a repeat of X-31A. And we don't want to explain anything to your men. Rumors, we don't need."

"What about IST? They don't know about this? Me?"

"We told you, no," said Wiley, Cox's putative commanding officer. "Not beyond their request for policing units. And you don't tell IST anything more, or let them find out. These two gentlemen," Wiley gestured to the pair of briefing officers, "went to a bit of trouble to get you out here without IST's knowledge. If IST's methods are at the bottom of this, we need to know that too. Does that answer all your questions?"

It didn't but it was going to have to do. "Yeah, I'll make up a shopping list with Locke, if that's okay?"

"Fine. You're both excused. We'd like your list," said the captain in black, "by nineteen hundred hours. We won't be available after that." He held out his hand and Cox shook it, then offered his to the other unidentified official.

There was too much callus in that handshake to make sense with the pecking-order here and the man said, "Come back from this one, Sergeant. I really want to see your report."

"Yeah, you bet," Cox promised and by the time he'd reached the door, Locke was right behind him.

Outside it, they looked at each other soberly and then Locke punched him playfully in the gut: "Come on, Det, let's go get skunked and compare notes. Christ, I'm glad you were in there."

There was something forced about Locke's manner, but Cox chalked it up to the draining tension: nobody wanted to sit in on meetings like that, let alone be the focus of them. Those guys in there were asking the dubious, if not the impossible. It was hard to tell them "yes sir" and "you bet sir," especially when you hadn't even scoped your men yet.

But with or without Cox's okay, they were going to drop him on X-66B with those guys he'd co-cooned in with, so what difference did it make how he felt about it?

The difference it made, he decided when he and Locke had found the mess and hunkered down over their beers, was that nobody was telling him there weren't aliens anymore.

CHAPTER 7

Work Camp

PAIGE BARNETT DREAMED about the landing at Morgan base long after she'd arrived there. In the dreams, she knew she'd died and gone to hell but that didn't make the fear any easier to bear or the shocks any duller.

She'd dream she'd waked, as she had in reality, from slow-freeze, stumbling and numb, to be herded into one of the drop trucks with only a respirator and an extra pair of coveralls to her name. She'd lost her paper bag with the comb and tooth-brush and she kept trying to go back for it but nobody would let her. She'd lost the big black man too—in fact, in the dream, she was sure she'd never see him again.

She was herded into the truck's cargo hold and she

found a seat on a slatted bench, cinched her harness, and strapped her respirator over her nose, just the way she'd done during the real drop.

But there all reality vanished from the dream. In the dream, there were *things* under the slats of her seat—crawly things and clawed things and gooey things among the filth collected there through the years. In the dream she lay down full-length on the slat and peered through them and she saw a horrid little creature like a wizened wrestler with a horny snout instead of a mouth, trying to burrow into the filth and the mulch and the writhing life there under her seat. Then it turned and looked up at her and opened its jaws malevolently. She started cursing, in the dream, as loudly and as quickly as she could because, in the way of dreams, she knew that if you cursed it horridly enough it couldn't get you. She cursed and yelled and screamed and then she chanted "Go a-way; go a-way," because that was what you did, to save yourself from the creature.

The creature was going to attack her otherwise, come right up through the slats and bite her on the behind and that would be the end of her, so she chanted for her life. And the creature, trying to get away from her chant, burrowed deeper until it burrowed into the steel beneath the mass of organic horror—through the spiders and the worms and the mulch.

Even though, when she woke, shivering, she was safe in a workforce tent on the frontier planet's surface, it always took her a long time to recover after the dream. Her heart would be beating fast and her throat as raw as it had been when she'd emerged from the bulk slow-freeze. And then she'd sit up, groping for her flashlight, to make sure there wasn't any *creature* under her cot.

The real drop hadn't been like that—the horror had been more muted. She'd had the breath squeezed from her; she'd been subjected to intense cold and barely-survivable depressurization. Her ears had felt as if someone was forcing litres of water into them and her eyes as if they were about to pop from her skull. Some had died, in the cold dark of the drop truck—hemorrhaged because they weren't strong enough to take it, or because they panicked and failed to use their respirators.

She thought, sitting cross-legged on her bunk a week after she'd arrived, that perhaps the black man had died that way. She missed him. She missed the transit hold, as well. The only thing she didn't miss was the bulk slow-freeze tanks, because she'd been so frightened.

She was frightened now, but it was a different kind of fear. She was Smith, no first name, work number XB340248. Smith had made too many waves when she'd been in the processing line at Morgan Base. Smith was an English speaker, where only the staff spoke English. Smith had thrown her extra coveralls at a foul-mouthed work boss with a cattle prod and demanded to be taken to the highest official in charge before she'd realized what that could mean.

Smith had looked around her, gasping in the thin air, up at the cobalt sky that never lightened, and then down at the thin soil and sparse brown grass that anchored the purple mud at her feet and raged. She'd looked up at the naked, jagged mountains that made Morgan Base cost-effective, at the sprinkled lights of oxygen-processing stations and mining facilities and terraforming platforms and, closer to hand, at the squalor of the workforce tent city, and she'd rejected all of it.

She'd caused so much trouble that three grown men had been necessary to frog-march her off to the commandant's office, a permanent facility of prefab composite. In it, under a naked fluorescent, she'd told her story to an impassive, pasty-faced man with a rolling gut who'd tapped a stylus against his lips and told the ruffians who'd dragged her into his presence to "wait outside. She's not going anywhere."

When she'd finished, the workforce commandant's aide rose ponderously from his plastic desk and strolled to the window, scratching the crack between his buttocks without regard to the presence of a lady.

Then he'd turned and said, "Listen here, Smith or whatever your name is, let's get some things clear: I don't know, or care, if you're telling the truth. It doesn't make any difference how or why you signed your contract. You signed it. You're here. Unless you can reach into your pocket and pull out enough spare change to pay for your round-trip, plus whatever prep charges are against your account, you're here for your whole tour. We could send a query back—if I believed you, which I don't—but it'd take six, eight months to get to Earth, and I'd have to pay for it. Which I won't, without a real good reason— better than you've given me. Plus, there's the elapsed groundsider time since you left: if you had a job, like you say, you don't have it anymore. Now, if you speak anything besides English, I could get you into liaison, if you make it worth my while."

The sexual innuendo was unmistakable. Paige shook her head.

He said, "That's what I thought. Listen up, then,

lady: you're just more workforce slime, as far as we're concerned. The reason these projects aren't wholly automated except for tech crews is real basic: you eat, you shit, the shit's great fertilizer. You carry bacteria of all sorts, the interactions of which are too complicated to bother reproducing through technology. So you're here to tote that bale and, if you're lucky, push some paper while your human-body factory does its little bit to aid the terraformers. You die here, that's even better: we can plant you, and it's real good for the soil, human mulch. You should know all this if you're what you claim to be—some hotshot from IST headquarters." Now the sneer he must have been suppressing for the entire interview broke out as he leaned his elbows on the windowsill and said, "So if you want me to go to all the trouble of checking out your story, you come back when you've learned the facts of life. Maybe you can convince me to send that query for you. Until then, we'll put you up on Knob Hill, where it won't matter that you're an English speaker."

She hadn't understood how bad a mistake she'd made until much later, as the ground trucks came and went, carrying workers to their billets. When numbers began to be called for the Knob Hill trucks, hers was among them. And someone came up to her and gave his condolences in broken English, a tall, thin man who handed her a card that said, *Worker Joachim Sanchez.*

The card was a smudged xerox. On it were some numbers. She said, "What's this, señor?"

He had graying temples and a hawk-nose and as he leaned closer, she could smell the rankness that bad diet had given his flesh and breath: "If I can help up there, señorita, give me a call."

Then she realized what he was: workers' union. She almost threw the card in his face but that was an old impulse prompted by the part of her that still was a loyal IST employee.

She got out the card now, in the dark, and read it again in the light of her flashlight. Then she shook her head and put it away. He'd want the same sort of incentive that the commandant's aide had. She wasn't going to let this place turn her into a zombie like the people around her. She was going to get out of here. She already had a plan. Knob Hill was a high-risk area because of its physical location: on a sheer cliffside, the workers tended heavy equipment. The noise and the dust kicked up by the drilling was horrendous. The dust, she knew, was necessary for greenhousing, as much a product as a by-product. But she coughed all the time now.

There was a chance, though, up here that she wouldn't have had below: the terraformers' headquarters was up here. The tech barracks, hermetically sealed, was here too. There were people in them who were English speakers, perhaps even some Americans; certainly someone, among the host of them in the bureaucracy, whom she could convince to help her. She had enough insider knowledge to convince another insider it would be not only prudent, but an opportunity for advancement worth taking, to notify Raymond Godfrey that his lost administrative assistant was alive and unwell at Morgan Base.

She kept going over the plan in her mind until her chest stopped heaving, but she couldn't go back to sleep. Not and have the dream again. She slipped off her cot and padded through the rows of fitfully sleeping workers. There were so many that their body heat had warmed the tent, and when she slipped through the outer seal into the night air, the cold hit her like a wet towel.

She gasped and hugged herself. And realized she wasn't alone out here. On the rock shelf that extended from the plateau was a knot of people talking in low voices, crouched against the livid dark, silhouetted in the dust-diffused light of the tech center across the chasm.

There were no guards patrolling this part of the work camp because there was no exit but a sharp, killing drop to the reservoir under construction hundreds of feet below. The fences and the guards were all over to the east, where a road had been cut out of the mountainside.

She stood listening to the rumble of voices, unable to make out the words. She told herself she was shivering because of the cold, that she should have put on her respirator and her other coveralls, that her agitation had nothing to do with a surreptitious meeting on the promontory by night.

Overhead, a triangle of lights left the tech center —a police VTOL or a tech bird—flying in her direction. It was hard to tell how high it was, but she could hear its roar already, and it was getting louder.

Impulsively, she headed toward the gathering on the shelf, not knowing whether she'd be welcome or not. There were two hundred workers up here, only a few of them new. They had a society of their own and they didn't exactly welcome you into it with open arms. Your mistakes could kill them, if you were at the right machine and pushed the wrong button. Still, she had nothing to lose and somehow she didn't want to be alone in the open when that bird came over.

There'd been rumors about surveillance; there were guards who came tearing through the tents on unscheduled head-and-bed checks, two kinds of guards: IST lifers, and rougher men, men Paige was sure were paramilitary—professionals looking for trouble to stop before it started.

She'd read the proposals; she knew more about what those hard young men with the weapons were looking for than most of the distraught men and women they turned out of bed on surprise inspections. And knowing what she did about unionization and IST's stand against it, she was out of her mind to head for that group on the shelf.

But she did. She was too angry and too frustrated and too bored not to. She skulked through the jumbled rocks, glancing up repeatedly at the sky to make sure the bird wasn't going to sweep down on them before she reached them.

When she was less than ten feet away, the bird came directly over and none of them dove for cover. They just stopped talking and sat very still. Smart.

When the bird had gone, they began talking again in the polyglot she was beginning to pick up, but hadn't yet mastered.

"...holy mother of...praise...every soul...holy father of...praise...every soul..." she heard them say together.

And since it was some sort of repeated chant, and among the voices was one she was sure she recognized, she kept inching toward them, curious, lonely, and somehow unafraid.

When she was almost upon them, the chanting stopped and one voice said in Spanish simple enough for her to follow, "To business, now, Jadeesh. We have fifty—"

Her foot hit a rock and every head there turned.

She was close enough to make out five men and two women, and a blanket covering a flashtorch. She froze, thinking they'd listen, hear no more, and go back to their discussion. She couldn't just pop out of the rocks, she realized now, and say hello, not after sneaking up on them like this. She'd be very still, and they'd forget about her.

But they didn't: there was a stacatto of monosyllables, and all five men moved at once, faster than she would have believed possible, toward her, spreading out as they came.

She turned and ran, scrambling among the rocks, suddenly terrified. They were obviously not IST, and just as obviously ready to deal with anyone caught spying on them. She was acutely aware of how far the shelf protruded over the construction project below, and how far the drop.

Struggling for breath in the thin air, Paige could barely hear over the pulse pounding in her ears. So she ran right into the chest of a man who grabbed her with practiced skill. Before she knew it, he had her in a bear hug and then had whirled her around. A hand came down over her mouth before she could scream, another across her chest, pinioning her arms, and then other men were around her.

Voices whispered together, unintelligibly except for the urgency in them. Someone shined a flashlight on her face. Someone said something more.

She couldn't see anything but the blinding glare of the flashlight, although she could hear the men moving around. And then she heard rapid-fire Spanish, and the voice she'd thought she recognized said in English, "If your lips are free to speak, you must promise not to scream, yes? Nod if you agree."

She nodded as best she could. The same voice gave a command. The hand came off her mouth.

She could feel the heat of the man against whom her backside was pressed, the way his muscles were tensed.

The voice behind the glare said again, "So, Smith, you decided to take me up on my offer, yes?"

"I . . . yes," said Paige Barnett, hardly recognizing the name as hers. "I'm sorry, it was an impulse. I'll just go away now. . . ."

"We must talk with you before we can release you. You agree? Come back and sit with us? Do not be afraid." The hands holding her let go completely and the man behind her stepped back, out of contact with her body.

Not until then did she realize what kind of bargain she'd made, and who the man with the familiar voice must be: Joachim Sanchez, the one who'd given her his card.

"Sanchez?" she quavered. "Yes, all right."

The flashlight went off, leaving her momentarily stone blind. And shaking uncontrollably. Men crowded around her and one touched her arm— Sanchez, because he said, "Yes, it is me."

She was escorted back to the place where their blanket was, and Sanchez told her to sit. She could see more than a green-black cloud now; she could see darker silhouettes against the night, sitting cross-legged. From the one parallel to her, Sanchez's voice came, talking fast in Spanish.

When the words ceased, she said miserably, "I can't understand you. You'll have to slow down or speak English."

He chuckled, said something in Spanish at which the whole group chuckled, and spoke to her again, this time in slow English: "I asked you how much you'd heard. I ask it again."

"I . . . some sort of chant, or prayer, then just something about business. That's all, I swear."

"And would you like to know more?"

"I don't know," she said honestly, trying to keep her teeth from chattering. "Would I?"

Again the voice from the silhouette had humor in it. "We could make things easier for you, señorita—now. But what we do is not without its dangers. You know this, I think."

"I know it."

"We could get you into the tech center, if you would do certain things for us."

"I—What are you offering, besides that?" And what did they want from her in exchange?

"A new life. Redemption. Resurrection. The holy way."

"What?"

"You will understand, later. Say now if you wish to join us—we are the workers' only hope. Or go back to your hopeless life. You do not yet know enough to hurt us."

Someone else interjected harshly, "She knows your name, Joachim."

"And we know hers; it has a balance."

"I want to know more," she said defiantly, cold and shivering and thinking about the tech center across the chasm, where there'd be employees of IST to reason with, not just sadistic work bosses and peasants. One thing she was certain of was that she didn't want to go back to her "hopeless life." Even engaging in unionizing beat that. And what could the workforce bosses do to her—send her someplace worse than Knob Hill? To her knowledge, there wasn't anyplace worse.

But looking at the silhouettes of Sanchez and the others, she suddenly remembered her dream, and the chanting in it that was the only way to keep the *creature* at bay.

CHAPTER 8

X-66B

———◆———

"COME ON, DET, talk to me," said Locke in Cox's ear. Cox tweaked his helmet transceiver's volume up and turned the EQ wheel with his finger to get out some of the static. Then he said, sticking his head out of the tunnel entrance, "Yeah, we copy, Muffdiver. We're just on our way back for that picnic lunch you promised."

They'd been deep enough in the tunnels that Cox's team could barely talk to each other if they got strung out around curves, let alone communicate with the bird Locke was piloting. But part of the reason X-66B was valuable was the sort of strata that made communications difficult; it went with the turf.

He'd kept his twelve guys strung on lines— breakaway lines, but lines nonetheless. He didn't want to lose anybody if this unsurveyed cavern decided to crumble under someone's feet. They hadn't seen anything like an alien. They hadn't even found the purported rebel base camp—the B target. But they'd found some signs of human exploration, or habitation, where no official exploration had been done.

Corporal Schultz had shot up the evidence before Cox had gotten down there, and scared the hell out of everybody. The DU shot had bounced around that rock so bad Schultz had thought somebody was shooting back, and there'd been a free-for-all with Cox screaming his guts out for a ceasefire.

Then everybody'd relaxed and they collected their shell casings and didn't find one more than their meters told them they'd shot. The packs and supplies Schultz had found in the cave were full of holes and singed where one of the privates had gone to plasma when his chamber jammed, but at least they had something to bring home.

It beat nothing, but not by much. The work bosses who'd been swearing up and down that they had a runaway problem could use the evidence to prove that they hadn't been trying to cover up an unacceptable number of field deaths with some story of escapes. But Cox wasn't here to make the work bosses' job any easier. What he'd seen at the drop point had turned his stomach: there wasn't any reason not to treat the workers better, except that the workers had the staff outnumbered and the staff was scared to death.

So it was one of those vicious circles Cox didn't normally have to think about. But X-66B wasn't normal. It had a revolution going on. He propped himself in the cave's mouth and pushed up his visor with his free arm, looking out over the bleak plain, full of heat-shimmer down here near the equator.

At least this terrain was deforested—or preforested. He watched the sky, waiting for Locke's bird. They hadn't dropped a ground carrier, not for subterranean work, and that meant they were without any but natural cover until Locke put the VTOL down to pick them up.

Sometimes all you did in this business was hike

and wait. Cox shook a cigarette from his belt and lit it, only a little concerned that some pocket of gas he wasn't briefed on would turn him into a human torch when he struck a spark.

It didn't and he was content to let the smoke relax him while he waited for his team to make it to the cave's mouth. Every so often, he could feel a tug or a tremor on the line at his waist, proof they were on their way.

It wasn't a bad team, really. It was a damned good one. All of them had shipped out-system before, and fully seven had worked together. So all he had to do was convince them of his competence and teach them his style—that and make up for the fact that Wiley, the real mission commander, wasn't going to get his boots dirty down here.

That left Locke the ranking officer, but Locke didn't do field patrol, so they were all Cox's, these twelve. And out of the lot of them, Schultz was the only nervous nellie, and that was because of something Cox could understand: this whole alien business.

Try as you might, you couldn't keep that sort of mission definition from seasoned rangers; the grapevine was too damned good. So they knew and he knew they knew but nobody talked about it. Nobody would talk about it until there was something to say about it—until somebody saw something or something happened. But he had to let them know that if somebody did, he wanted it priority one, day or night, even if they had to bust into the latrine to tell him.

He was going to do that tonight, after Schultz's little misfire down there. Sure he was. Maybe he could get Locke to do it—Locke was doing precious little else but keeping the armor and the firepower and the birds shiny.

Back before the drop, when they'd still been transiting to orbit and he and Locke had made their shopping list, the two of them had been sure they wouldn't get what they asked for. So they'd asked for the moon—everything they could think of. And damned if Locke's two pressure-suited friends hadn't read the list and looked at one another and said, Yeah, they thought they'd anticipated all of that.

So when the recon detachment had dropped out of orbit, they'd had a VTOL and a TAV in case they wanted to make a hasty exit back to the mother ship. They had twenty-four guys and redundant firepower, two ground-ready troop carriers with flame and shot, and enough electronics to put a girdle around the whole planet's equator. They'd had so much, in fact, that they dropped like a stone in a huge kangaroo hauler on chemical burn.

And once they'd made landfall at the equator, they'd had lots of red tape because they didn't have maintenance people of their own and Cox didn't want anything more to carry. Recon was light baggage. They'd left as much as they could at the equator base station, and they hadn't brought any of the local paramilitary along with them.

If the locals could have done any good here, IST wouldn't have called in the 203rd under the table. That was where Locke had come in handy—dealing with the local power structure; Cox didn't have the patience for it at the best of times, and lately the very sight of IST mission patches got his back up. Plus, he didn't want them to find out who he was.

He flicked ashes into his palm, crumbled them despite the heat, and squinted at the sky, where the VTOL was a growing speck. There wasn't much in the way of flora and fauna here to worry about, but he always felt better when the bird was there, the door open, and he was moving his guys inside.

When he used to have those dreams about X-31A, he'd always dream the bird crashed, that he couldn't make it aboard, or some such. Just because the only animals on the charts to worry about on X-66B were human or human-imported didn't mean you couldn't have a problem.

He'd asked Locke, back on the mother ship, whether Locke had had bad dreams about X-31A, and Locke just said, "I have bad dreams about lots of places." And they'd talked some about IST then, but not like later. Then, he'd only let out a couple of hints about being boxed for so long at IST's insistence, and that because he'd told Locke about how he'd been signed up for X-66B.

You had to tell somebody, and Locke's ass was going to be hanging on Cox's decisions once they got staged through, so Locke had a right to know that Cox wasn't real sure about some things. Like the hows and whys of the tactics used to get him here. Like whether Cox really was in perfect physical and mental shape and drugs were to blame for the rest of it.

He'd gone as far as telling Locke about the woman with him—the IST woman, Paige Barnett. He'd asked Locke if Locke had seen anybody like her, shipboard, because he'd had that glimpse of her being hustled onto the same plane at Hanscom. But Locke hadn't seen any woman like that and had said, very carefully, studying his beer's head, "Maybe you just thought you saw her—if you were drugged, I mean," making it plain he wasn't accusing Cox of hallucinating without chemical help.

Or trying to. Cox had checked the women among the rangers himself, and when he came up dry, admitted that he hadn't expected to find her there. She wasn't trained for out-system; she was probably just hitching a ride to some corporate vacation spot and what he'd seen had been her luggage.

But Cox relied on his senses to keep him alive. He knew what he'd seen and it bothered him that Locke was telling him he hadn't seen it, like it bothered him that Locke hadn't been put in some endless debrief program the way Cox had. Well, rank had its privileges. And anyway, Locke had never claimed to have *seen* an alien—Locke just saw Cox after Cox had seen one.

Now nobody was seeing aliens, when that was what they were on this shitball to do. Not even seeing revolutionaries. And Cox was about to pull the plug on the equatorial site and head north, where there was a larger concentration of workers and techs in close contact, and where it wasn't so goddamned hot. X-66B (actual astronomical designation classified) was tilted more than Earth, with gravity a fraction lighter, and Cox figured it must be a little farther from its sun, or else that sun was cooler.

The astronomy wasn't a burning concern for him; the US would give up all that data when it was time for statehood; until then, Cox neither needed nor wanted to know more than that his mother ship was up there, ready and waiting, and that his bird was coming in for pickup.

He could see the bird clearly now, and he put his index finger over the last coal of ash on the tip of his cigarette's filter before he ground it underfoot and slapped down his visor. Turning into the cavern, trying to give his signal as much direction as possible, he tugged once on his line and called out, "Hey Schultz, let's hurry it up. Scramble for pickup, girls. Repeat: proceed to pickup area."

He tugged on the line again and it didn't snap back right. In fact, it didn't snap back at all. His heart double-timed, stopped entirely, and started up as soon as his saliva turned to glue in his mouth.

"Fuck all," he muttered, and started pulling the line in, praying for resistance, his feet braced in the tunnel opening. He took three loops before it pulled tight. Please, Christ, don't let it be snagged somewhere.

Don't let there be nobody on the other end of it. He tried again, this time setting his com-channel on open so that maybe Locke would get some of what he was sending into the cave with its damned natural shielding.

"You sons of bitches call in, fall in, or I'm going to leave you here," he yelled hoarsely into his helmet.

There was crackle, then a dead spot. Cox could hear his blood rush in his ears.

Then Schultz's voice came clipping into his helmet "—ucking pants on, sir! We're comin', and we got somethin' for ya!"

Cox actually slid down the rock wall, limp with relief. He didn't want to lose them. He couldn't lose them. He was too close to the memories of losing everybody, including Reynolds, on X-31A. He just couldn't handle it—getting through it, writing it up, having to tell people about it, getting boxed again because of it.

He was still sitting like that when Schultz, looking armed and dangerous, came up out of the dark, all pack and full-auto with something hanging from his belt in a regulation sling that wasn't regulation at all.

And behind Schultz, Cox could see more phosphorescent line and another armored head. He slapped off his com-mike for a minute and cursed the lot of them. Then, having let off steam, he rejoined the com circuit, got to his feet and held out his hand. Behind him, the bird was landing.

"What is it, Corporal?" he said to Schultz, too gruffly.

Even with Schultz's visor down, Cox could see the man do a double-take. "Sorry, sir. We saw this thing and we thought we'd cut it out for you. Next time, we'll leave it. But we couldn't raise you round that last bend and—"

"Never mind, I just don't like to eat alone. Let's have it." Schultz handed over his sample bag and in it was a piece of rock with some scratches on it. Maybe letters. Maybe pictures. Maybe manmade. Maybe not....

For this those bastards had nearly scared the shit out of him. Cox shook his head in his helmet, but hooked the sample bag onto his belt. Now he had a worthy reason to pull these guys out and take them north: the real tech talent was all up at the terraforming center.

Behind him, Locke was so close that the sound of the bird putting down came right through Cox's helmet, and the amount of air it was pushing made him stagger. He yelled, "Okay, form 'em up. Let's head out," and stood back as Schultz did just that.

Cox leaned against the rock wall, rifle ready, until he'd head-counted his people. Then he followed the last of them toward the open slider of the VTOL, the sample bag banging against his crotch. Maybe it was revolutionary graffiti, but if it wasn't, even Locke was going to start taking this whole thing a little more seriously.

When he reached the VTOL, Cox looked back involuntarily, and in the tunnel he was sure he saw something glowing a little bit—a pale something about the size and shape of a naked man.

CHAPTER 9

Redemption, Resurrection,
the Holy Way

———◆———

"READY, SEÑORITA SMITH?" Sanchez whispered to her in the dark, three nights later.

"Ready," Paige replied, gritting her teeth against the wind whipping the shelf, her lips already numb from cold. She still wasn't sure what it was she was ready for, but now she was a part of the revolution. She wasn't supposed to ask questions of her new friends. She was supposed to do as she was told, to listen, to learn.

She'd learned that being part of the revolution brought you corporate-level perks among the workers. Her food was better; she had two new blankets. People saved her a place in the chow line and the latrine line. Women smiled at her and men didn't pinch her bottom. She should have joined up before and saved herself lots of black and blue marks.

Knob Hill's secret society was meeting tonight, and after the meeting, she was scheduled to "infiltrate" the tech center. Sanchez and his two lieutenants, Jadeesh and Ho, never spoke of their plans in specifics, to her or to anyone else, she was beginning to realize.

But she knew she was going across the spidery bridge, swaying there in the wind. The lights on the bridge jiggled and jumped like fireflies formed up for review and, watching them, her heart skipped a beat. It would be so easy to fall...But if Sanchez had meant her harm, he'd had plenty of prior opportunities.

So she stood where she'd been told, on the shelf, and waited for the others. When they came, they came from blackness, soundless and full of guile.

Sanchez, whose tall, stooped form was easy to recognize even at night, crooked his hand in her direction: follow me. No one was talking. She counted seven others in their party and then she was doing as she was bid, following Sanchez.

Sanchez seemed to be conducting a ritual suicide as he stepped off into nothingness, disappearing down the sheer cliffside. Or so she thought until she felt the step cut out of rock under her searching foot, saw him grab for a handhold in the cliffside and did the same. She inched downward, terrified by the abyss she was descending into. One false step and she would be in free fall, toward the reservoir project so far below. Climbers above her trailed along behind, dislodging the occasional stone. During that long descent down a zig-zag route, no one spoke.

The interval was interminable, so much so that Paige was startled when Sanchez disappeared entirely. She'd been following the beacon of his hiking boots and now they were gone. For an instant she was sure that at last he'd fallen soundlessly toward the reservoir below.

Then she raised her eyes from the vacant step

before her, that next step downward in an endless chain of steps, and realized it wasn't a step at all. It was a ledge. And on that ledge, as well as beyond, was a deeper darkness. In that darkness, in a cave's mouth, stood Sanchez, beckoning. Taking wide strides because suddenly she could, Paige realized that the cave was not merely a shallow depression, but an ·entrance to a tunnel whose mouth made a right-angle turn.

There, with Sanchez, she waited for the others. No wonder no one had found out how the revolution worked on X-66B. Nobody would have looked down here; from a bird this cave would have looked like a simple blemish in the rock face. Inside, if they went far enough, their heat signatures would be undetectable to the workforce guards.

And they did go inside, venturing deep into the cliff along a winding track that was so narrow in places that only one person could pass at a time. They trudged in silence, but for the sound of heels on stone and the occasional cough, until they came to a place where the tunnel widened into a chamber.

When she entered, Paige's hand raised reflexively to cover her mouth and nose. The stench was nauseating, putrid and sweet and nearly unbearable. In the center of the cave was a corpse, a black and bloated corpse. Around it were a dozen people, sitting cross-legged between flashtorches.

Sanchez led her to a place near the corpse's head and motioned her to sit. She did, her stomach roiling, her eyes fixed on the corpse. It was the black man she'd transited with, and he'd been dead far too long.

Sanchez touched her arm and whispered, "Be calm. Redemption, resurrection, the holy way."

Paige was trying not to breathe the stench,

which probably carried enough bacteria to start
an epidemic among the gathered rebels, or whatever they were. There were now perhaps two
dozen in the cave, maybe more, because they kept
filing in from the tunnel.

Some of them had blacked faces; some wore
handkerchiefs over their noses. One wore a makeshift robe and he was Asian—perhaps Pakistani,
maybe Indian or Mongol, but not pure Chinese.

This Asian got to his feet and began speaking
and gesticulating, his arms raised. First he seemed
to try to touch the ceiling and when he did, all the
gathered workers repeated the phrase he spoke.

Paige mouthed the syllables that were, to her,
meaningless, along with the rest because Sanchez
was watching her out of the corner of his eye.

Then the Asian turned forty-five degrees and
held his arms straight out to the wall, and spoke
again. Again, the crowd repeated what he'd said,
chanting his words.

He did this four times, arms straight out as if to
embrace the rock walls, and when he came back to
his starting point, he once more reached for the
rock ceiling above.

By then Paige had seen the scratchings on the
walls. She couldn't decipher them any better than
the chant, which was not in any language she
knew. But the tenor of the call-and-answer began
to build and now she could catch a few words of
Spanish, of Arabic, perhaps of Pashto, and Canton-
ese. At least some of it sounded like those tongues.
Her head snapped up when she heard in English,
"By the holy mother of redemption, in praise of
Resurrection, to save every soul through the holy
father of us all, we praise the holy way, that brings
every soul new life."

A whole sentence in English! At least, a long

string of English words: the effect of hearing her native tongue was unexpected: tears came to Paige's eyes. She wanted to go home. She wanted to wake up from this awful dream and be under her goosedown puff, in her own bed, listening to her alarm tell her it was time to go to work. She wanted to have bacon and eggs and get into her company limo for an all-expenses paid trip to the District. She wanted to go shopping and sit in her favorite fitting room smoking cigarettes while her salesgirl brought her clothes to try on and accessories to match and called the fitter up to make everything perfect.

She wanted to feel guilty because she was contemplating buying a coat made from an endangered species. She should have bought the damned coat when she could, before Paige Barnett became an endangered species herself.

The chanting kept up and tears ran unheeded from Paige's eyes. She didn't usually cry; she hadn't cried much here—it was a waste of strength. She hadn't cried since the transit hold. But now she did, overcome with a bone-deep sorrow, for herself and for the whole sorry human race of which she was a part. She wept with deep, wracking sobs and her eyes streamed tears which blurred her vision. All the while she kept mumbling the chant she didn't understand because it wasn't in English anymore.

When the chant stopped suddenly, the silence was like a physical blow. She didn't know how long she'd been chanting, or how long she'd been crying, or how long it had been since she'd looked at the corpse in the middle of the convocation.

But now she looked up—at the crowd, at the corpse lying in its midst, and at the Asian chanting over the body. Paige blinked. She looked away. She wiped her eyes hastily and started to speak.

As if he'd been waiting, prepared for just this reaction, Sanchez's arm went around her head so that his hand came down over her mouth and he could turn her face toward him. With his eyes and his frown he told her to be quiet, sit still, and wait.

Then he turned her head forcibly so that she saw again what had made her look away.

The corpse seemed to be rising, rising toward the ceiling. It wasn't levitating—it was being drawn upward by long, pale arms that seemed to come out of the rock ceiling. The brown arms of the Asian were reaching upward and the luminous arms of the rock were reaching downward and the corpse was as high as the Asian's head now.

She was sure she was going to vomit. She shook her head to dislodge Sanchez's hand but it did not come away.

Her eyes couldn't leave the corpse, anyway. She watched as, in the aching silence, the corpse rose toward the ceiling and into it.

Into it! She knew this wasn't happening. She'd been drugged, doped. Or she was dreaming again. She took a deep, quavering breath and the air she breathed was rife with the stench of decomposing flesh.

The corpse was being entombed in the rock ceiling of the cave, now. Dust and detritus fell from around it in a desultory shower. She kept watching and the corpse kept rising. It rose and rose and even though it obviously couldn't rise any farther, it continued on its ineluctable way, disappearing right into the solid-looking rock. The hands guiding it were visible, pale against the swollen black back, cradling the dead man, until even his backside disappeared and there was nothing there but rock once more.

Paige raised her hands to her eyes again and realized that Sanchez was no longer holding his hand over her mouth. He was watching her and smiling a paternal, welcoming smile. He leaned close and whispered, as if his words answered all the questions she hadn't yet formed, "Redemption, resurrection, the holy way."

And then the Asian in the makeshift robe sat down where the corpse had been and began to preach in workforce polyglot, giving thanks for the miracle in a way that made Paige know it wasn't a first-time thing.

She didn't remember much of the ceremony—indeed, she didn't remember much more until she was climbing behind Sanchez, up the footholds cut in the rock. By then she was wondering how they'd managed to dope her food and telling herself she hadn't seen what she'd seen.

But she knew she had. And she kept remembering the revolution on X-31A, and the religious overtones it had had, and the rumors of aliens. And the white hands coming out of the rock. And somehow she started thinking about Dennis Cox.

But it was all too crazy, and life was precious. She had to watch her step. If she fell and splattered herself over the reservoir project below, she had a feeling none of these miracle-workers could help her. Was this what Sanchez meant when he'd asked her to join "them": had she been asked to join a cult practicing mass hypnosis, not a revolution?

She wanted to ask but this bunch was maddeningly, completely silent as it climbed. You didn't want to let any sensors pick up the sounds of voices; meetings like this—groups of more than two or three—were against all the rules even when they were just outside a tent.

What she'd seen under the overhang tonight would be grounds for terminal procedures, if the work bosses found out about it. The part of her that still identified with IST knew damned well that, if any of this ever got home, IST would nuke the venue rather than risk the spread of this kind of cult. Resurrection!

She snorted and muttered to herself as she followed Sanchez out onto the shelf where she'd first stumbled onto his group meeting, and he said to her very softly, "We'll talk later, once we have you over at the tech center. Are you ready?"

She'd forgotten that there was a mundane method in Sanchez's madness. She'd forgotten about the swaying bridge in the gusty night, about the promises she'd made and the risks to come.

She just wanted to go back to her tent, pull her covers over her head, and go to sleep. But she was in way too deep to refuse Sanchez anything, especially tonight. And she wanted to go to the tech center, where she could find others of her own kind.

Her resurrection lay over there, among the ergostations and the freeze-dried steaks, among the technocratic elite who manned the tech bastion here. It sure as hell didn't lie in some cavern with phantasmagorically pale hands that reached down from the ceiling to give you a topsy-turvy burial.

The enormity of what she'd seen scared her: either it was mass hallucination, or it was worse. If there was something down there, something that liked human corpses, what possessed these crazies to make a religion out of it? They should be running like hell. But instead, they were ritualizing some phenomenon that IST would destroy every living thing on X-66B to eradicate.

It was way too late in the race for territorial space for aliens. She looked at Sanchez dully, realizing what he wasn't sophisticated enough to understand: eventually, this had to leak out. When it did, everybody who thought they knew about aliens on X-66B was going to die.

If the aliens didn't get them first. Assuming there were real ones, and not just hallucinatory ones. But, hallucinatory or not, the alien cult was doomed as soon as it surfaced. Paige Barnett, looking Sanchez straight in the eye, said, "Let's go then; let's hope your plan works."

And he heard the determination in her voice, although he'd never understand the reasons for it. Paige Barnett was now facing a deadline: she had to get off this ball of rock before word leaked; she had to get home, get the mistake that had brought her here rectified, before IST found out how big a problem this place was going to be and abandoned it, destroying as much as possible of the evidence as it pulled out.

"Come then, Señorita Smith," Sanchez said and led her toward the swaying bridge, alone. And all the way across it, Paige kept hearing the Asian priest's chant in the back of her mind. She heard it while she was sure that any minute a paramilitary bird was going to swoop down and shoot them off the restricted span; she heard it when Sanchez made solid ground on the far side and held out a hand to her. She heard it when, mysteriously but somehow predictably, a tall steel door marked, DANGER: NO ADMITTANCE opened to Sanchez's cadenced knock.

A white-faced man with a crew cut in a technician's smock was standing behind it. He said, "Damn, Joachim, what took you so goddamned long? This the woman? The English speaker? Come *on*, lady, hurry it up," and ushered them inside.

CHAPTER 10

Chasing the Revolution

———◆———

PRETENDING TO HIMSELF that he hadn't seen any white, luminous form worth reporting had been only half the fun Cox had had, once his team was ready to leave the equatorial zone of X-66B. Getting to Morgan Base with the evidence they'd found at the equator had been the other half. Cox had left local security forces guarding the equatorial tunnel site because of the piece of stone and the traces of rebel activity Schultz had stumbled on there. And they'd had to bury a string of seismic sensors that would beep the mother ship if anything human showed up there—Captain Wiley's orders.

Wiley was regular brass, good at giving ball-busting work orders from his comfy command chair miles above the action. Wiley had thrown in an extra one for good measure: mine the equatorial fault system; belt the whole planet with remote-detonation electronics and explosive ordnance.

If Locke hadn't been the pilot he was and if Det

didn't stand for Detonator, they'd still be at it, down there at this shitball's belly. As it was, the touch-and-go's they'd done around the equator ranked among some of the worst duty intervals Cox could remember.

His team bitched like hell about it, too: they weren't on this pocked rock for jump drill. But jump they did, with VTOL coverage, on strict rotation, placing what explosives they couldn't drop.

It was Schultz who'd wondered aloud, after the last packet was emplaced and the codes laid in to allow Wiley to punch the button from orbit, "What's to keep Cap'n Wiley from pushin' that button on a go order from higher-up without re-memberin' to evac us first?"

And Locke had replied, from the foredeck of the VTOL, "You don't know Det, Corporal. I'd lay odds he's got a bug in that system that won't let it go bang without his permission. Right, Det?"

Cox had rubbed the back of his neck, looked at his dusty boots on the bulkhead, and said, "Now look here, girls. Fucking with command electronics is against regulations. But anybody fucking with my life span is downright unacceptable. You pulled Locke and me," he let his gaze travel over the Alpha recon team in the VTOL, "precisely because we're real survival oriented. Just trust us to do everything humanly possible to get all our asses off this rock—or any rock—in one piece."

If that discussion had to go down, Cox was just as pleased to have it there and then, in the VTOL among the fourteen of them. With Locke on the flight deck, his thumb on the flight recorder's squelch button, nobody who shouldn't was going to hear any of what was said.

Leaving Schultz to fly the VTOL, he and Locke

had gone up-latitude with the fresh Beta team in the TAV.

They'd put down at Morgan Base, six hours before Schultz and the slower VTOL, and talked to the work bosses for a couple hours about the situation. Then he and Locke left the Beta team to feel out the lay of the land, collect stories about revolutions and religious cults, and wait for Schultz and the VTOL to arrive.

Cox and Locke went over to Knob Hill alone, toting their rock sample, leaving word for Schultz and his Alpha team to meet them there ASAP.

The Knob Hill tech center was as good as it got out in the boondocks: white rooms, clean rooms, rec halls, three restaurants, two bars, video inphones, and a theater as well as science modules and equipment shops.

The Morgan Base commandant had told them to talk to a Professor Singer, and when Singer couldn't see them, they headed for Knob Hill's best restaurant, where they showed their IST cards and ordered "Earth-range-fed Angus."

And it seemed real enough, when it came. But by then Locke was saying, "You know, we ought to face the possibility that this scratched-up piece of stone's going to mean something."

Cox looked at the pale blond man across from him and said, "Like what?"

"Like enough evidence to start the ball rolling."

"You mean the ball that goes bang?" Cox sat back and slid down on his spine, scanning the restaurant. It was pink and pale blue where it wasn't green with imported plants or depth-defying because of mirrored walls. There were only two other parties in the place, both white-smocked. Although he and Locke, in IST police coveralls, weren't remarkable, Cox turned on his belt transceiver and dialed it between channels, then goosed the gain for a little impromptu jamming before Locke could answer his question.

"Uh-huh. You heard what I heard in Wiley's cabin," Locke reminded him. "If we come up with artifactual evidence, what do you think they're going to want us to do?"

"I *know* what they want us to do: 'solve the problem.' What I don't know is that it's worth trashing this whole complex to do it. We'd have to be pretty sure there wasn't another way..." Locke was looking at him funny, his face all squinched up. "Or are you telling me I'm underestimating the situation?"

Locke rolled his silverware out of his pink napkin and started making a space station out of linen. "I'm just saying that those black operators who briefed us up there and gave us every little thing we asked for—*they* want any alien life or evidence of alien life eradicated. You think bringing this piece of stone over here fits that description?"

"Jesus Christ," Cox said, shaking his head. The rock sample hanging from his belt felt three times heavier than it had a moment ago. "Somebody say that to you in so many words—'eradicated'?"

Locke nodded.

"Well, nobody said it to me like that, but I'll take your word. Evac for someplace this populated is a long time away, even if we start now...."

Again, Locke gave him the "you-got-it-wrong" look. Followed by: "No evac. If we find something, we blow the presence. No matter the collateral damage."

"Didn't you learn anything after X-31A, buddy?" Cox's voice dropped an octave and Locke sat up straight. "I don't like this crap—if they want everybody who knows about this to become past history, where does that leave us and our Alpha and Beta teams?"

"In receipt of privileged information, but what's new about that?" Locke looked at him squarely, implying lots of things like special knowledge, power beyond his lieutenancy, and a faith in mankind that Cox just didn't share.

When Cox didn't answer, Locke said earnestly, "Come on, do I look like a suicide candidate to you?"

"I don't know what you look like. I couldn't find you for all that time. Tell me straight out what you're trying to say here."

"I'm trying to say that we don't want to tell this Professor Singer more than we have to, is all. Let's get that chicken-scratched piece of rock shipped up to Wiley in orbit and let the cryppie computer program work on it."

"Fine, so what do we tell the professor we wanted?"

"Show it to him, find out if he's seen any others like it, and let's allude that we think it's a code belonging to the revolution. Otherwise, let's just pump him."

"Don't let *him* pump *us*, you mean. Yeah, okay." But Cox was uncomfortable. He did just run recon; Locke obviously had his hand in other things.

"I'm glad you copy. We shouldn't have any problem. Just don't leave it with him—evidence, let's say."

"Are we telling him we're not IST?"

"He'll figure that out."

Sometimes Locke made Cox very nervous; this was one of those times. It wasn't just being outranked, it was the way Locke thought about things, the way he operated. When Cox was on the ground and Locke was in the air, Cox—or any ground commander—was boss. Here, in a situation where either of them might have been calling the shots, Locke had just made the pecking order clear.

And behind Locke was Wiley, up there safe in orbit. Cox didn't think sending that sample to the ship was any kind of good idea, especially if things were as tense as Locke was suggesting.

By the time their steaks came, Cox wasn't hungry. Only a bad case of nerves or intense physical pain could kill his appetite, and it wasn't the latter, not this time. He wanted to go out and roust the so-called aliens, or the rebels in alien outfits— right now, thank you very much. Or he wanted to go shoot off a couple hundred rounds of high-priced, high-kick ammo just to make himself feel better. He didn't want to try to chew the charred meat before him, cut into its bloody center, or talk to the civilian honcho he was here to meet.

But as he was chewing determinedly, a heavy-set, brunette woman in a white smock came toward their table. Above her right breast was a blue badge, and blue was top ranking code on Knob Hill. When she reached them, she was already smiling and holding out her hand to Locke by the time Cox read her name tag.

It said, Professor Singer.

She said, "Hello gentlemen, I've been instructed to give you full cooperation."

Locke was on his feet, shaking her hand and pulling out a chair for her like he'd expected a woman, telling her what an impressive station she had here.

"We like it," she said, letting Locke slide her chair under her buttocks and then pulling it forward. "Even though the men down at Morgan

Base are always trying to scare us with this revolution stuff."

"Stuff?" Locke said.

"The men?" Cox asked at the same time.

"Ah, Sergeant," she said as if noticing Cox for the first time. "I'm Elaine Singer. Because ladies outnumber gentlemen in the upper echelons at Knob Hill, we're very informal. Call me Elaine."

"Right," he said. "Det." He realized she'd just answered his question obliquely: administrative power at Knob Hill was concentrated among female staffers. It wasn't unusual at scientific installations; here it could cause some morale or political problems, what with the type of men running the work camp and Morgan Base. It also meant that Knob Hill's data was pretty secure from external espionage and the persons of its female executive officers safe from sexual harassment: all the doors he'd seen had scan bars. Where you wanted to limit the access to rated personnel and those personnel were female, you just coded-in a male-alarm. More sensitive screening, like card-access, came after the first test was passed.

And nobody he'd seen down at Morgan Base could pass a ladies-only barrier. Neither could anybody in Det's unit, with the exception of a pair of privates in Beta team. Well, if he wanted to sneak around in the labs, he'd rotate them into Alpha.

He realized Locke had been talking to Singer about her joining them for dinner only when Locke signaled for a waiter. When the servo came, he punched up the menu for her and gallantly insisted that she "At least have a drink, if you're not hungry."

Singer was on the wrong side of forty, biologically, but well preserved. Cox knew Locke well enough to know that Locke wasn't planning on sleeping in the TAV if he could help it. Fine, let Loche do that kind of recon. Cox just wanted to get this tricky political stuff over with.

He pushed his food around his plate until it was time to go to the lab, then followed Locke and the lady professor through a maze of neat white corridors, watching his steps because he needed to learn the routing codes set into the floor in a series of colored lines.

Cox had it down by the time they got to the lab tower, entered the elevator, and Singer started loosening up, talking about her "sanctorum" and how difficult it was to keep up a "good working relationship with those paranoid fellows down at Morgan."

"You don't think," Locke probed, "that there's any real problem with this workforce?"

When Professor Singer raised her eyebrows, a complement of worry lines appeared on her brow. "I think a lot of the problem there is due to... mismanagement." She bared bonded teeth. "I'm assuming—I've heard, actually—that you and your group are the real thing...nonpartisan investigators."

"Something like that," Locke temporized. "We're here at IST's request because both the government and IST are concerned that there *is* mismanagement here, that's all."

"Well, it's rampant. Those workers need something to give them hope. They're living in such squalor. The conditions down there are the worst I've ever seen. I don't blame them for trying to bet—"

"Ma'am, we're wondering about the religious angle? Do you know anything about cults at Morgan Base?" Cox interrupted. If Locke was going to romance this aging executive all night, Cox had better things to do than hang around.

The elevator stopped and opened onto an octagonal suite with window walls of shimmery kevlar-reinforced glass. Singer stepped into it and motioned them to follow, saying, "Why do you ask, Sergeant Det?"

"Plain Det's fine." Funny answer. But it opened a shortcut. He unhooked the sample bag from his belt and held it out for her. "We'd like to know what you make of this. Assume we don't know anything about it, and give it to us from the top. We found it at the equator."

She was already opening it and sliding out the piece of laser-torched stone that Schultz had found in the cave. And Locke was scowling.

As if she'd forgotten them, Singer headed through the suite, down a hallway whose doors got out of her way just in time, and didn't stop until she was at a workbench with lots of hardware on it. There she carefully put down the sample, pulled a remote from her pocket and aimed it at the doors, setting up a security block, and said, "Where did you two say you were dispatched from?"

"We didn't," Cox said, crossing his arms, before Locke could finesse a response.

The woman breathed, "I see," and turned to the sample on the workbench, running her fingers over the scratches. Then she looked up again. "I can't tell you anything much unless you wish to leave this with me. The language, if it is one, isn't familiar."

"But it's not natural striation?" Locke asked. "It's something man-made?"

"It's something made by an intelligent hand, yes," said the woman, who knew she was saying much more. "Do we want to discuss this, gentlemen, frankly and honestly? I have a great deal at stake in the success of X-66B."

"You've got your ass at stake if there's a problem, lady," Cox said flatly, hoping to jar her into something resembling a declarative sentence. "They didn't send us in here to play PI. They sent us here because there might be real trouble."

Locke shot Cox a warning glance over his shoulder and intervened. "I can't leave that here, and if I don't get satisfactory answers, I'm going to send it up to orbit and let our people work on it."

"Just whose people are those?" Professor Singer wanted to know.

"American government, ma'am," said Locke softly.

"O-kay," she said. "Let's go back to Elaine, for me, and nonconfrontational for both of you."

"Then talk to us. We haven't got much time and lives could be on the line here," Cox said, leaning against the worktable.

"What would you like first? The revolutionaries' meager attempts to better working conditions down at Morgan, or my assessment of the validity of their inspiration?"

"In English, okay?" Cox said.

"Shut up, Det. Take your time, Elaine. I've got all night. I just can't leave the sample unless I'm with it."

"I'm out of here, then," Cox said, decided. "Somebody call me if you two come up with anything I ought to know. I'll be at the TAV, waiting for Schultz and Alpha."

And he was, when Locke came down six hours later, bleary-eyed and blotchy-faced, to tell him that Morgan control said there was some sort of "incident" up at the Knob Hill work camp and wanted to know if they'd like a piece of it.

By then, Beta team and the VTOL were in place and Cox scrambled everybody and everything. Ten minutes later, with Alpha team in full armor and recon suits, they were screaming into the thin air of X-66B, in the VTOL for a bird's-eye view.

What Cox saw through his dopplered radars and infrascopes made him tell Locke to put the bird down and ready Alpha to drop, deploy, and derail the engagement in progress.

"And don't shoot the damned IST grunts. Set your cameras to select out and feed you good targets," he yelled into his com-mike, checking his own weapons.

He'd issued crowd-control stuff: rubber bullets and DU-shot, no plasma, no airfoil expanding rounds or thallium. But he let them have their whole battery of grenades, in case the workers were out for scalps. You couldn't tell when something like this would turn lethal. If this was the big blow-out, the rebels would be going for broke, willing to die to take their Knob Hill camp as a stronghold.

So he dropped with Alpha, laying smoke and CS-gas and generally running amok, feeding everything through his pack up to Locke, who was feeding to the orbital command post.

And got shot at by a workforce guard. He shot back, the guy dropped, and only then did Cox realize he'd used his ten-millimeter side arm, thallium tipped penetrators and all.

"Lethally aroused" was an understatement for what was going on here. He could quadrant his helmet's visor and get an overlay from the VTOL of "enemy" positions, but that enemy included the workforce guards. Cox's people didn't have gear sophisticated enough to do better than distinguish Alpha and Beta team members from the bad guys —everybody else.

He screamed at Locke on his throatpad to contact the work bosses and fix that, and kept shooting whatever popped up looking hostile, while his visor display insistently reminded him he had people on the ground to look after.

A lot of that was shouting orders, which he did, and keeping track of positions, which he did, until he shimmied over, around, and through a rockfall to come face-to-face with six hostiles carrying shotguns, side arms, and laser torches.

At first he thought they were IST paramilitary, because they were in those uniforms. But they saw him clearly and shot at him, so he shot back and called in for support, hunkered down between two rocks that showered him with bits and pieces every time a round came close.

He keyed his bullhorn and said quietly, "Put down your weapons and surrender and no harm will come to you," knowing his voice was blaring out of his computer pack at 120dB. One of the six took premeditated aim and tried to shoot his head off with an expropriated assault rifle.

Until then, he hadn't realized what kind of loads the guards were armed with for emergencies. Half the rock next to him blew apart. Fragments as sharp as needles went right through his sleeves, which could turn a bullet impact, leaving just a bad bruise, but couldn't deflect a concentrated point-entry so small.

He could hear his team, on its way, and he probably talked to them; he tended to keep up a running commentary when he was in that sort of situation. If he did, however, he wasn't conscious of it.

He was conscious of losing his temper, of needing to shoot back, and of taking careful aim at the biggest target, a tall, stooped form in a bloody stolen uniform—unless some guard had joined the revolution.

He used his pistol consciously this time, and shot for the throat, well aware that the airfoil round in that chamber was going to tear its target to bits if Cox got a hit.

He did, and the man went over backwards. The others scattered, all but one. That one, scrambling over to the fallen man, lost an ill-fitting helmet. He was shocked to see a woman's mane of chestnut hair spill out of it. Then she was up again and running after her friends.

She took one backward look though and, even at that distance, he could feel the hatred and the sorrow cast his way.

Right about then Schultz slid down beside him in a shower of stones, yelling, "Det's hit. Sergeant's *hit*, damn it. Get that VTOL down here! Evac. Say again: Evac."

"Ah shit, Schultz, it ain't nothing but flesh wounds—rock bits," Cox said, rolling over, out of the niche he'd been squeezed into, now that Schultz was here to cover the area. He looked at his left arm and his whole sleeve was soaked with blood. Well, maybe it was something.

He put away his side arm and used the front sight on his assault rifle to lift the armored sleeve away from his skin. Looked like something big and nasty had been chewing on him for a couple of hours—lots of free-bleeding holes, and dirty holes at that.

Well, couldn't be helped. He hit his beltkit and pumped some painkiller into himself, in case his adrenaline ran down and it started to hurt, still watching the aerial display that showed him who was where.

There were only a few rebel blips left moving; Locke had gotten enough of a fix on the local paras to make their blips orange and he had the right guys, because they were in obvious formation, chasing the single red blips of rebels from rock to rock.

He got on the horn to Locke, saying he wasn't hurt that bad, and then to Alpha and Beta, telling them to rally at the pickup point, and sat there while his computer pack did the rest of his job for him and his pharmakit got him high.

He got so high, in fact, that by the time the bird came he was seeing things: he saw the tall guy he'd hit with the airfoil move, as if he was sliding toward the nearest rock. He closed his eyes because next he'd be seeing white hands dragging the corpse away, like he had with Reynolds. When he did he saw, in his mind's eye, first the pale shape in the equatorial cave's mouth, then the woman rebel looking back at him with hatred in her eyes. And this time, she looked familiar.

"Nah, couldn't be," he told himself aloud. But Dennis Cox knew damn well what he'd seen. He just didn't have time to wonder how come he'd seen it, or the stomach to make a fuss in case he was hallucinating again.

Maybe Paige Barnett was out here on some kind of executive tour, but she sure as hell wasn't fighting on the side of the rebels.

"What's that, sir?" asked Schultz, all solicitous at the sight of blood.

"I said, let me have your undershirt, Corporal.

Want to bind this up with something before the wash from Locke's bird drives half the dust on Knob Hill into these wounds."

CHAPTER 11

Hidden and Revealed

———◆———

PAIGE THOUGHT THIS was the same cave in which the ceremony had taken place, but she couldn't be sure. Her lungs were burning and her heart was pounding as if it might burst from her chest. All around her was the ragged band of rebels, pathetic and beaten in the scanty light of flashtorches shaking because the hands holding them were shaking.

Her hands were shaking, too, especially the one still holding her rifle in a deathgrip. She didn't belong here. But it was too late to turn back now.

She leaned against the rock, realized what she was doing, and jerked away from contact with it, remembering the black man's corpse disappearing into the ceiling. Then logic reasserted itself: there was rock under her feet and it hadn't swallowed her up.

Everyone else was settling down. She could hear the polyglot profanity, the gasps, the stifled moans and groans of the wounded and the disheartened. Eventually she'd have to lean, to sit, to sleep—unless the fugitives moved on. And she was too tired to move on.

She settled into a squat and rested her head and shoulders against the rock wall, half-expecting to be sucked through into...what? She didn't know. She didn't want to know.

She knew that Sanchez had been killed and she knew what she'd seen as she'd run: white hands, coming out of the rock to embrace him. She knew the soldier whom she'd been faced off with, across Sanchez's body, had seen it too. She wondered what he thought.

Ho, the Chinese man who'd been one of Sanchez's confidants, had seen her face-off with the soldier. He'd given her a disparaging look when she'd broken and run. Paige Barnett might be a reluctant revolutionary, but she wasn't a killer; she didn't know anything about weapons. She'd probably only have succeeded in getting herself killed. She hardly remembered how she'd come to have the gun...

That wasn't true, she told herself savagely, slumped against the wall and gulping thin air and watching listlessly while Ho and a man she thought might be the Asian priest distributed meager rations of food and water to a score of shaken revolutionaries. She knew damn well how she'd come by the gun—Sanchez had shoved it into her hands when she'd come out of the tech center, skulking like a spy in the dead of night.

Which was what they made her, Sanchez and his workers. She was as guilty as any of these around her, as responsible for the bloodshed and the carnage and the...criminality. Perhaps more guilty. Sanchez had used her and now he was dead and she couldn't imagine why she'd let him make her do it.

Because she hadn't been thinking, she told herself—and because it had been a trade-off. Paige was used to trade-offs, even those with stakes this high. She simply wasn't used to being on the short end of the stick.

She'd done as she was told in the tech center. The code-clerk who'd guided her, a rebel sympathizer, had explained it all concisely through lips blue with fear:

"I can't get in the high-security operations rooms; they're male-secure. And all the file notations are in English, so you fit the bill: an English-reading female. Your job is to walk in there, use this cardkey on the door, find the file number I'll give you, and copy the file data onto this piece of paper." He'd held out a perfectly ordinary looking piece of paper in trembling hands, his voice low and sibilant with urgency. "Understand?" He'd shoved the paper at her.

"No," she said, taking the sheet of ordinary paper. "And I haven't told you what I want in exchange for doing you this favor, yet."

"In a minute, you can tell me what you want. If this screws up, I'll be transferred to the workforce, so listen closely: use the sheet I gave you, none of the paper in there. Every sheet in there is numbered and marked 'danger, eyes only/light sensitive paper' for good reason. Take it out of there, into the corridor lighting where it can react to unfiltered fluorescent wavelengths, and it'll explode in your hands. What you're to copy won't make any sense to you—it's in code. But make sure you get it right."

"What good is it if it's in code?" she'd whispered, looking around at the windowless supply room in which they were crouched beside a humming printer.

"Where do think you are? This is the coderoom. I'm a code clerk. When you bring it out, I'll decode it for Sanchez. You'll take it out to him. Make sure you get the right one."

"How will you know if it's the right one if it's in code, even after you get it?"

"Lady, did anyone ever tell you you're a pain in the ass? You act like one of those exec bitches I work for." His face blanched. He took deep breaths and she could see glittering beads of perspiration form on his upper lip. "The number I'm going to give you is of a coded transmission that came down from a government ship in orbit up there— US government—when I wasn't on shift. We have to know what it says, what that ship's planning to do, how come it dropped armed personnel here. Beyond the fact that I've got the right number and I'll know if you purposely screw up, you don't need to know anything more."

"But *you* need to know that I'm not going anywhere until I see you send a message for me— that's my price."

He'd gotten very quiet for a moment, long enough for her to wonder if she could tell if he only pretended to send her message. Then he'd said, "All right, let's hear it. Sanchez trusts you, and that's got to be good enough, but I can't do the impossible, lady. Remember that."

"I'm here by mistake—"

"Who isn't?"

"—and I want to get word back to IST's home office in Massachusetts that—"

"Massachusetts, *Earth*?"

"The IST Tower on Route 128; more specifically, Raymond Godfrey's office—"

"Oh lord, you're not saying this." The young man rubbed his face and seemed to fight down panic. "Look, lady, I don't know who you are or why IST would send an investigator out here like this, but let me explain how come I'm—"

"Relax, friend," Paige said, finally realizing he thought he'd been discovered by the enemy and that, in his terms, perhaps she was—or had been. "I was drugged, shanghaied, sent out here mass slow-freeze with false documents. Somebody wanted me to disappear. I want to let my office know I'm alive and rectify the situation. As far as you people go, rebels or not, you're helping me and we'll take that into considera—"

"We? Lady, can you hear yourself? If somebody went to all that trouble to put you on ice, how come you think they're going to get a communique from you—what, six, eight months, a year later—and be overjoyed about it? Doesn't sound to me like the sort of mistake IST's going to want 'rectified.'"

She'd been refusing to think about that. What did she want to say, and to whom? To God. To Ekberg? Jill Ekberg might be part of this, working under God's orders.

She'd massaged her forehead, staring at her muddy boots. She wasn't an IST executive assistant now; she was a worker. Or she was an ex-IST executive committing corporate espionage. But she was still an American citizen; she'd never been officially fired; she wasn't a criminal, at least not really. She was merely trying to correct an error that had turned her life upside down—trying to get home, get her name back, her life back.

She said, "Look here, maybe I was hasty, but I'm here under false pretenses, with a false name—I told you. I'm an American citizen in good standing, probably listed as a missing person." An important missing person. "So I'll settle for a priority

message to the captain of that American ship you
say is up there in orbit—who I am, that I'm in
danger, and that I request—no, demand—passage
back to Earth as a precursor to a formal inquiry."
She glared at the code clerk.

"All right, you really are one of them, talking like
that. I'll send your message. You better tell Sanchez what we're doing, though—and stay away
from the revolutionaries until you're picked up."
His eyes were pleading. "You've seen enough here
to know they've got good reason—and how much
everybody's risking. . . ."

"Don't worry, friend. When I get back, we'll put a
stop to this, I promise."

It had sounded like bravado even to her own
ears, but that was the only thing she had to offer.
Like the rebels, she was running on gut instinct—
the instinct to survive. The code clerk had gotten
out his copy pad and taken down her verbatim
message. She'd waited while he sent it. Though
she wouldn't have known if he hadn't sent it prop-
erly, he didn't know she couldn't tell.

An answer had come back, by the time she was
safely out of the male-secure file room with the
copied alphanumeric gibberish that the clerk assured her was the right code. The message told her
to wait at the Knob Hill workers camp, that someone from the ship's ground contingent would be
sent to interview her and make a "determination."
And it was signed, Captain A.J. Wiley, USS *Malibu*.

Then, with the glitter of imminent rescue blinding her to everything else, she'd been hustled out
the same door she'd come in through—out the
door and into the maw of revolution.

Sanchez was waiting there and that was when
he'd shoved the rifle into her hands and everything

had gone crazy. Now, in the cave surrounded by the battered rebels, she saw clearly that she should have refused, gone back to her tent and waited for the soldier dispatched to interview her.

But hindsight was myopic. Joachim Sanchéz would never have let her go; not then, not with a major confrontation only minutes away. Not once she'd seen the guns.

The guns weren't what really terrified her, she thought as she stared without focus at the pathetic rabble in the cave—it was what she'd seen when Sanchez had been shot. This time, she hadn't been in a cave full of the faithful and there hadn't been all that chanting, so it couldn't have been mass hallucination that produced the hands coming out of the rock, dragging Sanchez toward it...

Perhaps she'd been drugged or hypnotized the first time, but not this time. She sat up, away from the wall. Ho was coming.

Ho bent down in a gesture that seemed like an Oriental bow and handed her a canteen-cap full of water and a single cracker. His long eyes were full of worry He asked her, through unmoving lips: "Your mission, successful?"

She nodded and handed back the empty cap, which hadn't been more than a third full. The water seemed to go all through her; she could feel the moisture spreading out inside her. Belatedly she wondered if the water might have been drugged. Then she asked herself what difference it would make if it had been.

Here, now, she was no better than any of the rest of these criminals. Until there'd been violence, she had been, but not now, not when she'd taken up arms...

She had to get back to the Knob Hill tent city,

she just had to. Before she knew it, she was on her feet, threading her way through the huddled rebels, toward the cave's mouth.

When she reached it, a form stepped out of the dark to block her way. She yelped in surprise and then took a fearful step backward.

Before her, looming in the cavern's entrance, was a black man. He was tall and wide and nearly blue-black, and when he smiled she saw small, yellow teeth.

Paige must have staggered, for his hand came out and caught her elbow to steady her. Then she knew it was really the black man from the transit hold, the man who'd been so very dead. She remembered clearly his bloated corpse, levitating toward the ceiling, then into it. That was one memory she'd never forget.

"It can't be," Paige murmured and only knew she'd spoken out loud when the black man said, "Redemption, resurrection, the holy way. Come with me, please," in perfect English.

She was going to be sick, she knew she was. Her feet felt like they belonged to someone else: every concussion they made, slapping against the rock floor, was a surprise as she followed the black man who still held her arm.

He took her away from the rebels, away from the cave where everyone sat together and tried to help the wounded. He led her down a tunnel and to the right and to the left, guiding their steps with a flashlight.

Finally, in a small, round chamber unremarkable but for some glyphs scratched in an oval on the wall, he said, "Sit."

She did. "I didn't know you spoke English," she said.

"I learned," he replied in a soothing voice as soft as velvet.

"Oh," she said, as if that explained everything. Learned when? "I'm—it's good to see you. I don't even know your name. I thought you were dead—" She broke off and clenched her hands before she started biting her knuckles.

"My name... 'Freedom,' in English, will do. Ayoub is the surname I have."

She said, "I was sure you were dead. I saw a man who looked a lot like you and he was...his corpse was..."

"Resurrected," said the black man kindly. He was sitting opposite her; he held out his hand. "Feel me," he suggested. "Feel the warmth, the health, the strength in me."

She took the hand he offered and squeezed it. He squeezed back with gentle strength.

"Are you satisfied?" he asked her.

"Satisfied? What do you mean?"

"That I am alive."

"Of course you're alive. What I saw was..." What had she been going to say? A case of mistaken identity? A hallucination?

"My emptied shell. My unredeemed flesh. I was, Paige Barnett, that man you saw. Do not mistake the truth. I was a corpse and now I am a new man—a man who can speak to you in your native tongue."

All the hairs on Paige's body rose as if she were in the middle of an electrical storm. "That can't be," she said. "We're both mistaken. You're different but you've had a shock, some kind of trick. They've tricked us both."

The black man who called himself Freedom Ayoub shook his ponderous head. "Redemption, resurrection, the holy way." He got to his feet and walked to the place where the glyphs were scratched into the wall. Over his shoulder he said, "Come here, Paige."

She struggled on rubbery limbs and obeyed him, when all she really wanted to do was run the other way. But run where? Deeper into the caverns? She'd be lost forever. Lost, she might die. Dead, she might be vulnerable to the hands that came out from the rock . . .

She was crying when she reached his side and for the life of her she couldn't have said why those tears were streaming uncontrollably down her cheeks, as they had during the ceremony in which this man's corpse had . . . ascended . . . to the roof. And beyond.

He said, "This is Thai, you know. Nothing more exotic. The priest, the little brown man who was at my resurrection, he has given the words to humankind, in his own tongue." His fingers traced the glyphs, characters like sharp-edged serpents that seemed to writhe as she peered at the unfamiliar script through her tears. As his fingers touched the words, he repeated, "Redemption, resurrection, the holy way."

She heard her voice saying, "Did it . . . does it hurt?"

"Dying? If it is violent, yes. Redemption? Never. The light of resurrection, the path of the holy way, is pure and pain is impure."

He turned to stare at her out of black eyes swimming in yellow-and-red whites. And he smiled his yellow-toothed smile.

"What do you want from me?" Her voice had a tinge of panic, a treble of hysteria.

"I want to teach you the holy way, Paige Barnett."

"I'm not ready to die, thank you." She crossed her arms and took three backward steps.

He chuckled but it was a kind, velvet chuckle. "I want to teach you not to fear, teach you what lies beyond what you call death."

Her hand shot out of its own accord and grabbed his wrist. This time she squeezed as hard as she could and she felt blood pulsing in his veins, his rough and warm skin, muscle and bone. "You've got a long way to go—I'm scared half to death already. And I'm not going to be around here very long," she said defiantly. "I'm going back to the workers' camp as soon as I can—before head-check brands me as an outlaw, if I can. If I'm caught, I'll make up some story about running off when the shooting started. But one way or another, I'm getting out of here. I'm going back to Earth."

"I know," said the black worker. "And I will help you, if you'll help me."

"Help you, how?" Her voice was rasping; her throat was so dry it hurt to talk.

"I want to go with you to Earth," said the black man who had been dead.

CHAPTER 12

The Message

———◆———

"YOU'RE NOT GOING to believe this, Det," Locke cautioned as he sat down carefully on Cox's bed in the tech center sickbay.

Cox was sitting on the other side of the white-sheeted bed, his feet firmly on the floor, his coveralls down around his hips. "Oh, I might. The nurse started giving me fifty reasons why I had to stay here overnight, too. I just keep telling them they don't cut my orders." His arm was stitched, disinfected, and wound with gauze. He'd let them give him a pint of clear, synthetic blood and that was the most he was willing to take from the tech nursing staff, whose specialty was athlete's foot and migraine. The nurse had almost fainted when she'd looked at his arm, then tried to cut away his kevlar-reinforced sleeve—with a pair of regular scissors, no less. "All I need is another one of those steaks and I'll be ready to go back to the TAV." He grinned because he knew he was pushing this flesh-wound business for all he could get.

Locke didn't smile back. "Det, this is serious."

"And my wounds, sustained in the line of duty, aren't?" He used his right hand to lever himself around on the bed, facing Locke: "Lay it on me."

"Here goes. Two things. One: the damned sample disintegrated during Professor Singer's routine

106

testing—I saw the bits and pieces. There's nothing worth sending up to Wiley."

"Come on, don't tell me you're falling for that Cover-Thine-Ass bullshit. If she didn't make a photocopy of the marks, I bet I could sketch them from memory. It's not the stone, but the writing, we're interested in—isn't it?"

The question hung too long in the air before Locke replied, "I'll get a copy of the hash-marks and see what the shipboard cryppie system can make of it. Hell, I'll even bring the pebbles. But I don't like it, for the obvious reasons."

Locke's reasons were never obvious, Cox was beginning to learn. For all Cox knew, Locke had snuck up there and pummeled the stone fragment into dust all by his lonesome. Whatever Locke meant, it probably had something to do with exchanging fire with the rebels, though. "How's my Alpha team? Anybody seriously hurt?" Beta team hadn't gotten a scratch, which was why they were Beta team. Cox was beginning to think of them as "Locke's Beta team," and he shouldn't do that.

But Locke hadn't caught the proprietary inflection or the possessive Cox had used. The lieutenant said, "Nobody's hurt as bad as you—physically."

"Uh-oh." Here comes the alien stuff. Somebody else saw something. Cox could see it in Locke's face now, looking close: a couple extra centimeters of stubble on a set jaw because Locke was spooked enough to be shaken out of his grooming routine; a certain tightness to the mouth.

"Yeah, 'uh-oh.' Schultz says he saw the guy you put down—with a nonstandard and way overpowered round for this venue, by the way—go sidewinding along the ground into a rock, well after he should have been dead."

"Don't tell me: white hands came out of the rock and pulled him into it, right?"

"How'd you know that?"

"Learned it on X-31A, remember? Schultz is just looking for a long, all-expenses-paid R&R on Earth." The quippy tone wasn't cutting the tension, and Cox dropped it when Locke grimaced at him.

"We gonna talk about this, Sergeant?"

"Not more than we have to, here and now, no—Lieutenant." Cox started struggling into the good sleeve of his coveralls. "I told you a little about me seeing something, maybe a hallucination, on X-31A—Reynolds being pulled into a rock just that way, hands and all. Well, same thing's happening here—that's not real surprising, considering your spook buddies wanted me out here so bad. So what's got your rpms up so high?"

"Schultz isn't the only one who encountered something like that—we think Alpha team put down four rebels, but we don't have a single body to show for it. And the less seriously wounded all got away."

"Since Alpha team saw this thing, at least I'll have company when we get back and IST starts debrief—"

"What do you mean, 'thing'? You think there's only one? That it can travel between—"

"Get off my goddamn case, Locke. Help me with this sleeve. Let's get out of here, okay? Talk about it in the VTOL, or somewhere else safe." He was trying to get his hurt arm into his stiff and punctured left sleeve.

"Can't do that—at least I can't. I've got dinner with Professor Singer and I've got to hush this thing up somehow."

"You know, you're downright amazing sometimes. If you had hush orders on this, why bring down two teams of professionals to shoot the place up, make casualties, cause a repeat of all the parameters that started this—" Cox shook his head irritably and broke off.

Locke, without a word in his own defense, came over to help Cox finish dressing. When Cox had his left arm in the sleeve and was gingerly trying to see if he could move it without the kevlar-reinforced material snagging his dressings, Locke said, "Listen, Cox, I don't think we're going to stay here much longer. And I'm thinking we're going to get some very permanent orders regarding this place. So be ready for that, hear?"

Their eyes met. Cox said, "I don't want my people hung in red tape; I flat won't stand for it. They want a bang, up there, they better understand that I've got a team down here who's seen that stuff and I won't have anybody tellin' them they're crazy. Or any accidents that take out Alpha before they make it back to the ship, or funny orders that leave Alpha here to babysit the revolution."

His mind was jumping from treachery to treachery, because last time he hadn't seen this crap coming. This time, Locke was supposed to be on his side. "And I don't see what Singer's got that's so important now. How come you got more pressing business with her than with Alpha, if Alpha saw somethin' you want to keep classified?"

"I don't know why that sample got destroyed. Maybe there are sympathizers in the tech center."

"Revolutionary symps? Or cultists?"

"I don't know, I said. I'm staying here this evening to see what I can find out. You're welcome to join us for dinner, but maybe Schultz and Alpha could use a fancy meal, courtesy of IST..."

A bribe, but a tempting one. "I'll take that—and

we'll stay out of your way. *And* I'll tell them to keep this to themselves, at least until we get where we can take everybody's depositions on video. Good enough?"

"Great." Locke seemed relieved. "Let's blow this place, then."

Cox, on his way to the door, looked over his shoulder. "Not funny, under the circumstances." And: "Hey, was that the second thing I wasn't going to like—that we didn't take any prisoners?"

"Nope," Locke said, catching up with Cox and reaching past him to put a hand on the door so it wouldn't open automatically: "Wiley sent down a message that we're supposed to investigate a complaint from one of the workers—or from somebody in the Knob Hill camp who claims not to be a valid worker, but a US citizen here under duress. I left the transcript for you with Schultz. Take some of Alpha, if you want, when you go into the camp to check it out."

"Shit, why don't you just kill me here?" Going into the tent city after the kind of engagement Alpha had just had was anything but safe.

"Look," Locke said earnestly, "I'd do it myself, but I've got Singer and her screw-up to deal with. Send Beta, if you're too weak to handle it—they're fresh. But if there's some woman in that camp who has the right answers to Wiley's questions, we're supposed to bring her out. Over the work bosses' objections, if necessary."

"Woman? Bring her out?"

"Out: bring her with us when we leave. If she's what she says she is, she's getting a ride, courtesy of the United States Space Command, all the way back to Earth."

"What she says she is?" Locke could be a little more forthcoming, damn him.

"An IST honcho of some sort. So if she is that, you can imagine that we might run into a little resistance from the Morgan work bosses about taking her off X-66B, especially if they haven't made her stay here as pleasant as they possibly could."

"Okay, now I see why you want an armed presence when she's checked out. Got a name, by the way?" Cox said it very casually, because even though it couldn't be who and what he thought, it probably was.

"Slipped my mind. Schultz had the transcript, I told you." Locke let go of the door so that it opened. Then he said, "Wait a minute, I remember: Smith, XB340248. And it sure isn't a higher priority than Alpha's after-action dinner."

"I think I'll keep Alpha and Beta together," Cox said casually as he went one way, following the colored lines on the tech center floor, and Locke went the other.

To do any of the above, he had to sneak out of the sick bay without the damned nurse finding him.

CHAPTER 13

You Only Die Once

———◆———

PAIGE COULDN'T SEEM to summon the strength to argue when Freedom Ayoub gave her orders. Maybe she'd become a zombie. Maybe she'd died in the firefight and wandering in the black man's wake through this maze of tunnels was some sort of nightmare dreamed in life's last moments.

They'd left the rebels far behind, she thought, until they took a turn and she heard voices, down the tunnel. Then she thought that the man who'd been a corpse had been leading her in circles all this time. Furious, she considered picking up a sharp piece of rock, any of many strewn at her feet, and braining the man in front of her.

Then she'd see how the whole thing worked—if he'd rise up to the ceiling again, be resurrected again. But she just couldn't find the energy. She merely trudged in his wake until they rounded a final corner and she saw where the voices were coming from.

There, in a small widening of the tunnel no bigger than her bedroom back on Earth, were a half-dozen men huddled together, talking.

" ...work bosses definitely have sent guards into the tunnels after us. Armed guards. We must be ready to guide the people to the surface. And to the—" The speaker turned when Freedom Ayoub cleared his throat.

Paige walked right into Freedom because she wasn't watching where she was going. The black man grabbed her arm and she stood there, mute, staring at the little group which in its turn regarded her.

Among them were Ho, the Chinaman who'd given her water in the big cave; the Asian priest whose name she'd never learned, the one who Freedom said had made the scratches on the walls and who'd presided at his resurrection; Jadeesh, the Indian who'd never spoken to her in the whole time he'd been Sanchez's assistant...

...And Sanchez himself. Joachim Sanchez sat in the midst of his revolutionary brothers and smiled at her, beckoning. His shirt was open, exposing his ummarked throat, the hair of his chest. He said, "Señorita, welcome! Ayoub, just in time!"

She grabbed at the black man's arm and moaned. She rubbed her eyes with her free hand. How long had it been since she'd seen Sanchez die? Stood over him? Confronted an armed man over his...corpse? What was happening here?

Freedom Ayoub's strength guided her steps and soon enough she was so close to Sanchez that she could have reached out to touch him.

As if reading her mind, Sanchez extended his hand and she took it. The hand of Joachim Sanchez was cold, moist, and hard with callus from manual labor.

Paige must have whispered, "You're alive."

She thought he murmured back, "You only die once," but that couldn't have been what he said as he took his hand away.

In a louder voice, Sanchez asked Ayoub, "Is all prepared?"

"She has agreed," Freedom replied in his velvet voice and Paige wished she could find her own.

But she couldn't speak. Sanchez looked at her fondly and his eyes seemed to be exactly the way she remembered them. He said, "Thank you, Señorita. We haven't much time. The enemy comes after us. There will be much bloodshed. Be strong. You and Freedom are our witnesses."

The other men with Sanchez murmured assent now. Paige had a horrid intuition that every one of these others had been dead all along. How fast was the resurrection, anyway? On what did it depend? What did Sanchez mean, *You only die once?* The implications froze her tongue in her mouth.

She wanted to demand an explanation. She wanted someone to cut off a finger and show her that it would grow back. She wanted to be promised safety and...no, she didn't yet want what they had—not what Ayoub and Sanchez had.

She clenched her fists because she didn't know what she wanted anymore, and because Sanchez was talking of more bloodshed as if it didn't matter ...Because he was *dead*, damn him! She'd seen him die. Maybe after they were dead they didn't care about the living. Maybe they weren't human at all, just...phenomena. Maybe they were possessed by inimical forces, or animated by alien microorganisms wearing human bodies the way hermit crabs wore shells. Or maybe they were mere mimicry, some kind of physical or ectoplasmic joke.

If they were human—if Sanchez was the man she'd known, he wouldn't speak casually about guards coming down into the tunnels after the workers. These tunnels were the heart of the revolution, even Paige knew that.

Through gritted teeth, she managed to say, "Joachim, I don't understand."

"You will," he said. "Ayoub will go with you. Quickly now, before the guards find us. Go! Run!— And thank you, Paige, from all of us."

There was no time to answer before Freedom Ayoub's big hand was propelling her past the little knot of men, along the tunnel. His flashlight bobbled before her hypnotically. She followed, listening to her better self lecture the rest of her that this was all shock-related fantasy, that none of it was real, that she'd wake up back in her tent in the Knob Hill work camp and nothing whatsoever would have changed.

She lost track of how long they'd been running through the tunnels, following Freedom's bobbing flashlight. She could hear only her breathing, and

his, and occasionally the distant sounds of conflict.
Once, the conflict seemed to be coming closer. She
heard shouts and sharp reports, echoing off the
walls so that it was impossible to tell from where
it came or how much of what she heard was rever-
beration.

She ran until she got a stitch in her side and had
to stop. Freedom Ayoub stopped with her. He
wasn't even breathing hard.

He said, "Come, find your strength: we must
flee." His yellow eyewhites seemed luminous in the
cave's dark; his small teeth flashed like a Cheshire
Cat's smile.

"I can't. I can't go on."

"Do you wish to explore the mystery now?" he
said kindly.

And she said querulously, "What?" before she
could stop herself.

So again Freedom Ayoub told her patiently, "Redemption, resurrection, the holy—"

"Stop saying that! Of course I don't want to die,
you idiot! I want to get back to the camp!"

"Then you must either get up and run, or allow
me to carry you," said the black man as if he was
telling her what of two choices she could have for
dinner. "They are coming closer."

"Who? How do you know?" She pulled her
weary knees up and encircled them with her arms,
trying to envision herself standing and running,
urging her limbs to regain their strength. But it
was no good. She needed to rest.

"The workforce guards. I know because I can
hear them."

She'd heard something too. She rested her cheek
on her updrawn knees, for just a moment. She
closed her eyes. Suddenly she was being swept up

into the arms of the big black man and carried as though she was a child.

She protested, "But you'll never be able to hold out. There's a limit to even your—" Paige broke off. She didn't know this creature's limits. Her skin crawled, being carried by whatever sort of entity he was.

Paige wasn't sure she'd made the right decision, saying she'd take Ayoub with her if he'd help her. Seeing Sanchez had shaken her badly. Sanchez was somehow different. Well, hell, he'd died, hadn't he? she told herself fiercely. That ought to make you just a little bit different.

Paige couldn't sustain a rational train of thought when all these events were so far from what she'd learned to consider logical and rational. She wanted to get back to the camp, to wait for the investigator sent to interview her. But she wasn't sure that she wanted it enough to be carried there by a black corpse animated by a power she didn't understand.

Or by a player in some gigantic charade whose mechanism was beyond her. She wanted, increasingly, to go to her fate under her own power. Her skin began to tingle wherever she was in contact with Freedom Ayoub and she couldn't have testified under oath whether that tingle signified repulsion, superstitious awe, or anticipation. She did know that she wanted him to put her down, and that he shouldn't be able to carry her much farther.

Finally, she said, "Let me go, Freedom. I can walk now. You must be exhausted." Because he should be, he really should be—anyone human—anything physical—would be.

The big black man wasn't even sweating, not

breathing hard, she noticed as he stopped and gently lowered her to her feet.

"That's better," she said haughtily. "Now, where are we? How far do we have to go?" She was stronger, after the rest he'd given her.

"Not far, Señorita, but it is most dangerous for you from here on—"

"What do you care? If I die, you'll resurrect me, right?"

The torch was slung from his belt. She could see him shake his head.

Something made the whole cavern quake. Beneath their feet, above their heads, on either side, rock trembled. The noise was deafening. Paige clapped her hands to her ears and shouted, "Grenades! They're using explosives!"

Ayoub had already grabbed her hand and was running, dragging her, toward what appeared to be a dead end. The work bosses must have issued the guards some sort of crowd-control grenades, Paige's mind told her; the guards wouldn't risk being buried alive in here.

Would they?

Freedom was running headlong toward the rock wall ahead, it seemed. The light bobbling on his belt made it hard for her to tell just what she was seeing.

He had one hand outstretched. Stiff-armed, he collided with the wall, jerking her closer to him at the same time. Something gave way and they were in another passage.

He'd pushed through some sort of hidden door, she told herself, some rotating panel hewn from the rock. She could find no other explanation and everything was happening too fast.

They were running up rough-hewn stairs, now.

Running until she began to see colored sparks before her eyes—red sparks and green sparks and blue-white sparks that danced at the darkening edges of her vision.

But she kept following the bobbling light, the big dark form up ahead which had her hand in an unbreakable grip. She was sure that if she fell he'd drag her, or come back and carry her, up the stairs.

On leaden legs and then burning legs she pushed herself upward, gulping breaths of stale, dusty air. And then fresh, colder air.

She peered into the gloom, at the man who had her by the hand, at the place where the torchlight should be bobbling. The torch was off. The man was still. They had come out of the stairwell into a fissure between rocks and, above them, three workforce guards were poised, their rifles trained on them.

"Hands above your heads! Come out of there, one at a time! Move or you're dead meat!" screamed a young, nervous Spanish-speaking guard.

Freedom Ayoub let go of her hand, put both of his above his head, and meekly began to climb.

Trembling uncontrollably, she stumbled after him, calling out, "I'm Paige Barnett. Somebody from the Space Command is looking for me! I was just hiding from—"

A guard grabbed her by the collar, pulled her off her feet, and smacked her backhanded across the mouth, calling her something horrible in Spanish. For an instant, off the ground, her feet kicking, one of the guards ripping at her shirt, she saw Freedom Ayoub's eyes go wide and she managed to shout, "No, don't, Freedom," through her bleeding lip.

Then the guards thrust her against the big black

and used their rifle butts to gesture toward the rocks out of which they'd just come.

The guards' orders came too fast for her to follow as the two of them were pushed roughly against the rocks, spread-eagled, searched and handcuffed. Paige heard a rifle butt come down against Freedom's kidneys but he didn't make a sound. When someone jabbed her in the stomach, she grunted with pain. They were shoved, stumbling, toward the camp, ablaze with mobile searchlight batteries.

When they reached a small group of other prisoners, they were pushed in among them. Then the lot of them were roped together and taken, not to the commandant's office as Paige had expected, but to a holding pit blasted out of the rock.

When they'd been pushed into the pit, a trapdoor came down with a slam that locked out all light and every sound but the muted sobs of a single person weeping.

Paige was trying to decide whether that person was male or female when she realized it was herself. She stopped.

She rolled off the prisoner next to her and whispered, "Ayoub?"

"Here," she heard.

She'd been going to challenge him, taunt him, tell him, *go ahead, get us out of here.* But she didn't have the heart for it. She just untangled herself completely from the knot of prisoners and found a place to curl up against the wall.

The man next to her leaned sideways and whispered in a velvet voice, "Do not be afraid. I am with you."

Paige Barnett didn't answer the man who called himself Freedom. Her lip hurt and her pulse was pounding and she was beginning to worry that the investigator from the ship would never find her, locked away in this hole.

If that happened, and the ship left without her, at least she'd never have to make good on her promise of taking Freedom Ayoub to Earth.

CHAPTER 14

Ticket-takers

———◆———

"YOU THINK MAYBE they're shucking us some way, sir?" Schultz asked hopefully as Alpha and Beta team conducted their second tent-by-tent search of Morgan Base's work camp. "The revolutionaries, or religious fanatics, I mean—dressing up in alien outfits and pulling some kind of scam?"

"I wish I could say yes to that, Corporal. But I don't think so," Cox said.

They were sitting in the VTOL's open slider watching the teams deploying among the tents. Morgan brass was pissed beyond measure about this second surprise search, but Cox wasn't giving up on finding the woman who'd sent the message —not when the transcript he'd gotten from Schultz said she claimed to be Paige Barnett.

And anyway, he didn't have anything better to do. Locke was still occupied with Professor Singer. The pulverized stone sample and the photocopy of the glyphs on it had gone up to orbit yesterday, too soon for any revelatory answer from the cryppie program. And the Morgan Base brass had decided to mount a cleansing operation of its own without any help from the US government contingent.

The base commandant and Cox had had one monster of an argument about protocol and procedure, but it hadn't done either of them any good. Cox's idea of cooperation from the commandant in a situation like this was "you ceding me total unilateral control because I know my job better than you do." The commandant's version of that was "This is my turf, my problem, my workforce, my troops' morale, and don't you come in here telling me how to do *my* job, sonny. A week from now, you'll be gone and I'm not about to spend any longer than absolutely necessary cleaning up the mess you make with your gung-ho ticket-takers."

So the commandant had turned his own gung-ho ticket-takers loose on not only the revolutionaries, but on the whole godforsaken workforce, because you couldn't tell the rebels from the workers without a program. And nobody from Morgan Base or Cox's 203rd had a program.

Cox held his helmet in his lap so he could listen to the banter on Alpha and Beta's com-channel. He had a feeling they weren't going to find anything but a bunch of prisoners the workforce guards had taken at random during their early morning raid, because there weren't any other kind to take—because Cox's teams hadn't managed to capture any rebels and the base commandant was determined to do better than that.

So the local paramilitary had probably rounded up all the suspected troublemakers; prisoners were prisoners in a situation like this. You might have the right people, or some of the right people, by accident. The prisoners would swear they were innocent, of course, but it was only their word against the guards'. And the base commandant was ready to string up somebody—anybody—as a warning to the balance of the workforce. Terror tactics could only be fought with terror tactics, Cox knew. But he didn't like it. He was a combatant, and in his world, you went up against other combatants. Even if you outgunned them, they'd asked for it.

This sucked. What was worse, it was going to escalate matters by giving whatever portion of the workforce who'd stayed nonaligned a clear message: might as well join the rebels, because you're going to be treated as if you are one. But you couldn't tell the base commandant anything. He was too nervous, with the eyes of the USG upon him in the person of Wiley, in orbit, to do any different.

Cox had seen it all before; that didn't mean he had to like it. So he'd had a hidden agenda to pursue during these surprise searches: he wanted to make sure that any prisoners taken had at least a minimum of human rights.

And to that end, the women rangers of Beta were coming in handy. He could send them in where he wouldn't send a man—among the female detainees. The reports he was getting from them weren't the sort of thing the base commandant was going to want on his record. More to the point, they weren't the sort of reports IST would want bouncing around Washington.

So Cox was picking up a little leverage, sitting there with Schultz and running the search via his helmet com-link. If Locke had been available, they'd have routed everything through the VTOL's more sophisticated com-system, but Locke was closeted with Singer. The professor must be hell on wheels once she got her clothes off, to keep Locke so completely occupied.

Cox had Schultz set up an automatic patch that would beep him if any communiques came down from Wiley in the *Malibu* so that Cox didn't have to depend on Locke for his weather reports. Once that was done, he had only to wait for the telltale to alert him and carry on with his primary mission: finding the woman now identified in the ship's log as *Smith, XB340248, a/k/a Paige Barnett.*

He'd never been so glad to see a piece of printout in his life as he'd been when Schultz had handed him Wiley's directive. "Find and interview; establish credibility and evac if as advertised," Wiley had ordered.

Yes sir, Cox was trying his damnedest to do that. There was somebody named Paige Barnett here and that meant that Cox wasn't crazy, that everything he'd thought he'd seen had probably been as real as the woman who'd stared at him over the rebel corpse. It meant that everything else he'd seen was probably equally as verifiable, too. But one thing at a time. He wanted to perform his search and rescue and then he'd have time to gloat.

The only thing he didn't like about the prospects of finding the same Paige Barnett who he'd thought he'd seen boarding the transport with him at Hanscom was that, if everything he remembered was right on the money, then the aliens were too.

What he really needed, he decided, slipping off the lip of the VTOL's open slider door, helmet in hand, was an informant or two. But short of the woman listed on the roster as Smith XB340248, he couldn't fathom how to acquire one.

Beta Leader was telling Alpha Leader that Beta had gone through "every frigging tent in this sector with zilch result. Repeat, Alpha—no female paydirt." The voice was female because Frickey, the Beta leader for this, was one of the unit's two women. Frickey would probably make sergeant because of Cox letting her run Beta on the ground, and she knew it.

Frickey might be willing to show her gratitude, but all Cox wanted out of Frickey was a perfect job—he wanted to find his quarry. Especially because he was sure now that the quarry was Paige Barnett. Which meant he could trust his senses and his instinct implicitly. That instinct, honed through twenty-seven planetary out-system missions, was telling him that the base commandant didn't *want* the 203rd to find Smith, XB340248— that either the guards had her and had secreted her, or hoped they had her and were secreting everybody who might fit that description.

Still listening on the com line, Cox waited until Alpha had reported in turn, "Same for us—no lady prisoners whatsoever. And no women lookin' to talk to us; they're all happy as trained clams on a mud flat."

Schultz was looking at Cox expectantly, waiting for orders, still sitting in the VTOL, swinging his legs.

Cox said, "You know, I want to go up to the Knob Hill work camp, maybe we'll have better luck there."

"Right, I'll pull 'em—" Schultz's round, baby face smoothed with relief. He didn't like being down here among the workforce guards, where the hostility was palpable and the odds in favor of Morgan Base if push came to shove.

Schultz's stubby thumb was already keying his mike when Cox said, "Hold it!"

Schultz deliberately lifted his thumb and brought it down on the squelch button, shutting out all com-line chat. "Yes, sir." He looked at Cox calmly. "It's held."

"Good. Off the record, okay? Just you and me for a minute, Schultz."

"Sure, Det." Schultz's head seemed to retreat into his shoulders but his short legs didn't stop swinging.

"You saw something funny out there during the riot, like I did—what do you think's going to happen when we come home telling tales about white hands and aliens?"

Schultz screwed up his face and expectorated, just missing his own foot. "I'm gonna answer lots of dumb questions and look like an asshole, no matter how right I am."

"If you're lucky, that'll be the worst of it. Okay, if we have this woman—an ex-IST honcho, who's been here and gotten her nose in the revolution, maybe—nobody's going to bother with us. She'll take all the heat."

"I hear you, but we can't find her."

"How come, you think?"

"Aw—I see. You think they're hiding her?"

"I think they—IST, not just the Morgan Base brass—don't want her found, yeah. I think that's why she's here." Like that's why I'm here. "So maybe this is higher risk, and more complicated, than we've been treating it."

This time, Schultz squirmed where he sat. "Well, we been talkin' about that, 'mongst ourselves, sir —Det. We didn't want to say nothin'—high risk is what we're paid for. But we're gettin' less than no cooperation from these merc guards and we was wonderin' about tunin' some of 'em up a little?" There was a Doberman-like eagerness in Schultz's eyes.

"I don't want that," Cox said automatically. They

might not win a confrontation with these work bosses, not one-on-one; and Wiley would never let them use the heavy artillery on IST staff in good standing.

"Then why're you tellin' me this? We know what you did with the electronics, Det, and we appreciate it—it's just not real encouraging that you thought you had to."

"I'm telling you because I want you to volunteer to go up to Knob Hill with me and do some personal groundwork. I want to leave Beta with the VTOL and Alpha here, because we need a decoy, something for the staff to watch."

And because, asshole, you ought to realize that if we don't get positive proof, and get that proof back to Earth alive, well, and parade-ready, we're probably not looking at much of a future, any of us.

Schultz was nodding solemnly. "Okay, Det." He keyed his mission log recorder. "Sir, I volunteer for Knob Hill recon, just you and me." He gave the notation a security block and let up on his mike toggle.

"Thanks. Full kit, okay? We don't know what we're going to run into up there." Had to be up there, or else Paige Barnett was holed up with the rebels some place only high-tech electronics were going to find her.

"Balls," he muttered as the thought struck him. He walked to the VTOL's tail and looked past it, up the slope toward the pinnacle on which the tech center was built. There were birds flying in and out of there all the time. If he found out that Locke was doing aerial recon from the tech center and hadn't bothered to tell him, Cox was going to get real testy.

But one thing at a time. Schultz ordered Beta

back to the VTOL and Cox went inside to strap on his full kit, recon pack and all. He checked the levels in his pharmakit, put a new disk in his belt transceiver and plugged in a booster, so that the transcript would satellite up to the ship without having to go through the VTOL. Then he shoved a fresh cassette of film into his helmet camera, topped off his respirator tanks because you never could tell, and started checking his weapons.

By the time Schultz joined him in the VTOL, he'd broken out full assault gear. No rubber bullets this time. If he was going to be shooting, he'd be shooting workforce guards, and for that he wanted twelve-foot-spread thallium and as much plasma as he could pack in three extra magazines.

Schultz looked at the firepower and said, "Holy Mother of God, Det. You think we're going to need all that?"

"Nah, I'm just a slave to training. Want to take some of these?" He tapped a belt-feeding bandolier of ten millimeter before he shrugged into it.

Swearing under his breath, Schultz grabbed ninety pounds of hostility-neutralizing firearms and explosives to clip, belt, strap, and secret about his person.

All of that over armored coveralls ought to get them through a confrontation with the aliens themselves.

If that was what happened, Cox didn't want to be staring at his empty hands and wishing he'd come prepared. When both men were in full battle dress and had checked out each other for patching errors, Beta was waiting outside.

Frickey's eyes, shadowed under her visor, didn't blink when Cox came to the VTOL's slider and bent down to tell her, "You want to leave somebody else in command here and fly me and Schultz up to the Knob Hill tech center?"

"Yes sir," said the female corporal, her square jaw knotted with the effort of not saying, *Dressed like that?*

He left her to her job and slammed the slider shut.

When she came aboard, before she started the VTOL, she said softly to Schultz, "Anything I should know, Fritz?"

"Lots, but not about this mission. Just drop us, okay?"

Frickey strapped in and called to them to do the same.

The woman flew like a race driver but Cox hardly noticed. Schultz was up front with her anyhow; if she was cowboying beyond what he could stand, he'd throttle her down. Meanwhile, Dennis Cox needed the interval to decide just how far he was going to trust Locke.

It was a hell of a decision to have to make, this far into an operation where lives might rest on Cox's judgment call. As approach and landing patter started coming from the flight deck, Cox unbuckled and stuck his head up into the cockpit: "Just put us on the pad and leave, Frickey; we need you at Morgan with Alpha and Beta. Another hour, if they come up dry, you bring them in, back to the TAV, and give them three beers apiece from the kangaroo's stores. No more, hear? And everybody stays locked and loaded. Copy?"

"Yes, sir," said Frickey, all pilot and trusted officer as she put the VTOL down vertically on the designated X among four empty bull's eyes at the tech center strip.

"Thanks for the ride, Frickey," Cox called at the

top of his lungs as Schultz pulled back the slider and the noise became deafening.

The pilot waved and Cox swung out and down, beside Schultz, who was looking around him, rifle at ready, as if they'd just jumped fifty miles down into unreconnoitered enemy terrain. Which the tech center might be, from the way Cox's body was reacting.

He touched the corporal on the shoulder and Schultz followed his example, dog-trotting away from the VTOL, a hand on his rifle's receiver to steady it in its sling. By the time Frickey had clearance to lift, they were in the tech center's lounge and Cox felt the moment of decision close him in like setting cement.

He just stood there, watching Schultz watch him, and finally said, "Christ, I've got to at least try to put Locke in the picture. Come on." He led the way through the white-walled tech departure lounge toward the science tower as if he'd grown up there, following the floor codes he'd learned the last time he was here.

When they found Locke, he was in Professor Singer's private lab and Singer was with him.

Locke looked up and did a double-take. "Det, God, what's going on? An all-out boogie?"

"Nah, I'm just toting my security blanket with me," Cox said. "Professor Singer, this is Corporal Schultz. Schultz can't take off his helmet, presence of a lady or not, because we're going right back out and we don't want to recheck all these damned wires." Cox grinned at Singer from under his raised visor. At the same time he keyed his recording camera from his belt. Never could tell what he might want to study later.

Cox walked around the room as he asked, "Any

luck with decoding the secret message on that piece of stone yet? I assume you're trying down here, as well as having sent a copy to the ship. Or with your aerial surveillance? Find any heat signatures that might be revolutionaries—or a missing white woman?" He was just letting his mouth go on autopilot, intent on completing his circuit of the room, and throwing out a couple feelers.

But Locke said with a sigh, "I should have known you'd scope the extra bird traffic over the camps. Det, I just didn't want to have to coordinate those IST pilots with your people—apples and oranges."

Schultz, not used to this sort of gray-area double-cross, said, "You what—Lieutenant?"

Professor Singer piped up, "It's my fault, gentlemen. You soldiers don't seem to realize that there are other ways to solve these problems, besides violence."

"Uh—what ways are those, ma'am?" asked Schultz, drawing himself up to his full height, chin pulled in so that it doubled.

"What the professor's trying to say—" Locke interceded.

"I can tell Corporal Schultz what I mean, thank you, Buff."

On his subvocalizer circuit so that the words came only to Cox's ears through his helmet electronics, Schultz repeated incredulously, "Buff? *Buff?*"

On the same frequency, dipping his head to nuzzle his mike, Det said, "Don't ask me. Pillow talk, most likely."

Meanwhile, Singer was explaining, her square jaw outthrust and corded, "—and we can't just put our science station pilots and aircraft under the control of the military, you must see that. You're welcome to the fruits of our labor, though. For the life of me, I don't understand why you didn't implement some such procedures from orbit, although Lieutenant Locke has tried to explain it to me. Surely a ship that costs the government—"

"Lady, we don't usually go looking for missing persons. We usually get cooperation from the local outposts, though. Lots better than this here. It's going in my report, I don't mind telling you. And—"

"Stop bitching, Det," Locke warned. "When you see this, you'll realize you don't have any grounds for complaint. And you'll realize why I didn't come tearing down there to demand that Alpha and Beta teams explore these...possibilities. Frankly, in my professional judgment, no single person is worth this kind of risk."

"I'll be the judge of that, okay...Buff?" Cox was hot and uncomfortable in full kit; he toggled on his internal cooling system, but for maximum efficiency he'd have to snap on his respirator and slap down his visor. Which he'd have loved to do, but it just wasn't polite.

When Locke got out the topographical map with the tunnels on it and showed it to Cox, Cox felt like he had to apologize: "Sorry I doubted you. You say this whole network is intermittently impenetrable because of natural shielding?"

"That's what Professor Singer tells me."

"And only marginally explored," Singer added. "These are computer simulations based on what exploration we *have* done. Whatever you may think, Sergeant, Corporal, the last thing IST wants—the last thing I want, or the science contingent here wants—is anyone getting hurt here.

Have you realized what the repercussions would be if your personnel were killed or injured here? IST would pull out quicker than a superforce jump. And there aren't that many US-staked claims that have the...peculiar characteristics of X-66B." The woman's face was covered with tiny lines that seemed to deepen as she spoke.

"Yeah, just X-31A," Cox said, "and this place, and—"

"What do you know about X-31A?" Singer demanded before Locke could intervene.

"Nothing, nothing at all." Cox fended her off with his free hand. The other, naked on his rifle's receiver, was beginning to sweat. "Except it had this same natural shielding and an unusually rich concentration of titan—"

"Of all elements worth mentioning, soldier," Singer enunciated precisely. "This innocuous, unpleasant sphere contains every element mankind is interested in mining—all the constituents of a main-sequence star, in fact, including heavy metals..."

"Big deal. So does the human body," Schultz shot back, and everyone turned to stare at the corporal, who added nervously, "I heard that somewhere, that's all. Stuck in my mind—the same stuff's in a man's body as makes up a star, except it isn't volatile. A friend of mine knew somebody supposed to have died from 'spontaneous combustion,' so everybody in the unit was talkin' about it..."

"Can we table the science lesson? Locke, I want one of those birds and your best guess as to where I ought to look up here for the lady Wiley wants me to interview. We've turned those camps down at Morgan upside down and come up dry—twice." Cox wasn't about to tell Locke publicly that Locke had been wrong to withhold the topo map with all the caves on it; it was Cox's prerogative to decide what was too dangerous for the 203rd down here.

The caves *were* too dangerous. And all of a sudden it seemed hopeless to try to find anyone here —not the woman who claimed to be Paige Barnett, not the revolution. Unless you wanted to seal off the tunnel entrances and gas everybody in them, or blow them with Cox's shaped charges, there was no way to win this.

Cox hated no-wins but he'd learned to live with them—when necessary. What was bitching him was the realization that he'd been sent out here to document just that: the impossibility of solving X-66B's problems by anything less than thermonuclear means. Which he should have known when he'd busted his balls setting those charges.

But you never think they'd do that to you—run you through the motions in order to document a foregone conclusion. It happened, Cox knew, all the time, but he didn't have to admit it, most of the time.

"Okay, you didn't answer me—can I have a tech bird and all this fancy geological sensing stuff of yours to find my missing person, or not?"

"No," said Singer with pursed lips and Cox thought about a high school teacher he'd hated who wouldn't let you go to the bathroom during class time.

Locke shot Cox a rueful look that told Cox not to push it. Then the lieutenant said, "Look here, Det. Try the Knob Hill tent city; there's a worker contingent over there, too. And then I'll do my best to finish up the business I've got here and fly a recon with you—in our VTOL, if I can't prevail on the professor to let me have one of her birds for a couple of hours, off the record." *And get out of here,*

Cox, before you irremediably screw up things you don't understand.

"Yeah, I'll do that," said Cox, starting to back from Singer's now hostile presence as if she were armed and dangerous. "Come on, Schultz," he said into his com-mike, irrationally wanting to slam his visor down manually as a comment to the woman on what he thought of her civilian autonomy and corporate decision-making and scientific independence.

As the doors sighed open to the tower elevator, Schultz said, subvocally, "Hey, I've got the *Malibu*'s burst-transmission in my com. Cryppie program says the writing's in Thai...y'know... Thailand?"

"Tell me later, Schultz. Right now, I just want to get out of here."

He didn't like the way Locke had left him on his lonesome, without even an offer of a ride over the high-altitude footbridge connecting the Knob Hill work camp to the tech center. If he had to blow this place in the end, he wasn't going to feel one bit sorry for the staff. It was the workers he felt bad about—the poor fools who hadn't known what they were in for out here.

CHAPTER 15

Witnesses

———◆———

PAIGE HAD BEEN so close to salvation—to the investigator from the American ship, to regaining everything she'd lost—that she simply couldn't accept the trick that fate had played on her.

And neither, it seemed, could Freedom Ayoub. In his beautiful voice, Ayoub talked to the other prisoners in the pit about redemption, about the revolution, about making sacrifices and choices and forgiving little men their little evils: and Paige found herself helping him.

She hadn't realized what a good revolutionary she'd become. Together, she and Ayoub worked to buoy the spirits of the frightened workers around them: Doom was in your mind: The struggle was everything.

"Emancipation," said the man who called himself Freedom Ayoub, "comes from the soul. Throw off your fear, and weakness will depart your person. Risk your life, and it will be given back to you. No one can take anything away from you that you do not give up."

And Paige echoed, "Don't give up. We'll get out of here," without knowing why she was so sure they would.

There were reasons for her courage, she told herself during a sleep period, reasons beyond stubbornness and the need to stay sane. Food was brought, occasionally, by the workforce guards; thrown into the hole where people scrabbled for it in the dark. Freedom Ayoub made sure everyone got some; she helped him because she believed now that he was right: to be human, you must practice your humanity. They must not turn into animals simply because they were captives.

No one had been shot; they weren't being starved, at least not completely. And Paige still clung to the hope of being found by the investigator who certainly must be searching for her.

Freedom Ayoub held out a different sort of hope to these workers: he talked of spiritual redemption and moral resurrection, because what was in the body followed the lead of what was in the mind. Make your mind pure, your soul clean; cleave to life and create your own hope, Freedom taught. The rest would follow.

His words struck a chord so basic and so deep in her that she was even able, at times, to forget that he'd been...dead. At other times, she told herself that it was because he'd been dead that his words had such a ring of truth. She no longer disbelieved the evidence of her senses; they were all she had.

Freedom believed that "rescue" was imminent; he told the workers so over and over. And Paige had come to believe it too. So when there were sounds she couldn't explain or catalog, sounds that seemed to come from the very rock against which she leaned, at first she wasn't frightened.

She'd been listening to other sounds, more disquieting sounds, from above: thuds and cries and the occasional boot heel on the trapdoor itself. Just because she was brave during the waking periods didn't mean she wasn't aware that at any moment someone could pull open that door and kill them all as easily as shooting fish in a barrel.

The sound from the rock came again, and this time it was a creaking noise, as if the bedrock itself was shifting. Paige had been in an earthquake or two when she'd been working on the West Coast, and she knew what earth tremors sounded like. But this wasn't Earth. She reached out to touch Ayoub in the dark and found only empty air.

Had she been asleep when he'd gotten up to move? Where had he gone? It was pitch black in the pit, the scant light that came through the trap door in daytime totally absent.

She wanted to call out Freedom's name, to crawl around until she found him, but she couldn't, somehow. She was staring at the spot where he should have been and it was getting lighter. It was definitely paler than the deeper dark around it.

The spot where no man leaned against the stone was beginning to glow, as if light were shining through leaded glass, light from the other side.

The other side of what? She pinched herself roughly on the arm to see if she was truly awake. It hurt. She gritted her teeth and started sliding toward the pale spot on the rock wall, careful not to wake the others.

She sidled over a little and she could feel a difference in the temperature of the wall. She thought she could feel a difference in the texture of the rock—there was a sort of "give" to the stone, which should have been solid and unyielding against her back.

Paige inched forward, and found the rock at her back had a consistency somewhere between that of human flesh and gelatin. Again, she heard the deep rumbling. She couldn't see the light now because her body was obscuring it.

But she could feel the difference in the stone. She was tensing to inch still farther along the wall when two things happened:

From above, from the trapdoor, boot heels echoed and sounds of men arguing escalated.

From the wall at her side, something brushed her arm. She stifled a scream and her head jerked around so fast and hard her skull hit the wall. The impact was almost nil, as if she'd leaned back against a pillow. And from the wall, on her right and on her left, hands were emerging, pale hands that glowed on arms that were much too long.

Paige was paralyzed with fear. She couldn't make a sound. She wanted to shout, *But I'm not dead! I'm not dead!* but she couldn't unclench her jaws. Her tongue was immobile.

She grabbed the pale hands as they came together, clasping her around the waist, and she was filled with a sensation of overwhelming peace and joy.

She couldn't struggle against that feeling. She knew she was being drawn into the wall by the cool hands at her waist and the cool arms around her but she couldn't protest. It was as if she were being drawn into a great warm bed full of safe, childhood dreams.

Then she couldn't breathe. Her nostrils were stuffed with something. She tried to open her eyes but she couldn't lift her lids. She was hot and cold and pulsing all over, as if she'd stuck her finger into a live socket.

She couldn't find her limbs' controlling mechanisms. Oh, she could feel them and she knew that if she could just move one—any one—she'd regain total control. But she couldn't remember how to do that. She was a prisoner in a body she couldn't command. Panic rose in her, but it was far away from the part of her that felt peaceful and resigned, as if the panic belonged to a younger, more foolish person than she now was and she felt sorry for the frightened part, but she couldn't seem to reach it to tell it everything was all right.

Her lungs were burning but that was unimportant. And then they weren't. She fell hard, on her back. Her skull cracked against stone of normal density; her mouth opened and she gasped for air. Her heart was pounding so loudly she couldn't hear anything but the resounding of her eardrums.

Then she opened her eyes to see Freedom Ayoub and Joachim Sanchez bending over her. Sanchez had his sleeves rolled up and both men were smiling. To Paige, those smiles were inappropriate, death's-head grins.

She was merely terrified now, in the wake of the peaceful feeling that had passed as abruptly as it had come. The rock under her was cold, hard, and glowing softly in places.

She shuddered on the stone and raised her hand to her head, brushing away Ayoub's touch as she did so: "Am I dead? Is this it? Am I...what you are?"

Sanchez laughed. "Señorita, you are not dead. You are what you are."

Freedom Ayoub said, "Redemption—"

"Cut the crap. You scared me half to death." She sat up too quickly and a blinding headache overcame her. She lowered her head and put it in her hands. "So you weren't kidding about the rescue," she heard herself say. "What about the others?"

"We are making a doorway for the others, Paige," said Ayoub gently. "You started to fall through it, so we caught you and guided you. Soon, that will not be necessary."

Her skin crawled. She wanted to go back to her nice office where the worst things she had to worry about were interoffice squabbles and badly conceived memos and security breaches and her unrequited love for Raymond Godfrey.

She didn't want to be in a world where rock could turn to jelly and men came back from the dead.

Sanchez's Spanish-accented voice said, "Please move away from the doorway as soon as you're able."

She raised her head then and the first thing she saw was Freedom Ayoub's hand outstretched to help her. The black skin of it was pale and glowing. She began to shake. She scrambled to her knees, away from his touch, away from the wall of rock Sanchez had called a doorway. She scrabbled on her knees all the way to the opposite side of the tunnel.

It wasn't until she huddled there against hard, normal, cold, dark rock that she realized there were three others in the passage. She didn't recognize any of them but she knew they were revolutionaries—dead ones. She was certain of it. Every toxic-zombie movie from her childhood rushed in on her rational mind and her teeth began to chatter.

Ayoub looked over his shoulder at her and said, "Don't do that." Then he went back to what he was doing, now that she was out of the way. He and Sanchez were running their hands over the rock in a synchronized motion as if they were a pair of window washers who'd worked together for years.

With every pass, the rock seemed to glow more. Its texture changed visibly.

Paige put her head back against the wall and she could feel the pulse in her throat making her whole body quake. She put her hand over her heart and counted the thuds of her terror. She wanted to close her eyes but she couldn't take her eyes off the two men who were making the rock go away—or at least seem to go away.

Occasionally there was a groan from the stone around her, as if the whole planet were shifting to accommodate the two men's demands.

And then she realized she could see through the rock and into the pit, where the prisoners were sleeping.

God, it couldn't be true. They weren't digging a new entrance, not without power tools and laborers—not by running their hands over the stone. She noticed, at the edges of the hole they were making, places where the rock had piled up like mud.

None of this was real. She probably was dead. She sat and watched and shivered until Freedom Ayoub turned to her and said over his huge black shoulder, "Paige, come help me wake the prisoners. We must keep them quiet."

When she reached his side, she noticed that his hands were no longer glowing, that they were black hands once again. She knew from the look on his face that she was expected to take all this in stride. She reached out to touch the passageway and its edges were still warm. But where there should have been rock, there was nothing—just empty air.

She could barely follow Ayoub through the opening. She was afraid it would shock her flesh again, that she'd feel the resistance, be unable to breathe, become euphoric, and then be paralyzed once more with fear.

But it was only a passage between the pit and the tunnel, and Paige ducked through as if it had been there all along.

She looked back at the tunnel and saw Sanchez, still smiling his bemused and encouraging smile. He waved. She scuttled around the corner and began helping Ayoub wake the prisoners, one at a time.

First you put your hand over the prisoner's mouth, then you whispered, "Ssh!" then you pointed to the opening, beyond which torchlight shone bright enough to hide the weird glow. And they went, one by one, their eyes full of slavish thanks and admiration.

Paige knew while she woke them that all of these were now full-fledged revolutionaries from this moment on. And she also knew that, if she went with them, she might never encounter the man from the *Malibu* who was looking for her.

When the last prisoner had been roused and shown the way out, Paige hung back, leaning against the normal stone, her arms crossed over her chest.

Freedom Ayoub looked at her questioningly and gestured.

She shook her head, no.

He took quick, wide strides to her side and whispered, "Come, hurry. The guards may open the trap at any moment."

"What about the ship?" she whispered back. "What about going to Earth? I thought you wanted to go to Earth with me? We'll never find the man the Americans sent if—"

"Paige, you must come now. He will find us, or we him. It is written in stone."

"Don't give me that spiritualist bull—"

The crack of heels on the trapdoor stopped her. Again, she heard arguing, perhaps gunshots, and maybe the distant wail of an alert siren.

"Come," said Ayoub and reached out to take her hand.

She shook him off because she was sure his hand wasn't as black as it should be; that it glowed pale and awful around the digits. "Don't touch me, you...you, whatever you are. I'm coming—for now."

He made a sweeping bow and held it, his arm outstretched toward the tunnel beyond, in which the others waited. She could see their anxious faces. She looked again at Ayoub and realized he was as stubborn as she; he wouldn't precede her.

She couldn't have his capture, and that of all those others, on her conscience. Anyway, she was afraid of what would happen if she was the only one left when the trapdoor opened next.

Again, above her head, she heard footsteps.

"*Now*, Paige, or all this is for nothing," said Freedom Ayoub, a calm and determined shadow in the light spilling from the revolutionaries' tunnel.

"All right, all right." She ran, and he ran after her.

As they came through the passageway, Sanchez and the revolutionaries she didn't recognize were already massaging the rock back into place.

Someone had formed the prisoners into a column and that column was moving, slowly. From its head she heard a voice repeat in a dozen languages, "Don't push. Don't hurry. Move on, close up your line."

From behind, beyond Sanchez and his friends and the rock arch that was only beginning to glow, came the loud creak and slam of the trapdoor being opened. And shouts, because the guards saw an empty pit.

"Leave it. Run," Sanchez told the man massaging the rock with him. "Paige, run." Ayoub was already sliding between the column of prisoners and the rock, toward its head, calling softly up the line, "Hurry, hurry. Run!"

CHAPTER 16

Splatter-vision

———◆———

SCHULTZ AND COX ducked into the tunnel that the prisoners had used to escape the holding pit after only a cursory examination of the rock, which seemed fused around its edges.

At least no one was bullshitting them any longer about no prisoners being down here—it was true. But the look of surprise on the face of the work boss when push-and-shove had resulted in Schultz opening the trap while Cox held five workforce guards at bay had been all the explanation Cox had needed.

Those guards were so freaked that their prisoners had escaped that they forgot all about Cox's "unauthorized entry" and ran off, screaming for help. Even through his helmet, Cox could hear the camp sirens wailing as he'd shimmied down the ladder, gun at ready.

Now they were way into the tunnel, past two branches, and listening to each other breathe. Singer had been right about the shielding properties of this rock—like at the equator, one forty-five-degree bend, and you lost touch with the world, at least by radio.

Up ahead, Schultz was going slowly, all his electronics up and running, scanning everything for hostile implications. Cox was doing the same, his visor displays quadranted and sweeping for life-forms as well as explosives, booby traps, automatic sensors, or passages where heat-signatures of recent travelers might remain.

All Cox was learning from his metering was that the big heat-track he was following on infrared had some places where it wasn't registering right —it was too hot in some spots, too cold in others.

Infrared of the sort Cox's helmet was giving him could show you a car in a parking lot hours after it had been driven away, if you knew what to look for. Here, it showed just a distorted polyglot, a serpentine conga line of uncertain composition, though occasionally a human form would separate from the mass and be clearly defined.

"Anything interesting up there, Corporal?" Cox said, trying to relax his grip on the rifle he was carrying. There was something wrong with this infrared telltale and he didn't like it one bit. Schultz, on point, could be seeing a less disturbed track— maybe a normal one, since Cox had to subtract for Schultz's own presence, his equipment, the whole recon suit's spectrum.

"Just rock. Wonder when those workforce guards are going to come down and give us some company?"

"Never, I hope. They weren't really happy, not about us finding their pit, or about the prisoners being gone."

"They still didn't admit to any prisoners," Schultz reminded him in a tight voice.

"That's true," Cox agreed. "But what with the empty pit and the nice new exit, what are they going to say, after they swore up and down they didn't have any women prisoners?"

"I still can't tell that—whether they've got any women. My readout's a mess. Probably a glitch in my—"

"I'm getting the same thing. We'll fix it later, if it turns out to be something we can fix."

Schultz just grunted and pressed on. A bit later he said, "Hey Det, what do you think made that passageway—it sure wasn't there before, the way the guards reacted. And did you see the way that rock was fused? What could do that?"

"Nukes, but this rock ain't hot," Cox said. He'd checked for radiation before he entered the tunnel, looking at the glassy edges of that arch and thinking about the future he wanted to have some day. "Heavy-duty terraforming equipment, maybe. Supports the theory that the revolutionaries have techs on their side."

"That's all?"

"What, you want me to say it for the record? Maybe it's whatever pulls dead guys into apparently solid rock. If it does the one, it can do the other. Maybe the rock's alive, for all I know."

"Jesus, Det!" Schultz stopped in his tracks, shook his helmeted head slowly, then pushed on. "C'mon, you don't think that, do you?"

"That it's alive? I dunno. I hope not—I don't know how to kill something like that." He fanned his fingers on his rifle, checked his plasma cartridges, and trooped on behind Schultz, farther into tunnels his helmet was busily mapping so that he could find his way out, eventually.

At a place where three tunnels converged into maybe thirty meters of open space, both men

paused by unspoken agreement. "I'm going to re-
wind and check my mapping; I'm not going any
farther unless I know I can get us out," Cox said.

"Great," Schultz replied and squatted down
where he stood. A bit later, while Cox was still
scanning the results of his mapping program,
Schultz got up, walked purposefully to the center
of the chamber, checked his tank feed, and fired a
stream of plasma point-blank into the far wall.

Schultz kept firing at one spot so that Cox's visor
went to near-black to keep the glare down, until
Cox finally yelled, "Okay, Schultz, okay! Let's see
what we've got."

Schultz didn't immediately lay off the trigger,
but complied soon enough that Cox didn't mention
it. Anyway, he wanted to see what the stone looked
like where Schultz had shot it.

By the time he'd cleared his visor of the mapping program and checked the air for oxygen de-
pletion and residual fumes in case any noxious
byproducts had resulted from firing that much
flame in so small a space, Schultz was already giving his target spot a thorough once-over.

"So?" Cox asked, coming up behind Schultz but
keeping an eye on the tunnel they'd just come out
of and those branching ahead.

"Looks like I shot the shit out of it, sir, but
doesn't look nothin' like the arch we came
through."

"So call it an experimental datum, and don't
waste any more ammo," Cox said with all the
commiseration he could put into those harsh
words meant for the sortie record. "Let's go, Corporal. I'll take point from here."

And he did. Let Schultz look at something
human in front of him. The corporal was doing a
good job; Cox probably would have tried that him-

self, to see if he could make the rock melt. It should have worked, he thought. The more he thought about it, the more he was certain it should have worked. The piece of rock Schultz had attacked was just regular rock, and it had blackened and shattered and cracked. But it hadn't run together like the arch they'd come through. Maybe not so much silicate here, Cox told himself. But he wanted to be finished with these tunnels as soon as possible. He'd give it another hour and then turn back, having done his best to find the woman Wiley wanted.

He wasn't thinking of her as Paige Barnett anymore. She was with the rebels, obviously—if there was such a woman. Maybe he was getting paranoid, but Cox wouldn't put it beyond IST to have come up with this whole "Paige Barnett" scenario to get Cox in deeper here than Cox could get himself out of.

He was beginning to wonder if both his Alpha and Beta teams weren't in jeopardy on X-66B now that they'd seen the aliens. Especially since Locke was holed up in the tech center, doing mysterious "business" with the science types.

Cox was about to tell Schultz to pack it in when the heat-signatures he was following became more coherent. He tracked the infrared and tapped fixer codes into his belt computer to tune up the images.

They were much closer to whatever they were tracking, to maybe twenty or thirty life-forms—people. Revolutionaries, he corrected himself savagely, because he kept seeing Reynolds and hearing those spooks in the black pressure suits telling him how they'd "scratched" everybody on X-31A and started over.

What in hell had made Cox think he was going to be the exception to security procedures of that magnitude? He was sweating in his suit and he snapped his cooling up a notch, but it didn't help.

As soon as he and Schultz got out of here, he was going to evac his people up to the *Malibu* on the basis of a verbal report that there was no stopping this revolution, given the attitude of Morgan Base, and ride out the ensuing storm. Once he got shipboard, Wiley couldn't order him back down without a damned good reason. And Alpha seeing a rebel corpse or two pulled into rocks by white hands wasn't anywhere near enough reason to buy your lunch on a godforsaken shitball that he was beginning to think the government wanted to nuke anyhow...

Up ahead, there was a blind corner and Cox nibbled his mike: "Whoa, Schultz. Let's treat this like there's armed hostiles around that corner."

Schultz came up behind him. "Yes, sir. Ready, sir."

Assault rifles could even lots of odds, especially with rebels. Cox didn't realize that Shultz hadn't gone to thallium shot, but stayed with plasma, until the two of them sidled up to the blind corner and Schultz started shooting, full auto, at whatever had moved beyond.

Cox couldn't hear himself yelling until Schultz had emptied his clip and Cox's hoarse scream of, "Cease fire, damn you!" reverberated in both their helmets.

Then he jerked Schultz bodily back around the corner and slammed him against the rock wall, waiting for his helmet to adjust to the absence of blinding flash and flame.

Schultz's breathing was ragged and the corporal was telling him, "I saw somethin'. Shit, I'm sorry, sir. I just ..."

"Shot it, yeah, I noticed. It's okay. I just want to get another look. You ready? Up and running?"

Cox's visor was back to normal. Too bad these systems couldn't side-look around this kind of corner. When Schultz said, yeah, he was ready enough, Cox said, "I'm going first."

It was his job, after all. Once he'd peeked around the corner at the mess, he stepped out into the center of the tunnel, sure from his quick scan that nobody left alive in that carnage had anything heavy enough to penetrate his suit, let alone be worth the kind of hosing Schultz had given them.

There were maybe ten dead people, if you thought about matching up this and that piece of barbecue. Beyond the dead ones were another ten or twelve wounded, and at the rear, backs against the rock, were five or six healthy enough to have their hands laced above their heads.

Cox said into his bullhorn, as matter-of-factly as he could, "You're in the custody of the United States government. Surrender any arms and come with me. We'll send somebody back for those who can't walk. Let's go. Form a line against the wall."

He didn't like this one bit, but he couldn't risk having Schultz go to pieces because the corporal had just roasted a bunch of defenseless workers. There was no way to tell that they *were* defenseless—not even if they were unarmed. That many people jumped you, recon suit or not, you were in deep shit.

So he switched to his com-link and said, "Good shoot, Schultz; we're just barely going to be able to keep the remainder subdued enough to get 'em back to Knob Hill." He didn't feel that way, but you had to read the right things into the record or the review boards (who'd never been out-system and scared to death and outnumbered twenty to one) might make the wrong call.

Schultz knew what Cox was doing and choked up a little when he said, "Glad you think so, sir. Wish I'd brought about sixty feet of rope."

"If we need it, we've got the rappelling line." Cox didn't think he'd need to tie these people up: those that weren't burned to bits or burned into a state of shock were half-blind from the flash and flame.

And they were used to being muscled around by armed guards; they didn't have the sense to use their numbers. The ones against the wall, the unhurt ones, started helping up the ones who could stagger back if somebody had an arm around them, and in Cox's display it looked like an animated Bosch painting.

So he shunted his display over to targeting, and his captives became stick figures with numbers by their heads. Helped a little. But he still had to remind himself that these were the revolutionaries who'd shot up his arm and tried to do worse to him.

Schultz did a good job of rounding them into a queue and then Cox had to take his system off targeting because he needed real-time photos of those he was leaving behind, both the wounded and the dead. Cox reconned the casualities and when he was done, he picked up a position in the back of the line so that Schultz wouldn't have to look at anything but clean tunnels and his mapping display.

It was going to take forever to get this bunch of sorry souls back to Knob Hill.

And there was some kind of holdup, near the front, before the tail end of the line that Cox was babysitting had even made it around the corner of the tunnel.

He didn't know just what it was until he got the stragglers past the blind corner so that he could talk to Schultz in his helmet again. When he heard Schultz swearing, he felt an immediate wash of relief, and then he said grumpily, "Corporal, you keep these bastards bunched up good—I don't want to find out I can't hear you again, not the whole way back. Every time we come to a sharp corner, you wait 'em up until I get close enough and then we'll all go around together."

"Yes, sir, sorry sir. Hey, if you didn't hear, Det... I mean, I forgot you couldn't hear. I got this woman up here who says she's the one we're looking for."

"She hurt?" An awful feeling came over Cox. He'd forgotten all about his primary mission as soon they'd engaged that many of the rebels—hell, he'd forgotten as soon as Schultz had started blasting anything that moved.

"Not much. Blisters, burns. Talkin' crazy, though. About not leaving any dead back there because they'll turn into...well, talkin' crazy. Says we'll see those ones we leave in the cave again. Want to hear some of this? I'll patch it through to you?"

"No, send her back." Shit. That was all he needed, was this woman's on-site hysteria read into his sortie record.

"She says..." Schultz's voice now had a sharp edge. "She says that she's not goin' nowhere without this big black guy she's leanin' on; she says she's gonna fry all our asses when she gets back to Earth and she's takin' this black guy with her as a witness."

"Send her back here, with the black guy."

Cox toggled his system onto area input and began taking audio and video readings in real time of everything going on. With his visor giving him one quadrant with light-intensification, one with the targeting stick figures he'd designated previously, one of mapping so that he could see just where they were and where they were going, and one of infrared, he had to use splatter-vision to see anything at all in his real-time field of view.

But he managed, focusing beyond his display readouts, at the farthest head he could see— Schultz's, because Schultz was a big boy in recon gear and the top of his helmet had its homing beacon engaged so that a red light blinked intermittently.

Consequently he saw the big black guy and the woman sidling back, pressed against the tunnel wall, as the rest of the captives moved forward. Then he said, "Goddamn," and turned off his recorder for a full minute while he considered his options.

Well before the two had reached him, he could tell that Schultz was right, the woman wasn't seriously hurt. As they came closer, he could hear her angry, horrified voice and the ragged edge to it that tears gave.

When the two got real close, Cox keyed his bullhorn. "That's far enough. Mister, you fall in at the end of this column. Lady, you're gonna walk with me for a while."

She looked at him with ice-cold eyes and her face was puffy from crying. He'd thought, somehow, she'd recognize him by his voice but of course she couldn't, not the way it blasted out of his speaker pack. And guys look pretty much alike in full recon gear. But for his stripes and the "Det" stenciled above his visor, he probably looked just like Schultz to her untrained eye. And she didn't know him as Det.

She was telling the black guy to be cool, thinking Cox couldn't hear her. He tapped his gain up so that he could catch every whisper between them.

She said: "We merely have to be strong until we reach the tech center. I know I can get us that far. I'll find the investigator, and we'll put all this right. I'm sorry, you don't know how sorry, about the killing...Americans aren't usually so vicious—"

And the black guy whispered back: "Why should you be sorry for the dead? Redemption, resurrection, the holy way. As for your promise, I have no fear. All our futures are in your hands and I have faith in those hands."

The woman actually looked at her hands before she left the black and came up to Cox.

By then, he'd restarted his recorder. Whatever he thought he might want to say to her, he'd do it later. Now, he couldn't miss the chance to get this stuff recorded, even if it turned out to be embarrassing.

She was standing before him, her head high, one cheek pebbly with blisters, soot smeared over her chin, hands on her hips. Her hair was longer than he remembered it.

Beyond her, he saw the black man at the end of the line move away.

"Here I am, soldier. I demand to know your name, rank and serial number. And I demand to be taken immediately to the investigator assigned by Captain Wiley of the USS *Malibu* to find me. I'm a very important person and you're going to swing for this, buddy. Cold-blooded murder. You don't know what kind of mistake you've made here!"

Cox muttered to himself, "Christ, shut up!" because he didn't need this sort of thing on his transcript and considered not letting on that he knew her, turning her over to somebody else. But he couldn't. And the line of captives was getting farther away.

Decided, he pushed up his visor and said, "Oh yeah, I do know. But look, Paige, I've been bustin' my butt trying to find you. You don't make things easy for a guy." He thumbed his squelch button as she blinked like a startled cat. "You don't push this 'murder' bullshit and I won't let on that you're part of the revolution, okay? And maybe then we can pick up where we left off—I did rescue your ass at great risk to life and limb."

He didn't know what he expected, but it wasn't her throwing herself into his arms. "Cox," she kept saying. "Dennis Cox, my God." And he was sure he saw joy in her eyes.

CHAPTER 17

Revolution

————◆————

PAIGE BARNETT FOLLOWED the shambling line of silent prisoners through the tunnels toward the Knob Hill pit, with Freedom Ayoub's broad back always before her and Dennis Cox's unyielding, gloved hand on her arm.

Her face where she'd been burned hurt as if a swarm of wasps had stung her. She'd witnessed the callous incineration of innocent workers and revolutionaries of conscience by one American soldier, and been warned to keep silent about the travesty by another.

Yet somehow, because that second ranger was Dennis Cox, she was feeling better, not worse. Cox was the investigator sent to find her; she was safe now. She knew it with more certainty than she'd known anything since she'd okayed Cox's vital stats when Dream Date proposed their meeting.

And she knew it was irrational to feel the way she did. When he'd pushed up his visor and looked down at her, nothing else seemed to matter—not the death and destruction, not the horror of the burned innocents back in the tunnel . . . nothing but getting home to Earth in Cox's care mattered.

Paige told herself that her feelings were excusable because she believed—because she knew— that those casualties in the tunnel would be resurrected. You only die once, Sanchez had said. Sanchez hadn't been there when the smoke cleared. As if by magic, he'd disappeared. So had the others she'd known instinctively to be like him . . . resurrected ones.

Keeping pace with Cox in the tunnel, she wrestled with her guilt and won: she didn't have to feel pity for the dead; they were going on to a better life. All her old emotions seemed suddenly outmoded and she kept her attention fixed on Freedom Ayoub's back. Because that was her task: to get Freedom Ayoub to Earth, as she'd promised Sanchez.

Where Sanchez was, or why, or even how were not her concern. She was an executive; she was well-versed in compartmentalizing her emotions and making hard choices. The worst was over; the sorry line of prisoners before her seemed haloed in gilded promises. Beside her, Dennis Cox moved easily, armed and dangerous, part of the unenlightened forces arrayed against the revolution.

And yet she'd never been so glad to see anyone in her entire life. She'd thrown herself into his arms, overswept with unreasoning joy, with personal triumph in the midst of so much pain and death. Although Cox seemed much larger than she remembered, more forbidding in all his armor and weaponry, she hadn't been afraid for a single instant since she'd seen his face.

The only trouble was, he couldn't talk to her now—he'd made it clear that anything they said would somehow go on the record; that his equipment automatically recorded everything that happened. Well, she'd already grabbed him like salvation on the hoof. And before that she'd told his homicidal companion just what she intended to do—take Freedom Ayoub to Earth with her, press charges...

She slowed her pace and the helmeted head beside her turned slowly, its insect-eye visor rising.

"Something wrong? You hurtin'?" Cox asked.

He wasn't wearing his respirator; she could see his face clearly in the light from his belt torch; his gaze was unwavering. She replied, "I've been thinking about what you said. And what I said to your friend." With her free hand, she made a throat-cutting motion, hoping he'd understand. "And I want you to know I'll do whatever you think best."

He nodded and took his hand from her arm, tapping his belt keypad as he said, "Good. That's gonna save everybody lots of trouble. And you'll get further, quicker, cooperating." His eyes flickered to the line of captives moving away. He stopped stock still and said even more quietly,

"Okay, what is it? We're squelched but I can't do it long—we're keeping real-time records." Again, his attention flickered to the line ahead. "And we don't want to get separated."

"I..." Now that she could say whatever she wanted, she didn't know what, exactly, she wanted to say. "The black man, Freedom Ayoub, *must* come with us. Please, don't ask me why. Not yet."

"Yeah, Schultz told me what you said. I'll do the best I can. That it?" His hand was poised on his belt.

She reminded herself that Cox was a soldier in a combat situation; this was no place to have the discussion she wanted to have with him. "That's not *good* enough. Freedom has to come with us."

"Great. I said I'd fix it. Later. Now, we don't want to get too far behind..."

"Then let's walk. Give me just a few more seconds to talk to you—we'll have security considerations later, too—won't we?"

His lips quirked. "I forgot how slick you are. Yeah, that's right. Let's go. But spit it out, okay, Paige?"

"Certainly. Have you thought at all about how and why this happened—to us, I mean?" She was on dangerous ground now. She asked herself why she was trusting this man and couldn't find an answer. But trust she did; every fiber of him told her she could.

"You bet. Lots. Especially since nobody was admitting you were out here and what I thought I remembered was sounding crazy." He looked at her, away toward the line, and back again. "Look, this is one very nasty situation. You don't know how nasty. Now that I've found out you're really here, I'm beginning to worry that whoever pulled the strings to get us here doesn't expect either of us to ever get back in-system to tell anybody anything. You read me, pretty IST lady?"

"I...I guess that was what I wanted, to warn you about that very possibility."

"You don't know the half. I keep thinkin' that maybe it wasn't just a wrong number I got when I was tryin' to find Locke and got Dream Date instead. You ought to start trying to figure out who set this up on your end—and why. I hate to think it was just because you happened to be hanging out with me."

"It wasn't," she said flatly, then just walked on, not elaborating.

Cox sighed sibilantly. "I can't stay squelched much longer. But you and your revolution are about to put this shi—chunk of rock in jeopardy of one serious hosing. I want you—"

"It's not the revolution that they're afraid of, it's the—"

"I know what it is. Let's not talk about that till we get to the VTOL, where I'm sure about security. Now, you do what I say, don't ask questions or make threats. There're only so many cocoons on the *Malibu* and if evac's in order, there's a science staff in the tech center who'll probably try to get my Alpha and Beta berths—"

"What?"

"Rides home are going to be at a premium."

"Freedom Ayoub must—repeat: *must*, Dennis—come with us."

"I hear you. I also heard him say something about 'redemption, resurrection, the holy way'... we just decoded some rock hieroglyphs that say that in Thai. Is this a Thai cult?"

"It's...too complicated to explain now. You're right, we'll talk about this later." She rubbed her arms, suddenly cold in her tattered coveralls.

Leaning toward her, Cox said in his husky voice, "Hey there, I didn't mean to scare you. I'll get you back. It's what I do—get back. Every time." He grinned and it was infectious.

She reached up to touch his face, stopped because somehow it didn't seem right, not here, and he signaled that he was going to turn his equipment back on. Down came the visor, and she was looking at a forbidding, unidentifiable ranger again.

His gloved left hand slipped from her arm, across her back, and squeezed her briefly against him. Then he let go of her entirely for the first time since they'd started walking together at the end of the line of prisoners.

Through his helmet speaker, his voice came again, clipped and noncommittal, "We're falling behind. Let's pick it up." Cox started to jog, watching to make sure she could keep up with him.

By the time they'd caught up to the others, she was winded. He noticed and once again retracted his faceplate, this time to wordlessly unfasten his respirator and play out its hose until she could, standing on tiptoes, bury her face in it. The cold, pure air was rich and heady. She gasped greedily, and he pulled it out of her hands, saying, "That's enough, you'll get giddy," before he took it away.

It was foolish to regret, after Cox's single generous gesture, all she'd left unsaid, Paige told herself. Cox had that air supply whenever he wanted it; this was the first time he'd offered her any. He was a soldier, whatever else he was, and used to danger—willing to make a living under these conditions. Just because she had a notion where Sanchez went and what to expect next from the revolution didn't mean she had to warn Cox. If she did, now, she would go on record as a conspirator. If she had, previously, she'd have made him one.

So she held her peace, telling herself that she and Freedom and Dennis Cox and his murderous ranger companion and all the prisoners would be safe before Sanchez launched his next offensive.

But she didn't believe it and her hands started to shake. Simply because she'd witnessed mass murder in the tunnels and hadn't cracked under the pressure didn't mean she was profligate where her own life was concerned. The last thing she wanted was to die on this blighted sphere and find out firsthand what resurrection was like.

She almost blurted out something stupid when their party finally returned to the pit. As she ducked through what remained of the arch, she recalled how it had come to be there and sucked in a loud, quavering breath. But Freedom Ayoub was right in front of her, watching. His yellow eye-whites seemed to glow in the light of Cox's flash-torch as the ranger at the head of the column climbed up the ladder, swearing loudly and with much bravado about what he was going to do if the workforce guards had locked the goddamned trapdoor on him.

Freedom moved close to her and whispered in her ear, "Be prepared. Be calm. You only die once."

"Oh, crap," she said brazenly because she was suddenly frightened again, even with Cox nearby.

Then the ranger on the ladder had the trapdoor open and into the pit poured light and sound. He stuck his head up, then climbed down the rungs quickly. Then he hung there, halfway up, halfway down.

Paige didn't hear Cox communicating with the other ranger; she didn't know when the two men realized that there was trouble up above; the fighting was still fairly far off, the shots muffled, the screams too faint to have penetrated the trap-door.

The other ranger climbed up again and out the trapdoor. His amplified voice urged the prisoners to climb the ladder single file, telling them not to scatter, to reform their column on the surface and march toward the footbridge leading to the tech center.

By the time she and Freedom got to the bottom of the ladder, sirens were audible, and the roar of tech birds swelled up out of nowhere so that she wanted to clap her hands to her ears. Cox was yelling through his bullhorn at everyone to move along, keep together, keep low, head straight for the suspension bridge.

His gloved hand pushed her roughly toward the ladder where Ayoub waited for room to climb. She looked over her shoulder at Cox, startled at his roughness, and saw his rifle pointing straight at her. It was as if Cox had forgotten who she was, as if everything in the tunnel had been a dream.

"Move, damn it! Climb!" his bullhorn roared.

Behind Ayoub, Paige climbed up the ladder and right into the path of Sanchez's revolutionaries swarming up the hill from Morgan Base, headed for the tech center.

CHAPTER 18

Stand-Off

———◆———

"SCHULTZ, LET THE bastards go! Get down to Morgan if you can. I can't raise Frickey on my com! Get Alpha and Beta and all the airpower and evac to the tech center. Repeat: evac to the tech center!" Cox yelled while he was reloading a plasma clip from his belt.

Around him, you couldn't tell who the hell was fighting who. Some of the rebels were in guards' uniforms, some had guards' weapons, some of the guards had been rousted out of bed so they were in civvies. "Paige, you and your friend get over there." He pointed to the tech center, across the bridge. "Go on, go!" Cox was crouched down behind one of the struts at the bridge, returning fire only when he was sure he could get a hit.

Mostly, he was keeping the bridge approach clear and covering Schultz, who'd almost gotten himself killed trying to protect the prisoners. Funny what you do in a situation like that, even when the last order you got doesn't make sense anymore.

Cox's helmet wasn't telling him anything he wanted to know. It was showing too many hostiles in all fields of view and there was some kind of interference on the radio bands. He tried frequency-hopping but the jamming was too complete.

He kept waving when the tech birds went over, but none of them stopped for him. Some of them had .50 caliber under-wing guns that the guards had installed for crowd control, and strafing an area is never neat and clean.

But nobody up in the tech center was ready to blow the bridge, thank God. Not yet. He punched up "rearview" and checked on Paige and the black through a combat window centerpunching his quadranted screen because he wasn't about to look away from the contested area in front of him.

The two were halfway across the bridge, crawling over a couple of bodies. The bridge was swaying wildly and there were six guards at the far end of it, which accounted for the corpses. He'd already ID'd himself at full volume, so the guards weren't going to shoot him or his charges. At least he didn't think they would.

He punched off the combat rear window. You had that capability like you had the ability to suppress the sound of external firing from the audio you were getting—had it, even though, except in very exceptional circumstances, you were a fool to use it. The rear window blocked the exact center of your field of view so that you couldn't splatterlook and you had a blind spot in your forward viewing area; looking backward too long could get you real dead, real fast. But so could not hearing somebody shouting at you and Cox never used that bang-suppressing function, even though his hearing suffered.

Better to be alive and temporarily deafened than dead with healthy ears, he reminded himself when his helmet rang from the noise of a tech bird's strafing run. Too close for comfort; rock flew in all directions.

Involuntarily, he closed his eyes as flying bits of

stone struck his visor. When he opened them, Schultz was just a telltale, out of sight on a downhill race to find Alpha and Beta.

Where the hell were they? Why weren't they responding? Cox brought up an oscilloscope and tried again to get around the jamming, but he just couldn't. When he downloaded the scope he heard Schultz's ragged transmission: "—VTOL in sight, Det. Can't find Frickey or the TAV, but maybe they're holed up in the kangaroo. No, wait, there's—"

Then all Cox could get was static. While he was listening to it and yelling to Schultz to talk to him, three rebels came at him with shotguns and he flat fried them with a steady burst of plasma, no neat single shots.

He was getting nervous. "Schultz, you batfucker, you come back and talk to me or I'll bust your ass to private! Please, Fritz, say somethin'!"

All he got was white noise and his imagination was giving him lots of additional static. Had Schultz meant he saw the VTOL, or that he didn't see it? That it was fine, or screwed? There was no way to find out and more rebels were topping the hill.

Cox had two choices: hold his position and pray for a tech bird to swoop down and save him, or fall back until he could get his com-lines up and working.

He wanted to do neither of those: he wanted to go after Schultz. But he knew he shouldn't. He punched up his rearview window again and saw Paige and the black, Ayoub, on solid ground across the bridge, being hassled by the workforce guards over there. Both their hands were on top of their heads and one of the guards was patting them down.

"Assholes, that's all I need," he muttered, and said for the record and because maybe Frickey or somebody else from Alpha and Beta could hear him even though he couldn't hear them, "Det, falling back to tech center with Barnett, Paige and Ayoub, Freedom—cognizant witnesses. Alpha and Beta, fall back to tech center if you read me. Repeat, if you copy, evac, with or without aircraft. Just get there, guys. ASAP. Det, out."

And he was just about out—out of ammo, out of adrenaline, out of patience and out of control. He knew damned well that Alpha and Beta would be a significant presence in this melee if they were physically capable. Which meant they weren't. Which meant these rebels were personal enemies of Dennis Cox's.

As he got ready to retreat over the swinging suspension bridge he paused, hunched over, only long enough to toss a dozen grenades—his whole fruit salad: time delayed, anti-personnel, blow on impact . . . everything he had.

If it weren't for Schultz and the missing Alpha and Beta teams, he'd have used them to blow the bridge once he got across.

He counted seconds aloud along with his digital time-to-detonation readout, and wheeled to run, diving after three steps because that first bang was going to be a big one.

It was and he didn't want to think about what showered him as he scrambled to his knees and ran like a cockroach, bent low, his pistol in one hand and his rifle butt pressing against his stomach. When he reached the bodies on the bridge he kicked one out of the way, jumped another, and thought he saw the third one move as he dodged by.

His hostile-fire indicator was lit up like a pinball

game, and he was the ball: five degrees to the
right, two to the left, avoiding projected points of
impact by a hair's breadth. He didn't have time to
wonder if he'd really seen that dead guy move, the
guy whose chest was half-blown away. He couldn't
think about it. He had to get Det Cox across that
tricky span without getting part of himself blown
away.

When he reached the far side, he sank down beside one of the bridge's stanchions, and gasped in
his bullhorn, "Let those people go, you assholes.
They're mine. You got plenty else to do."

His sound pressure level must have been about
135dB. The workforce guards froze and backed off.
Paige, white-faced and shaking, ran to Ayoub and
hugged him. Cox blinked that sight away and took
another deep breath: "Barnett, Ayoub. Keep your
heads down. What do you think, you can't get shot
over here? Head for the blue door to the right of
the ramp, on my signal." And, after a quick scan
through his rearwindow for incomings: "Mark!
Goddamn you!"

All three of them ran. He caught up to the
woman and put himself squarely behind her: his
recon pack, his kevlar body armor, and finally his
body could offer her some protection. But she was
a slow runner. The black guy kept slowing down to
wait for her so that Cox screamed at him to look
after his own ass and get the damned door open.

Then he holstered his pistol for a free hand,
caught up to her, came alongside, grabbed her
around the waist and with his fingers twisted in
her belt half-dragged, half-carried her the rest of
the way.

Paige's big worker buddy had gotten the door
open, despite a guard behind it who was looking
doubtful. Cox bashed his way in there, stumbling

over the threshold, dragging the woman, and let them both fall where he could lie still and breathe awhile.

"Shut the damned door, asshole," he panted, lying on his side, his rifle over one arm and sighted down the ramp at the bridge because there were lots of rebels on it now. He wanted more oxygen than his mix was giving him and he wanted that door shut, about equally as bad.

The workforce guard and some tech there wanted to wait until the guards on this side of the bridge got in safely. Cox, still lying on Paige where he'd sprawled them both, concerned only with his weapons and the tactical situation, jacked up his oxygen mix radically, slapped his pharmakit hard. And said, suddenly rushing as synthetic adrenaline flooded his system, "Either you close that door now, or you and those guys you're holding it open for are dead so I don't have to make any choices."

His bull horn's gain was full up and the result must have been painfully loud in that small, enclosed antechamber, with its white walls and inlaid floor.

Cox didn't even need to emphasize with the pistol he'd grabbed: the tech, with a word to the guard, closed the door.

Paige wriggled under him and he remembered to get off her. He turned down his bull horn, zeroed all his meters, checked his damage report for any fried circuits or blown fuses or punctures or just plain odd readings, and everything came up clean except his ammunition level. He hadn't needed his auto-counter to tell him that. Besides what was in his pistol, he had one plasma clip and forty rounds of thallium left. He had an hour's worth of combat-level life support. He needed, as soon as he could, to get to a recon resupply station and put himself back in working order.

But his suit wasn't penetrated and nobody knew he was a couple quarts shy in the ammo department.

As soon as his chest stopped heaving he got to his feet and pushed his automatic visor release. When he could, he rubbed his eyes and looked around.

The antechambers's front and rear emergency exits were both closed and bolted. He could hear noise outside that he chose to interpret as rebels trying to break in rather than workforce guards trying to get away from rebels.

The workforce guard inside the chamber kept looking at him accusingly, but Cox ignored it. He just wanted to stand against the wall, propped up by his recon pack and the stubborn streak that wouldn't let him quit while he didn't know his team's status, and be alive a little while longer. Then he was going to put Paige Barnett and the black she was so fond of somewhere else. After that he was going back out to look for Schultz, Frickey, and the others.

But for just another minute, he was going to stand right here and watch nothing in particular happen.

He watched Barnett getting her strength back and the big black cooing to her like some wet nurse. He watched the white-faced tech in the smock take a call on the intercom that Cox couldn't make heads or tails of. And he watched the workforce guard glare at him as if Cox had started the whole revolution all by his lonesome.

Then the tech in the smock palmed the mouthpiece he was holding and pointed to the intercom grille with its lit floor indicator. "Ranger, your lieutenant wants to speak to you."

"Why not?" Cox strode as energetically as he could across the floor and Paige, sitting there with her arms encircling her knees, touched his calf as he passed. He looked down and winked at her like everything was fine.

And then he said, "Sergeant Det, here," and listened to Locke demanding all sorts of answers Cox didn't have yet.

"How 'bout I come up there and we talk about who can do what about what, in person. I got a couple of collaterals here and I want to make sure they're logged in as safe, sound, and delivered as promised."

"What do you mean, Det?" Locke said, the iron going out of his voice.

"Paige Barnett and a witness we picked up."

"Witness to what?"

"Locke, I'm on my way up and then we can exchange situation reports. When I get there, I'm going to ask for a tech bird and the answer you and Singer give me this time better be 'yes.'"

CHAPTER 19

Situation Report

———◆———

"LOCKE, I OUGHT to fry your ass right here—and your lady scientist's, too." Cox stood with his knees slightly bent and his hand on his gunbelt, opposite the blond man called Locke, in the office of a woman named Singer.

Over in one corner, apparently forgotten for the moment, Paige leaned on one of the packing crates stamped with security classifications, Freedom Ayoub by her side.

The argument had started over her and Freedom, and whether there would be room for them on the *Malibu*. Cox had said he'd been following Wiley's orders, that was all, and as far as he was concerned the orders still stood. Locke had said Cox ought to be concerned with his Alpha and Beta teams: that they'd discuss the "workers" later.

Cox had replied, "Fine, then give me the tech bird and I'll get going."

The horse-faced woman named Singer had looked at Locke meaningfully and shaken her head. The big blond man had said, "Listen, Det— we need those birds to pick up tech staffers stranded in the field and get them to the center in time for evac."

Cox had replied, "I thought we weren't going to

171

evac—that we were going to solve this on site, one way or the other."

Locke had replied, "Come on, Det, be reasonable. The situation has changed. We'll be taking the science staff and their research with—"

"Cut the shit, Locke. The situation hasn't changed one bit—you knew you were going to pull this, all along. That's how come you've been spending so much time here, preparing for it. I want to know just what you're going to evac these —how many? twenty? thirty?—privileged people *in?*"

Paige had watched, fascinated, as the man named Locke had gotten up from the ergo chair he'd been sitting in and come around the woman's desk. He too was wearing a side arm. Ayoub had shifted closer to her and Paige had found her knuckles handy to gnaw on. The tension between the two rangers jumped like visible electricity.

After a pause, the blond in the black coveralls had said, "You know the answer to that, Det. And you damned well know the situation calls for it—we don't think there's enough left of your Alpha and Beta teams to cart home. And that's as much your fault for leaving Frickey in command as it is the jamming we had to initiate to cripple the tech birds the rebels expropriated—"

And that was when Cox had threatened to shoot Locke, there and then.

Now Locke said soothingly, "You don't want to do that, Det. You don't want to do anything crazy. As it is, maybe we can squeeze all the survivors into—"

"Into what? Your tech birds? Or are we going to—"

"Frickey's in orbit with the TAV, Det. I cut the

orders, since you were out of contact in those tunnels and we had to have—"

"You son of a bitch. You *let* Alpha and Beta get wasted. You planned for it. Without the TAV, they couldn't coordinate anything past that jamming your..." Cox broke off, shook his head once, and his shoulders slumped. He turned away from Locke and made a slow circuit of the room, his left hand trailing along the neatly stacked packing crates. When he passed the place where Paige and Ayoub were standing, he didn't acknowledge her.

Finally he came full circle and stopped in front of the laconic lieutenant in the black coveralls. Cox said slowly, "You know, I had all these questions about you I kept tabling, 'cause you pulled my ass off X-31A. Now I've got answers and I don't like them." His right hand went to his belt and suddenly there was a weapon in it, pointed at Locke's belly.

The horse-faced woman in the science smock bleated in surprise and her hand covered her mouth. Ayoub took Paige's arm and held it.

"You know, Locke, these damned pistols are so tricky sometimes. I've been shootin' all morning and I'm in Condition Zero—cocked and unlocked, because in a firefight you just plain don't want to lose that extra fraction of a second to take a pistol off safe. This goes bang by itself, who's to say it wasn't an accident?"

"Det, you're jumping to conclusions. This isn't going to do Alpha and Beta any good." Locke was perspiring but his voice was steady. "Maybe we could come up with one tech bird. But don't crash it—we need you for the detonation." Locke smiled in a conciliatory fashion and Paige recalled numerous meetings back on Earth wherein Godfrey had slit someone's throat or killed a lifelong dream of a project with a smile like that. "We're off the record, this whole conversation, by the way. If you were worried."

"I'm not worried. Not about that. And not about my own ass—you're damned right you need me for the bang."

"Then let's leave it at this: You can take your special interest cases, there," Locke's chin flicked toward the corner in which Ayoub and Paige were huddled, "up to the *Malibu*, and I'll take mine— Professor Singer and however many of her staff we have room for. We'll count heads and come up with an evac—"

"Not until I've personally determined the status of Alpha and Beta. If I've got wounded, I'm taking them, no matter how bad—"

"Fine. Professor Singer will have a tech bird and a pilot standing by for you. You can leave your prisoners with me until—"

"They're not prisoners. I'm taking them with me. I wouldn't want anything to happen to them, or them to get misplaced. And I'm flyin' the bird myself. And before any of that, I want to talk to Frickey. Alone. *Now!*"

"Easy, Det. I know it's hard to lose friends. It was hard on X-31A: it's harder here, a second time. But we do need you. Try not to get paranoid about—"

"Now, fucker!"

Paige saw Cox's form fairly shiver; his pistol was still in his hand. She caught Ayoub's eye and his expression counseled patience.

Locke licked his lips and said, "I'll patch you right through, from here. Best I can do—'alone' will take time. Satisfactory?"

Cox merely nodded, but he holstered his weapon and his body relaxed.

Locke picked up his desk instrument and began patching procedures, talking to someone in central switching. It took what seemed to be a horrendously long time, given the animosity in the room.

Paige was no soldier, but she was quite certain that what she'd heard was an irremediable break between these two officers, and that each man had something on the other, which, if charges were pressed, could ruin both careers. In her world of corporate maneuvering, the phone call to the TAV that Locke was arranging and the fact that Cox had holstered his weapon would have signified that some compromise had been struck—but in her world, arguments weren't settled with firearms, so she couldn't be sure.

When Locke held out the handset to Cox and said, "Frickey," Cox shook his head: "Put it on the speaker."

Professor Singer propped her chin on one hand and swiveled her chair away, facing the tower window and the sporadic fighting still going on below.

"Det? Hey, Det? You okay?" came a voice from the speaker and Paige started: it was a woman's voice.

"Frickey, shit, what're you doin' up there?"

"Orders, sir," came the woman's response, tight and hard. And then, "Aw, Det...what was I gonna do? Came straight from Wiley via Locke and I couldn't raise you or Schultz. All hell's broken loose, but then you know..." The woman trailed off and Paige was sure she heard a strangled curse, although it could have been static, given that the TAV was, according to Locke, in orbit.

Cox didn't say anything. He was looking at his feet and again shaking his head.

The speaker burped and Frickey said, "Det, the TAV's the only capable evac, with the VTOL shot to shit. They're right, I guess, but...I feel so bad. How is...everybody?"

"That's what I was callin' to ask. Give me a personnel scan, if you have to cripple the tech center's jamming to do it. I'll be in a tech bird—Give me a call number, Singer."

The woman in the swivel chair got up, went to her desk, toggled a screen, and gave Det the numbers he wanted.

He repeated them to Frickey. "And do everything twice. I'm gonna evac whatever you find, but if there's anybody down there too hurt to call in, it's just you and me left to find them. You copy, Frickey? Either we pull them out now, or they'll fry with the rest of these fish. So give me your maybes if you have any. I'll need it in, say, fifteen minutes."

"I'm on it, Det. And...thanks for not blaming me."

"I got somebody else for that. Let's see if we can fill those cocoons with the guys who shipped out in them. And one more thing, Frickey."

"Yessir?"

"Don't take any more orders from Locke unless I tell you different. I'm not sure he's workin' from the same copybook as the rest of us."

"Ah...yes sir, if you say so, sir. In that case, you want to give me an ETA when you'll want me?"

"Yeah, okay—two hours and...let's say fifteen hundred on the tech pads. Get with Wiley and give him my timetable—make sure he knows it's my call."

"Yes, sir."

"Over and out, Corporal." Cox tossed Locke the handset.

The blond man looked like he'd just eaten something very sour. "You're pushing this too far, Cox."

"Your opinion. You've got two hours to pick who

and what you're taking and get it ready to go. Prioritize your line because I'm not making any exceptions—all of mine go home, or nobody goes."

Singer leaned forward, palms on the desk and said in a sharp, argumentative tone: "Lieutenant Locke, you can't let—"

"Professor, the man's got his finger on the button and I know him well enough to know he's not bluffing. Let's just do what he says," Locke told her in a very calm, very professional voice. Then he looked at Cox and said, "Det, I'm telling you, I'm on your side. You're reading this wrong..."

"You bet. Paige, Ayoub, let's hustle—you two are coming with me."

Again, the professor began to protest, but Cox had already turned his back on her and Locke and was heading for the tower elevator door.

Paige tugged on Ayoub's hand and the two fell in beside the ranger, who was fiddling with his helmet. As the elevator opened to swallow them up, she said, "Dennis, I have to talk—"

"Det," he said abstractedly, absorbed in calibrating his helmet's electronics. "And this is no place to talk."

She clamped her mouth shut, knowing that if she couldn't tell him now, she wouldn't until much later. Freedom was already giving Paige his warning look.

But Dennis "Det" Cox, grieving over his lost Alpha and Beta teams, had a right to know that they weren't really dead—at least, not in the way he was used to thinking about death.

If Freedom Ayoub wouldn't let her tell him now, she'd have to find a way to get Cox alone. She wanted to do that anyway—she had so many questions, especially about "the button" that Locke had mentioned.

CHAPTER 20

Last Recon

———◆———

THERE WAS ALWAYS the chance that some of Cox's people had escaped in one of the all-terrain vehicles from the kangaroo carrier, Cox kept telling himself as he settled Ayoub and Paige Barnett in the tech bird and gave it a walk-around and a thorough instrument preflight, then swung aboard and checked everything again.

He left his channel to the TAV open and his tower channel as well. The bird's com-gear wasn't affected by the jamming the tech center had used or else they weren't jamming anymore. It could be either one. Somebody had set the countermeasures system in the twenty-place bird before Cox had gotten there.

When he was ready to taxi, he told Paige to look in the overhead lockers for anything she could find. She came up with light pressure suits and respirators, there for crash support or night recons or whatever the techs did on X-66B's mountainous peaks where the terraformed air wasn't thick enough yet for breathing.

He told her absently to "Put that stuff on. Ayoub, too. And there ought to be food, coffee, maybe other goodies. Don't drink any booze, but otherwise take whatever you want. This baby's ours and they owe us."

He wasn't at all certain that he wouldn't try to

make it to orbit in the tech bird, if he saw what he thought he was going to see down at Morgan Base. It wasn't a good shot—the plane was hypersonic, but basically an air-breather. He wasn't sure he was mad enough to risk all their lives just to screw Locke around like Locke ought to be screwed.

But it *was* a shot. He kept it on his list of options. Another was enlisting Frickey in the time-honored game of "frag the incompetent officer," out-system style. It wouldn't be the first time. Assuming that Cox could trust Wiley, the idea of leaving Locke to fry along with everybody the lieutenant had deemed expendable was looking increasingly attractive.

Since Cox was thinking about it so much, he probably wasn't going to leave Locke behind. But he was trying not to dwell on the moment when Wiley was going to order him to blow the charges he'd placed at the equator—whether Dennis Cox was willing to live with so many deaths on his conscience.

It hurt to think about it. He didn't want a repeat of X-31A. He flat couldn't handle it. And twice... he'd get his butt grounded, if not worse. There'd be inquiries and hearings and more therapy because of the alien angle. He just wasn't ready.

While he pulled the bird up through the thin air and leveled her off just fifty feet below the "maximum indicated ceiling" in case the rebels had birds in the sky around him, he kept wrestling with his own, limited options. And he kept coming out on top in only one scenario: Dennis Cox wasn't going in-system. He'd get Wiley to drop him someplace, anyplace he could where there was a ranger base, and file his reports from there. Then, if he was busted out of the service, he wouldn't have to sweat getting clearance, or passport restrictions removed, or the money to get out-system. He'd *be* out-system. He'd had enough Earth this last time in to suit him. He didn't want, under any circumstances, to be marooned on that world, more hostile to his way of thinking than even X-66B.

Well, he knew what he wanted now, and that was something. He slumped back in his seat and punched the autopilot he'd set: the bird would fly above the action until it reached Morgan, then go into scan-and-search circling, slowly corkscrewing downward. If Cox had to engage any rebel-flown aircraft he'd have plenty of time to spot them before they saw him.

Guys never looked up for trouble, not those kinds of guys. They looked down, where the obvious targets were. And the sun would be some advantage, because Cox was going to be flying right out of it. He wasn't up here to strafe the rebels or engage their airpower. He was up here to do one last recon and bring out his wounded, if any. To do that, he had to have an undamaged bird. So he'd do his best to sneak in, and he'd do his best to sneak out again, whatever he found. He had Paige Barnett and her worker friend on board because he didn't think they'd be safe with Locke. Therefore, they had to be safe with him.

He couldn't sync his recon electronics to this IST tech bird's, so his helmet was on the copilot's seat. When Paige, in a gray pressure suit whose tab hadn't been pulled yet, came up and touched it, saying, "Mind if I sit?" she startled him.

"Don't touch that gear. Don't ever touch any of my gear."

She retreated quickly and he had to look away from his console to call her back: "Sorry. I'm jumpy, that's all. Come back up."

The black guy was sitting in one of the science

bays, a sandwich in his lap, his feet in the integrated gray boots of his pressure suit, his tab also unpulled.

When Paige Barnett came forward again, she said, "Would you like something? A sandwich? A cold drink?"

"Nah, not till I'm done with this." Cox reached over and snagged his helmet, putting it between his own legs. "Any hardware back there? You've made a pretty thorough search."

"Hardware?"

"Guns. Ammunition." There were under-wing cal .50's, targeted and fired from the pilot's console, but that was all he'd found on the flight deck.

"Nothing but a flare gun, I think it was. Freedom said it was a flare gun."

"Has he got it?"

"No, we left it where we found it."

"Good. Why don't you pull your tab?"

"Excuse me?"

He leaned over and pulled the tab on her suit's sleeve and her eyes went wide as it plumped up around her.

"Oh," she said. "Am I going to need this—and the helmet that's back there?" Her eyes were still very wide, he noticed.

"Don't be scared, okay? I just want you as protected as possible. When you go back, get the helmet out and the two of you run through hooking each other up. I'm not thinking of trying to take this bird to the *Malibu*—yet. But if I do decide to, you'll need whatever protection that suit will give you."

"Den—Det, I want to talk to you about—" She swung around, as if to see whether Ayoub was watching, then back. "About your friends. They're not de—"

"Jesus, wait a minute." He shut down the cockpit recorder, the flight recorder, and his own suit's systems with three practiced stabs. "Okay, say whatever you've got to say."

"The rebels say, 'You only die once,'" she told him and her face was bone white, so white the veins in her temples showed blue.

"Sounds good to me," he quipped, glancing back at his cockpit. She didn't understand that he couldn't give her his full attention. But she was smart, and she'd heard the row in the tech tower. "What's it mean?"

"I'm trying to tell you—they'll be resurrected, your friends—reborn."

"You don't understand what's going to happen to X-66B once we leave it," he said savagely, watching his windscreen now because he didn't want to talk about it, not yet. And not with her. He especially didn't want her telling him that Reynolds was alive, or post-alive, some zombie Reynolds back on what was left of X-31A with a bunch of other zombies made by the USA when they scratched the rebels from the gamecard out there.

She stared at him, after he'd said that, for a long time. Then she said, "Well, I'll get out of your way."

He caught her wrist as she got up. "It's not my ...I don't cut the orders for the whole goddamned 203rd, lady. You're IST, you know what your people did on X-31A. And you know more than I do about what's happening there. Tell me one thing."

She inclined her head, yes.

"Is this the same as X-31A—what happened there, I mean? Is the same thing happening here?"

"Yes," she said. "The very same thing."

"Then you know more about what's going to happen than I do—you said you were the dissenter on the X-31A thing, that the vacation you were going to get was because of some flap over X-31A you got caught in."

"Do you remember everything?"

"Only important stuff."

She tugged her wrist away. "We need to talk, before we get back to Earth." Her eyes flickered to where Ayoub sat. "I just want you to know that the people you're worried about are . . ."

"Yeah, you said. Makes me feel lots better."

She didn't respond to that, just went aft and he was glad she was gone. What difference did she think that was going to make? Now he had something else to worry about—you couldn't leave the bodies, because the zombie-hands would get them. He wished he hadn't brought her.

He was still wishing that when his telltale told him the tech bird was over the target and she started into his preprogrammed corkscrew downward.

Then he got real busy, punching up magnification scans and waiting for Frickey to call in with her life-scans.

Frickey was exactly on time, and her news wasn't good, or unexpected. "Det, I can't find a living soul. I can get three-quarters of the suit-positions ID'd, but they're all . . . dead." Her voice was too shaky.

"Come on, Frickey, you're all the support I've got in the solar system right now. Don't get womany on me."

"I'm not, sir." She sniffled. "I—found Fritz . . . Schultz, is all."

Oh, boy. So Schultz and Frickey had been an item. Cox's luck just couldn't get any better. He asked her because he was asking himself and maybe she'd have some feeling about it: "Want me to try for a pickup, bring the bodies back? Make *me* feel a lot better, but I've got lots of hostile tracking down there."

"Yeah, lots—don't try picking up bodies on my account."

Morgan Base looked like it ought to after that much fighting, all torn up and shot up and you couldn't find the administrative prefabs except by zeroing on the coordinates where they should have been. Frickey was feeding him her better-resolved photo-return data and he was bringing it up on his bird's little screen as they talked.

He had better gear in his helmet than they had in this whole plane, but he couldn't fly his suit. They worked at the imaging for some time as the bird circled lower and lower, and finally he saw why Frickey was so choked up: the kangaroo carrier had exploded. Its extra ammo must have ignited when a rebel got a lucky strike.

The pieces of exploding kangaroo had crippled the VTOL and suddenly Cox remembered Schultz's last transmission, and this time he imagined he heard Schultz saying clearly what the static had masked, "...wreckage of the VTOL in sight, Det."

Cox said, "Frickey, stay with me and I'll feed you close-in stuff," and took the bird off autopilot. He buzzed the wreckage as low as he dared and as slowly as he could without stalling, hoping for a twitch, a muffled groan, anything that the bird's sensors, or the TAV's better analysis of the bird's data, could find. Or anything Cox's naked eye could pick up and interpret as a sign of life. But there was nothing.

There was nothing human whatsoever. There weren't any bodies, although there were empty suits. Cox's finger stabbed for the cameras instinctively and blacked everything out.

Frickey's voice came rattling through almost instantly: "Det? Sergeant? Talk to me, please sweet Jesus, talk to me!"

"Keep your pants on, Frickey, I just lost the cameras, that's all. Some damned short. This bird's tech is lower than a frog's butt."

"Sorry, sir, I don't want to lose you too."

"Yeah, I know. Well, ride shotgun for me," he told her carefully, "I'm coming in. When I get back to the tech center, commence evac. Repeat: I'm stepping up the timetable."

"Shall I call Locke, then? Or will you?"

"I don't care if nobody calls him. We've got some extra berths and I guess he can fill them with his science people, but it doesn't mean squat to me if all of them fry along with this mess they made."

He was prayerfully glad he'd forgotten to restart the cockpit recorder and flight recorder. The only record of those empty suits down there was the TAV's. "And hey, Frickey, wipe that last bit of scan, would you? My tattletale's off down here and I bet we can get the Alpha and Beta families better benefits without that last funny picture."

"Yes, sir," said Frickey in a voice that let Cox know she hadn't understood why he was asking what he was asking.

He signed off with her and pulled the bird into a straight-up climb, still alert for hostile air power, headed back to the tech center. He had the whole ride to think about what it meant that those suits were empty like that, in light of what Paige Barnett had told him. And what, if anything, he was going to tell Locke about it.

This time, Cox had to make sure he didn't damage his own credibility. This time, Locke wasn't going to be the only guy who went home with a believable story to tell.

CHAPTER 21

One on One

———◆———

"ARE YOU WORRIED that some of your men might still be down there, in one of those wrecked vehicles you saw?" Paige asked Cox when he'd landed the bird among half a dozen others at the embattled tech center's pad port.

Cox was sitting there, slouched behind his controls. He'd made no motion to leave; he hadn't released the locks on the doors or cut his engines. Back in the passenger compartment where Ayoub waited quietly, the seatbelt indicator was still lit.

So she'd come forward on the pretext of asking Cox if he wanted a cold drink now, but one glance at his face had told her to skip the inanity.

He was slow in responding, and he didn't look at her, just kept watching the instruments before him. "Nah, I'm not worried about that—we did a thorough scan; we didn't miss anybody. There *isn't* anybody." Then he did turn to her and the intensity in his eyes was desperate, angry, and cold. "Unless they're...what you said...or down in the tunnels. I don't like it." He shook his head.

Paige was worried herself. She'd asked Freedom about the casualties and his only answer had been a slowly drawled promise that none of the newly dead rangers would come strolling into the Knob Hill center at the last moment, revealing every-

186

thing Sanchez and Ayoub so determinedly wanted
to keep secret.

Paige didn't understand how Freedom could be
so certain. But certain he was. And the more certain he seemed, the more commanding he became.
The closer they got to that moment when they'd
board the *Malibu* and the die would be cast, the
more Paige worried about the implications of what
she was doing by helping Freedom Ayoub transit
to Earth.

She didn't know anything about the resurrected
ones, not really. She knew only enough to have become an uninformed conspirator. But the ranger
before her knew less. Paige was willing to keep
Freedom's secret from the entire world if she must,
but not from Dennis Cox.

She said to Cox, very softly, "We still need to finish our talk."

"That's why I'm waitin' here. When Frickey
brings down the TAV, you, me, and your buddy
there are going to trot straight over to it from here
—no detours into the tech center. I don't trust
Locke worth a fifty-cent round. So we won't go
back in there, where the science types and their
muscle have the advantage."

They'd stay here, where *he* had it, she realized.
And then she understood why he kept one hand on
his control panel, next to a joystick: the underwing
guns. If Cox had to, he was going to shoot his way
to the TAV.

"So we can talk now, Den—Det?" As she sat sideways in the copilot's seat, her glance flickered involuntarily to Ayoub, sitting so quietly back there.
This wasn't the way she wanted to do it.

Cox must have noticed, because he said under
his breath, "When we get to the TAV, Frickey'll cut

me all the slack under heaven. I got everything figured out. Just hold on to what you've got to say, unless it's got to be said before we get off-planet."

"Only if that 'button' you have that Locke was talking about has to be dealt with before then," she dared.

"Nope. Now just watch the pretty meters, okay?"

She did and soon she began worrying about what they might be trying to tell her. She could see little blinking red lights moving across what seemed to be a schematic, or a streamlined architectural drawing. And occasionally there was the sound of aircraft overhead, or an explosion loud enough to penetrate the bird's soundproofing. "What if we're overrun while we wait?" she asked, twisting her fingers in her lap.

"They're your guys, aren't they? That happens, I expect you and your friend to get me diplomatic immunity or whatever." When he smiled to take the sting out of his words, there was no humor in it.

"They're not exactly 'my' guys," she said huffily and crossed her arms.

Before he could respond, a thunder of static came from his radio, and a woman's voice followed it. "You ready for me, Det?"

"You're lookin' good enough to eat, Frickey. Come on in, the door's open," he replied, and then he was too busy to bother with Paige for an interval.

She watched the TAV come down in the big clear space ahead of them fearfully: it could crash; it could be hit by rebel fire, intentionally or accidentally crippled. They could still be trapped here. To her layperson's eye, it didn't seem like the big plane had enough room to taxi.

It probably didn't, really, since smoke came from its huge tires and it halted in a shriek of tortured mass just yards short of one of the parked birds.

The woman whose voice came from the TAV said to Cox, "Det, the next time you want somethin' like this done, I'm gonna find some dumb guy to do it for you."

"You did great, Frickey. I'm coming over from your six o'clock bird with two civilians; let us in before you even talk to Locke. Then I'll take it from there."

The woman's sigh of relief was audible. "I can't wait. Ready to switch to your recon hailing frequency whenever you are."

Cox reached for his helmet, noticed Paige, and said, "What are *you* waiting for, lady? Go pull your buddy's tab, get each other into those helmets, and be ready to break for the TAV's forward door. You'll see it open."

"What about you?" She was out of her seat already, suddenly shaking. She didn't want to die here, especially when there was something called a "button" ready to be pushed.

Cox was settling his helmet over his head, one hand on his respirator, the other pulling an assault rifle from beside his seat. "I'm going to cover your asses, like I know how to. You just run, that's your job—get there."

"What about the reb—"

"Don't pay those meters no mind. None of those blips got over the bridge, did they? And they won't. We got fifteen, twenty minutes before the ones coming up the far face get close enough to start scaling the walls or trying to break those doors down. The incoming blips you saw were workforce guards who got lucky, that's all. Now go on, this ain't no training run. Scat."

He twisted out of his seat and slapped her roughly on the bottom. She yipped in outraged surprise but she was already moving, away from his touch and toward Ayoub, who'd heard Cox's instructions.

There was a sigh as the pressure dogs released the doorlocks, and that was the last exterior sound she heard before her helmet came down on her head.

Freedom's dark fingers moved tentatively, checking its seals, and then Cox was there, deft and cursory, snapping latches and pushing studs.

Static erupted in her helmet. She jerked her head. Cox's lips mouthed: "Hold still, damn you," and then she heard, "—like the goddamned civilian you are. Signal if you can hear me."

She nodded.

He turned his back on her and made the same adjustments to Ayoub's suit. Suddenly she could hear both of them.

Freedom was asking, "—why we must wear these?"

"Cause I say so," Cox's voice decreed inside her helmet. "And because now they're all the protection you've got against anything flying through the air. Later, they'll make two less of you types to worry about during a depressurization emergency in the TAV. Now, do you trot over there, or do I drag the lady by the scruff of her neck and leave your butt behind?"

Freedom's luxuriant voice said sardonically, "I am yours to command, Sergeant Cox."

"Gee, thanks, buddy. *Move it!*" And Cox pushed flathanded against Ayoub's shoulder.

For a moment the two men were stock still, and

then Ayoub reached out familiarly for her hand:
"Paige, we go."

And they were running, down the ramp that
came folding out of the bird's door as Cox opened
it and across the tarmac. The TAV's door still
wasn't open, Paige noticed fearfully. She couldn't
hear anything outside, now, just the breathing of
the men.

Then there was someone else there, a workforce
guard cutting across to intercept them. Ayoub
jerked her by the arm, away from the other man,
putting himself between her and the fellow running full tilt in their direction.

As she realized that the workforce guard wasn't
just any guard, but was the commandant's aide,
the man who'd treated her so shabbily when she'd
first arrived, she saw the gun in his hand.

Freedom did too, and stopped in her path. The
man kept running toward them and the ramp now
descending from the TAV's fuselage.

Suddenly and without warning, the workforce
boss stumbled, his shirt blossoming red. Paige
screamed in her helmet; at the same time, Freedom jerked her forward once more.

When she stopped screaming she heard Cox's
voice in her ears, telling them both not to "get rattled, folks, just keep running. That's what I'm here
for, so we don't sweat the small stuff."

She'd forgotten that Cox had that gun; she'd forgotten, transiently, that he was behind her. She
couldn't get it out of her mind now: that he was
there, with that weapon, and would use it at the
slightest provocation.

Her feet propelled her clumsily up the boarding
stairs in Freedom's wake. Inside the cavernous TAV,
it was dim and empty. She threw herself into an
acceleration seat and panted, limp and quivering

with reaction, watching dumbly as Cox came charging up the ramp, rifle in hand, and slapped a button by the door.

She could see his helmeted head turn her way but she couldn't see past his faceplate. The TAV's door was closing, the ramp folding into it automatically.

Freedom's soft voice reminded her to take off her helmet. She couldn't manage it by herself. He helped her, and when she looked around again, Cox was nowhere in sight.

They held onto each other, she and the resurrected man, once they had their helmets off, simply clinging for warmth and human contact. Held on until she heard Cox, behind her, say, "If you want to have that one-on-one, Paige, now's the time."

She slipped from Ayoub's grasp and saw Cox, bareheaded, leaning against the hatchway where the TAV narrowed. He motioned her toward the flight deck. She followed him, ducking through two tiny, cramped, "crew-only" sections full of electronics until, where a bathroom would have been in a commercial TAV, Cox stopped before a door on which someone had scrawled, "Ranger Powder Room," in sloppy black script.

He pushed the door open and said, "Here you go. Secure as it gets."

At first she thought there were other men inside, but when she entered she saw that what she'd thought were men were hanging suits. Then she noticed that Cox had stripped off his own suit, and that it was there among the others. She knew it was his: the helmet said "Det" and the suit was hooked up to a whirring machine that seemed to be testing it.

Cox closed the door and the room turned red. He

leaned against the closed hatch, demonic and much younger looking in the red glow, and said, "Let's hear it. We don't have much time."

"Time before you...press the button." She didn't know why she said it; she'd wanted to tell him about Ayoub, about resurrection, about what lay ahead for them on Earth. But the "button" had stuck in her mind.

Cox pushed away from the bulkhead and sidled toward her in the room's close quarters. "I've got to suit up while we do this," he muttered, squeezing by her, and then past the suit she knew was his, to crouch down before a cabinet from which he started extracting rifle magazines and grenades. "Frickey's going to come looking for us any minute."

"Are you going to shoot her?" Paige's attention was riveted on the assault rifle, handgun, and plasma pack that came and went in Cox's hand.

He stood up. "Nah. But I'm going to strip down and get into my suit, now that it's spec'd up. You want to turn your back, it's fine with me."

She did, because he suggested it.

Then he said, close behind her, over the rustle of suiting and the clink of composite on metal: "You've got a right to know, I guess. You've probably guessed, anyhow, seeing as you were in on the flap over X-31A. We mined the fuck out of the equatorial faults, in case we had to blow this shit-ball wide open. And Locke's not kidding—Wiley's going to give me that order."

"You can't." She spun around and he was half into his suit. "All these people—"

"Yeah, right. The science staff, at least the keepers, are comin' with us. That makes it pretty clear what Locke wants to do. But I figured way back that there might be somethin' funny here, and when I saw you I was sure of it. So it's a good thing I put a bug in the detonation program..." He shrugged into the sleeves of his suit and zipped it to the waist. "But then there's Alph—the folks that do get left behind, and all your revolutionaries."

He moved toward her and her mouth dried up. The moisture there went to her eyes and she knuckled them, suddenly afraid she was going to cry.

Cox was only a step away. His arms went around her. "Come on, you're tough enough. We blow the planet, once we're far enough away that we're sure we're signed on for the whole ride home. That's all I wanted, was to make sure I—we—get home. Nobody at IST expects that, you can bet. You'll have Wiley to back you up, and Ayoub there for a witness. I'll see you as far in-system as Cerberus or Io, and by then the cat'll be out of the bag or you'll have cut some deal—"

"You can't," she gasped, pulling away from him because his touch was no longer comforting, but the embrace of a traitor. "We'll never make it without you, Det. You know that. Not two civilians... against IST. Because that's what this is, isn't it: IST covering its tracks, erasing an error? Especially if you...destroy an entire colony, kill an incalculable number of Fourth Worlders and surely some techs in the process—without you, nobody's ever going to hear from us."

He dropped his hands and they twisted in his equipment belt. "Yeah, I guess I know that. I'm in here topping off my tanks like I'm going to need all this firepower shipboard. I probably don't have to warn you about Locke, or Singer. But maybe I do about Wiley. He's regular—"

"Det, say you'll come back to Earth with me. If

only to help me get to Raymond Godfrey. To tell
the truth about what happened here ..."

His sour expression stopped her. "Truth, shit.
Maybe I'll go with you to Godfrey, but to get
even. For Reynolds and Schultz and my Alpha
and Beta teams. If they'd decided this place was
expendable, they didn't have to give away
two ranger teams to justify the bang they
wanted." His voice was razor sharp. "How come
you're not shocked, or pleading to save your
rebel friends?"

She looked into his suspicious, disapproving face
and said, "I told you, I worked for IST. I also told
you what the resurrected ones say: 'you only die
once.'"

He shook his head at her. "Let's not talk about
that, okay? Or I'll begin wondering if you're not
really one of them. Maybe I can help you find out
who's responsible for railroading us both out here,
but if I do, I want it understood that I choose the
means."

"Means?"

"Yeah. Once we target the bad guys, you're out of
it. I put you somewhere safe, and the rest is mine
to do—my way."

She looked into Cox's eyes and there was less humanity in them than she'd seen in Freedom's when
his were blind and staring in death. She didn't
know what to say to him, how to begin to explain
about resurrection, about Freedom Ayoub, about
the holy way. And she wasn't sure anymore that
she should: Dennis Cox was going to blow X-66B
to bits and he wasn't particularly concerned with
the consequences beyond his ability to survive the
event. He was, however, concerned enough with
her to be willing to come back to Earth with her,

to protect her. If she started explaining about Freedom, and Cox panicked, what then?

She took a step toward him, hands outstretched, and he met her more than halfway, pulling her against him so fiercely that she struggled for breath. His lips met hers. Then he was all fire and hard edges, and his recon suit jabbed her as he gathered her up.

He'd pulled the zipper on her suit and was helping her with it when the light in the tiny suitroom changed colors. They blew apart like a miniature explosion and she scrambled to her feet, shrugging into her suit's sleeves, as the door opened.

A bareheaded woman in a recon suit stood silhouetted in the doorway. She said, "Hey Det, Locke wants to come aboard—oh, sorry." She nodded stiffly at Paige. "You're the white woman, right?"

"Excuse me?" Paige's heart was pounding.

"The IST lady?"

"Yes."

"It's okay, Frickey, you can talk in front of her," Cox told the female ranger. "She's more on our side than theirs."

"Yessir. Will you come forward, sir? I need some help on the flight deck." Ignoring Paige as if she didn't exist, Frickey's eyes stayed fixed firmly on Cox, who was slipping into his recon pack and buckling hardware about his waist.

When Cox nodded, picked up his assault rifle and helmet and said, "Let's go then, Corporal," the female ranger asked, "Should I take something extra up front?" and indicated the storage magazines.

"No. We'll just change the combination lock again—you and me only, copy?"

"You bet, sir." Frickey stepped back, into the

body of the TAV, and Cox motioned Paige to follow the other woman out. "And Frickey, if I get into any trouble, this lady here, and her black friend, are your responsibility—all the way to Earth. She's the only one can get us straight for Fritz and the others."

For the first time, the freckle-faced female soldier looked at Paige with something more than disdain. "If you say so, Det. Now can we go get Locke's people on board and commence evac before I run out of excuses or the rebels break through and we both get busted to private—sir?"

Her unspoken critique of what she'd glimpsed in the suitroom hung in the air only briefly before Cox said, "I'm with you, Corporal," and, to Paige; "Go pick a seat and belt in like you live there. Don't get up for anybody or anything. You need help, push the middle button on your right armrest and yell. Me and Frickey'll come running. And Paige—relax. Worrying doesn't do squat."

And he left her there, following Frickey to the cockpit.

CHAPTER 22

Judgment Call

———◆———

"WHAT ARE WE going to do, Det?" Frickey asked flatly, her finger white on the TAV's cockpit squelch button, the band of her headset, upside down, dangling under her chin.

Cox didn't answer immediately, just leaned over

and stabbed at the button that would open the TAV's passenger door and lower the ramp to admit Locke and his chosen survivors. Then he said, "Locke's our ranking officer once we're airborne. He wants to fly this broom, we let him."

Frickey's recon helmet was propped on her headrest. She leaned back against it and eyed him. "You know that's not what I'm asking."

Cox shifted in the copilot's seat, watching the windscreen where recon-quality site intelligence was displayed: tiny color-coded dots running amok among the tech center buildings, trying to defend or assault it; other dots, and bigger shapes of conveyances, crawling up the precipice. Then he said very quietly, "We decided not to collect our dead, remember?" *Keep it neutral, you don't know how bad she's hurting over Schultz. Probably no worse than he was, over losing twenty-three of his twenty-four rangers.* "We live with that, because we've got the privilege. We follow our orders and, when we can, we write Locke up for cutting you the order that probably killed Alpha and Beta."

Corporal Frickey reached out toward him and then hesitated. Her hand came to rest on the TAV's throttle. "And the EO?"

Explosive ordnance. "We'll get orders."

"I thought you might..." Frickey stopped and shook her head.

"Fake it? Too many repercussions. Personal ones. This way, I'm just doing what I'm told. But if we're going to create an asteroid belt, sterilized for easy mining later, and do it under the guise of military necessity, I want to be out of pulse range and in my assigned cocoon when I execute those orders. Clear, corporal? I intend to come through this alive, well, and squeaky clean as far as any evaluation team is concerned. You better do the same."

Frickey's chin was quivering as she nodded her head.

"Hey, come on, Frickey—there's nothing worth saving down there that we've got the clout to save. There's us up here, and saving us might still take some doing. Hang with me, okay?"

Frickey's thumb was still on the squelch button when she said, "But when we get home, we'll file charges, right? So maybe we should enter some dissenting opinions about the blow—"

"I dissented my ass off, on the record, in the tech center with Locke. If we push 'em, we're going to step right into the kind of intelligence-puckey that never comes off your shoes. And you don't want that if you want to keep your rating, Corporal— and I'm betting you do."

The woman who'd executed Locke's order to take the TAV up into orbit and out of support range favored Cox with a tortured stare and said softly, "Whatever you say, Det. You know this game better than I do."

Better than anyone. He'd spent all that time grounded on Earth for seeing less and doing less. He said only, "You'd better let up on that privacy button and get ready to play spit-and-polish. But for your own sake, whatever you do, don't start volunteering anything about that alien presence we thought we saw down there, not unless somebody's threatening to dope it out of you."

"I hear you, Det," she sighed, and he saw her finger come away from the button. It was game time. He clapped her on the shoulder as he got out of the copilot's seat, telling her to prepare for take-off as he went aft.

Opposite the suitroom he paused, his recon helmet latched to his belt, rifle slung over his shoulder. He'd gone to shipboard ammo: airfoil rounds and rubber in his handgun, thallium and plasma/lexan in his rifle. He could probably hijack the *Malibu* with what he was carrying, if he could think of some place to hijack it *to*. Or a reason beyond his unventable anger at Locke's performance.

He moved past the storage magazine, through the two crew-only compartments, and paused in the hatch that opened onto the passenger-carrying fuselage. A ghost-image of Alpha and Beta, spread out with their equipment strewn around the big cabin, popped up to torment him. He blinked it away.

In its place appeared Locke, and Singer, and the Morgan Base commandant, and a score of techs from the Knob Hill center. What Locke was doing wasn't right, by Cox's standards, but neither was lifting off with empty seats. He told himself that if he wanted to shoot Locke, he could do it later. He just had to live until later. He had real qualms about surviving slow-freeze intact, considering the kind of information he had in his head and the way the brass seemed intent on limiting those privy to that information.

He told himself that, if the 203rd or the Space Command or their interface with IST wanted to really keep a lid on things, all these techs wouldn't be scurrying around in the TAV's belly looking like they'd just reached the promised land. The thought made him feel enough better that when Locke came forward and stopped three feet in front of him, he didn't just haul out his handgun and shoot the lieutenant there and then.

Anything could happen in slow-freeze; some of the pods' suspension controls weren't internal to the cocoons. Cox had the same chance to screw up Locke's life support as Locke did to screw up his.

Hell, maybe they'd both stay awake the entire flight, watching each other.

And maybe Locke was innocent of everything but pisspoor judgment in an emergency he wasn't spec'd to handle. Locke saw Cox eyeing him, walked over to the hatchway Cox was blocking, and said, "Everything nominal, Sergeant?"

"Close enough," Cox replied, not getting out of Locke's way. "Frickey's a good pilot."

"You lay off Singer and the techs, hear me?" Locke said under his breath and took another step forward. "While I'm busy on the flight deck. You have complaints, we'll hash it out with Wiley when we get these folks settled in and the bang's confirmed."

"Before the bang," Cox said, still not moving out of Locke's way.

"You're the ordnance expert," Locke said, and Cox could see a sheen of sweat where Locke's black pressure suit collared his neck.

"You bet," Cox replied and stepped aside. Locke squeezed by him and Cox's weapons belt nearly fouled with the other man's. Locke wasn't underestimating the situation.

Cox watched the lieutenant disappear forward and kept watching that doorway until he heard unintelligible exchanges that meant Locke and Frickey were about to get under way.

Then he went aft, threading his way through the techs still milling around. Singer threw him a nasty look but he ignored her, heading for the vacant seats around Paige Barnett and her black companion.

There were plenty of those, still: none of the techs were about to sit near the pair if they could help it. Singer was already realizing she'd have to assign those seats and call her people to order.

Cox slid down into the window seat next to Paige and looked out over the sweep of the TAV's wing. No hostiles on the tarmac, yet. There were some workforce guards there though, men that somebody must have lied to, saying they'd be picked up later, or they'd be storming the TAV themselves.

Cox watched the fools ready to protect the TAV with their lives impassively. He wasn't so different from any of them. A little smarter, a little more experienced. But a sucker all the same. And the woman beside him, who reached out to tug on his sleeve and then smiled encouragingly when he turned his head, was part of the command structure that routinely pulled this sort of crap—had pulled it on X-31A and gotten away with it. Cox was kidding himself if he thought that it would be any different this time. IST and the Space Command were going to do exactly as they pleased out here, answerable to nobody but their own.

Paige Barnett, who'd probably be bonused and returned to her old job within an hour of touchdown because she was too visible to scratch and too knowledgeable to risk having as an enemy, now told Cox not to worry: "We'll be fine. Freedom and I have talked about it. Don't feel guilty. You're not really kill—"

"Christ, shut up." Once an executive, always an executive. He leaned his head back, toying with his recon helmet. He hated passive danger, where something Frickey or Locke might do could crash him, and nothing he could do could stop it from happening. Usually, he closed his eyes and let his pharmakit do the rest. Today, there was too much tension in the passenger compartment, and there was Wiley waiting, once they got back to the *Malibu*. And Paige should know enough not to try to talk to him about anything important where they might be overheard.

So he looked again at her and encountered a dual stare from her and the man who called himself Freedom, two pairs of eyes trying to impart some special knowledge Cox couldn't quite grasp.

He rubbed his jaw irritably and lay his head back once more, watching Singer and the Morgan Base commandant hustle people into their seats as the "seatbelt" light lit and the TAV's engines began to roar. His attention still focused on the horse-faced lady scientist, he said to Paige, "Put your head back. This thing's milspec: she's gonna go almost straight up with enough g-force to puree your lunch if you'd had any."

Out of the corner of his eye, as the TAV started to taxi, he saw Freedom Ayoub's dark hand reach out and enfold Paige's pale one. Then the plane surged starward and, outside his window, Cox got a last glimpse of the workforce guards on the tech pad before X-66B dropped away into oblivion beneath him.

CHAPTER 23

Freedom Speaks

———◆———

PAIGE WAS DREAMING again, aware that she was, and yet frightened of that awareness: if she hadn't known she was dreaming maybe she could wake up, because the dream was so horrid and she couldn't seem to end it.

She was lying on the slats again, in the mass slow-freeze hold, only this time Cox was beside her and so were all the techs from the Knob Hill center. Through the slats, she could see the glowing mass of decomposing life, writhing like it had the last time she'd dreamed this dream.

She could smell the decomposition and the heat from the organic mulch warmed her face. In its midst was the digging thing, like a spider, that had tried to bite her the last time. She started to chant her litany, *Go a-way, go a-way.* Only this time, the creature looked straight up at her and it had Freedom Ayoub's face. Around and below it in the quivering mass of mulch, she began to see other faces among the worms—the helmeted faces of rangers, the white faces of techs with mouths opened wide as if they were screaming, the placid faces of Sanchez and the Asian priest.

And Freedom was reaching out to her with his spider's foreclaw, beckoning her to join him—

"Easy there, easy," she heard and realized she was struggling in her seat, trying to shake off the black hand clamped on her wrist. And another hand, on her other side: Cox's. There was someone leaning over her with a pharmaceutical injector: the woman named Singer.

Someone had unzipped her suit and pulled it down over one shoulder. She could see the angry red blotch where drugs had been injected into her body. Her breath was coming fast; her mouth was dry. With as much strength as she possessed she jerked her wrists free of the two men, saying loudly, "I'm awake. I'm all right."

Singer straightened up, eyes on the empty injector she held. Everyone else in the TAV was staring at the four of them. It was wholly and totally quiet. So quiet that Paige realized they must have docked with the *Malibu* while she'd been asleep.

She couldn't find a place to rest her eyes or a way to avoid the discomfiting stares coming from her fellow passengers. She said loudly, "What did you give me?" to Singer.

The scientist replied, "An anti-depressant. No tranquilizers, with slow-freeze coming up. Don't worry, it'll just normalize your chemistries." The older woman flashed Cox a no-good-deed-goes-unpunished look, and strode away, back to her seat.

Everyone was still watching Paige and the combination of their scrutiny and the drug entering her system made her dizzy. She leaned back and stared up at the ceiling, looking neither to her right nor to her left.

A hand came down on her arm. She shrugged it off angrily and turned to her left: "Keep your hands to yourself, soldier!"

Cox held up an open palm as if to fend her off: "Yes sir, ma'am." Cox leaned across her. "Ayoub, you want to tell your ladyfriend here that we're berthed, and as soon as she can handle it, I've got to take her to Wiley? Sometime in the next few minutes, she's got to debark unless you two want to be the only ones riding home the hard way? We've got to get our pods and check 'em out and—"

"We'll be right with you, Sergeant," said Freedom dismissively to Cox.

"Terrific," muttered the soldier, standing abruptly and gathering his equipment. "Cause I got a job to do, you know? I can't hang around here while her drugs cycle..." Cox stepped past them, into the aisle crowded with techs getting ready to debark.

Paige watched him make his way forward and caught a glimpse of Corporal Frickey and Lieutenant Locke, waiting for him beyond the open passenger door.

Paige started to rise, but Freedom stopped her: "Wait until the crowd has thinned."

"Fine. I'm just a little dizzy from whatever that bitch gave me. She doesn't like me, you know."

"She doesn't like us, I know." Freedom's yellow eyewhites were very bright, glistening. The red veins in them reminded her of the worms in her dreams. "You had a nightmare, Paige. Do you want to tell me about it?"

"I want," she blurted, thrusting her face close to his so that she wouldn't be overheard, "to understand what you meant when you said those people back there—the living and the dead—that they'd be all right. I want to know what you meant when you said—" She sat back suddenly, shaking her head, her hand to her forehead. "I don't know what I want."

"We only die once, you know this. You believe this. Forms may change to suit the environment, but survival, for the resurrected, is eternal." Ayoub's voice was like a priest's, like a parent's; it entered her soul and while he was speaking she couldn't doubt him.

She peered at him dumbly, telling herself that most of what she was feeling must be the result of the drug Singer had given her. What she wanted to say seemed somehow out of place, sacrilegious, but she couldn't stop herself: "You forget, I'm not ...one of you. I'm taking all this on faith. I—Do you understand what they're going to do—what Cox is going to do—down there, do to X-66B? How can anything survive—?"

"How can anything *not* survive? Do you have

knowledge of nothingness? Do you have experience
with nonbeing? Or do you know only life? Do not
be afraid of change, Paige Barnett. It is your im-
mortality. And all of ours. It is the holy way. You
have begun on the path to redemption. You have
witnessed resurrection. You need not even have
faith, for the faith you need is in the very cells
of—"

"You two ready?"

Cox was back, standing over them, and behind
him were two men with *Malibu* patches on their
uniforms. Near the passenger door, Locke and
Frickey still waited. Everyone else had debarked
while they were talking. And all Paige could think
of was the last thing Ayoub had said: *the faith you
need is in the very cells of* . . . Of what? Her body?
Was she already infected, or imbued, or trans-
formed with whatever had made the resurrected
man beside her so different from the non-English
speaker who'd been her companion in the
freighter's transit hold? Her flesh was suddenly
cold. She got clumsily to her feet while Cox was
explaining why Wiley wanted to see her:

"Just a formality, to confirm my ID and your
story—and to get you, Mister Ayoub, cleared for a
pod."

Freedom stood also, and preceded Paige into the
nearly empty aisle. "Pod?"

"Slow-freeze cocoon, remember? Like how you
got out here, but probably nicer. Not that I think
they'll give us any trouble about it, what with
Paige on your side. But regulations—"

"I will not need one."

"Right. Alone, awake, for four months plus, real-
time. Looking a superforce jump in the eye, with
nothing to speak of in the way of life-support. It'd
be a first dumb step for mankind, that's for sure.

Come on, buddy. Just keep your mouth shut and let us take care of you, okay?" Cox waved Ayoub into the custody of the two *Malibu* crewmen, then said to her, "You look like you could use a little help, but I don't want to get you mad again ...?"

"I'll manage. It's just the shot Singer gave me." Her legs were rubbery and she was hardly aware of Cox pacing her, or how slowly they were proceeding out of the ship, until she encountered the ramp descending endlessly below her gray-booted feet and she teetered.

Cox's hand clamped on her belt. "You be superwoman some other time, Barnett. Right now, you lean on me and nobody'll think the worse of you."

Somehow, he got her down the ramp and into a cargo cart. Then there was just the cavernous ceiling of the docking bay with its dotted lines of light, and a freight elevator in which her stomach lurched and her ears popped. She was vaguely aware of Ayoub and one crewman behind her in jump seats, and Cox to her left. On her right, the other crewman was driving and on his arm she could see an MP band.

When the elevator door opened, the driver said to Cox, "Your stop, sergeant. We'll be down in the cocoon bay with the others."

"Give Frickey my beer," Cox said with a grin and a wave as he helped Paige out and the elevator door began to close.

"Freedom—" But the doors were closed and Ayoub was gone, along with the cart and the crewmen.

"What is it with you and that guy?" Cox asked irritably. Then he added, when she didn't answer, "Let me show you how to get around up here where only hotshots dare to tread," and began explaining to her about the upper decks of the Malibu, where "if I understand the pecking order, you'll be quartered," as he ushered her to their meeting with Wiley.

Outside the captain's door Cox offered, "It's a good sign he wanted to have this talk in his quarters. Don't be nervous. It's just a formality."

"If you'd stop reassuring me, it would be easier," she said.

Then Cox pushed a button, pressed his hand to a plate, and the door slid aside.

Inside, the captain seated behind a desk at the end of a long, narrow gray room stood up. On a black couch to one side sat Locke. Neither man was smiling. Locke didn't stand; he had a portable terminal open on his lap.

Paige and Cox stepped in, the door closed behind them, and as Paige walked forward to shake the captain's outstretched hand, she realized Cox wasn't beside her. She risked a look around and saw the sergeant, arms crossed, leaning against the closed bulkhead door.

"I'm Captain A.J. Wiley," said the balding man with the small mouth and large teeth. "And I understand you're the woman who sent us the exceptional message."

"I am." She grasped his hand firmly. "Paige Barnett of IST—Raymond Godfrey's administrative assistant...at least I was, before all this happened."

"Please sit down, ma'am," said Wiley kindly.

Paige took one of two seats before the desk. Behind it were pictures of other spacefaring vessels, and one of the U.S. President; in one corner was a flag hung with battle standards.

When she volunteered nothing, Wiley cleared his

throat and said, "As a corroboration of your identity, may I impose upon you to repeat your original
message verbatim?"

She did that, and added: "I intend to file formal
charges against whoever drugged and abducted
me. Your Sergeant Cox was with me at that time
and saw the men responsible. He's a material witness—"

"That's true, Cox?" Wiley's voice seemed to am-
plify. "On Earth, you knew this woman and were
present at the...event?"

"Uh, yes sir, Captain." Cox's reply was barely audible. Paige shot a glance at Locke, who was busy
with the terminal on his lap.

"So I need," Paige said brutally, "Cox present on
Earth for the investigation. And I also need the
'cognitive witness' I brought with me, one Freedom Ayoub, who was among the unfortunates
transshipped out here in the same transit hold. I
expect—no, demand—every courtesy and assistance from the Space Command. I also want IST
notified."

"We've done that," Locke said laconically and,
from behind her, Paige could hear Cox swear
under his breath.

Wiley, ignoring both other men, favored Paige
with a most professional smile. "Ms. Barnett, another ship headed in-system took your initial message. They'll retransmit as soon as they've jumped
through to the solar system. But we won't be that
far behind them. In the meantime let me assure
you that, as the ranking IST official on board, we'll
do everything we can to make you comfortable
during transit."

"And Freedom Ayoub."

"And your witness, of course."

"And I don't want to wake up after the jump and

find that Cox has been transferred somewhere on some sort of mission—not until I can get a neutral deposition taken from him in front of witnesses." Her voice choked up. It wasn't that she didn't trust Dennis Cox, it was that she didn't trust anything at the moment. Her head was spinning from the drugs and there was something wrong about this meeting. Wiley wasn't anywhere near conciliatory enough. She *was* the highest IST official within light-years. Wiley should be treating her like one, not like somebody hitching a ride on the beneficence of the Space Command. The Space Command was only out here because of IST.

"You'll be quartered up here in our guest suite, which I hope will prove satisfactory," said Wiley drily, "until we jump—for the next few days, anyway. I'd be honored if you'd have dinner with me tonight."

Paige, knowing the meeting was over, stood up before Wiley did and went through the hand-shaking ritual again. "That's fine, as long as I have free access to both Mister Ayoub and Sergeant Cox."

"Sergeant Cox has a job to do, Ms. Barnett. A classified job. When we meet at dinner, we'll block out some time you can spend with him, if you really need it. Now, if you don't mind, I've got a ship to run and a crisis, you're well aware, down on X-66B. The steward waiting outside will see you to your quarters and try to provide whatever you may need."

"Thank you, Captain," she said stiffly, and strode to the door, ignoring Locke.

Cox got out of her way without meeting her eyes, his face cold and set.

By the time she'd reached her quarters and the young steward was fussing over her, explaining that the best he could do for her in the way of clothing was some women's uniforms, she regretted putting Cox on the spot like that. But she needed him. And she needed to see Freedom.

The young steward looked doubtful, but agreed to take her "down there. They're all bunked into the recon quarters, ma'am: it's nothing like this. And I can't pass any of them to these decks—we're restricted to brass and specialists up here. So if we could make it quick?"

She made it as quick as she could, because the bed in her stateroom had clean sheets and there was a stocked bar and fresh fruit on the table and she wanted nothing more than to eat, drink, and go to sleep. But she had to see Freedom, make sure he wasn't being discriminated against—make sure he was still aboard.

She did find him, on a top bunk in one of the tiny recon sleeper cabins. While the steward waited like a watchdog, she managed to ask him if he was comfortable, but little more: there was no privacy here, the steward had told her the truth.

"Do you need anything, Freedom?"

The big man, still in the gray pressure suit they'd taken from the tech bird, rubbed his arms and said, "Do not trouble yourself, Paige. Not about me. You have kept your promise and we are on our way."

"If you need me, you know where to find me."

"I do. And know that I'm watching over you. All the way back to Earth."

This was no place to start discussing that. "Det was right," she told him; "you'll have to take a cocoon like everyone else. It's not like the mass freeze hold, I promise. Don't be afraid." She couldn't say any more, not here; but Freedom was smart. He'd know she was trying to tell him that she'd made sure, on the record, that no one would try to deny him passage—that his importance was clear, a matter of record.

"Afraid? Never that, Paige." Freedom Ayoub smiled his small-toothed, beaming smile. "What is there to fear, once death is conquered?"

He'd whispered it, but Paige's body hair horripilated. "I'll come down to see you after my dinner with Captain Wiley. Until then, get some rest."

And she left with the steward assigned to guide her, aware that everyone was watching her and that "everyone" did not include Professor Singer, who wasn't among the techs billeted in the recon teams' quarters. And equally aware that perhaps she'd drawn too much attention to Freedom Ayoub, the way she might have to Dennis Cox up in the captain's quarters.

But Paige had to proceed under the assumption that her IST status would protect her, now that she was aboard an American vessel. She had to, or else she'd begin to believe all Cox's innuendo and start wondering if she dared hope she'd ever make it home alive to tell her story.

CHAPTER 24

Classified Job

———◆———

"YOU BET I'M insisting on going on the record with this. Sir." Cox was leaning stiff-armed on Wiley's desk. Locke was still sitting on the couch, above which was now displayed a freeze-frame of recon intelligence taken from somebody's helmet that

day Cox had smoked one of the rebels on
X-66B.

In the frame, you could see the weird white
hands coming out of the rock, ready to drag the
Hispanic revolutionary toward it as soon as Wiley
let the tape run at speed again.

Cox's words had been a hoarse, muffled shout
although Wiley was only a desk's width away. In
its wake, silence reigned too long.

Then Locke finally got off his butt, came over to
the corner of the desk, and said with intense sin-
cerity, "Det, you're not thinking about what you're
asking Captain Wiley to do. With your permission,
sir?" His head swiveled to Wiley, who grimaced
and sat back, playing with a stylus.

Cox was already replying, "Look, 'Buff,' don't
tell me what I'm thinkin'. Me and Frickey, as the
two surviving members of a unit you fucked over,
are going to take your butt to the cleaners, by the
book."

"Det, there aren't going to be any reports about
this—not about what's on that screen, anyway."
Locke jerked his head toward the frozen frame of
site intelligence. "It was my call to pull the TAV out
of danger, and I'm not apologizing. You were
smart enough not to transmit site-pictures of that
last recon—or to bring back any bodies. Can't you
add up the rest, man?" Locke's intense face jutted
toward Cox. "This isn't the first time. You saw
Reynolds. We've got that data too. You're sent out
here and the same thing happens. If you'd been
stupid enough to try and bring back KIA's, we'd
have found a way to leave them behind. We'll
probably jettison the TAV, in case it's contaminated. We don't know what we're dealing with
here and there aren't going to *be* any written re-

ports of the kind you can add performance notations or complaints to. You copy, Sergeant?"

Cox ignored Locke. "That true, Captain Wiley?
We can't nail this bastard for probably killing my
Alpha and Beta teams?"

"Sergeant—Dennis," Captain Wiley said as his
chair came forward. "Why don't you sit down?"

Cox did. "I'm sitting."

"This has become a highly classified mission;
Lieutenant Locke is right. We can't risk the spread
of this...whatever it is." Wiley's beaver-face
turned to the wallscreen over the couch, then back
to Cox. "Lieutenant Locke maintains, and events
tend to support his thesis, that keeping the TAV out
of the action was the only way to ensure the timely
evacuation of what personnel we did save."

"Except the *Malibu*'s lifeboats." Cox shifted in
his chair so that he could keep Locke, who was
moving away from the desk, in sight.

"You know that was never a possibility," Wiley
said. "I have my responsibilities, too. They don't
include stripping this ship of her emergency capa-
bilities."

"And what about the ship you told Barnett
about—the one that took her message when it left
for Earth?" Cox hadn't known about the other
ship, but he had an idea what Wiley was going to
tell him.

His idea was right, but it was Locke who confirmed Cox's suspicions: "Come on, Det, you're
battle fatigued. You sat with those briefing officers
yourself. Where do you think they came from,
some closet on the *Malibu*?"

So the men in the black pressure suits that Cox
had met in Wiley's office had had their own spacecraft—jumpcraft. Which meant that there had

been an intelligence presence on X-66B prior to the arrival of the *Malibu*. Which meant that all Cox's worst suspicions about Locke, and the way they'd lost Alpha and Beta, weren't just paranoia. You send some guys down to die so you've got a reason to do what you wanted to do before your "recon" team reported any damned thing at all. It sucked. Cox kept remembering Fritz Schultz's eager face, and the way Frickey had looked at him in the TAV when she'd been trying to get Cox's help to put Locke on report.

"Nah, Locke, not from some closet aboard this jumpbucket. I'm just surprised you didn't run back home with 'em, instead of chancing 'contamination' yourself."

"That's not the way I work, Cox. You, better than anyone, should know that."

Cox shifted to face the lieutenant and the two men seemed to exist then in a separate space where only their personal conflict mattered— where there was no Wiley, no jumpship around them, no passengers and crew to be concerned about. A shot up on this command deck, if it penetrated a bulkhead, could cripple the *Malibu* if it hit the wrong wiring panel. Cox had loaded rubber and airfoil for just such an eventuality, but you still didn't start plinking away on board ship at random, not with everybody's life-support at stake.

"Yeah, I know that—now. Maybe I should have, before, when you were so careful not to get your hands dirty, stayin' in the tech center the whole time. But you better realize that just because we can't crash your butt through channels doesn't mean this is over. Not for me. Or for Frickey." Not when there were casualties on two X planets because of Locke and his kind. "My dead better get at least as good as Reynolds's family did."

"I guarantee it, Sergeant Cox," said Wiley as he inserted himself between the two men. "And you have my condolences, Dennis, as well as my sincere regret that I was prohibited from putting you more completely in the picture earlier. Now, we have a job to do here and you're both professionals. I let this go on as long as I did precisely because, in my estimation, failing to air these grievances before some authority you both recognize would impair your further performance. Now, as far as I'm concerned, your decks are cleared and I expect wholehearted cooperation. That goes for both of you."

"That was never in doubt, sir," said Locke.

"Right," said Cox.

"Fine," said Wiley with a sigh. "Then start acting like it. We've got a detonation to accomplish, orders to execute."

"Can I ask whose orders those are?" Cox wanted to know.

"The highest authority. But what difference does it make to you, soldier? I'm in command here." Now Wiley's voice had an edge Cox recognized.

"I just want somebody to tell me," Cox said, turning with the captain as Wiley made his way back to sit at his desk, "that when I get home, me and the rest of these poor suckers aren't going to find out we've been 'contaminated,' or that we're going to be in debrief for the rest of our natural lives—however long that is." Except for Locke, of course, who'd come through X-31A without a hair out of place.

Wiley leaned forward, clasped his hands over his blotter, and banged his joined fists down hard on his desk top. "Sergeant, if I thought I couldn't give those kinds of guarantees, I wouldn't be out here myself. The three of us are the only ones with the total picture. The science people have rationalized away everything but the revolution, and most of them are in shock."

"And Frickey?"

"His corporal, the other surviving ranger," Locke prompted Wiley.

"I know who she is, Lieutenant. Frickey is in about the same position you were after X-31A, Sergeant. Her—"

"—ass is in your hands, Det," Locke interrupted. "Along with Barnett's. And this Ayoub's. If we can blow X-66B to bits, then we don't have a problem. We have apocryphal stories about a planet that no longer exists. And we don't have a threat we can't analyze that could force the entire Space Command into mothballs and cause American corporations doing business in space to suspend operations indefinitely. Which in turn would cause a monetary crisis of proportions you're not informed enough to evaluate."

"Fuck you, Locke. I don't believe a goddamned word you say. Captain Wiley, you promise me, if I blow this shitball for you, nobody's going to restrict the movements of those civilians we went to all this trouble to bring up here—not Barnett, not Ayoub. And that Frickey'll get her sergeant's stripes, not unlimited therapy, out of this."

"You have my word, Sergeant Cox. Now, can we talk about the safe pulse lead you'd recommend?"

"Safe? For the ship? Or for any supposedly contaminated personnel from the surface?"

Cox was intent on Wiley. He didn't see Locke come at him, opened handed, until the lieutenant had slapped the trank toggle on Cox's pharmakit and it was too late.

Cox caught Locke's wrist and Locke pushed

against his grasp. Cox's buttocks hit the back of Wiley's desk but he didn't topple. "Cute, Locke."

"You needed it, Det. You're revving way too high."

As the trank function normalized his chemistries, Cox's anger fled. His pharmakit wouldn't jolt him beyond his normal range, even if Locke could hit the toggle again, which he couldn't, not with Cox holding his wrist. Cox considered breaking that wrist. A simple snap would do it, the way his fingers were poised. But he didn't. He let go. And he said, "Okay, maybe I'm out of line—hell, I know I'm out of line. But you back off."

Locke did, all the way to the couch.

Wiley was chewing his stylus, simply watching from his command chair. "Can we continue, gentlemen?"

"Yeah," Cox said sheepishly. "Well, I don't want to blow the target until we're ready to jump—up to speed, not just out of normal pulse range. X-66B's so rich in elements, and those elements are so varied, we could end up with a volatile reaction, not just hurtling chunks of rock." He'd thought this through long ago. You didn't say to a spacecraft commander that you plain weren't going to follow his orders until he did what you said. And in this case, what Cox wanted to say had more to do with his distrust of Locke and his general estimate of this mission's survivability than it did with the actual safety of the *Malibu*.

But he had to lay out his conditions, and hope that Locke and Wiley had enough respect for Cox's expertise in demolition—or insufficient expertise of their own—to swallow the bullshit he was about to put forward as his rationale. So he continued, "My feeling is, given the volatiles in the geologic structure down there, that we ought to be all set to jump, in our pods, even, before we go bang. Then, even if we get a baby nova down there, we'll be popping out of normal space before the pulse, let alone any possible plasma, can get to us."

"So you want," Wiley said with a frown, "to be all the way out at the edge of this system."

"Yeah, accelerating outward toward half-C. And I want you to jump on my mark, if you can set it up. We'll laser the detonation command back. Even if we've emplaced a couple duds down there, she'll blow. You won't have the luxury of hanging around to verify it, is all. X-66B's satellites'll be fried with the first pulse, so they'll be your best telltale. Only I really don't want more than a hundred pico-seconds of verification time. Run a loop program to the satellites, if you need to confirm: when it cuts out, she's gone. And we should be too, within one second thereafter."

"Nice," Locke said ruefully, because he understood the implications, if not the fabrications in what Cox proposed.

"You've convinced me," agreed Wiley. "I've got family back on Earth; Wiley men have commanded US vessels for five generations and never lost one. I have no intention of being the first."

"Speaking of first and last, I've been thinkin' about that." Cox saw his chance, and went for it. "If we get everybody ready for slow-freeze and in their pods, leaving, say, just you, Captain, me, and the flight engineer, then I can rig up a system so I can detonate, and you can verify, just before we close our own cocoons. Gives us some extra time." And Locke'll be snoring peacefully in his pod. Also gives me a chance to go over the guts of my pod to make sure nobody's tampered with it.

"Any objections, Lieutenant?" Wiley wanted to

know. "Normal automation for superforce jump, computerize the confirmation signal? We're hardly in a position to go back to X-66B and reinsert Sergeant Cox to tweak his ordnance if for some reason the charges don't detonate."

"None that I can verbalize, Captain," said Locke, and turned to the couch under the screen which still showed the white hands reaching out to the Hispanic rebel, with Paige Barnett blurry in the background.

"Good. Then can we get on with this?"

Locke picked up a portable terminal from the couch and lifted its lid. "Yes, sir. Cox, this picture, and some others, shows your IST friend aiding and abetting the rebels. If we ignore this evidence, certain problems arise."

"Not like they would if you tried to crop that picture to show her doing whatever you think she's doing, but not to show those alien—or whatever those white hands are."

"Easy, Det. Whatever you think, I'm on your side. Tell the lady we've got this data, and we've classified it along with the rest of the putative 'alien' material. Try to make her understand that if she opens up this can of worms, the worms will eat her alive."

"She's having dinner with Captain Wiley. Maybe he could tell her." Tranks or not, Cox wasn't going to be tricked into doing Locke's dirty work. "I bet you'll be there to, along with Singer and the rest of the honchos. That's the drill, right?"

"Cox," Wiley said, "I'm running short on patience. You're verbally and officially constrained, as of this moment, from discussing the purported alien presence on X-66B with anyone, for any reason." His voice softened. "Like the rest of us. I'll take care of Ms. Barnett for you. And now, you've got about eight hours before I put you together with my flight engineer and we start jury-rigging the system you think you need."

"Thanks, sir." Cox wished his head was a little clearer, but he thought he'd done okay. Wiley shook his hand, anyway. And Locke tried to. When Cox ignored the gesture, Locke said, "How is it that you were with Barnett, anyway, back on Earth, that night she claims she was abducted?

"I thought I told you," Cox said in real surprise. "A dating service put us together."

"You don't mind if I quote you on that?" Locke was pecking at his terminal.

Cox realized then where Locke was leading the question-and-answer: the two men who'd doped his drinks back at the Solar System Bar & Grille had been the same two spooks who'd had their own jumpcraft out here. Paige had loudly declared she was going to find them and charge them with everything in the book.

Dream Date, if there still was—or ever had really been—such a dating service, would cover for the two spooks with the black pressure suits who'd been caling the shots on this mission. Whether Locke and his friends could cover for Raymond Godfrey and IST the same way remained to be seen.

On his way out, Cox was fervently hoping that Locke *could* find some way to keep IST's name out of any ensuing investigation. Otherwise, if Paige pressed hard enough in the right places, Dennis Cox wasn't sure that either of them would survive long enough for Cox to keep his promise and square Alpha and Beta's account with IST.

When Cox woke from a dreamless sleep eight hours later, in the bunk above Frickey's, he was still wondering what, if anything, he could do to sandbag Paige until the time came to make a move.

He hadn't seen her; she was still up there with the brass. He'd seen Frickey, all of Frickey, because they'd needed to wind down and they'd both lost so much and, damn it, there was always privacy to be had in the suitroom, if you were a ranger.

When they'd wound down enough that they were just holding each other for human comfort, Frickey had giggled against his chest.

He'd asked her what was funny, and she'd replied, "Nothin'—yeah, something. Fritz told me once you two were talking about me and you said you'd rather soul-kiss a bat than screw somebody who shoots as good as I do."

"Yeah, well, I didn't want to crowd him," he'd replied, and he could feel her tremble. Too bad, getting involved with another ranger in the same unit like she had. But not on the same team, he reminded himself. And here he was, doing pretty much the same thing with her. Although they both knew they were just decompressing, now that they were safe aboard the *Malibu*. But how safe was that? You never thought you were going to lose friends. It wasn't that much worse for her, over Schultz, than for him, over his two teams—unless crying made it easier for her.

Frickey had sworn him to silence about the tears, making self-deprecating remarks about women in combat, and they'd sat around in their underwear checking their gear and cleaning their weapons and trying to pump each other back up to spec until he'd remembered he had to see the flight engineer in a little under four hours.

So they'd racked and when he went blearily stumbling for the galley, he was already late. Late enough that he'd pulled on his recon suit instead of ship's coveralls, which meant he could hit his pharmakit and skip breakfast.

The flight engineer lived his life in hearing protectors and gave Cox a pair of electronic earmuffs, first thing. They still had to shout at each other until they got through the engineering bay and into the man's office. It didn't take the rotund career officer long to see where Cox was headed:

"You worried about your pod, boy?" The flight engineer, Clough, had jowls and basset hound eyes and five hairs pulled over his pate. "We don't tolerate monkey business on this deck. You and I got a job to do, we do it. My boys'll be on the lookout for anything funny. You got a possible perp in mind?"

"I don't want to say. All those people we're hauling saw stuff maybe they shouldn't have seen: let's leave it at that."

"I can't put somebody on every cocoon, son."

"I know that. I also know what I'm lookin' at when the cover comes off the guts of one of those."

Clough pulled at his lip. "Still, pick out two or three pods and I'll guarantee to get you and them through in good order—I can't just switch you with somebody else's pod at the last minute, because of the mods we're going to make."

"I know that. That's why I'm worried."

"Well, you can't stay up all the way home, like that crazy bastard from Deck Seven is going to do."

"What?"

Behind the flight engineer were some girlie calendars, a couple schematics, and a hand-scribbled note. Without looking around, the engineer pulled the note off the board and handed it to Cox.

It said, in childlike, rounded handwriting, *"To whom it may concern: I will not be using the slow-*

*freeze pod. Do not prepare one for me. Freedom
Ayoub, Deck 7, Bunk 3.*

"Oh boy." Cox shook his head. "Well, I dunno. We
can't make him, I guess."

"Sure we can, son. This is government property.
Without a cocoon, he'll go nuts. That's what pods
are for, beyond lengthening your functional life-
span."

"He's nuts already. Let's see what we can do
about rigging this system."

Ayoub's note bothered Cox all through the technical discussion. When he and the flight engineer
had reached a "meeting of the minds"—which
meant that they couldn't really satisfy each other's
requirements but had hashed out a compromise
that had a good chance of working—Cox left the
flight engineer's office, looking for Deck 7, Bunk 3.

Ayoub was sitting on it when Cox found him. It
was lunchtime and everyone else billeted there
had gone to the galley.

Cox knocked and Ayoub waved him in. The big
worker was sitting on the top bunk, swinging his
legs. He gestured expansively, "Welcome, Sergeant
Cox. I was hoping you and I would have a chance
to talk."

"That's what I want to do. Look, I told you in the
TAV, you've *got* to slow-freeze. People don't adjust
well to superforce jumps...it's not space and time
like we know it. Things don't have the same phe-
nomenal logic, as I understand it." He stopped,
wondering if the Fourth Worlder could grasp what
he was saying, and began again only when he saw
rapt attention in Ayoub's eyes: "Take messages,
say. You can't send a message through a superforce
jumpspace—it doesn't go straight through, not to
where you send the light beam, anyway. Or it does

go straight through but it's real slow, still traveling
at the speed of light, and we haven't been in space
long enough to receive one traveling that slow. Or
we just flat don't know."

"Do not worry, Sergeant Det Cox. I will stay
awake during the jump and protect Paige and
yourself."

"Nobody's going to do anything to us during the
jump. You don't understand what I'm telling you.
If we have a problems, it'll be mechanical, and you
can't solve that. Can you?"

"Not . . . mechanical problems, no. That I cannot
solve." Ayoub's big lips worked.

Cox looked at his own feet and leaned back
against the wall. "The people problems—the kind
we might have—we won't have. I just took care of
that. I'll be the last one to go beddy-bye. We'll be
jumping a couple seconds, max, after I . . . finish
what I've got to do. Everybody else but the captain
and the flight engineer will already be asleep.
Everybody. So you don't have to worry."

"And what is it you have to do, before you
sleep?" Ayoub's eyes pinned Cox's with unexpected
force.

"You know what," he mumbled. "If Paige didn't
tell you, you must have guessed." He tried to drag
his gaze out of the other man's and somehow he
couldn't. That scared him and he tried again, succeeded, and then couldn't find anywhere else to
look but at Ayoub's black face.

"I've got to," Cox nearly pleaded. "Everybody's
scared to death of . . . you know. What's down
there."

"There's no need."

"The hell there isn't. I lost—" Then Cox realized
that Ayoub meant there was no need to be afraid.

Freedom Ayoub nodded as if Cox had spoken

aloud. "Paige has told you not to feel guilt. Your friends will be reborn, in one form or another. They want life. Life wants them. It is the holy way."

"Aw, shit. Kill yourself stayin' up in jump phase, you crazy—" Cox was halfway out the door when Ayoub called after him: "You believe me, Sergeant Cox. You know truth when you hear it."

"I don't believe any of what I hear, buddy, and only about half what I see." Cox wheeled, hands on hips. "You stop fillin' Paige's head with that garbage. Dead is dead, mister. Not just here, but on X-31A, and on Io, and on—"

"Dead is not dead on X-31A," said Freedom Ayoub.

Cox closed his eyes against the memory of Reynolds being pulled into X-31A's rock by white, translucent hands. Then he opened them. "You know, if I did believe you, I'd space your black ass. Everybody's nervous about contamination. You talk about this much more, you're going to find out what happens when you make the USG nervous. God knows, what's going to happen down on X-66B ought to be lesson enough."

Cox couldn't figure out why, when he stalked down the corridor toward the mess, he wanted to cry. So he changed direction and went looking for Frickey. Maybe Frickey would cry for him. Christ, she'd made it clear she'd do any damn thing he wanted, back there in the suitroom.

But he couldn't find Frickey without paging her on the intercom. He couldn't find Paige, either. And he didn't want to find Locke. So, without really thinking about it, he got his helmet, checked his tanks, and headed for the nearest airlock.

In it, his respirator on and all his systems checked out, his gloved finger hesitated on the se-

lector keypad, then pressed for exit. He sat out
there a long time, wedged firmly against a gun-
port, his fingers wound in the catwalk strutting,
watching the starfield as the *Malibu* headed out-
system and thinking about Reynolds and Schultz
and what Freedom Ayoub had said about life
wanting them.

And he remembered Schultz telling him that the
scratchings on the tunnel wall had been Thai for
redemption, resurrection, the holy way.

Maybe Locke and the spooks were right. Maybe
the only thing to do about whatever was down
there on X-66B was to incinerate it. If that were
true, then what was Cox supposed to do about the
suspicion growing in him that Freedom Ayoub
wasn't just spouting Fourth World ideology?

He sure as hell didn't want to be the guy who
refused to kill something like those white hands
before they spread.

CHAPTER 25

Slow-freeze

———◆———

"WHAT WOULD YOU like first, the bad news or the
worst news?" Cox had asked Paige when she'd encountered him and Corporal Frickey during the
slow-freeze orientation.

Paige had said, "The worst news," with as much
insouciance as she could muster because there was
Cox, in full battle dress, with the female ranger so

close to him their hips grazed, and Paige didn't like the proprietary air the other woman radiated.

She also didn't like the way the two were armed to the teeth. They were safe here on the *Malibu*. Captain Wiley and Lieutenant Locke had gone to great pains to assure her of that, during her first dinner in the captain's quarters and thereafter.

The *Malibu* was under way, headed toward the edge of X-66B's solar system, where gravity wells wouldn't complicate the imminent superforce jump. So the bunched muscles in Cox's jaw just didn't make any sense.

Didn't, until Corporal Frickey took one step away from him, turned her back to face the cocoons and the people milling about in the center of the large gray jump-bay, and Cox said, "You got it: worst news first. Your crazy friend Ayoub is determined to stay awake the whole ride home."

"You're taking Freedom too seriously," she objected.

"You see him here, IST lady? Or you think it's cute that he's playing hookey from the only training run he's going to get?"

"No one needs a 'training run,' Sergeant Cox. You know as well as I do this whole charade is simple government posturing, an assertion of control, an attempt to force by-the-numbers discipline on people who aren't accustomed to following orders by rote."

"Civilians." Cox shook his head, indicating the whole room full of IST science staffers getting into their cocoons while *Malibu* crewmen with clipboards and headset transceivers instructed them in government transit regulations and emergency procedures. "You don't know what you need, Paige —not if you've been hangin' out with Locke."

"We've misjudged Lieutenant Locke, Sergeant—
Det." The effort to unbend, to recapture some of
their former intimacy, made Paige stumble over
her words. Behind him, Frickey stood watch,
spread-legged, keeping at bay any possible eaves-
droppers. And any chance, Paige realized, that Cox
was going to unbend. "He's been very kind, very
helpful. Accommodating, in fact—"

"Did he accommodatingly tell you about the
site-intelligence with your face plastered all over it
that he's got classified? And that he's willing to use
against you if you get out of line? That's the bad
news."

"Out of line? I don't think I under—"

"Push IST too hard, honey. And I don't want you
to, either. It was bad enough you didn't trust me to
keep my word and told Wiley how you need to
have me there, on tap, on Earth, for your goddamn
inquiry."

So it was what she'd said to Wiley, not Frickey
or the fact that Paige had been spending time with
the officers on the upper decks, that was bothering
Cox. She said honestly, "Det, I had to. For both our
sakes."

"Not for my sake. The last thing I want is to be
tethered to you, lady, or anybody who's going to
insist on lots of time Earthside. I told you I'd help
you, but you couldn't leave it at that. Now that
you're so cozy with the brass, I figure I'm only
doing what I get orders to do. You set it up, now
you play it by your own rules." There was dry ice
in his gaze and it burned her.

"Det, I had to make sure you'd be there. You
haven't got the rank to keep those kinds of promises if—" And then she stopped, because she'd said
the wrong thing. Again.

"Yeah, I keep forgetting you're some kind of

high-powered executive twit." He glanced down at his chronometer. "Look, you're slotted for that cocoon over there, number 22. Don't let anybody switch with you, okay? Not for any reason. Somebody tries to change billets, you come to me about it. Not Locke, hear? Or I can't be responsible."

"Fine. Whatever you say. You know I trust you implicitly."

Frickey chose that moment to look over her shoulder and say, "C'mon, Det, it's gonna be crowded here in a couple minutes."

"What about Freedom?" Paige asked quickly, because Locke was coming in the far door and Cox, squinting past Frickey, stiffened when he saw the lieutenant.

Cox said impassively, "Now you're askin'? You left him to fend for himself with the rest of us humble folk. I talked to him. You think you can do better, try. Let me know if he changes his mind. Now go get your pod-drill like everybody else. Never think you don't need an equipment runthrough. Something goes wrong, all the clout in the world won't matter to a fried circuit."

And he turned away, murmuring, "Let's go, Frickey."

The two of them moved off through the crowd like workforce guards through a tent city.

Paige was so hurt, so angry, and so confused that she sat on the edge of cocoon number 22 and gnawed her knuckles, oblivious to the drill around her. She'd managed to put the horror of recent events out of her mind through the simple mechanism of making herself at home in the guest suite on the *Malibu*'s command deck. She had new, clean overalls, fresh fruit and vegetables, congenial dinner companions in the persons of Wiley and his officers. Lieutenant Locke had joined them that first night for dinner, and again the next night, and proved to be a well-educated gentleman with very real and well-conceived concerns about the situation on X-66B.

Both Professor Singer and Lieutenant Locke had been at pains to make clear to Paige their regrets over her "unfortunate" and arduous stay in the work camps. They'd discussed the revolution in a civilized fashion, especially the Thai litany they'd discovered scratched on a wall.

Paige was the expert on X-66B, as far as Locke was concerned. His interest had been flattering, his questions penetrating. She'd nearly been able to forget about the atrocities, the horror—and the resurrected one waiting below decks in the crew quarters. She'd avoided discussing Sanchez, or resurrection, because it was beginning to seem as if she might have hallucinated the whole thing. She'd sat drinking Montrachet with the captain while Locke talked about revolutionary politics, occasionally baiting her to dispute him in congenial fashion.

It had been, in point of fact, an interval reminiscent of her life before she'd met Cox and been shanghaied into a nightmare. She told herself that she hadn't divulged anything crucial to Locke or anyone else abovedecks, even if Cox was right and they were all her enemies.

It was true that Locke had warned her that some of their recon photos showed her in the company of rebels, and those pictures might demand some later explanation to a very low-profile committee, but Paige was used to security, to committees, and to endless meetings. She welcomed the prospect of an inquiry into X-66B, and she'd said so.

She had to speak her mind. She knew, she was sure, what not to say. She also knew that cooperation was the best course. She wanted to make an ally of Locke, because that was the way one did this sort of thing. If she was to stand before Raymond Godfrey and demand an accounting, she'd need all the help she could get.

And the help she'd need wasn't the sort Dennis Cox had shown himself capable of giving. He was so angry that she'd used him as a bargaining chip with Wiley that he couldn't see the wisdom of it. It was, she knew, a matter of perspective—where Locke was concerned, Cox didn't have any.

"Pardon me?' she said and looked up because someone had spoken to her.

Before her was a *Malibu* crewman who asked again, "If you're ready, ma'am, I'll walk you through the basics. This cocoon isn't too different from your civilian pod so if you'll just stand up so I can show you how to operate your internal controls—"

"Yes, fine."

And it was, until Locke, who'd been wandering around the room, stopping here and there to listen or to make a comment, approached her with Professor Singer in tow.

"Hi, Paige," Locke said with a taut smile and a wink of one blue eye. "We've got some sort of problem with your witness, Mister Ayoub. He doesn't want to take a pod."

"Oh really? I'm sure we can convince him. He's had a hard time." Paige crossed her arms and nodded at Professor Singer. There was something about the woman she just didn't like.

"You want to come down with me and see what you can do? Professor Singer, why don't you take this pod and—"

Was Cox psychic? Or just a psychotic who'd made a lucky guess? All Paige's earlier fears rushed in on her and she replied firmly, "I'm almost done here, and twenty-two's my lucky number. So if you'll wait a moment." She turned to the crewman: "Let's hurry this as fast as we can, please."

She watched Locke's face out of the corner of her eye and his expression didn't change. He simply took Singer's arm and led her toward another pod.

When he came back alone, Paige was ready to go with him, a simplified sheet of cocoon instructions clutched in one hand. Locke seemed guileless once more as he guided her toward the hatchway and Ayoub's quarters.

In them, Freedom Ayoub was adamant: "No, Paige, not even for you. I will be fine. Your government has detailed the dangers. Surely it has no more responsibility to me than that."

Locke said, "We can drug you and freeze you, friend. Nobody wants any problems with this jump," and Paige heard the roughness there that had been lacking on the upper decks. It was as if Locke were two people. And this side of him Paige recognized as the enemy.

She wanted to find Dennis Cox and apologize, but this was not the time. She and Locke spent nearly a half-hour trying to convince Ayoub together, and then Paige said, "Let me speak to him alone, Lieutenant."

When Locke had left and closed the door with elaborate deference, she whispered, "Freedom, don't make such a spectacle of yourself. You can lie in a pod and not push its activation button— look." She held out the spec sheet she'd been given, on which were all the instructions necessary to operate a slow-freeze cocoon.

Ayoub's thick yellow fingernails traced the lines of print. When he finally looked up at her, he said,

"It will be easier to watch over you in the slow-freeze bay."

"Then you'll agree?"

"To lie in one of the cocoons, yes. But that is all. I—"

"Great!" She didn't wait to hear the rest. She opened the door and told Locke, "He'll do it. Let's get him up there so he knows *how* to do it."

"He will?" Locke ran a hand through freshly-trimmed blond hair. "Okay, fella, let's go get you set up."

And off they went, back to the slow-freeze bay. As the two men began Ayoub's orientation, she hung back and found herself alone, looking at the array of closed and open cocoons, some with people in them. It was quiet in the bay, and eerie beyond description. In an hour or two, it would be time to do this for real.

She wanted, abruptly, to hurry the process, to lie in her cocoon and push the buttons and see the top come down and go to sleep. Then she desperately wanted to see Dennis Cox before she did that. But Cox wasn't anywhere around, and Locke and Freedom Ayoub were huddled together over a cocoon going through the orientation.

Again, and this time with rising panic, Paige fought a sense of disorientation: had everything she'd thought happened on X-66B really happened? Was Freedom Ayoub what she thought he was? And if so, did she have any right to aid and abet him?

She wanted to get it over with, close her pod and awake where it would be too late for second thoughts. But second thoughts were all around her. She saw Sanchez in her minds' eye, and all the suffering in the work camps. She saw Ayoub dead and Ayoub reborn, as well as the Ayoub before her.

And she saw Raymond Godfrey's face as he'd told her to let the X-31A matter lie. Only this time, Jill Ekberg was looking over his shoulder at her, offering Paige a blind date.

She struggled to recapture the sense of righteousness and determination she'd felt previously, to find someone whose motives were certain and whose good nature was unquestionable. Someone —or something—to believe in, because suddenly she didn't believe in herself, or her assessment of right and wrong in this situation. That person wasn't Ayoub, who carried within him either the seeds of redemption, resurrection and the holy way—or destruction. It certainly wasn't Locke, whose agenda was so completely hidden.

But she'd promised to get Ayoub to Earth. She had her own agenda. And she'd have to determine right and wrong for herself, not look for it around her—especially not here, where there was something drastically wrong.

For a long interval she sat by herself, trying to isolate the nature of her feelings. And finally she thought she understood: these were the rangers' cocoons, in this bay. The *Malibu* crewmen and the officers' cocoons were separate, a function of military redundancy: if one bay was for some reason inoperable or even destroyed, the entire ship wouldn't become an immediate ghost, devoid of life.

None of the techs and science staffers now making final preparations for their long winter's nap would be here if not for the death of all but two of the Alpha and Beta rangers.

She had to find Cox. She went to Freedom, touched his arm, and that odd look of his that seemed to pierce her soul told her not to tell him where she was going.

Paige fled through the ship's lower corridors, following the color-coding on the floor that Cox had taught her.

And she ran into Cox and Frickey, taking off their helmets as they came out of an elevator.

"Hey, hey, what's up?" Cox waved at her. Frickey didn't.

"I . . . came looking for you. Freedom's in the cocoon bay with Locke; we've convinced him to at least lie down in one."

"Nice work. We're going that way anyhow. You all ready to jump?"

Paige fell in between them, noticing that Frickey had a folder under one arm and that Cox's suit was very cold to the touch, so cold a film of condensa-·tion had formed on it and was evaporating while she watched.

"I . . . you told me, number 22. Locke tried to give it to Singer, but I kept it. I'm sorry for doubting you about Locke—you were right."

Cox's eyes met Frickey's over Paige's head. Then Frickey said, "Det told me about your worker friend. We'll do the best we can."

Told her what? About Ayoub's hesitancy? About . . . the rest? Paige didn't dare ask. She wished she hadn't come looking for Cox at all. She wished Frickey was still down on X-66B. "Det," Paige blurted. "Did you do it? The explo—"

"The EO?" Frickey answered before Cox could. "Not yet. But we will."

Not "he" but "we." Well, what had there been between Paige and Cox, anyhow? A blind date that had devolved into an unending nightmare, a rescue that had been ordered by his superiors, a kiss in the suitroom. Nothing more.

Then Cox said with surprising gentleness, "We're going to have plenty of time on the other side of the jump to feel bad, lady. All of us. And to see how your friend comes through this."

"If he does." Frickey's voice was even softer. "If any of us do."

"Don't scare her, Frickey. It's fine, Paige."

And it was, in the cocoon bay, with Cox there to open the plate in her pod's belly and check it personally. He stood up finally and said, "Okay, let's tuck you in."

She scrambled up and into the pod, only at the last minute thinking about Freedom. She looked around but didn't see him. Half the pods were already closed, whirring, their red lights on and their lexan covers clouded with interior condensate.

"Nighty-night, and don't forget to hold the little red button down," Cox said with a humorless smile before he backed away and gave her cocoon cover a smart whack that seemed to hurry it closed.

For a moment she could see him through the lexan. Then she could see only her interior controls and the white puffs of sweet air she was exhaling. Then she couldn't see anything at all.

CHAPTER 26

Detonation

No MATTER WHAT he'd told anybody, including Frickey, Cox still had a choice about blowing X-66B. He could fake it, engaging the fallbacks he'd rigged in his detonation program: the satellites would likely go down with the pulse from the more limited detonation. Nobody would find out, if his luck was good, unless and until IST or some salvage company came back out here next year, or the next, to mine what was left.

But if he did that, the remaining survivors on that hard-luck ball of rock would be in for a long slow death, instead of a nice clean one. It wasn't worth it, just to make himself feel better, to put those people down there through hell. And it wouldn't ease his mind any: Cox considered himself a good soldier; it was not his habit to disobey a direct order. He didn't want to be bounced out of the service, or worse, when somebody did put the pieces together. Which somebody would. Locke would, if nobody else.

Indecision had chased him back outside to hang on the *Malibu*'s skin, watching the stars again, until Frickey figured out where he was and came to get him. But it was good to parse things out where a false move could get him spaced because the *Malibu* was picking up speed. His body's reac-

239

tion to imminent physical danger always cleared his head.

Det Cox didn't want to leave things as he'd found them on X-66B. He flat wanted to blow the place to bits. He didn't want to ever see anything like he'd seen down there again; if he could, he wanted to keep any other ranger from ever seeing it. Freedom Ayoub's face kept popping into his mental field of view, like some target image on his visor display.

Hell, if he could, he'd have spaced Ayoub in the bargain, just to be certain that all those poor bastards down there weren't going to die for nothing. If they were going to die at all.

Maybe he was beginning to see the USG's point of view in all this: maybe he was just seeing Locke's. But by the time he'd tucked Paige in her pod and his suit had reached room temperature, he couldn't wait to get it over with.

If he thought about X-66B and what Ayoub had said too much more, he was going to lose his clarity again. What the fuck were they bringing all these types back with them for, if they didn't know what they were dealing with? And were they really going to let everybody go afterward? All the techs, the science staff, who might have been exposed to whatever it was down there? Paige, and Ayoub, who'd certainly been?

Paranoia's only crazy if you're wrong about the odds. Captain Wiley had looked Cox straight in the eye and promised there'd be no detention for him or his on the other side of the superforce jump. If Wiley was lying to him, Cox would deal with that when the time came.

Right now, he wanted to push his button and verify that bang himself. He wanted it so bad that he was pacing, in the corridor outside the ranger

cocoon bay, waiting for his chronometer to show
the time hack he'd set.

He couldn't hang out in the cocoon bay; the
memories were too painful. They were letting
these civilians slow-freeze fully dressed, and nobody'd explained to them about the ejection procedures. It was weird, but it didn't mean foul play.
It just meant that nobody wanted to advertise the
differences between milspec and civilian equipment.

In fact, there was nothing Cox could find in any
of the procedures he'd watched, or the electronics
he'd checked, and nothing Flight Engineer Clough
was admitting to having found, that was outside
normal mission parameters—except for the
changes Cox himself had demanded.

He checked his watch again and started wondering where the hell Frickey had got to. Then he remembered he'd stationed her in the cocoon bay.
He swore at himself and went in to find her.

Frickey was the only moving thing in there.
Maybe Cox ought to have thought about how it
would be for her, posted in there with all those
shut cocoons which had been Alpha and Beta's,
but he wasn't as sensitive as he should have been
—getting straight with blowing a planet full of civilians can make you a little absent-minded.

Frickey's eyes were real wide in her freckled
face, the freckles were standing out like spattered
mud against her pale skin, and her over-under rifle
was cradled in her arms. She said, "It's like a goddamned morgue in here, Det."

"I know. We're two minutes, thirty-five seconds
from ready. You all set?"

She sighed. "I guess. That Ayoub's pod isn't operational. We gonna let him do that?"

Cox looked where Frickey's chin jutted, to where

Freedom Ayoub could be seen lying in his cocoon. There wasn't a bit of mist on the lexan; the poly hadn't frosted up at all.

"I dunno." Cox, out of habit, walked over to one of the three remaining open cocoons and started to strip: rangers didn't slow-freeze clothed. Frickey followed. He was packing his suit neatly in the undercarriage locker when she knelt down beside him, nude as well now, but still holding her rifle. "Is Locke really coming down here with us?"

Locke's was the third open cocoon. "I expect. Don't wait to snooze until I do, okay? I'm going to wait Locke out, see his cover fog, at least. It'll make me feel better."

"Hey Det?"

"Yeah?"

"We did good. Best we could. You did, for all of us."

"Thanks, Frickey." His eyes flicked to his wrist chronometer, then to hers. "If I had more time, I'd show you how much I appreciate you sayin' that."

She leaned toward him and her rifle jabbed his gut as she hugged him. Cox kissed her forehead, then her lips. "We'll be fine—and we'll play this thing out, for Fritz and the rest of 'em."

Frickey nodded wordlessly and jacked into her cocoon with jerky motions, still carrying her rifle. It wasn't regulation, but Cox didn't blame her. He just didn't think a rifle was going to help him get out of the kind of trouble he might be about to have.

He watched as her cocoon's lid came down and she waved before she closed her eyes.

Then he was by himself, in the cocoon bay, listening to his heartbeat pump. Kneeling by his locker, he fingered his workbelt one last time, tossed it into his open pod without getting up, then slapped the locker cover down and palmed the lock. There really wasn't anything a weapon could do to help him in slow-freeze, but slow-freeze wasn't all he had to worry about.

He straightened, resting his buttocks on the edge of his pod, and waited with arms crossed for he didn't know what—Locke and a bunch of crewmen intent on ejecting every cocoon in this bay, or shooting all the civilians while they slept. If somebody tried, he was going to reach for his workbelt and do his best to stop it.

But nobody came before his sweep hand hit the hack. He pulled himself into his cocoon, settling his workbelt by his control panel and his jury-rigged headset over one ear.

Then Locke showed up, just as Cox was running com-tests with the flight engineer and Wiley, both in their own pods abovedecks.

Standing over Cox's open cocoon, Locke said, "Do a good job, Det. It's probably the most important thing you'll ever do."

Locke had his clothes on. Cox suddenly felt naked. He sat up in his pod, one eye still on his chronometer. "You got fifty-nine seconds and change, Locke. Move your ass."

Locke stared at him like looks could kill and slowly shook his head. Then he walked over to his cocoon, stripping as he went. It was the one beside Singer's. Cox had memorized every pod's occupant and read them, along with his reasons for modifying the pods holding himself, Frickey, and Paige, into his recon pack's log. Nobody could jettison his pod or theirs. Nobody could abort the time clocks, or screw with the life-support, of those three cocoons.

Maybe it was arguable that Cox had thoroughly

and completely protected the lives of Frickey, Barnett and, most importantly, Dennis Cox. But there was always something you hadn't thought of. In his entire life, Cox had never been afraid of slow-freeze before.

Wiley, from his pod on the command deck, was saying into Cox's left ear, "Approaching designated safe distance...now. Half-C minus thirty... twenty-five...twenty..."

Clough cut in with his "all stations automated and confirmed" report and Cox started to slide down into his pod.

He just had time to settle his head on his pillow, adjust his physiosensors against his neck, and get ready to punch the extra keypad that Clough had wired into his pod.

One last look around and he was going to let it happen. He craned his neck. Locke's cocoon was clouding up normally. Frickey was lost in her personal mist. And then, just when he was satisfied, Freedom Ayoub's pod-cover started to open, like some damned mummy coming out a tomb.

It was the last thing he needed to see, and Wiley was calmly counting, "...six...five...four..." in Cox's ear.

Cox came up on one elbow and Ayoub raised his own head at just that moment. The whole idea of sealing himself into his pod with that crazy bastard loose on the ship, alone and free to wreak any kind of havoc, became completely and resoundingly unacceptable.

Then Ayoub saw Cox looking at him and smiled that childlike smile: "Sergeant Cox, I will be watching over you while you sleep. It is the holy way."

"Shit," Cox whispered, eyes darting to the panel before him, then to Ayoub again. He thought crazily that even Ayoub couldn't get at him through the high-impact lexan/poly composite, and then he was one second from go or no-go.

He shoved himself down flat, hand extended. His fingers found the keypad and the plasma-display above it verified readiness. Fighting the impulse to close his eyes, Cox punched-in the sequence that would detonate the charges that they'd set around X-66B's equator, then hit the button that would close his pod's cover.

The rest was automatic: he told Wiley, "Signal executed, sir. Repeat: detonation signal sent. Let's get our verification. Now. I'm cycling for slow-freeze."

And he heard Wiley's response, already distant as the cool, sweet, drugged air in his pod started to do its work, "We've got it, Cox—the bang's good. Repeat: detonation confirmed. I'm ready for freeze. Have a good flight. See you on the other side."

Cox thought he said, "You bet, sir," but he wasn't sure if his lips moved, or he was already dreaming.

CHAPTER 27

Awakening

———◆———

A RED FLASHING light interrupted Paige's sleep, pulsing urgently beyond her tight-shut lids. She shifted, stretched, and encountered the unyielding walls of her slow-freeze cocoon.

Claustrophobia gripped her, chasing away her

drowsiness. When she opened her eyes, the pulsing red light was still there, beyond the closed canopy of her pod. All the risks and the unspoken warnings she'd seen in Cox and Frickey's faces before the jump rushed in to panic her.

She was shaking, pushing at the increasingly transparent lid of her cocoon, before she remembered she had buttons to press. She felt around for her instruction sheet and found it, crumpled by her thigh.

She thought she remembered what to do in a normal situation, but she wasn't sure. She was frightened. She didn't want to make any mistakes. And she didn't think this was a normal situation, not with that red light flashing out there.

What if the ship had had a mishap? What if the bay around her was depressurized? The interior of her cocoon was lit only by the LEDs set in the keypad and what light was coming in from the bay, making the instructions she held hard to read. And the crumpled words on the page seemed to offer no alternative to the terror she felt.

But there were instructions: *In case of depressurization emergency, joystick and switches 1–7 will cease operation. Emergency lights 1A-7A will be lit, allowing operator to initiate Escape Procedures. (See Field Supplement 3A for Protocols.) During Escape Procedures, internal access to undercarriage lockers is potentiated by B Code (FS3A, iiv-1.2). TO DEFEAT SEAL: open lexan/poly cover by entering Special Release sequence (FS3A, 23–3.4). WARNING: Special Release option functions only when exterior pressure readings are life-supportable.*

First she thought, I never could read technical manuals. Then, They didn't give me a Field Supplement 3A. And lastly, Okay, where're Emergency Lights 1A-7A?

When she found them, she realized she hadn't seen them before because they weren't lit. She took deep, tremulous breaths and said aloud, "All right, idiot, calm down. It *isn't* a depressurization emergency." Then what was it?

"For all you know, it's a wake-up alarm," she told herself through gritted teeth. Then she remembered what Cox had said about the red button. And blushed though there was no one there to see.

Chagrin flooded her. She balled the instruction sheet in her fist and tossed it against her cocoon's fully transparent lid. Cox had told her all she'd needed to know: squeeze the red button. She found it, away from the emergency controls, conveniently placed near her hip on the pod's joystick.

She wasn't risking anything, Paige told herself. If the bay out there was depressurized, the red button wouldn't work. Then there'd be time to panic all over again. So she squeezed the joystick, taking a deep breath as she did so.

And holding that breath, as the cocoon around her began to whir, her cheeks puffed out and her throat muscles began to ache, anticipating a struggle against the vacuum logic told her wasn't out there.

In came the smells of a working spacecraft— processed air, hot electronics, human body odor. And with them, an ear-splitting siren that hooted in time to the red flashing lights.

She came up out of her cocoon as quickly as it raised, her hands pushing against the motor-driven canopy as if she could hurry it.

Six pairs of eyes fixed on her. Three weapons' muzzles trained on her. The nearest weapon was in the hands of a crew-cut man who wore an MP armband. The hooting of the siren made speech impossible.

The rifle in the man's hand jerked eloquently: get out, stand on your feet.

She did, facing the crewman holding her at gunpoint and two of his companions, who were sitting on a closed cocoon that had lights running across a telltale on its plinth.

Beyond them, and looking her way, was Lieutenant Locke, also holding a gun, and Professor Singer, each before an open cocoon. Locke seemed to smile at her and call out something. Whatever he said was lost in the siren's wail. Locke turned away from her, to Freedom Ayoub, who was standing behind his open cocoon, back against the wall, both hands laced above his head.

Paige's eyes darted around the slow-freeze bay. Its exit was firmly shut and two *Malibu* crewmen were posted before it. Other crewmen, nearly a dozen, were stooping among the closed cocoons, sealing them with distress-orange tape that said SECURITY/SECURITY/SECURITY on it in bold black letters.

Paige found herself gulping air, her hands at her throat. She glanced surreptitiously at her own cocoon and saw that it hadn't been taped. Neither had the one that two of the MPs were sitting on Neither had Freedom's, but then, he was already out ...

Out, and she was out, but where was Cox? Paige slumped back against her own pod, realizing that the two MPs intermittently revealed in red by the flashers were sitting on Cox's pod.

She yelled at them, "You bastards," against the din, knowing they couldn't hear her. Cox had been right, and now he was trapped in that cocoon, despite everything he'd tried to do to protect them ...

Just then she caught a motion out of the corner of her eye.

Another cocoon was opening. She'd never be sure of what happened next: of exactly how many men with weapons were in that bay, or of whether the story they told later was true.

What she saw was Frickey's freckled face, with its close-cropped red hair, and her rifle's barrel, coming up over the opaque lip of her pod.

Then there was a naked woman leaping, and an exchange of fire Paige was unable to follow in the strobing cocoon bay, and deafening reports that cut through even the siren.

And Frickey, propelled half by her initial leap and half by impacts of bullets, exploded out of that cocoon toward Locke, Ayoub, and the far wall.

"Frickey!" Paige screamed, in that instant realizing she'd never bothered to learn the other woman's first name.

By then Frickey was falling against Freedom. He caught her in his huge arms and together they slammed back against the wall to slide down it.

Paige did remember, though, that Frickey's rifle was lying where it had skittered across the floor after she'd dropped it, right between Professor Singer's legs.

"Oh God," she said, and as if He'd heard her, suddenly the siren and the red flashes stopped. The silence shocked everyone momentarily. Then the men with tape went back to work as if someone hadn't just been shot here.

Paige found herself halfway to Ayoub, who was cradling Frickey in his arms like a child, before Locke's shouted, *"Hold your fire!"* penetrated to her brain. Locke's hand came down on her arm, jerking her backward, away from the black man and the naked white woman covered with bright blood.

"Let me go, you bastard." Paige tried to shake off

Locke's grip, but he wouldn't shake. His fingers pincered her arm and he pulled her closer: "Stay out of this. Your crazy friend has been up through the whole jump. This sorry mess is the result. I'll explain later."

Professor Singer, cradling Frickey's rifle, seemed to loom: "I'll take her, Buff." Singer's free arm went around Paige's shoulders as Locke let go.

It didn't make any sense. She could hear Frickey's breath rattling from here. And there were the two men still sitting on Cox's cocoon, and so many others, all with guns. "Freedom didn't do this—whatever you say 'this' is. He doesn't know anything about spacecraft or slow—"

There was a muffled explosion and a scream from the direction of Cox's pod. Paige wheeled in time to hear a second bang and see both men who'd been sitting on that pod roll off it in different directions. One was screaming.

The pod's canopy was fractured crazily, Paige saw as its motor raised it up, whining. Inside she saw Cox, a second before he came vaulting out of his cocoon with a weapon in his hand.

Singer pulled her out of the way and both of them stumbled and fell. Frickey's rifle slid out of reach, under a pod-carriage. Paige got a glimpse of Cox, diving among the closed cocoons, and Locke suddenly dropping out of view.

The two MPs who'd been sitting on Cox's cocoon were groaning and bleeding and someone was yelling at the men who'd run over to help them to "Leave 'em for later, damn it!"

There was so much confusion and yelling that only later did Paige realize that this time not more than three shots had been fired, after the initial ones that had cracked through Cox's pod-lid and into the buttocks of the men sitting on it.

When Paige raised herself up on stiff arms she saw Cox, quite naked but for a gunbelt, with the muzzle of his gun in Locke's ear and his other arm around Locke's neck, dragging the lieutenant backward toward Frickey and Ayoub, who were still slumped against the wall.

A quiet seemed to radiate from them, silencing everything in the room and bringing activity to a halt, even before Locke said, "Freeze, everybody, okay? Weapons on the deck, nice and easy." Cox was whispering in Locke's other ear. After a pause in which men disarmed, Locke said again, "Sergeant Cox doesn't understand the situation yet, that's all. He won't mind if we take care of our wounded, though. Will you, Cox?"

"Yeah, fine." Cox seemed to notice her for the first time. "Paige, get away from Singer. Good. Over here."

"Det," Locke said, his voice choked because his neck was bent to its limit and Paige could see his pulse beating in his throat as she threaded her way through the cocoons to join them. "Det," Locke began again, "don't get too close to that black son of a bitch. We don't know what he's capable of. While we were all out—"

"Don't bullshit me, Locke. You're as predictable as a morning piss." Cox let his gaze flicker to Frickey, by Ayoub on the floor. "Paige, she dying?"

"I—" Paige knelt down, opposite Freedom, and their eyes met. Freedom's hand seemed to be cupping Frickey's left breast and blood ran under it.

Paige blinked at the black man's grasp. At first it had seemed that Frickey's chest wasn't rising and falling, now it seemed that it was. "Will she live?" Paige asked the resurrected one.

"Forever," Freedom Ayoub said with a strained smile. "Redemption, resurrec—"

"Freedom, dear god, don't give me that," Paige pleaded. She reached out to take Frickey's wrist and search for a pulse there because she could see only white under Frickey's lids.

There *was* a pulse. It didn't look to Paige as if there should be—could be. But there was. This was no cave on X-66B. This was no ceremony with believers present. This was just, she told herself, a trick of fate.

But the joy that overswept her made her blurt, "Det, quick! Let's get her to a doctor! She's breathing, but there's so much blood—"

Not until she'd finished saying that did she pay any attention to what was going on around her.

Locke was telling Cox, "—four lightminutes from Cerberus, and we've got new orders. You're in enough trouble already, soldier. You let me go, we'll forget about this. A misunderstanding."

"Yeah, like Frickey was a misunderstanding?"

"That's right, Sergeant. Like Frickey. Asshole came up out of that pod like the Lone Ranger, waving a weapon. Let me go, maybe we can save her if Barnett's right."

"What about the others?" Cox's voice was completely without inflection. His face seemed all bone and corded muscle.

"Those others—all those cocoons, no matter whether what's in them is alive or not—are security sealed until we off-load them at Cerberus for debriefing."

"C'mon Locke, cut the crap. For quarantine, you mean. For interrogation."

"Call it what you want, soldier. You've got the gun. And you're holding it on a superior officer. Some of those cocoons aren't reading normal lifesigns. We've got to take Ayoub into custody until we look at the log and see if he had anything to do with that. You want to keep him company, that's your choice. Right now, and for the next thirty seconds, you've got a chance to keep this off the record. You fuck with me any more, mister, and the rendezvous team from Cerberus that's going to dock with us—the ship that was going to take you and Barnett and her pet nigger to Earth—is going to take you to hell instead."

Ayoub shifted and Frickey groaned softly. There were little pink- and red-flecked bubbles at the corners of her lips.

"Det, she'll die!" Paige looked up, and around, and realized how many others were waiting to see whether Cox would let Locke go: too many, including the MPs at the doors. "We'll never get out of here otherwise. Do what he says," she pleaded shamelessly, wanting only to live to get home, and for Frickey to live long enough to see a doctor, and for Freedom Ayoub to live to set foot on the planet Earth.

Ayoub nodded at her as if he was pleased and took his hand away from Frickey's breast. The wound wasn't as large as Paige had thought. And she saw something in his palm, something very much like what she supposed a bullet looked like.

Cox said, "Locke, you gotta promise me, no reprisals. And help for Frickey, right away."

"That's what I've been offering, Sergeant. She could be in sick bay by now, except for you and your one-man show."

Cox pushed Locke away from him, very hard, very abruptly. Locke stumbled and Paige saw his hand go to his hip, where he wore a holster, as if forgetting the holster was empty. He called, "Okay, you heard me. Call sick bay. Let's get those cocoons sealed so we can open the room and get the corporal up there. Call Wiley and tell him the emergency's under control and we're back on normal operating procedures. And pick up your weapons, assholes. I'm glad I'm not going to write this up— two rangers hold a whole complement of MPs at bay! Look great in your jackets, gentlemen!"

Cox was already kneeling down over Frickey, staring not at her, but at Ayoub. He called Paige's name.

By the time she'd leaned close, Cox was saying to Freedom, "—what you did to her, but it better be either nothin' or somethin' she's happy about. As for Locke's charges: any of that's true, your ass is mine, buddy, no matter what the fuck you are."

"Det, what is it?" Paige said softly, to remind him she was there.

"Get me my suit—Frickey's. In our undercarriage lockers." He reached out and gently lifted a thin steel chain from Frickey's neck. The woman didn't move.

Paige thought, Please God, don't let her be dead. Please. And please don't let her be—

"Stick the tab in her locker and her ID will open it. Take mine, too." He slipped his own chain off his neck. "I want my suit, my helmet, my pack— everything that's in there. And take this, in case anybody gives you trouble."

He reached behind his hip and came up with a stubby gun, holding it out.

"I can't. I don't know anything about—"

"You take it. Just threaten. Nonregulation .500 magnum—how I shot through my poly-cover. Equivalent of a suicide pill in my business. Shoots through anything we've got worth piercing, with enough foot-pounds at the muzzle to scare anybody on board who wants to keep breathin'." He bared his teeth at her, then his lips pressed into a tight, thin line. "C'mon, IST lady. You don't want me spending the next few days in the brig naked as a jaybird, do you?"

She went, fumbling through his instructions, and it seemed to work. At least, none of the MPs busy taping the quiescent cocoons so much as made a motion in her direction once they saw the gun.

After she'd given Cox everything he'd asked for, she realized that Singer and Locke were huddled together in a corner where there was an intercom. Locke waved her over.

She looked down at Cox, just zipping his suit, and at Freedom, holding Frickey, and hesitated. "Det—"

"Yeah, I saw. Go over there, if you want. Just remember, they're going to want you to tell this story their way. And I'm going to want you to tell what you saw, without any frosting." He rubbed his forehead with the back of his hand. And squinted at her. "Go on. It's a small ship. Try to come up to the sick bay, if you can. And don't worry about me—" He stopped, swallowed. "Keep your fingers crossed for Frickey. She's the last one —last of Alpha and Beta; last one who ought to have taken a fall over this goddam..." He trailed off and, when she didn't move away, added, "Get out of here, I said! This is ranger business. Go make your brass-only deals about who says what and just tell me how I'm supposed to play it."

Paige left him, chiding herself for not realizing that Frickey was more than just another ranger to Cox: she was the single survivor, in his mind, of his lost teams, the difference between acceptable losses and total failure. She might be even more than that.

The vision of Ayoub's hand over Frickey's bloody breast, and the piece of twisted metal Paige thought she'd seen in his palm, haunted her well after Locke had assured her that "all the repercussions from this are containable, if we work together like professionals."

"Even Freedom Ayoub?" she demanded, in a clean white elevator on the way to the upper decks where, she assumed, Frickey would be treated in sick bay.

"If the tapes scope out," Locke had said bluntly.

"If Ayoub wasn't...responsible for any tampering with the cocoons, he means," Professor Singer added. There was a spattering of tiny blood droplets on her face.

"What if there *was* tampering but you can't prove who did it?" Paige retorted. "That was what Det...what Sergeant Cox was trying to prevent— tampering. That was why he went to all that trouble."

"Ms. Barnett," said Professor Singer, seeming to grow an inch taller. "You're jumping to conclusions unworthy of your station. Of course we're keeping the balance of the staffers in slow-freeze in order to debrief them thoroughly without the chance that they'll homogenize their stories by too much fraternization. And there's the danger of... contamination by other than verbal means. No one knows, right now, why some of those pods malfunctioned." She crossed her arms.

Locke said in a low voice, "Cox and the flight engineer, Clough, were the last people to access the pod electronics, but we've got plenty of time to run our checks. We'd like to start with you, Paige."

"Start with me?"

"We need to get an exhaustive, on-the-record interview with you that covers everything you remember about X-66B. Its ranger policy in a situation like this—government policy. And we need to do it before your own memory blurs. If you'll cooperate, and let Professor Singer and me take your deposition, then when the patrol cruiser that's going to be space-docking with us shows up, you can leave with them. Free and clear. Back to Earth the way I promised."

"Leave with them," she parroted dumbly. "And everyone else?"

"They're IST workers," Professor Singer reminded her. "You know IST policy, the way we cooperate with government agencies. We've agreed to keep everyone at Cerberus—"

"Cerberus?"

"A classified staging area in-system, very secure," Locke answered before Singer could. "When we've checked them out, they'll be reposted."

"But they're not going to Earth?" Paige hugged herself.

"Certainly not in a group, as disaster survivors —survivors of a disaster we need to minimize."

"You mean pretend it never happened, like X-31A?"

"Just exactly like X-31A," said Locke while Singer smiled at her encouragingly from a seamed horse-face without a trace of humanity in it that Paige could find.

The elevator stopped and opened onto the command deck; Paige recognized it right away. "Where's the sick bay up here? I promised Cox—"

"Frickey'll be in the below-decks sick bay," Locke said, urging her out of the elevator. Singer followed and the elevator closed. "Don't worry about Cox, he's got plenty to keep him occupied."

"What do you mean, don't worry? Cox and Ayoub and Frickey are going with me to Earth on that patrol cruiser. Of course I'm going to—"

"If you're still insisting on that, we'd better get

started right away. The best way you can help them is by being as forthcoming and as cooperative as possible. They've all got charges to be cleared of, before we can let them go anywhere like Earth."

"But you promised him! I heard you." She stopped in the hall and her voice was loud enough that someone peeked a head out of an open office door to see what the commotion was.

"Yeah, I promised him. He had a gun stuck in my ear and he was about to shoot up the whole pod bay, like his girlfriend tried to do. Cox has to get through a stress evaluation, one way or the other. We promised you that you'd have him for a witness. And Ayoub. I don't remember saying anything about Frickey, but we don't know whether she'll make it, let alone be fit to travel."

Paige glared away the hand that Locke extended to her.

Singer said, "Ms. Barnett, let's be professional about this, shall we? You know exactly what is going on here, and you know why. Now, can we go get our question-and-answer started, so that all of us can get on with our lives?"

There was no alternative, Paige realized, but to go with them. To be cooperative, to remain alert, to show herself to be reasonable, a good team player. If she didn't, she was liable to find that she, too, needed to pass a stress evaluation before she was allowed to return to Earth.

If that happened, and she got shunted with the rest of the cattle to a restricted military base called Cerberus, she had real doubts that she'd ever see Earth, or Dennis Cox, or Corporal Frickey, or Freedom Ayoub, again.

CHAPTER 28

Lone Ranger

———◆———

"COME ON FRICKEY, don't die. Damn it, Corporal, can you hear me?" Cox put his head down on the clean white sheets next to Frickey's pale arm. In her arm was a drip feeder; she'd had lots of clear blood, lots of drugs, and lots of sad headshakes because no matter how they tried, the medics couldn't find the airfoil round that ought to be inside her somewhere.

Now you just waited it out. Cox brushed his lips against the cool flesh of her arm and tasted salt, and antiseptic, and death.

He'd had to disarm to get in here; they wouldn't let him see her otherwise. He didn't care much about that anymore. There was no way he was going to hold the entire *Malibu* at bay. He wasn't fool enough to try.

He'd just been running on instinct back there, that and his basic hostility toward Locke. And Frickey; god, Frickey—all he had left to show for X-66B and it had been enough, to bring one soldier through. He'd been holding onto her, hard.

"Come on, don't die," he murmured into the sheet by her arm and somebody behind him cleared a throat.

He raised his head and there was Ayoub, black as doom in this all-white area cordoned off with movable baffles of sheeting, with three MPs on his tail to keep him tractable. They'd all been shot up with tranks, which was probably another reason Cox had let his weapons be taken from him, but Cox was used to tranks.

From the look of Ayoub, he was too. The big man sat down on the other side of Frickey and the MPs backed off before Cox had to ask them.

Ayoub peered at the bandaged, unconscious woman and then extended his closed fist, over her unmoving body, to Cox.

Cox reached out to take it, just to show there were no hard feelings, no matter what this sucker had done or tried to do while the rest of them were in slow-freeze, and Ayoub opened his fist. Down onto Cox's palm dropped something his educated flesh had identified before he took a look: a badly mashed airfoil round out of somebody's shipboard rifle.

"Jesus, you find this on the floor?" Slugs did funny things. They tumbled, they deformed, they couldn't be predicted. Maybe this one had gone in Frickey's chest and come out her open mouth. Cox had known somebody once who got shot between the eyes and the bullet had run down a sinus and popped out his mouth, breaking some teeth. But Frickey's teeth were unbroken and there was no exit wound in her back. The airfoil was specially designed not to achieve anything like the degree of penetration that could be dangerous in pressurized craft.

Ayoub didn't answer, just kept watching him.

"We better tell the doc, you know?" Cox got up and the MPs readied-up. He raised both hands, the airfoil displayed between two fingers. "Just want to show this to somebody. Maybe it'll change her prognosis."

Or change something. He waited while the MPs

got permission, muttering into the transceivers they wore. He didn't have that anymore, either—no access to Wiley, or Clough, or anybody.

He knew he was probably in more trouble than he could handle, but nothing they could do to him would be as bad as Frickey dying. He pushed at everybody and everything until they let him see the chief medical officer and then got into a ballistics argument with the man about whether this was or wasn't the same bullet that had torn up Frickey's chest.

It didn't occur to him until too late that maybe he ought to stay with her. And when he got back there, she'd died on him with only Ayoub there to see her through it.

Cox slumped against the wall, looking at the corporal with the sheet pulled up over her head, wishing he'd been there. He didn't know why, but it was like he'd deserted her.

And he didn't like it that Ayoub had been there. Ayoub had caused this whole mess that got Frickey killed. If he'd just gone into slow-freeze like everybody else, the security boys wouldn't have gotten so jacked-up and Locke wouldn't have been able to pull off what he had—if he had.

Maybe it was just bad luck, but whatever it was, if Cox didn't do some damned thing, he was going to cry. And this time, Frickey wasn't around to cry for him.

Shouldn't have given up his weapons, that was for sure. Maybe if he wrecked the med bay they'd put him in the same holding tank with Ayoub and he could strangle the guy. But that wasn't any good, either.

Ayoub was over in one corner, watching him.

Cox brushed at his eyes and blinked and said, "What you starin' at, sucker?"

"Love," said Ayoub.

"Shit." Cox got off the wall, took a step toward the black worker. The three MPs moved an equal distance toward Cox. He said, "I'm okay. I just need a drink. Take me wherever I'm sleeping, and send a message up to Wiley that I'd appreciate a chance to tell my side of this."

One thing Cox had going for him was that he knew how the system ran. Another was that death made him mad.

The way it felt, what it did to him, what it did to everybody it touched—death was the real enemy, and it won every time, no matter what you did. He'd been proving that he wasn't afraid of it all his life, going one-on-one with it since he was old enough to get into ranger school, but that made him an expert only on giving and taking the suffering associated with dying. And there was no expert's rating for losing. Against death, you lost every time.

Freedom Ayoub looked across Frickey's bed with eyes that had seen the inside of a superforce jump and said, "I read in your ship's library what one man named Donne wrote: 'Death be not proud, though some have called thee/Mighty and dreadful, for thou art not so,/For those whom thou think'st thou dost overthrow/Die not, poor death.' "

"Tell it to Frickey, if you can make her hear you. I'm gonna go see if I can kiss Locke's ass enough to get her body shipped back to her family."

And he was out of there so fast that the MPs assigned to him came tumbling from the sick bay after him, sheepish and bitching, trying to at least look like they had him under control when he half-wanted to prove to them they didn't, so they'd shoot his ass and he could find out where it was that Frickey had gone.

But they didn't want him dead—it would screw things up with Barnett, and with the investigative agencies. He knew they didn't and it gave him an edge he was grief-stricken enough to push without thought to whether or not he could push too far.

He wanted his weapons back. He got them. He wanted his full recon panoply; he got that. He wanted a goddamn private room and he wanted to get drunk, and they gave him that too, although a medic came by warning him that he'd been tranked up too much to be drinking.

Until they'd gotten a statement out of him—one they could edit into something to support whatever conclusion they decided they'd most like to have on the record—he could do pretty much what he pleased, as long as he brought his MPs along.

And since he figured that he had three or four days to kill before rendezvous, calculating from what Locke had let slip about the lightminutes from Cerberus, he was intent on killing them as completely as possible. It was, after all, what he did.

But he couldn't seem to get drunk. It must be the tranks. It couldn't be what Ayoub had said to him; nobody could scare you flat sober.

Still, he was sober, having aced an entire fifth of 100 proof, when Locke decided to "look in" on him, as sober as he'd been when he was sitting with Frickey.

Locke said, "You want to see Wiley. That's fine. I simply need to make sure you realize that Wiley ought not to be brought into the picture on this any more than necessary."

"So?"

"Det, I'm doing the best I can for you. You're not helping."

"How's Paige? Frickey's dead. Paige dead too yet?"

"Are you drunk?"

"Nah. Tried, but it didn't work."

"You and Clough, and Ayoub, have some serious explaining to do."

"Tell you what, Locke," said Cox expansively, leaning back spread-armed on his bunk. "You explain it all for us and I'll get the other two to sign off on whatever you want, short of death sentence or court-martial."

"You will? Just like that?"

"Sure, if you put Frickey's body on the next Earthbound ship so she gets an honors burial. One of us ought to."

"That's all you want?"

"All I can think of. I'd like to keep my rating, if you can manage it; but shit, I've had a good run."

Locke stared at him, stood up, and said, "I believe you. And I think we can work something out. Stay put and for chrissakes, don't shoot anybody else."

"Not even Ayoub, promise," said Cox, and he meant it. Then.

When Locke started interrogating him for real, though, it was harder than he'd thought to play dumb and swear to stuff that hadn't happened, while ignoring things that had.

Getting Ayoub to sign the garbage deposition was a piece of cake—the Fourth Worlder really did want to see Earth. And Flight Engineer Clough told Cox straight out he'd "do anything to keep my head above water on this one."

That head, with its five long strands carefully arranged across a perspiring pate under the briefing room lights, was bowed and Clough wouldn't meet Cox's eyes.

By the middle of the Q&A Cox was pretty sure he'd never get out-system like he'd always wanted, with a nice retirement check and a clean slate.

But he'd get to Earth with Paige, like he'd promised. And he'd get Frickey back home. You couldn't be a ranger forever—there weren't any old rangers. One way or another, you became *ex*.

Frickey's way seemed a whole lot cleaner, the way he was feeling during the debrief. He knew they'd have gotten what they wanted from him somehow, but he hated like hell to "yes-sir" and "no-sir" Locke like Locke deserved it.

Locke had beaten him, square and fair in Locke's terms. Locke was going to get to fly more missions, probably get promoted, keep his clearances and his recon pack under his bed and jump when the bells rang. Cox was going either to Cerberus for disciplinaries, or to Earth with Paige Barnett, and even the choice was out of his hands.

He saw Ayoub only once, and Paige not at all, until the patrol cruiser rendezvoused and two guys came out of the spacedock tube.

They were the same two men he'd seen first in the Solar System Bar and Grille and again during the *Malibu* briefing before he'd taken Alpha and Beta down to X-66B and they waved like Det wasn't under close arrest wherever he went.

One, the blond, came up to him and said, "Sergeant, my condolences. You've had a rough time and we're all grieving with you. But right now we're going to need your help with that female exec you brought in-system. Are you in shape for a little quick improv?"

"Sir?" This was the last thing Cox had expected from these two. From the look on Locke's face, Locke hadn't expected it either. The man who'd spoken to Cox was the one everybody'd called

"Captain" during the initial briefing in Wiley's office, and when that man just looked at him, waiting for a better answer, Cox said, rubbing his jaw, "I'd like to help, but I don't know that I'm in any position to, sir."

"How's that?" said the blond captain.

"You better talk to Lieutenant Locke, sir. I guess the brass here feels I pegged a couple too many meters, comin' out of slow-freeze."

"I see. Well, at ease, Sergeant: you haven't got any problems I can't solve." And the captain clapped him on the arm before he took Locke off into a private huddle.

The darker of the two officers who'd come through the docking tube, the one whose rank had never been specified, looked from Locke to Cox and the left side of his mouth pulled down sharply. "Whatever you've done, Cox, it just unhappened."

When Locke, scowling, and the blond captain rejoined the small welcoming party, the dark man said, "Let's talk to Wiley; get the woman, the black, and out of here. I'm on a tight schedule, Lieutenant." His words cracked like a whip.

Locke said, "Det, go with these two gentlemen. The rest of you," he told the MPs, "come with me."

"Sergeant Cox, you'll have to show us how to get to the command deck," the dark-complexioned officer in the black pressure suit confided in friendly fashion. "And when we get off this cow, you can count on telling us what really happened down in the cocoon bay—and back on X-66B. Will you do that?" he asked, his blue eyes startlingly candid, as Cox led them to an open elevator.

In it, Cox said, "Yes, sir. I'd like to do that, sir. I'd also like to make sure that Paige Barnett—that's the IST woman—and Freedom Ayoub get a chance to do that. And I'd like to get my dead—one body, name of Frickey—back home with me, sir."

"Is that all, Sergeant?" said the blond captain in an odd voice.

"Sir, beyond that, I really don't give a shit."

Then the elevator opened, and Paige was stepping out of one on the other side of the corridor. She ran up to him and, standing on tiptoes, took his face in her hands, "Dennis. Dennis, are you all right? I was so worried about you. They wouldn't let me see you. You didn't sign anything, did you? I—"

"Yeah I did, but it's okay." He was uncomfortable at the display, in front of these officers. He reached up, took her wrists in his fingers, lowered her hands, and let them go. "I'm fine," he said, very low. Then: "Paige, these are...serious brass, going to take us to Earth. Freedom, too. And Frickey's body. So be nice, okay?"

"Sergeant Cox," said Paige Barnett primly, straightening her borrowed coveralls, "I'm *always* nice. Gentleman, as you may have gathered, I'm Paige Barnett of IST and I've been waiting quite a while to talk to you."

CHAPTER 29

Debrief

———————

PAIGE HAD AS many questions as the two black-suited men presuming to interrogate her, but she got fewer answers.

The two men who'd whisked Paige, Cox, and Ayoub away from the *Malibu* in their Space Command patrol ship claimed to be from something called the Joint Special Science Task Force. Cox, when she'd told him that during a meal in the ship's galley, had laced his hands behind his shaggy head and shaken it pityingly: "Ain't no such thing, but if it makes you feel better about what they did..."

The two men had identified themselves as Major Kipling and Captain Ross, Ross being the blond. And they'd tried to explain shanghaiing her, drugged and helpless, to X-66B as, "...a screw-up, plain and simple, ma'am. Crossed wires of the worst kind." Or at least, the blond named Ross had. Kipling wasn't the sort who made excuses or apologies.

He'd said, "We're rectifying the error—in person. Starting with you and ending, I hope, with IST's CEO." Kipling had paused to offer her another glass of white wine. "We'll be with you all the way up the chain of command, Paige." No "ma'am" from Kipling. The dark man with the blue eyes wasn't used to treating people as anything but subordinates. Paige knew the type.

She knew the type well enough not to need Cox's warning that "these guys are covering their asses, best case. Worst case, they're arresting us and we don't know it yet."

So when Paige's interrogation was forestalled for a "quick stop at Cerberus, just to take on fuel and clean up some loose ends," she was understandably nervous.

So was Cox, who paced the passenger compartment of the twenty passenger in-system cruiser in full recon gear, asking her questions she couldn't answer.

"Did these guys tell you whether they really sent that first message of yours up through channels?"

"No. But would you believe them if they had?"

Cox turned, his hand on one of the seats. "Look, I'm the bad boy in this mess, and they're just about ignoring me. I could probably shoot up this cruiser and nobody'd say boo to me. You don't find that a little odd?"

"No. Yes. I don't know." She looked desperately aft, hoping for assistance from Freedom, who seemed to be napping; the black man's eyes were closed and he didn't move.

"What kind of stuff are they askin' you? You know that, don't you?"

"About...X-66B. About the revolutionaries. About...you know. Freedom. Sanchez. Resurrection, redemption—"

"—the holy way. Christ, you're tellin' them that shit? I told somebody a story like that once. You met me on the tail end of what happened to me because of..." Cox's senses must have been augmented in some way by his recon helmet, even though its faceplate was up, because he was suddenly facing the other direction, where Ayoub was moving.

Freedom came up the aisle, hands gripping each seatback in turn as if he were climbing a ladder. His yellowed eyewhites seemed very bright. "Sergeant Cox, I want to ride in the hold with Corporal Frickey."

"I told you before, wingnut, it's barely survivable in there—pressurized for the body, yeah, but cold as vacuum. You can't—"

"In a suit, I can. I must. You must let me. For Frickey's sake."

Cox's arms crossed; his hands gripped his upper arms as if he were hugging himself. He said, "Don't do this to me, Ayoub. Don't make me think she's not...that there's somethin' we could..." He broke off and Paige saw his helmet slowly angle downward. "Crazy bastard," he muttered, and sat on one of the seat arms.

Ayoub's gaze fixed on her imploringly. *For Frickey's sake.* This wasn't happening, she told herself. Her heart went out to Dennis Cox, bent over where he sat as if he were studying his booted toes.

"Det, you have to let him try. We can't not..."

"Paige, I can't handle this. I'm going to shoot him if he keeps this up." Cox's helmeted head raised to Ayoub. "I let you back there, fucker, and you screw around with that body some way—or if what I think you're saying doesn't work out just right, then you're dead meat. I promise you."

Freedom Ayoub said, "I will get ready," and headed aft, where the tanks and helmets were stored.

Cox's helmet swiveled slowly after him. Paige wished she could see the sergeant's face. Then she did see it, when he turned toward her, and wished she couldn't.

Cox's eyes were red and his jaw was set and his cheeks were pale white and splotchy where his two-day beard didn't shadow them. "You think this is smart? You want to do this? What do we tell those bastards from intelligence, if it works? 'Gee, they made a mistake back on the *Malibu*'? And if it doesn't..." His lips quirked. "I'm not thinkin' straight. I don't know what...I can't believe it's possible—or that she'd want..."

He pushed himself back, sliding from the chair's arm into the seat to sit there with his knees crooked over the aisle arm, and his visor came down with a snap.

She knew he could still hear her. She said, "Det, I don't know if it will work either, but we should try."

Through his recon suit's speakers, Cox's voice came at low volume, "The two of you are breakin' my goddamn heart. How come you can't let Frickey be?"

She didn't say anything else. Neither did Cox, until Freedom was ready to enter the cargo bay, at which time Cox's expertise was required. He checked out Ayoub's suit, his helmet, his seals, and his tanks, then said, "Okay, mister, I'll get you in there," and took Ayoub aft, to the cargo lock, and through it.

Once the bulkhead door had closed and the airlock began to cycle, Paige felt a paralyzing sense of loneliness descend on her. She ran to the emergency locker, got herself a helmet, an airpack, and then walked slowly back through the empty passenger compartment, toting her equipment, looking out the windows at Cerberus base beyond.

Cerberus' lights were bright out there, against the blackness in which she could barely make out the *Malibu* in its parking orbit around the asteroid. Cerberus station was built into the regolith; very little but docking areas were above ground, and those were airless swathes with large numbers painted on smooth, composite landing pads. Although the *Malibu* wasn't down here, her lifeboats were. Men in space suits were off-loading cocoons with security tape all over them. Paige found herself hugging her own arms.

What if something had changed? What if Major Kipling and Captain Ross had gotten new orders —orders to leave them here after all? But no, she told herself, they weren't through debriefing her.

She was glad now that she'd been so reticent. When Cox came through the airlock, she jumped at the sound of the bulkhead door drawing back. "Dennis."

Up came the visor and Cox palmed his eyes. "You know, I really wanted to shoot that bastard in there, just to see if he was tellin' the truth. I asked him about somebody I knew from X-31A, and he says, 'You only die once.' Hope it gives those poor suckers back on X-66B some comfort, now that they haven't got more than a couple feet of ground left to stand on that's in one piece."

He came up and stood right in front of her, hands on his hips, "Don't you think it's time you told me what's going on?"

"I . . . don't know, for sure. I saw . . . a resurrection. Ayoub's. Long after he was dead."

"So it doesn't have to be right away?"

"I . . . guess not. And he wasn't a believer, as far as I know. But he was . . . there. I'm not sure if even Freedom understands the process, or if it will work in space—work anywhere but on a place like X-66B."

"If it does, and those two spooks find out about it, we'll be in a heap o' trouble, lady." He grinned bleakly.

"We're in that already," she said, surprised at herself.

"Christ, I wish they'd come back—get ready to lift. I don't like this." He sat sideways again in an aisle seat, rubbing his arms. "If they decide there's a real threat of contamination, we'll never get loose."

"I know." Then something struck her. "But when they find out Freedom's insisting on riding back there—"

Cox pushed himself to his feet and muttered as he went, "I'm glad somebody's thinkin'."

She didn't understand until she saw what he was doing, and then not until an inflated pressure suit with gloves attached and a helmet on it was arranged in one of the rear seats to look as if Ayoub was sleeping there, his helmeted head turned toward the window so that the emptiness within wasn't apparent.

Cox stepped back from the effigy he'd made and said, "You realize, all this is on the log tape, if anybody bothers to run it."

"I . . . no, I didn't. Will they?"

"Not until they get where they're going, probably."

"Where they're going—you mean you don't think it's back to Earth? They said—"

"Oh, I do think it's Earth. Someplace nice and safe around the District, or Pax River maybe."

"They promised me IST headquarters—"

"And we'll deliver," came Kipling's modulated voice from the exterior airlock. "It took us a little longer than we thought to get Cox's tail out of the proverbial door. Sergeant, the next time you're in up to your neck on something like this, don't be so anxious to sign away your rights—we went through a paper-pusher's hell in there with the Cerberus base commander."

"Sorry," Cox said as Kipling came in and Ross followed with an ingenuous smile at Paige. Neither man gave the effigy of Ayoub more than a cursory glance.

"No, you're not. You're suicidal. Happens sometimes, when you lose as many men as you did," Kipling said.

"Crap," Cox said under his breath.

"For future reference," Kipling continued as if Cox hadn't spoken, "listen up: the truth is always worth something—more than you'd think, often. Especially in a situation like this, soldier."

"And," put in Ross, without missing a beat as he picked up where his superior left off, "you're not exactly a soldier any more, either. We had to second you over to Special Science to get you out of Locke's pecking order. He's inordinately sore about you shooting up that bay like you did—probably has something to do with his allegiance to IST and its project guidelines."

"That's enough, Ross. They don't have to sort this out. We do. Cox, you're stuck with us for a while—only thing we could cop for you but a medical, which you don't want, I'm sure. But your transfer to us means you've sort of dropped out of sight."

"And Paige—is she 'unhappened,' too?" Cox asked.

Paige noticed how stiff Cox was, the way his hands hung loose. Behind him, Ross was still projecting success at her with every fiber of his person. She was suddenly afraid that Cox was suicidal, as Kipling had said, after all he'd lost.

Cox shouldn't be asking these men questions, not with the effigy of Ayoub in his seat and Ayoub in the cargo bay. Unless Cox wanted to be discovered, this was not the time for questions. It was clearly and resoundingly not the time.

Kipling stared, unspeaking, at Cox as if he hadn't heard Cox's question, and then said precisely, "Mister, we went to lots of trouble to get you out of IST's clutches after X-31A and back to work —where you wanted to be, doing what you know how to do. Whether you knew it or not, then, doesn't matter—you've been part of this team since we hauled your sorry tail out of that Hanscom bar. Now, maybe the lady deserves an apology, and shouldn't have been mixed up in this, but you're a soldier. You went down there, tried your damnedest, lost some personnel. Too bad. Happens all the time. It's not up to you to decide whether you've failed and if it was worth it and where your loyalties lie. It's up to me. And I'm good at my job. So you sit down, relax, and enjoy the ride until I'm ready to let you spill your guts. When I've heard everything I need to hear, I'll let you know how you did and what happens next. You copy, ranger?"

"Yes sir, Major," said Cox levelly and stepped out of the aisle, his visor already down before he slid into a window seat and started strapping himself in.

The major smiled at Paige as he squeezed by, on his way to the flight deck. And Captain Ross said, "Now, ma'am, if we can go on to the sleeper cabin and pick up where we left off? I've got the rest of your deposition to take."

Leaving Cox, alone in the passenger compartment and even more alone in his helmet's confines, was difficult. What the dark Special Science major had said about Cox being suicidal made her hesitant. But there was Ayoub, in the cargo hold, to consider.

She could barely keep her mind on Ross's questions, she was so disturbed. Could Freedom bring Frickey back to life? Here? Between the worlds? Would it be better if he could, or if he couldn't?

There were repercussions in either case. Some of them were personal, for herself, for Dennis Cox, for Freedom Ayoub and his holy way. But if Ayoub succeeded, what then? What was she bringing to Earth, anyway?

She'd never really thought about it, because it had never occurred to her that the phenomenon of resurrection wasn't in some way intimately connected with X-66B. If it could be exported, what then? Not only Singer and Locke, but the powers who had decreed the extreme measures taken on both X-31A and X-66B, had obviously thought that the revolution so intimately tied up with redemption, resurrection, and the holy way was containable—and dangerous enough to justify those measures. An entire cocoon bay full of IST workers was confined indefinitely to Cerberus to make sure that not even word of what had happened leaked out.

And yet here she was, being assured by a well-bred blond man from a low-profile government agency that everything possible would be done to redress her grievances, return her to her former status, and even punish those responsible for her suffering, despite the fact that he himself had been a party to her abduction.

And all she had to do was cooperate, tell the truth, lend his task force her experience and her expertise. Both she and Cox would be well compensated.

She wasn't sure that Cox could ever be compensated; she knew she couldn't. She almost said that, and then she remembered Freedom Ayoub—the effigy of him strapped into its seat and the real Ayoub, back with Frickey's recon-suited body in the cargo hold. There in that hold lay either compensation beyond her wildest dreams or punishment beyond her darkest nightmares.

Was it salvation or contamination they had with them in the hold of this unnamed patrol cruiser, making its way to Earth?

CHAPTER 30

The Holy Way

————◆————

COX HAD BEEN certain he was going to look out the wing window of the cruiser sometime during the first few minutes after liftoff and see Cerberus base and the *Malibu*, close by in a parking orbit, go bang right before his eyes. A nice, clean, inexplicable accident at a classified ranger staging area—an accident that nobody'd ever hear about except the bereaved families of the IST and ranger personnel who'd died in it.

He'd been sure that was what Kipling and Ross had been doing on Cerberus so long—setting up the ordnance. It was what he'd have done. You could blame all the X-66B casualties on the Cerberus blowup and never have to mention X-66B in a single communique. And you wouldn't have to worry about decontamination or leaks.

So he watched and waited and when the explosion didn't come, one sort of nervousness left him and another took its place: he really didn't have a pulse on what was going on here, even though he was up to his neck in whatever it was. Only when Cerberus was out of his recon suit's targeting range did he switch his electronics off magnification and onto standby mode.

He kept wishing that Paige would come back from the sleeper cabin and her debriefing, and that Ayoub wouldn't come back, ever. If he could have jammed the cargo intercompartmental airlock, he probably would have. But it would start all sorts of warning lights blinking on the flight deck. The last thing Cox wanted to do was alert Kipling and Ross that something was wrong—you don't give aid and comfort to the enemy; and until proven otherwise, Kipling and Ross were the enemy. An enemy Det Cox didn't have any idea how to fight.

So he was waiting, with every capability of his recon suit on line, for the other shoe to drop. His visor displays weren't giving him much but straight optical, since there weren't any targets, but his snooper band was operational—he'd pick up any message traffic to or from the cruiser, although he might not be able to crack the encoding. No matter how much frequency-hopping he did, Cox wasn't hearing anything but standard flight-band chatter and vectoring beeps.

Then he did hear something, and at first he thought it was his own breathing. Then he thought that somehow he'd managed to sweep his way into the microwave band and was getting some of what was going on between Paige and Ross in the sleeper cabin.

Then he realized he was picking up another recon suit and he sat bolt upright, alone in the huge passenger compartment. Easy, don't jump to conclusions. He slid out of his safety harness and got a solid wall behind his back, up near the forward bulkhead, and leaned there. His own breathing was so loud by then it was hard to tell if he'd heard anything else at all.

But he knew he had. A groan. An intake of breath. A mutter. Then nothing. He was pretty sure there was only one other ranger on this ship and that one was dead. There hadn't been any recon suits in the emergency locker. It was possible that Kipling had one—with Kipling, anything was possible—but Cox didn't think he'd heard Kipling.

He tried to wipe his forehead with his wrist and banged his hand against his faceplate. He was really rattled. He took deep, measured breaths and when that didn't work, tapped his pharmakit onto monitoring mode as if he were ready to go into combat. His imagination was running away with him, suggesting all sorts of things going on behind the aft bulkhead door, where the cargo bay was.

The airlock was two-staged, so there was no warning light or bell to alert those in the passenger compartment because there was no danger of depressurization when the lock opened. There was, however, a green-light/red-light sequence that let you know if anyone was in there, and when it was time to push the cycling button. He watched that display through a half-magnification window he set up in the upper right-hand corner of his visor display, and asked for infrared scans in his southwest quadrant.

He got imaging right through the bulkhead, which was no surprise: under conditions like

these, his suit's system could give him a rat burrowed behind a crate fifty miles away, and if it was
a pack-rat, he could estimate the value of its stash.

But the second life form he was reading in the
cargo bay was too big to be a rat and it wasn't
Ayoub. Ayoub was Target A. Target B was climbing to its feet because previously it had been
longer than it was tall, and now it was taller than
it was long. Lots taller.

He really didn't like the way his guts were
churning. He actually considered emergency self-
relief procedures, and that pulled his imagination
up short. This wasn't an emergency for anybody
but him. Not yet. Maybe not at all.

So there was something back there that read like
a life form, and it was moving. Warm and moving.
It didn't have to be Frickey.

But the breathing he was hearing in his helmet
intercom did. Jesús, Frickey, don't do this to me.
Don't be some kind of monster. Don't be a zombie.
Don't be . . .

He jacked up his volume because both blips
were moving toward the airlock and he thought
he'd heard something like a vocalization from the
other recon suit that his was tracking. The damned
suits were supposed to do this for you—keep you
in touch with your team, with your buddies, with
the only other life that mattered when you were up
and running. Even on a standby, you were only a
whisper away from one another.

In his com, he heard, "Fine." That was all, the
one word, spoken in a voice enough like Frickey's
to have fooled her mother. Cox began to sweat and
his suit started cooling procedures with a whir
loud enough to nearly block out the breathing
sounds.

But by then it was steadier breathing—steadier

than Cox's own. He felt his pharmakit prick him and wondered what his readouts looked like. He wanted to shoot whatever was going to come through that door, because nothing had any right to—nothing but Ayoub, and he wasn't feeling real friendly toward Ayoub right now.

He wished Paige were here. Paige understood this resurrection stuff, and then grunted aloud. He didn't need any help. Whatever had stepped into the lock and started it cycling was going to come through to his side and Cox was going to make a judgment call.

He slid his gloved hand around to his pack, opened the pocket of his rifle case, and slipped it out without really thinking about it. Only when he realized he was resting the folded buttstock on his hip did he truly think about what he'd done.

And by then, the light on the lock had cycled to green and its door was drawing back.

Two human forms, both suited, came through, bold as hookers on New Year's Eve, and the lock shut automatically behind them.

Ayoub was carrying his helmet, so it was easy to see which one he was. The other, the one in Frickey's recon suit, was reaching up to disengage hers. Cox took his weapon off safe.

Ayoub waved and called to him. The words were muffled because Cox had his suit's intercom up so high. He split his channels and brought the ambient volume up so he could monitor the room, then cut the helmet feed completely because the other one had its helmet off now, and his suit's intercom was useless.

Frickey's red hair flashed at him and she called out, "Det!" as she moved toward him.

He dumped his scans but kept his visor down. She didn't move right. She was unsteady, her motions jerky. But it was definitely Frickey's face. The smile on it was uncertain, but she'd just died, hadn't she?

The muzzle of his rifle drooped until the barrel rested on his flexed knee.

All the while, the Frickey thing was moving closer and he couldn't decide what to do. Ayoub, lagging behind, was dismantling the effigy of himself in the aft seat and returning the equipment to its locker.

Still she came on, Frickey in a recon suit, hands extended to him. The length of the passenger compartment might as well have been a landing strip, for all the resolution Cox could get with his naked eye. His vision was unaccountably blurry. He was having trouble breathing because his chest was so damned tight.

He moved his left hand to punch up a magnification scan and then realized she was too close for that. He wanted to take off his helmet, to really get a good look at her face, at the eyes in that face. He didn't remember putting the rifle down to do that. He just did it.

And then she was hugging him, their bare cheeks touching. If it was some contagious evil, he'd just caught it.

He grabbed her arms and they felt solid. He pushed back enough to see her face and he could smell her breath. She smelled scared, but not alien. Her face was Frickey's broad, freckled face; her lips were pale. Her eyes were deep and very bright, as if she was going to cry. She shivered, staring back at him, and then seemed to slump.

He had to catch her around the waist before she fell and then he was saying, "Jesus god, Frickey, is it really you?" and she was saying, "Det, I don't understand—"

"Neither do I," said a voice from behind them and Cox instinctively put an arm around her as he shifted them both to face Kipling.

Behind him, Cox could hear Ayoub slam the locker door and come toward them, his footsteps loud on the rubberized decking.

Cox reached desperately for a response and said, "Neither do *we*, Major. Ayoub heard something back there, so I sent him aft. What's the matter with those medics on board the *Malibu?* It's bad enough to take so many casualties, but to have live people logged out as dead—We're lucky we got to her in time. And we're lucky I insisted on keeping her in her recon suit, or she'd *be* dead, and those bastards on the *Malibu* would have killed her."

Frickey didn't say anything. Her eyes were half-closed now; she leaned against Cox with comforting weight and unashamedly human weakness.

Kipling's eyes went slowly over her, and Ayoub, who was standing beside Frickey, and Cox—and came to rest on Cox's rifle, lying on the deck.

Cox followed his gaze: "Didn't know what the fuck it was. I stayed here, in case whatever came through that lock needed to be shot. Ayoub went back. And here she is." Staring steadily at Kipling, Cox said, "Say hello to Major Kipling, Corporal Frickey. He's probably the highest brass you're ever not going to meet."

Kipling's face said he wasn't sure he was buying this. But Frickey was real enough, and she rolled her head on Cox's shoulder and said, "H'llo, Major," before she sagged bonelessly.

"Passed out," Cox announced. "Ayoub, help me with her. Get one of those seats reclined. Let's make her as comfortable as we can." Cox started suiting his actions to his words, telling himself that Kipling wasn't going to pick up Cox's rifle and shoot Frickey out of hand. He didn't have enough information to make that kind of call. None of them did.

Kipling did pick up the rifle. He'd safed it by the time Ayoub and Cox had Frickey stretched out in a seat. Cox was trying to decide whether to strip her out of her suit. She seemed too light, but that could be because it had been so long since she'd eaten. When Cox looked up, already saying, "Can we get her something to eat—soup or an intravenous drip if your med bay's up to it?" he found himself looking down the barrel of his own rifle.

Kipling let its muzzle drop desultorily. "Don't leave your lethal gear strewn around like this, Sergeant, in future. And if anything else unexpected happens back here when you're alone, I'd appreciate being informed. Let your friend Ayoub see to the corporal. I'm ready for you now."

"Now?" Cox looked over his shoulder at Frickey, whose chest was definitely rising and falling where she lay.

"Now, Sergeant. If the corporal's going to make it, she'll make it without your help. She made it this far. And we'll send Barnett aft."

"Right, sir," said Cox. Leaving Frickey—or that simulation of Frickey—was one of the hardest things he'd ever done. But brass was brass. He went forward with the major until they reached the sleeper compartments. The door to the one across the corridor was closed.

Kipling knocked on it. It opened and Ross peered out. Kipling said, "You're done for now, Ross. Let Ms. Barnett go aft, and you go with her. Autopilot's on. I want you to make secondary recordings of what's going on back there."

"What's going on back there?" Ross asked, already moving. Beyond him, Cox could see Paige getting out of a chair.

"That dead body we're hauling turned out not to be dead." Kipling held up a hand to forestall the question on Ross's lips. "Don't ask me stupid questions I can't answer. That's why I want you back there. Do the fullest med scan this boat can handle, and bring me the report. Soonest."

"Yes sir," said Ross to Kipling's back as the major ushered Cox into the opposite sleeper.

In it was a slow-freeze cocoon, an emergency exit, a redundant navigation console, as well as the things Cox had expected to see: desk, chair, sleeper bunk, underbunk toilet, minifridge. The perks jarred him enough that he thought, Okay, these guys have got clout and a ship but that's all they've got. They don't have any more of a handle on this than I do.

That made him relax a little. He'd get this over with, go back to Frickey, and they'd solve their problems together. He'd never really believed in God, but now he had Frickey back, and it was easier to think that way than to think that Ayoub had actually done something to a corpse in the hold...

"Sit down, I said." Major Kipling's voice had an edge to it.

"Sorry. That shook me—I mean, we might not have found her in time."

"Let's start with something simpler, Sergeant. Space Command, 203rd Ranger, wants to commend you on a job well done out there on X-66B. Let's see if I can make that impulse realizable."

"Sir?"

"When we sent you out there, you were briefed. You were detailed to solve the problem that X-66B represented. In your opinion, have you done that,

Sergeant Cox?" Kipling was sitting, now, behind a desk on which a display was lit, reading questions from it.

This was a formal inquiry, Cox realized. He tried to care, but he wanted only to get back to Frickey. He said, "Yeah, well, that depends on your definition of the problem. The revolution—what we were told to do was suppress it—is pretty much history, so I guess we did that."

"Your memory's faulty, Sergeant. I told you to solve the problem, the problem being any element contraindicating a successful colonization effort, remember?" He was paraphrasing the transcript before him on his terminal. "And I told you that, if IST's methods were at the bottom of the X-66B mess, I wanted to know that. And that we didn't want a repeat of X-31A."

"Yeah, well, you told Locke too, didn't you?"

"Yes we did," said Kipling, whose five o'clock shadow was blue over his jaw. "And I'm sorry about that. We'll have Locke and Singer up on charges before this is over. Now, you start telling me what I want to know."

"As soon as I can figure out what that is sir, I'll be glad to. We couldn't not blow the venue. You can't colonize what's left there, but you sure can mine it. That was Locke's order, and I guess I thought it came from you—from Wiley; from up the ranks, anyhow. I forgot about you saying you wanted to colonize it—or I was faked into believing you really wanted to blow the place from the gitgo."

Cox paused and squinted at Kipling's face, hoping for a clue as to how he was doing. He did remember all that talk, now, about wanting X-66B to be annexed by the US.

"Go on, Det," said Kipling noncommittally.

"Well, I was only the ground commander. We got into more than we could handle. Wiley was backing Locke, and Singer was too. I assumed it was government policy—you did say you didn't want a repeat of X-31A."

"But that's what we ended up with."

"Yes sir. Well, I refused to execute the bang order as long as I could—until just before jump. I didn't know . . . I still don't know what the command structure wanted out of me, beyond the verbals I got. Or wanted on X-66B. It's not my job to know. I'm supposed to execute orders, not question them. I still don't know what you want me to say here. And I don't know what the Space Command—if that's what you are—is looking for out of this mess."

"Det, at this point, we want to pin IST's ears back—hard. We want to know exactly what they've been covering up out there—what they tried to destroy on X-31A and X-66B, beyond the much-vaunted 'revolution.' We want them in line, under control, acting like a good American company. We don't want them withholding intelligence or discoveries. We want, quite simply, Raymond Godfrey's butt in a basket and out of the CEO's chair over at IST headquarters. And you're going to help us do all of that, aren't you?"

"Yes sir, I think I can help with that, sir. Some of it, anyway. Is that why Paige—"

"That's way above your security clearance, soldier."

"She's had a rough time, sir, one she didn't deserve. And you-all were at the start-up. She's not going to cooperate unless she sees something in it for herself. I know her."

"She'll get plenty, Cox. We did play along when

somebody at IST wanted her shanghaied out there —to find out why she was making them so nervous, partly, and for our own credibility."

"So this is some kind of sting operation?"

"Things start out one way, then they escalate. Sometimes they get nasty. This got nasty. Your IST lady's been out-system better than a year, Earth time—she's been stricken from the payroll because she didn't report back to work after her three-month leave. Godfrey claims to have no idea where she is. We're going to help him remember. Now, are my motives clear enough that you feel free to cooperate, Cox?"

"Ah—yes sir. I wasn't sayin' I wouldn't. I just think that it's going to take a long time to go through everything the way you were startin' to—one bit at a time."

"We've got a long time, Det. We've got the whole ride back to Earth."

"Okay, then, whenever you're ready, let's go back to the top and start again." It wasn't that Cox trusted Kipling any more now than he had previously, although what Kipling said rang true to him. It was that Frickey was out there, and more than anything, Cox wanted to get back to her. He was afraid she'd make some mistake, or Paige or Ayoub would, that could let the cat out of the bag.

And that, Dennis Cox was sure, would change the friendly look on his inquisitor's face. There was no chance of Cox getting any of his charges— Frickey, Paige, and Ayoub—back to Earth if Kipling realized that Frickey had been resurrected, brought back from the dead by Freedom Ayoub in the patrol cruiser's cargo bay.

CHAPTER 31

Born Again

ACCORDING TO CAPTAIN Ross, Paige's "out-passage was masterminded by IST; as a co-venturing government agency, we were misled. By the time we realized what IST was up to, for security reasons we had to play along. We couldn't have gotten you off X-66B much quicker if we'd been more overt, and there was a chance we'd have succeeded only in getting you killed. You have the apologies of the United States Government."

Ross had said it that way, in capitals. And he'd also assured her that her initial message had been "intercepted by us and checked out by us before it was rerouted by us. In other words, Godfrey and his hardballers aren't going to have any warning when you show up. So if you'll cooperate with us, we'll give you Dennis Cox and whatever other—"

Kipling had come to the door at that moment and Paige's world had changed radically once again. She'd known by the look on Cox's face, and by Kipling's wry comment about dead bodies, that Freedom had had some success in the cargo hold. Nevertheless, she was ill prepared for the shock when Ross had escorted her aft, into the passenger compartment, and she saw Frickey.

Frickey was stretched out on a recliner with a towel over her eyes. Her chest was rising and falling in her recon suit; the electronic belt at her waist was alight and blinking; her helmet and pack were on the next seat. Beside her was Freedom Ayoub, who smiled tenderly at them when Paige and Ross came in.

"What the hell?" said Ross softly.

"Freedom," Paige choked. She'd almost blurted out, "It worked!" She'd caught herself just in time. Her legs were rubbery and yet they propelled her toward the two resurrected ones as if they had a will of their own.

And Freedom responded to Ross's question, as Paige was hoping against hope he wouldn't: "Redemption, resurrection, the holy way—not hell, but everlasting life."

"Freedom," Paige said again pleadingly. She grabbed an aisle seatback to steady herself. Didn't Ayoub realize what he was risking? If the Special Science men got frightened, it wasn't too late to turn back: They were still beyond Mars' orbit. Or the two resurrected ones could be spaced... "Freedom," she began again, "we have a long way to go." That didn't sound right. Ross looked at her askance and his body language was pointedly defensive. "What do you need to keep Frickey comfortable until we reach Earth?"

"Full med scan," Ross found his voice. "Into the med bay with her, quick." And he strode forward to help.

Paige found herself sitting in the seat opposite Frickey, watching the corporal's chest rise and fall. Would Ross know when he touched Frickey that she wasn't...normal? If he did, what then?

She followed behind the two men who improvised a stretcher from the recliner cushion; they carried the corporal forward, to the med bay beyond the sleeper compartments.

In it, Paige sat on a white stool and watched Ross execute instructions by rote from a computer terminal called SPACEDOC. Freedom watched too, from his position by Frickey's head.

Ayoub caught Paige's eye and told her not to worry while Ross was mumbling to himself that "something's wrong with these instructions. I'm getting garbage."

Frickey's vital functions were about to be displayed on the med computer's screens and Ayoub was telling Paige not to worry? She chewed her knuckles and prayed.

Finally, the readings came up and Ross said only, "Fucking-A," and then: "Sorry, ma'am. I'm not a med tech. According to this, she's barely alive, but I guess that's to be expected."

"She needs nourishment," Paige's unwieldy tongue suggested. "She's been in that hold—"

"Yeah," said Captain Ross, looking doubtfully at the instructions for intravenous feeding he punched up. "Maybe you'll help me with this, ma'am?"

Paige, grateful for something to do, went to join Ross and Ayoub's voice said, "She is born again. She is gaining strength. Nourishment is in the air. Do not be con—"

"Freedom, shut *up!*"

Ross stopped what he was doing and looked at Paige, not at Ayoub. Then he said, "It's okay, ma'am. We know he's one of the rebels. We're not fools. He's your witness, we'll cut him plenty of slack."

"Call me Paige," she suggested. "Captain Ross, I can handle the intravenous feeding. I'm sure you're needed on the flight deck."

"Well, I don't know." Ross rubbed the back of his blond, well-shaped head. "And it's Dalton—Dalton

Ross. If we're dropping formalities. Kipling wants a full med scan and I should stay here to make sure he gets it. But if you want to nursemaid the computer, just send it on to the next screen whenever it's finished. I could get a decent dinner cooked up—the corporal might be fine on an IV, but I could use something solid."

"Certainly. Just advance the program when it pauses, right?"

"That's right. Okay then, I'll be back in a flash to ring the dinner bell."

When he'd gone, Paige let out a long-held breath and put her face in her hands. From between them, she said to Freedom: "This ship is keeping a continual log—everywhere, Cox assured me, but in the cargo hold. Please keep that in mind, Freedom. Everything depends on—"

"—Redemption, resurrection, the holy way. There is no need to fear now, Paige. Corporal Frickey is gaining strength every moment. Soon she will be up and around."

Paige couldn't find an answer to that; the questions she wanted to ask Ayoub all seemed too risky. She raised her head and stared at the woman on the examination table, feeling as if she were punishing herself by doing it.

She wanted to turn away, to go somewhere and cry, to screw up Frickey's IV and see if it was true that you only died once.

But she had a feeling none of it would do any good. Finally, because she had to say something and Ayoub was not good at small talk; because she had so many questions that if she didn't find a way to phrase them she'd burst, or run amok with a fire ax to find the answers, she asked, "Freedom, in your religion . . . what happens if the body of someone who's been resurrected is destroyed?"

"It cannot be." Ayoub shook his head and folded his hands in his lap. "Only the organization of the body, but not the body itself."

"I see. If...if there were believers on X-66B, could they survive the destruction in their... former forms?" She was trying to ask questions she didn't want on the cruiser's record. She kept seeing Cox in her mind's eye, telling her to be careful. But she needed answers. She didn't want to be the person who destroyed civilization as her kind had always known it. She needed to believe that what Ayoub—and now Frickey—brought with them was good, not evil.

"The form is not important. Survival determines the nature of the form." Ayoub left Frickey and came to her.

She found herself backing away from him.

"Paige, do not be afraid. Have I ever given you cause to fear? All the goodness that is Frickey is born again, and left behind is only what was imperfect."

"So—" Still she backed away from the black man, retreating until a wall at her back stopped her. "It's really Frickey—Cox's Frickey?"

"Paige, there is so much we must say to each other, and never the time or the place." Ayoub was so close now that she could see the folds in his wide dark lips, the occasional bubble on his pink tongue.

"You've been in the Fourth World, Freedom, and in the Third. You've seen enough suffering to know that humankind isn't...kind, as it is. With this— gift, if it is one...I don't know. Will it make things better, or worse?"

"On X-66B you were not asking such questions. You saw for yourself—"

Frickey moaned. Her hand came up, pulling at

the cloth over her eyes, at the sensors stuck to her temples.

"I've got to see to her," Paige said and ducked away from Ayoub.

But by the time Paige reached the exam table, Frickey was already sitting and the med-tech computer was beeping wildly.

"Lie back, lie back down!" Paige put a hand on the other woman's chest.

Frickey's fingers grabbed her wrist with inarguable strength. "Where's Cox? Where am I? What ...? Freedom, take these things off me before some—" Her eyes were wild and her grip painful.

Then Ayoub was there, soothing the patient: "Lie back, corporal. You are gaining strength. You are newly resurrected. You must wait, and listen, and learn."

Paige stumbled away from the two of them as soon as Frickey's grip loosened. Forgotten by the two resurrected ones and forgetful of the recording equipment monitoring all that went on in the bay, she listened while Ayoub's soothing voice told Frickey not to fear.

"There begins life, and life pushes back death, and finally goes beyond it. You are the promise of life everlasting; you are the expression of faith. You can do as I did for you, and you will live forever by so doing. It is the holy way. We share life, we get life."

"Forever?" Frickey's face worked. "Like this, right?" She shook one arm and the IV in it rattled. "A freak. What happened to me; what did you do to me?"

"Look at my face, Frickey, and think about what happened when you awoke. Think about the gift of life you were given. Think about the universal intelligence of which you are a part."

And there was more, much of which Paige never would remember. She was watching someone come from disbelief, through fear and hostility, into a calm that Paige Barnett had seen only in the eyes of Freedom Ayoub and his kind. In the eyes of Sanchez on X-66B.

She wondered if, in the cargo hold, Ayoub's hands had extended, become translucent, glowing, capable of molding steel and composite the way they'd molded the rock in the tunnels. She wondered if she had any right to facilitate this. She wondered if Ayoub and Frickey were human. And she wondered if there was any way to stop what she'd begun.

Stop it for a moment of reflection. Stop it because Frickey was a trained killer, a creature of war—not gentle like Ayoub. Stop it because Dennis Cox wouldn't be able to see danger now, if it was here in the person of Frickey—not if that person looked like Frickey did.

She slipped out of the med bay, into the hall. The cruiser was small compared to the *Malibu*, but it was bigger than a TAV. And it didn't have color-coded floors. What was she doing out here? She was supposed to be handling Frickey's med evaluation.

She'd had some vague urge to find Ross, or Kipling, or Cox. But now she realized this was the worst thing she could do. She must play her part, at least until she had more than unanswerable questions. Life and death were at stake here—not just hers but everyone's, perhaps. If Ayoub could resurrect Frickey in the cargo hold, he could certainly do the same on Earth. Could Frickey do it too? Was it salvation they were bringing home in this patrol cruiser? Or was it something so alien that she couldn't even recognize it in time? Did

Ayoub and Frickey only appear to be human? Were you human if you could only die once—and live to tell about it?

She palmed her eyes. She couldn't make this kind of decision, not for everyone on Earth. Yet, to sound alarms and allow these carriers of the holy way to be destroyed—or to join in an attempt to destroy them—might be to deny humanity what it had always longed for, what every great religion had offered and couldn't produce: everlasting life.

Life at what price? Should she run screaming down the hall that Ayoub and Frickey should be spaced immediately? See if they could swim to Earth through vacuum? Then this—whatever it was—wouldn't be her fault.

But she'd sound mad. What she'd be counseling was murder, if it worked, not only of Ayoub and Frickey, but of everyone alive who might choose redemption, resurrection, and the holy way, if given a choice.

Everything would be different, once this ship landed, if Ayoub's promise meant what she thought. And humans were most afraid of what they didn't understand, she as much as any other.

No wonder IST had been scared witless—frightened enough to try to silence her when she'd objected to the measures taken to sterilize X-31A. And foolish enough to choose a way to do it which seemed foolproof, because there was no capital crime involved, no body and no investigation beyond a cursory missing-persons report. IST had viewed the evidence and decided the human race wasn't ready for what the revolution promised.

Paige wouldn't place herself in that company; she couldn't become one of those who'd decided, unilaterally, to destroy out of hand what Ayoub had to offer.

She couldn't. But she couldn't go back into that room, either. That room where Frickey was. Frickey frightened her in a way that Ayoub had not. But then, Paige had seen in Frickey someone who'd been resurrected only minutes before, an unprepared unbeliever.

Maybe it would be all right. Maybe the violence she sensed in Frickey would fade away. Ayoub was increasingly different from the non-English speaker she'd met in the mass-freeze hold. Perhaps Frickey would change too. For Cox's sake and all of theirs, she hoped so.

She turned resolutely on her heel and strode back to the med bay, where she pushed open the door with her palm.

There she saw Ayoub, bent over Frickey, kissing her. No, giving her mouth-to-mouth resuscitation. Or doing something to her that Paige didn't understand. All the med computer's meters were spiking wildly. The whole bay was beeping urgently.

"Freedom!" she gasped, and he straightened up. He smiled pacifically. He went back to his stool by the examination table. The meters calmed. The woman on the bed turned to Paige and she smiled too as she pulled the IV out of her arm and dropped it on the floor.

"You can't do—"

"Look at the readings," said Frickey in a voice somehow deeper than Paige remembered it. "I'm fine: ninety-eight point six, one-twenty over eighty. I need to get up, walk around, eat solid food—see Cox." Frickey swung her legs off the table and Paige couldn't think of anything to say to stop her.

Behind the corporal, the med screens were reading out, *Sequence complete.*

Paige watched dumbly as the female ranger pulled on her recon suit, checked her pack, shouldered it and clasped the quick-release buckle around her waist, all while Ayoub helped like a handmaiden.

Then, helmet under her arm, Frickey said to Paige, "Comin'?"

And off they went, wandering through the strange cruiser, until they ran into Ross.

"What the hell?" the blond captain wanted to know.

"I couldn't stop her. She says she's fine," Paige began, "and she wants to walk around, see Cox, get something to eat—"

"Fine, are you, corporal?" The blond captain stared Frickey up and down.

"Good as anybody who's come back from the dead," said Frickey fliply and Paige winced. "You know, sir, when I woke up in that coffin I was some spooked. There ought to be something we can do about people declaring you dead before your time..." Frickey grinned at Ross and winked.

Paige shivered with relief. Ayoub sidled over to her and touched her arm the way he'd done so often on X-66B; strength and calm seemed to flow into her. She looked up at him and his eyes were there for her, sending her an unspoken message of love and peace.

Only this time, she wasn't so anxious to believe it. The corporal was saying, to Ross's inquiry, "med computer read me out fit to fight, sir. So there was no use sittin' in there. I'm a little queasy. Need to move around is all. And get some solid food."

It was Frickey, and it wasn't Frickey, this woman who had Ross hurrying to oblige her, stumbling over his words to assure her that he had "a great meal cooked up, in your honor, corporal. I want to hear all about it—you had no vital signs for some time, according to the *Malibu*'s report. Do you remember anything about what it was like when you were in the coma? I've always been interested in that sort of thing."

Ayoub's hand on her arm urged Paige to follow. She did, meekly, full of confusion and doubts, wondering where Cox was, if he was going to join them for dinner, and whether he'd think that Frickey was different.

Because she was. Very different. It was something Paige couldn't put her finger on, and after a time she stopped trying, telling herself that of course Frickey was different—she'd been resurrected. A brush with death, a trip beyond the knowable, was bound to have a certain effect.

But how different was she? Was she human? Was she . . . inimical? Cox wasn't at the dinner.

Ross said he was still with Kipling, and they'd eat when they were ready. And: "You're not eating yourself, Paige. My feelings are hurt. I could have just heated up a pre-pack."

"I . . . this whole matter has come as something of a shock." She looked right at Frickey when she said it. Perhaps her distrust of the woman had more to do with Cox than with Frickey. Maybe Paige was jealous. She didn't think so. She was asking herself if she, Paige Barnett, would willingly be resurrected when the time came, and her answer was that she didn't know.

She excused herself early, while the others were dawdling over their coffee, and went looking for the med bay. She could find out something, in there.

And she did. She pulled the diagnostics on

Frickey and when she'd read them, she slumped over the console. As far as the computer was concerned, Corporal Frickey was a healthy human female.

That information wasn't comforting, somehow.

CHAPTER 32

Redeemed Ranger

————◆————

COX'S FIRST DEBRIEFING with Kipling lasted forty-eight hours straight, broken only by the occasional meal and once by Ross's report that Corporal Allie Frickey was a healthy ranger, fit for service, despite her ordeal.

His second interrogation session lasted nearly as long, and by the end of it Cox's hands were beginning to shake. This was just what he'd been afraid of, all this time.

Kipling had the pictures from X-31A with Reynolds being pulled into the rock by the white hands—the recording Cox had sworn up and down he'd made and everybody on Earth had told him he'd imagined. Kipling had everything from X-66B too—the recording with Paige and the downed rebel leader on it; the whole nine yards. And Kipling wasn't stupid.

The confirm-or-deny component of Cox's assignment on X-66B was the part that could weigh Cox down like cement boots—keep him playing Q&A for the rest of his natural life. On the in-system flight, it kept him isolated from the other passen-

gers until he wanted to throttle Kipling with his
bare hands, or start screaming, or shoot the major
who hadn't had the sense to disarm him, and take
over the goddamned ship just so he could get some
sleep.

Kipling wasn't sleeping either, but Kipling was
on the other side of that desk with its computer
terminal and its bright light and its voice-stress
analyzer. Kipling wasn't going to let Cox out of
that room until Cox admitted that he'd encountered aliens both on X-31A and X-66B.

But Cox couldn't do that—not with Frickey at
risk. Not until he'd seen her again, talked to her at
length, satisfied himself that his corporal was safe,
sound, and untainted by whatever had saved her.

Otherwise, he was consigning her to a life as a
top-secret guinea pig—or the quick and dirty classified disappearance of an unquantifiable risk.

Cox considered sacrificing Ayoub to the wolves
of intelligence and red tape when Kipling started
talking about the "revolutionary factor on X-31A
and X-66B" in terms of societal impact and hostile
threat indices.

"Whatever the reputed alien presence and the
revolution have in common," Kipling confided,
"they're stirring up unrest of the sort that brings
governments crashing down. That's our concern,
Cox—yours and mine. To analyze what you saw
and heard there and find out whether it's export-
able."

Cox said, "Whatever it is, it gives those poor bastards some human dignity—frees 'em from fear.
When people aren't afraid, they can't be treated
like animals, not jacked around the way IST likes."
He couldn't help it. He was tired. This was going
to go on until he gave in, gave up, or gave out. He
needed to see Frickey, needed to decide whether it

was worth fighting Kipling, and the indefatigable line of Kiplings waiting for him on Earth, to keep a secret that he wasn't sure should be secret.

For all Cox knew, Ayoub or Paige or Frickey herself had already put a foot wrong, and Kipling was just looking for confirmation. "On X-66B, I half felt like throwing in with the rebels myself, the way those IST slave drivers were workin' them. It ain't right, not for an American company." Cox shrugged irritably, ran his hand over his stubbled jaw, and added, "It especially sucks that they can call in rangers to do their dirty work when the Fourth Worlders just plain can't take the hardship anymore. People who don't have squat to lose can be real feisty."

"People who think they can't lose their lives, you mean?" said Kipling in a soft voice.

"People whose lives are so hellish it makes no difference," Cox replied stonily, his throat tight. Kipling hadn't asked him for his weapons; he still wore his recon suit. But Dennis Cox couldn't shoot his way out of this one. He peered at Kipling's pleasant face, trying to decide if Kipling knew; if Kipling was baiting him into stating for the record that Ayoub was...what Ayoub was.

"Just how volatile do you perceive this 'redemption, resurrection, the holy way' ideology—or religion—to be, Cox? Religions have killed more people than any other single historical cause. Do you think that's what starts it—that the believers figure they're immortal, going on to a better life? Like Islam? Or Christianity?"

Kipling didn't know, then. "I'm no psych warrior, no professor. They fight when they're backed against the wall—it's human. When living conditions are flat intolerable." Cox nearly closed his eyes as he spoke. He was trying not to lie—lies would show up on the polygraph and voice-stress equipment. If this went on much longer, he was going to lose it, one way or the other.

He tried to think about what he should do if Kipling finally got the whole truth out of him, and then realized he wasn't sure what the whole truth was. He was bleary-eyed and exhausted. And his pharmakit was jabbing him so regularly he wasn't sure how he felt about this interrogation from one minute to the next. So he leaned forward and said honestly, aware of the meter Kipling was eyeing every time he spoke, "Look, sir, I'm beginning to feel like a prisoner in enemy hands. I had lots of trouble handling this kind of thing when IST was calling the shots. It doesn't feel much better with you doing it. And if this is what I've got to look forward to on Earth, I'd as soon skip the landfall..."

"What are you trying to say, Det?"

"I'm trying to say I need a break, or I'm gonna lose it. I'm trying to think of you—and this—as necessary and friendly, but it's tough. I want to wash my face, lie down, see Frickey. I really want to see Frickey, sir. Can't we quit for a while? I'm not goin' anywhere." He hated to beg, but he was telling the truth: he was armed, and an armed response was beginning to seem increasingly attractive, just to put an end to these questions.

Kipling looked at his displays, at Cox, and back at his desktop. "Det, you've got eight hours. Then we'll have one more session before we touch down at Hanscom. I needed to do this with you now— need to do more of it—to save doing it later. You and I have some tactical matters to discuss, too: about Barnett and IST. So go see your corporal, get some sleep, and we'll reconvene at...twenty-one fifty hours."

"Great sir, thanks." The relief in Cox's voice made it quaver. "And sir, can I use one of the sleeper compartments—me and Frickey?" He met Kipling's eyes boldly and allowed a lecherous smirk to quirk his mouth. "It's been a long time since I had her to myself." He wanted Kipling to think there was something like that going on— something he'd want privacy for. Otherwise, he couldn't talk to Frickey the way he wanted to.

"Ah...use Ross's. I'll tell him." And, when Cox picked up his recon helmet and turned to leave: "Cox—you're doing a good job in a trying situation. I'm aware of how hard this is for you."

"Thanks, sir; I know you are," he said to Kipling, but he didn't mean it any more than he thought Kipling had.

You did the best you could, was all. Kipling wasn't the worst ally he could have, it was just that Cox couldn't trust any ally right now. If Ayoub was responsible for Frickey's redemption, or whatever it was, then all hell was going to break loose when the truth surfaced.

And Det Cox was going to be right in the middle of the ensuing ruckus. He'd rather be holding off a brigade of rebels in any hostile venue in the universe than trying to fight his way through the kind of war Ayoub and Frickey and Barnett were going to start on Earth—a secret war, a psychwar, a war of wits.

His own were slow and frayed, ragged from the numbing interrogation. He knew what interrogation could do to you, and by the time he found his way to the passenger compartment where Ayoub, Frickey, and Paige were all asleep on recliners in different parts of the bay, he was wondering if he hadn't already screwed up with Kipling beyond hope.

Did Kipling know about Ayoub after all? Was
Cox blowing his only chance to be let off the hook
as a conspirator? Were there statutes about intro-
ducing hostile alien life forms to Earth? If there
weren't, there soon would be, and those statutes
would be retroactive enough to put Cox in a five-
by-eight cell in some stockade for the rest of his
life.

He tiptoed through the dimly-lit passenger compartment, past Paige's sleeping form, and she
shifted under her blanket.

Cox froze. He couldn't handle Paige Barnett
right now. He couldn't handle more than one thing
at a time right now. And the only thing he wanted
was to talk to Frickey. Talk to her before he went
into his next debrief session; talk to her before they
landed and she and Ayoub stepped onto the soil of
Earth. Frickey wouldn't lie to him. She'd tell him
the honest truth.

And he needed to hear something he could believe in from somebody he could trust. He needed
to see if Frickey was still Frickey, or some alien
Frickey-clone he ought to burn where it stood. Before it was too late.

He told himself he was paranoid from all the
questions and too little sleep and his pharmakit's
attempts to keep him alert. But that was what the
pharmakit was for: to make sure Cox remained
within normal limits. Unless he asked for better.

And he hadn't asked. Not that whole time with
Kipling. He hadn't asked because the only responses he was good at were combat responses.
The situation with Kipling, in which Cox felt helpless under attack, unarmed in a battle of words,
was the kind of thing that frightened him the way
nothing else could. He'd ended up in therapy the
last time the brass had done this to him.

He couldn't risk it again. Above all else, he had to save himself from a replay of the aftermath of X-31A.

"Frickey!" he whispered when he reached the blanketed woman on the acceleration seat. "Frickey, wake up." He shook her shoulder gently, leaning down so close his breath stirred her hair.

Her eyelids fluttered. Her eyes opened. In the dim light her eyewhites seemed to glow. "Det!" she whispered back, a smile on her lips, and touched his face.

"C'mon, Frickey, I got us a place to talk."

She nodded. He moved out of her way and she got up, grabbing her helmet when she saw him tap his. There might be redundant security logs all over this ship, but they weren't capable of defeating a recon suit's countermeasures.

The two of them slipped through the corridors silently, like they were sneaking up on a target. Frickey was behind him, at his left shoulder, and he didn't have to look back to know it: the maneuver eased him; it was something he knew how to do.

Ross had already vacated the sleeper when Cox found it; the door was ajar. There was beer in the underfridge and a note telling them to drink it, with Ross's compliments.

Cox shut the sleeper's hatch and locked it, watching the corporal with as much attention as he could muster. He wished he wasn't so tired. He wished it wasn't so spooky, looking at somebody you'd seen dead.

He said, "Psst," and pointed to his helmet, then put it on. As soon as he saw her follow suit, he cut the lights.

He ran a test code and she sent one back. He walked over to her in the dark, pulling up his infrared, ready to punch hers if she didn't realize what she should do.

But she did. He took her hand in his and led her to Ross's pull-down cot. They sat on it. He tapped her visor with his finger, then the scrambler on his belt when he was sure she was watching.

He held up fingers to help her determine how to set her countermeasures. Then he said, "Christ, I wish I could have got to you sooner. You okay?"

He couldn't see more than her reddish form with its bubble-head on infrared; he couldn't see into her helmet.

Her voice came back, "Yeah, Det. Okay. Captain Ross's got lots of questions."

"Kipling, too," he said. Then: "Look, I need to hear it from you straight, no bullshit. You don't have to tell me what happened back there, but I need to know from you whether...whether it's true about Ayoub and—you."

"Det, are you frightened of me?"

"Nah." He shook his head and stopped trying to look at her through his helmet. He reached out and took her hand instead. "I'm scared of what's going to happen on Earth though. To you. To us. Crap, to me—I'm not good at cat-and-mouse. Kipling's really pushing me."

"Tell him the truth."

"Yeah, great. What's that? That you're a zom— that you're..."

"That I've been redeemed, resurrected."

"You're Frickey, but you ain't. Is it going to happen to me too when I—check out?"

"Resurrection? You mean is it automatic? a virus? No. You have to want—want to live. You have to be...near a source. But I want it for you, Det. I don't want to lose you."

"Lose me? Then be cool, because they're going to

throw all our asses in some holding facility forever if they find out—" He bit his lip. He wanted to pull away from her; part of him wanted to draw his weapon. She'd just flat admitted to him she wasn't...wasn't what? Alive? She was. Human? She seemed human. But his hand was still in hers. Her naked fingers began stroking the skin of his palm.

"Lose you, forever. You don't have to cease to exist, Det. You can be reborn when you die. If you want."

"Reborn as what? Are you human, Frickey? Are you like you used to be? Do you know?" His voice was ragged and her fingers stopped moving against his palm.

"I'm human, just better. I'm not afraid any more, Det. Nobody ever has to be afraid any more. We just have to be...better at being people. Better to each other. Better to ourselves."

"Yeah." Their hands seemed cold where they touched. He was cold, that was for sure. "Well, if that's true, you and me are going to be out of work—there'll be no need for rangers."

"When? In a hundred years? A thousand? It's going to take so long, Det, to spread the gift. Redemption, resurrection, the holy way—it all starts with desire. Desire to live. And love. I loved you, Det Cox. I still love you, but in a different way. A better way."

He was blinking hard behind his visor. He said, "I liked you the old way," thickly. "I liked us both bein'—what we were. I can't—"

"Det, please don't be afraid of me." Now her voice was husky. "Let's go off line. I want to get out of this suit. I want to see your face. I want to touch you and prove to you that there's nothing to be afraid of."

He mumbled, "I dunno. I can't trust—" But her hands were already at his seals.

By the time they were out of their suits, he was regretting it. What if she was lying? What if it was something communicable? What if, by touching her, he was doomed to become whatever it was she'd become?

And then she pressed herself against him, warm and as human as she'd been that day in the ranger powder room aboard the *Malibu*, and he told himself that if he was going to catch it from her, he'd already caught it, when he'd held her after she'd first come out of the cargo bay.

He held her again now, wracked with emotions he couldn't name. She was here and now, alive and well, when he'd thought he'd lost her. She was everybody he'd lost out there, a symbol of something like God's grace. And then she was Frickey who wrapped her legs around his buttocks and thrust against him with as much passion as any woman he'd ever had.

When it was over, he was panting. She was lying on top of him, running a finger around one of his nipples, toying with the hair there.

He couldn't help it; he said: "Hey, Frickey, does your equipment still work? Can you have little Frickeys?"

"Do you want to?" she said in an odd voice. She propped both her elbows on his chest and her chin on her fists.

"I was just askin' . . . Allie."

"I don't want to lose you, Det. Promise we won't get separated, whatever happens. That you'll help me and Freedom stay together, not end up some freaks in a lab somewhere."

"I . . . yeah, I'd have done that anyhow, without this." He shifted under her and she rolled off him, sideways against the wall on the narrow pull-down. "About whether you can have—"

"I'm just like I was, Det, only better. This isn't the end of anything for us—or for anybody else. It's a beginning. Life conserves life, that's all. And begets it, just like always. Only difference is, maybe you don't become obsolete and get replaced. Maybe you go to the next step."

"That's what you and Ayoub are? The next step?"

"Me and Ayoub and your Colonel Reynolds from X-31A and everybody on X-66B who wanted to survive. That's all you have to do now, Det, is want to survive, and be where I can get to you when the time comes." Her eyes were very bright and he hoped it was just tears.

She vaulted over him like an athlete on a trampoline and started getting into her suit.

He sat up and he was trembling all over. "You know we probably just read this into the record, after everything I tried to do to keep that from happening."

"It's okay, Det. They know, inside anyway. They'll know the rest soon enough. It's too late to stop it now. We brought home somethin' from space, that's all—what everybody's been lookin' for since the beginning of time: a course correction, a commutation of the death sentence of a race, an end to the reason half of us are so mean and the other half so crazy. Look at me and tell me it's bad to offer salvation to the world, when it's all anybody really wants."

He looked at her, half into her recon suit, and said again: "You're Frickey, but you're not Frickey. Frickey doesn't talk like that. You're different. It scares the fuck out of me."

"I've been through some shit, Det. You still gotta

go through it. You still gotta die, only now you
only—"

"Die once," he interrupted. "Yeah, I know. Well,
let's go finish up with Kipling. Now that I'm gonna
tell him, he probably won't believe me. Maybe nobody will, you think of that? If Jesus Christ came
back today, he couldn't get his ass arrested, let
alone a permit to feed the multitude."

"It's started, Det. Belief of that sort doesn't matter. Getting onto the ground does, where we can
mingle with the biosphere."

"Thought you said it wasn't a virus." He was
looking at her, like she'd asked. He was seeing all
sorts of things, probably as a result of too little
sleep and too many drugs and too goddamn much
stress he wasn't built to handle. She was Reynolds; she was Fritz Schultz; she was every rebel
Schultz had fried in the tunnels and every poor
soul Cox had banged into a different kind of eternity when he blew X-66B.

"It's not, Det. It's a bridge for your soul. It's a
genetic correction. It's…redemption, resurrection, the holy way."

"It means that all those people I blew up on
X-66B don't need me feelin' so damned guilty I
can't even think about it?" he said, very low.

"It means that death is a gate. You unlocked
their prisons, Det. That's all. You don't have anything to feel guilty about. When this is over, you'll
be a hero."

"Yeah, I bet. That's what all us rangers are." He
got up abruptly, before he curled up in a ball and
covered his head with his arms, or started to cry,
or shot her out of hand. "Look, we got a strategy
session before final approach. Tell Paige it's going
to be Hanscom—she was worried it might not be.
I'm goin' back and roust Kipling, give him what he

wants myself before he runs this log. Then we see what happens."

"You promised," she said, suited up now with her helmet under her arm, a dim figure in the low-lit sleeper cabin, "that I wouldn't lose you. That you'd stay with us."

"I'm in. I said so. All the way to the finish. I just hope you're not going to spend that eternity of yours in little tiny pieces that I can't get my arms around." He strode past her, hit the lightswitch and the lockplate, and banged on Kipling's door, across the hall.

When it opened, he said to the major, "Sir, I hate to disturb you, but I got somethin' to tell you that just can't wait." Kipling let him in. He saw Frickey wave as she went by.

He didn't know what he'd let himself in for when he'd promised Frickey his protection down there on Earth, but it beat meekly standing around while the worst happened. And it beat trying to lie his way through whatever was coming. He said to Kipling, "Better turn your collar around, sir. You're about to hear more than you ever wanted to about redemption, resurrection, and the holy way."

He had to put Kipling in the picture before they landed. Or else they'd be walking into whatever IST might have ready for them, if Locke had gotten a message through to Earth from Cerberus. Maybe Ayoub and Frickey had been redeemed, but Cox and the rest of them on board, including Paige Barnett, were still mere mortals.

CHAPTER 33

Touchdown

———◆———

"AND WHERE ARE *you* going to be, Major Kipling?" Paige asked the man leading the strategy session that had been postponed until just before Earth reentry. Everyone on board the patrol cruiser was present in the passenger compartment; no one else had offered to argue with Kipling. Cox was looking at his feet. Frickey was looking at Ayoub. Dalton Ross was looking out the wing window. When Kipling didn't answer immediately, Paige pressed: "You've assured me up until now that I'd have your full support against IST. Suddenly, you're backing off."

"What do you want me to do, Ms. Barnett?" Kipling said. "I'm giving you Cox and Frickey, and they'll have full recon capability—your physical security's as assured with the two of them as—"

"Glorified bodyguards." Paige didn't look to the right or to the left to see how her words affected Cox or Frickey. She glared steadily at Kipling. "I want the US Government to join in filing charges against IST and you know it. I want you to confront Raymond Godfrey alongside me, with the evidence we have. I don't want you conveniently dissociating yourself and all official support beyond a deniable pair of rangers whose stability

313

might be brought into question. I don't want you leaving us swinging in the breeze."

"I'm going to do all of that. You must realize that this has to be handled delicately. You've got to file criminal and civil charges. I'm not even sure of the procedure on my end, yet. The Justice Department may want Mister Ayoub to make an additional statement. Space Command might not be the proper agency—we don't have police powers on home-planet soil."

She'd heard this speech a hundred times from a hundred deft professionals on a hundred matters of life and death to strangers; she'd never dreamed she'd be the subject of Implemented Avoidance Doctrine. Kipling was going to throw them out there and see what happened. Then he'd act, all right, but subject to the results she got—or to a clearly criminal and prosecutable response on the part of IST.

"'Leavin' us swinging in the breeze,'" Cox quoted Paige under the excuses Kipling was still shouting, and when she looked at him: "Nothin' we weren't expecting."

We. Cox and Frickey, certainly, because Paige had spent all this time with Ayoub and Dalton Ross and neither of them had broached the subject of how to proceed if the Special Science people withdrew their support.

"...you need to get through the paperwork, file your charges," Kipling was saying placatingly. "I'll file mine. When you're done confronting Godfrey at IST headquarters, come down to the District. I'll set up a meeting at the Pentagon. We'll work together on this. It just takes time. There's red tape and protocols and—"

"Did someone pull you off this, Kipling?" Cox asked bluntly. "Or was it somethin' I said?"

"If you mean do I believe your story about Mister Ayoub and Corporal Frickey being a couple of Lazaruses, that's beside the point. I'm going to ignore the other accusation. I'm in the same chain of command you are, Det. You know how the game works. My letting you take these civilians where they want to go—that in itself is stretching regulations. You've got a week before you're due to report to 203rd headquarters at Hanscom for new orders and a physical. Show up in DC with Paige and her witness before then. If you get into anything you can't handle, call us and we'll intercede."

Frickey and Ayoub kept looking at each other across the seatbacks like a pair of dimwitted lovers.

Paige said, "Major Kipling, for the record, I'm disappointed. Off the record, that's nowhere near good enough."

"Ma'am, it's the best I can do. You're not the only...fallout from X-66B, you know. Assigning Frickey and Cox to you, when they're the on-site experts, is stretching things as far as I can—that's why I can only give you a week. Of course, if you'd be satisfied with some security coverage from a groundside agency, and willing to wait until I can get my end together before confronting IST personally, then we're free to discuss alternatives."

"If she waits, there's no telling what Locke's IST connections will have cooked up," Cox said wearily. "We've been through this twice, Kipling—surprise is the only edge we've got, unless you can guarantee me that Locke's been incommunicado in the Cerberus stockade ever since the *Malibu* put in there—and that Wiley's not on Locke's payroll, and that whatever story they've cooked up won't make what you think you'll be able to do for us impossible because of 'political sensitivity' and that shit."

Paige didn't know whether to kiss Cox or shut him up.

Kipling responded, equally wearily, "Do I look like a four-star general to you, Cox? Or the President, maybe? You know I can't do any better than I'm doing. You ought to know I'm way out on a limb as it is. Have you ever been detailed to guard civilians before? Issued full kit for street wear in an urban venue in the goddamn Northeast Corridor? Just try and keep out of the newspapers—correction: keep *my* name out of them. You and Corporal Frickey are officially constrained from using deadly force except in your own and your charges' defense. And from using inappropriate force under any circumstances. Is that clear?"

"Yep," said Cox with a wolfish grin that came and went too fast.

"Sir," said Frickey—the first word she'd uttered during the entire meeting.

Freedom Ayoub made no comment, but he swept the gathering with a paternal gaze that made Paige feel braver and better when it touched her. Ayoub was still changing, Paige was certain of it now, after having spent so much time with him. So was Frickey, she assumed; but Frickey was Cox's problem.

Dalton Ross, whom Paige had increasingly come to like, cleared his throat. "If that's settled, we've got some stuff for you, Cox—something we hope will keep you out of jail and guarantee you the number of phone calls necessary to reach us in an emergency." Ross bent his blond head, sorted through a folder, and came up with a pair of credit card sized plates. He held out one to Cox, who stretched to take it, and the other to Frickey, who got up to get hers. Once she'd taken it, she perched on the armrest of Cox's seat, turning the card in her hands, frowning.

"I can't read this," Frickey said; "it's just a computer card."

"We're not set up to cut photo-ID's here. Those are bearer cards," Ross explained to Frickey. "You know, 'Do not interfere with, detain, or question bearer in performance of national security duties, nor deny access to classified areas or check or confiscate or refuse to issue special equipment or weapons.' Those are ours, so go easy, okay? The best we can do on such short notice. And welcome to the Special Science Staff."

"Gee, thanks," said Cox sarcastically, tapping the plastic against his knee. "What's my per diem? Can I charge hotel rooms and food to this, or are you going to give me cash too?"

Paige didn't like Cox's tone of voice. She wasn't happy with this turn of events either, but she'd spent enough time with Dalton Ross to be sure he wasn't lying—this was the best he could do.

Ross held out a blank envelope. "We don't carry much cash, and there's no way to get any at Hanscom without raising your profile. So you owe us, personally, off the record, for this." He held out the envelope and Frickey took it, looked inside, thumbed the bills, and put them away.

"If this gets any more deniable," Cox said in an uninflected voice, "I'm going to stay right here on the ship. How about we stop over at the Hanscom 203rd HQ and cash out from the X-66B tour?"

Kipling stood up, saying in disgust, "Cox, you do that if you want. Paint your butt blue while you're at it, you might as well. We're trying to get you off-base without putting a tracer on you, in case you're right and not just paranoid. This is the only way I know to do that. You don't like it, go piss into the wind by yourself. Me, I'm going back to the flight deck and start thinking about covering my own ass on this one."

"Major Kipling," Paige said to the man headed forward in silence. "Thank you for all your help. We'll see you next week in the District, God willing."

"God willing," Kipling replied from the forward hatch. "Ross will give you everything else you need, including my card. You be careful, ma'am. And if at any time between now and touchdown you reconsider and want to do this my way, I'll be glad to take you right down to Washington with me, where we can stick it to IST the civilized way."

"Thank you, Major," Paige said again. "But you know I've got to do this my way." Cox had been adamant about not going to Washington, not placing their fates in the hands of a government agency. It was his contention that they'd never see the light of day again if they did so. Frickey agreed with him; Frickey always agreed with Cox.

But it was Freedom who had convinced Paige not to go to DC. He wanted to walk on the streets; he wanted to avoid being prodded and questioned. He wanted to "mingle with the biosphere."

Paige was outvoted, even if she'd been amenable to Kipling's most recent offer. If she'd known beforehand what the major would put forth as an alternative, she might have tried to convince Ayoub. Now, after they'd made such a fuss about it, it seemed to be too late.

Ross scratched his blond head and said, "I'd better get up there—he'll need me soon. Here's the bottom line, if you haven't guessed: you've got one week, unless something happens. Then we expect you to report to us in DC, and the timing is crucial:

the *Malibu* will be spacedocking then. We've got what we need in the way of your depositions, but the major's put his career, and mine, on the line to give you this free time. We can't sanction any of this; we don't know about it. You're a civilian, Paige; so's Ayoub. Frickey and Cox pulled some R&R and decided to spend it with you. But you must be there when we need you. If something happens, you get your tails down to Washington *before* you've found your lawyers and filed your paperwork."

"That's what is hoped, yes?" came Ayoub's deep voice from behind Frickey. "That something will happen—because of us or to us—which will bring IST's evil to light?"

"That's right, buddy. Right now, it's your word against theirs on a lot of this. Not good enough for the government to get involved. You've got ranger backup, it ought not to be too dangerous. But for chrissakes, don't go around telling people you're . . . what you say you are . . . unless you want your credibility to be zilch, legally. The kind of interest that'll get you isn't the kind you're going to want."

"Perhaps not," Freedom Ayoub said.

Frickey leaned down and whispered in Cox's ear.

Ross was telling Paige, ". . . try and keep at least one ranger with you at all times. They've got enough electronics on them, in those suits, to ensure an unarguable transcript if you can get Godfrey to admit to anything. Don't worry about whether any evidence is admissable. Just see if you can get him to corroborate your story. If you do, you're going to be one very rich, very famous, and very heroic young lady, when the smoke clears."

"If she ain't dead," Cox said sourly.

"That's what you're here for, Cox, to keep that from happening. And if what you told Kipling is true, none of you have to worry about dying any-how."

"That's not true, it's just you only die once..." said Dennis Cox.

"Det, I don't get this," replied Ross candidly. "Do you think we die more than once any other way? Never mind—I don't want to get into the fruit-and-nut bowl with the rest of you. When this is over, we'll see if we can get you declared psycho-logically sound. I hope we can. I hope you and the corporal are torqued-down tight enough to do the job for Paige." Ross dipped his blond head and a shy smile crossed his face. "I really do." He straightened up. "And Cox, get some loose clothing or biker gear or whatever you can find to camou-flage those suits. Something to make you and Frickey look less like a recruiting poster, if you're going into that corporate tower, or you two will find yourselves stationed outside the door while somebody runs a check on those cards we gave you. Understood?"

"Affirmative," said Frickey, and got off Cox's armrest. Cox said nothing, just slumped bonelessly where he was until Ross had shaken Paige's hand warmly and gone up to the flight deck.

Then Cox said, "Well, we're fucked, beyond what we can do for ourselves: you realize that." He was staring at the plastic card he held.

"I don't see it that way at all," Paige objected.

"You don't. Well, what they want, near as I can figure, is to put you out there where IST can take shots at you, and they can see what happens. Sound like fun to you, Paige? Doesn't to me. Maybe Frickey and Ayoub don't have to sweat lit-tle things like dying, but for my money, death's still the same: there's no good death, there's no dignified death. Death's still a waste and a damned shame and I'm not convinced that I ought to be lookin' forward to it, just so I can start my new life as part of the revolution." His tone was no less harsh than his words, and he got to his feet as soon as he was finished, brushing by Frickey roughly to stalk aft, into the head.

The door slammed.

The remaining three looked at one another. After a time, Frickey raised an eyebrow and said, "He's right to be nervous. I don't know what he thought they'd do, though. Me, I'm glad they didn't put us all in nice safe cages. If we can't take care of ourselves, that's our problem, right?"

Paige didn't answer. Neither did Ayoub. Freedom had come forward and was leaning over the aisle seat, looking out the wing window at the blue Earth below.

"I never thought," he said, "to see such a sight. It is so beautiful." His nappy head shook slowly back and forth, then turned to Paige. "Thank you, Paige Barnett, for fulfilling your promise and bringing me to Earth."

His eyes were shining more brightly than the world below; from the bulkhead speakers, Dalton Ross's voice warned them, "Okay, folks, sit down, raise your seatbacks and strap in. We'll have milspec touchdown at Hanscom in forty minutes, give or take."

As if to prove the truth of his words, the *FASTEN SEATBELTS / EXTINGUISH SMOKING MATERIALS* light above the patrol cruiser's door lit. Cox came out of the head, a cigarette between his lips.

"Det," Paige called.

He'd been going toward the seat next to Frickey's. He came to her instead. "Don't worry about going to see Godfrey—I know how to handle IST." She almost added, I know how to handle government bureaucracy, too. But she didn't. She said only, "Don't blame Kipling. I might have done the same thing, if I were in his place. He knows how his machine works. I know mine. It'll be fine."

"That makes me feel lots better," Cox said testily, but squeezed her shoulder before he took a seat by himself, up near the main exit, across from the locker in which his recon pack and heavy weapons were stored.

Paige looked around once more, as she began to feel the patrol cruiser meet the upper atmosphere, and saw Frickey, head back, eyes closed, chest rising and falling as if she were asleep. And across from her, leaning his forehead against the wing window, was Ayoub.

Freedom must have sensed her watching him. He turned his head and Paige could see tears streaming down his face, glistening streams above his small-toothed smile. "Home," he said.

Only that, but Paige nearly wept as well.

CHAPTER 34

Groundside

COX WAS THE first one out of the patrol cruiser, in full kit—everything but a rifle at ready. There was something about Earth's runways, her aprons and tarmac: they always felt more solid underfoot, more right and more righteous, than anywhere else.

He knew why that was: the gravity you were

born for was the gravity of home. No superforce
simulation or space station rotation or near-Earth
venue could compare to standing on solid terra
firma.

He forced the feelings away. He wasn't going to
take up residence here; Earth held nothing for him
but disorientation, once he got off-base, and a con-
certed hard time. He could parlay this Science
Staff assignment and the card that came with it
into something to get himself back out-system
when all this was over. If he lived through it.

If he didn't end up getting his ass shot and either
dying or becoming one of whatever Frickey and
Ayoub were. He was damned sure that if that happened, Dennis "Det" Cox was going to be on classified display for the rest of his unnatural life.

The sun was bright out here; bright enough that
his helmet's visor started polarizing. He'd reset his
wrist chronometer for Earth time during final approach and as always, it had distressed him to give
away a chronological year and change to the laws
of relativity.

Well, so it would be a little more different here
than last time. Last time, it had been different
enough that he'd felt like an alien. This time, he
had something alien with him—something in
Frickey and Ayoub, or something that *was* Frickey
and Ayoub.

Frickey deplaned next, once he'd waved an all-
clear, shouldering a gear bag along with her recon
pack. She had her helmet under her arm, though.

He snapped up his visor and shouted, "Suit up,
ranger, damn you!" over the cooling noises the patrol cruiser was making. He'd tried once to reach
her on his com circuit and gotten a zero. He didn't
want to keep yelling.

She still seemed not to hear him. He tapped his

helmet, his other hand on one hip. There was lots of noise out here: other aircraft, fuel and maintenance trucks, the general clatter of a working field. He knew why she was slow to respond: she and Ayoub were determined to "mix with the biosphere."

As Ayoub appeared at the head of the ramp, Frickey reached the bottom and put on her helmet. As soon as she had a com circuit he could engage, Cox snapped at her, "Corporal, don't pull this shit on me again. I need you up and running. Unless you're not planning on soldiering for this mission."

"Sorry, Det. I just wanted to breathe the air. I . . . breathing's important."

"Yeah, you said," he reminded her. "Well, you can 'teach the biosphere' on your own time. I don't care how many molecules go through your system, not like I do about security and discipline right now. Here they come, that blue sedan there. Get the civilians on the tarmac, make sure they're ready with all their gear."

"Yes sir," said Frickey coldly.

Couldn't be helped. The car Kipling had promised him had no Massachusetts license, just yellow letters that said SCSS-HAFB on a blue plate, and above those, on the trunk, a serial number.

Not exactly a low-profile vehicle, but he was supposed to be something like a glorified MP. It would have to do. The guy in it got out, saluted brusquely, and opened the rear door.

Frickey hustled Ayoub and Paige inside, then helped the driver put their luggage in the trunk while Det stood watch, really wanting to bring his rifle out in the open, but not quite daring. Low-profile didn't allow for openly armed guards.

Frickey got in the back, behind the driver, just

like you learned in training for a situation like this.
Cox said, "Secure?" into his helmet mike.

"Secure,'" she replied, all business now.

Cox took one look back at the big black cruiser, a
milspec super-TAV with jump capability that
Kipling had let Cox know wasn't anything you
talked about riding in, and he saw Ross in the
open hatchway.

Ross raised a hand and then pulled the door
shut. That was the drill. Everybody went their separate ways. If he ever saw those guys again, it
would be too soon, because if he did, it'd be in the
District when they prepped him for hearings.

Cox had to do well enough with this that there
wouldn't be any hearings. He wasn't sure that
Paige and Kipling had the same objective, but they
ought to. Nobody who understood what was happening here should want to make it public.

Ayoub was sitting in the car, breathing deeply,
with a bemused and happy look on his wide, black
face. Cox sidled over to the car, jerked open the
passenger-side door and got in front, ducking low
to accommodate his helmet.

The driver had an MP armband and faced front
determinedly. Cox turned on his suit speaker and
said, "Okay, get us through the gate, then I'm
takin' the car."

"Yes sir," said the MP, a sergeant like Cox, without turning a hair. If you had a passenger equipped
like Dennis Cox who didn't raise his faceplate
when he talked to you, it meant that you weren't
expected to give a description of that passenger.

It was the best Cox could do for himself and
Frickey. Ayoub and Paige were probably the people
whose photos had been studied by anyone hostile
from IST or elsewhere, but that's why Ayoub and

Paige had Cox and Frickey. Cox was aware that it looked like he was escorting dangerous prisoners, and equally aware that maybe he was.

He'd been half-expecting Kipling or Ross to slip him sealed orders, or pull him aside and tell him just when to drop the other shoe—when to reel in Paige's leash. But it hadn't happened: he hadn't received delayed detaining orders or any other kind, beyond what everybody got during the last strategy session.

So maybe Kipling was straight up; or maybe Kipling didn't think giving Cox any such orders was a good idea; or maybe there really weren't going to be any such orders. But Cox had to assume there might be, any time now—if not for him to execute, then for somebody else. Somebody like this hotshot MP driver.

So he was beginning to diverge from the agreed upon gameplan as quickly as possible. He was taking this car, leaving the driver at the gate.

When he did that, the MP didn't say boo, just wished him, "Good luck, sir," once they'd reached the far side of the checkpoint.

As Cox drove away, he could still see the MP, leaning against the guardpost, watching.

He knew Hanscom and its environs. He knew what he wanted to do: get lost as quickly as possible. But it wasn't possible. He couldn't get a rental car without a credit card, and the Special Science Card was the closest thing he had. If it was flagged, any car he rented, any hotel he checked into, anyplace he ate, was on display.

So he just drove toward the highway. Once he got on Route 128, he said to Frickey on his com link, "Sweep for bugs and if we're clean, take the helmet off."

He took his off before hearing her results, because he was attracting too much attention. He knew he should get them rooms somewhere, try to get motorcycles, because the only civilian transportation that allowed a driver to look like he did was a bike. But he didn't want to. He wanted to get this mission up and running.

"Paige, how about going to IST now? Chances are better for surprising them now than later."

In his rearview mirror, he could see Frickey's helmet coming off and Paige and Ayoub. Ayoub was staring raptly out the window. Paige was squeezed between the two bigger people. Cox kept thinking about the biosphere, hoping he was right in helping this thing spread.

If Kipling had believed him, would things have gone differently? He tried not to wonder about it as he waited for Paige to answer.

She seemed dazed, confused, or choked up with some sort of emotion; he couldn't figure which. When she finally did respond, she said, "Det, I need to think about it. Can't we go get some rooms—"

"No, you don't have to think about it," said Frickey. "He thought about it. He just wants to know if you're up to it."

Cox saw Paige's shoulders hunch, between the two resurrected ones. He thought he saw a trapped look cross Paige's face. "Hey, it's okay, either way, Paige. I just can't see that we can avoid being traced, whatever we do. If we're fast enough, we can get this over with before anybody figures out we're tougher than we ought to be." He gave her an encouraging grin and started looking for a rest area.

He cut across two lanes of traffic toward one before she answered, keeping the car on manual despite an angry red dashboard warning light that kept blinking at him to "Enter automated traffic pattern." Like hell. The rest area had no comfort facilities. He cut back into the middle lane and horns honked.

He wasn't giving up any more control than he absolutely had to. Not of the car, not of the people he was supposed to be protecting, not of his own future. He'd had enough debrief in the patrol cruiser to satisfy ranger SOP three times over; if they wanted more from him, the reasons weren't the sort he cared to contemplate—the same sort that had got him into this mess in the first place.

The same sort, maybe, that had gotten him Dream Date, the supposed "wrong number," when he'd been trying to find Locke.

Finally, Paige said tiredly, "If you think it's best, Det, let's try it. Take your next off-ramp east."

"We'll grab something at a fast-food place on the way," he promised. "Frickey can go in for it." Frickey had their cash. He flicked a glance at his chronometer. "It's lunch time. You think he'll be there?"

"Who? Godfrey? By three . . . by fifteen hundred. If he's in town."

There was that. This whole thing was crazy by anybody's standards, unless it was a set-up. He'd thought about that too much during the cruiser's approach. He told himself he wasn't going to think about it any more. If Kipling had orders to get them dead, there were easier ways. Safer ways, if you accepted just the possibility that what Ayoub and Frickey claimed was true.

Ayoub had said something, during a dinner break on the cruiser, about how they were going to be "teaching the biosphere how to give life" from the moment they got on the ground. If you wanted to stop this thing, and if any of what Ayoub said was true, you had to have done it before now.

Cox wasn't willing to trust Ayoub as far as he could throw the big man, but he knew Frickey wasn't lying to him. So he was driving around with two people who were doing things to his planet just by sitting there.

How much they were doing, he wasn't sure. Frickey had been concerned that they not be out of reach of one another, if something happened to Cox. So she could fix him. God, he hated to think about it.

And the car was getting more and more angry at him because he wouldn't give up control to whatever computer was doing the traffic controlling. For all he knew, refusing might be illegal by now. He was just starting to look for troopers with flashing lights when they saw a fast-food place at the next rest area, just before the off-ramp.

On impulse, he wheeled the car across two lanes to get there and saw people shaking their fists as their cars automatically avoided his, and each other's, by inches.

Not good. He was sweating by the time he'd parked. He was pumped up enough that his pharmakit was engaging, so he took it off monitor mode. He couldn't eat if it hyped him. It thought he was in a combat situation from the way his body was reacting. So did he.

But it wasn't. It was a sunny summer day on Earth, in Massachusetts, and there were kids with balloons in bright clothing, with dogs on leashes and frowsy mothers in see-through pants and cars crammed with summer necessities packed by families on their way to their beach houses.

There was even spilled strawberry ice cream by

his left front tire, a whole scoop, with ants formed up in columns, trying to carry it away before it melted.

This was no place to feel like shooting the enemy, that was for sure. He sat in the driver's seat and watched the ants and the melting ice cream while Frickey went in to get sandwiches and coffee. So he didn't see the kid's dog jerk its leash free and run out after a car until the kid screamed and the car's tires screeched and Freedom burst from the back seat.

"Damn," Cox said as he grabbed the keys, opened the door, and went after the big man.

By the time he got there, Freedom Ayoub was holding this dead tan cocker spaniel and there was blood all over both of them; the kid was crying; the mother was yelling at the dog-murdering driver who was yelling back and getting out his license and registration.

There was a lot of blood—a cocker spaniel's worth. Cox put a hand on Ayoub's coverall-clothed shoulder and said, "Come on, let the kid have his dog. There's nothing we can do." Cox's hand felt funny, as if he was getting a hundred little shocks. He let go.

The sobbing boy was kneeling in the blood and Ayoub was holding out the dog to him. "Cradle him gently. He loves you. He won't leave you. Hold his head and don't let anyone take him from you."

Cox got down on his knees too and said, "You asshole," under his breath. "Come on, man, don't turn this into a side show. Let's go."

"The dog wants life. The boy wants the dog. Everyone is sorry. No one meant this."

"Look at all this blood," Cox whispered desperately. "That thing gets up and walks, we're going to be stuck here for—"

The kid was still crying, his cheek pressed to the dog's face. Then he screamed, "Mommy! Mommy! Gruff licked me!"

"Oh boy." Cox grabbed Ayoub and pulled him to his feet, hoping everyone was watching the kid and the dog. Hand to the flat of Ayoub's back, he pushed the other man roughly, once, then again.

Ayoub kept watching, and Cox kept pushing, all the way back to the car.

When they got there, Frickey had returned with the sandwiches and Paige was bitching about the blood all over Freedom's gray coveralls and Ayoub was still looking back the way they'd come.

Cox didn't risk a glance until he'd manhandled the black man into the car, slammed the door, slid behind the wheel and keyed the ignition.

Then, on the way out, he did. He couldn't help it: Paige was demanding to see what happened, Frickey was watching him imploringly, and to get back on the highway they had to drive past the crowd that had gathered.

The damned cocker spaniel was sitting there, in that pool of blood, calmly licking it up, with the kid's arms around the dog and the mother standing by, crying.

"My god," said Paige Barnett in a voice full of wonder and surprise as if she hadn't been the one who brought Ayoub here, "look at that!"

"It's begun," Frickey said, and reached out across the front seat to squeeze Cox's arm. "It's really begun. Thank you, Det."

Ayoub was examining the blood on his knees as if he didn't know how it had gotten there.

"Frickey, you got coffee?"

She did, and it was a good thing: Cox's hands were shaking. Before he drank it, he snapped his pharmakit back on: maybe this wasn't combat the way he'd come to know it, but he was going to need all the help he could get, keeping these people out of harm's way.

Frickey helped him with his coffee. When he'd had a swig, he said, "Ayoub, you can't do that again. You can't. We got an objective: Raymond Godfrey and IST. You can't put everything and everybody at risk for somethin' like a dead puppy."

"You have one objective—an agenda, I think. IST may have another. Your government has its own. But I have mine, Sergeant Det Cox. I have mine."

And Ayoub gave Cox that shit-eating grin again that made Cox want to haul out his magnum and shoot the bastard there and then. In the head, to see what would happen when his braincase was spread all over the back seat.

"Talk to him, Frickey," Cox said instead, and accepted a cigarette from the corporal, while Paige tried to convince him it wasn't a problem that they'd just performed a miracle in a fast-food parking lot.

CHAPTER 35

IST

———◆———

SOMETHING DET COX had said while they were all still aboard the patrol cruiser kept bothering Paige: *Death's still a waste and a damned shame and I'm not convinced that I ought to be lookin' forward to it, just so I can start my new life as part of the revolution.*

It had bothered her throughout the interval with the cocker spaniel, and it bothered her all the way to IST headquarters. It bothered her enough that everyone in the car noticed her uncommunicativeness, but she couldn't tell them why.

Cox, in his inimitable fashion, had cut to the heart of the problem that IST and undoubtedly the United States government in the persons of its representatives, Kipling and Ross, were most worried about.

The revolutions that had overtaken X-31A and X-66B were symptoms of a cause, and that cause was redemption, resurrection, the holy way. Its carriers were seated in this blue mid-sized sedan, and Paige Barnett had helped bring them here.

When Cox pulled the car up in front of the tower that was IST/128, Paige was cold despite the summer day around her.

There was no alternative but to go ahead. There was no choice but the holy way, once it was offered. Yet it was going to change not only her life, but America's, and the world's. For the United States, as hard as it might be over the next few years, the changes Ayoub and Frickey represented would be easier to metabolize than for many other nations. America still paid lip-service to her Constitution. She was a republic, a democracy at her heart. After Ayoub and Frickey finished "mixing with the biosphere," she would be one in truth.

But being the catalyst for a second American Revolution was none of what Paige Barnett wanted for herself. She wasn't even sure she understood the holy way. Unlike redemption and resurrection, which were physical processes, the holy way was some sort of philosophy. Maybe you had to die to understand it. Millions would, in the totalitarian states and even here, during the upheavals and class struggles that seemed to go hand-in-hand with freedom from fear of death.

She knew now why Ayoub had chosen his first name. He'd said to her, in the car after he'd resurrected the spaniel, "Even if we were all to be blown to bits now, in this car, and the pieces were buried by unbelievers, it would make no difference. The very soil of this world will carry on the work; it will learn to give life back to those who love it."

"And what would become of us?" she'd whispered back.

"Whatever we wish, in our hearts," he'd answered.

Paige hadn't had the heart to continue the conversation. What Ayoub had said made her understand how the whole thing must have started: on X-31A, X-66B, and perhaps on other worlds where the conditions were right, the constituents of resurrection had been waiting for millenia. X-31A and X-66B were exceptional geologically in their richness, but devoid of atmosphere until man came to mine them. Then someone had died, someone who wanted to live, and the knowledge in the holy ground itself had done the rest.

So it was just as Frickey had said: begun. The dog was probably enough, on his own, to spread the gift they'd brought home. Frickey had undergone a battery of tests meant to detect anything abnormal, anything as small as a virus. So it was no virus; they hadn't lied. It was a molecular code for rebirth, a natural spelling lesson that taught earth and air and fire and water how to renew life.

With the car idling in front of IST's familiar portico, Paige suddenly wanted no part of what they'd brought back from X-66B. She didn't want to learn to mold rock like clay, as she'd seen Ayoub and Sanchez do in the tunnels. She didn't want to seal mankind's fate and force him out among the stars, as must happen now because otherwise there would simply be too many people.

And there would be anarchy before there was peace. Before there were enough resurrected ones to overcome resistance, to change long-entrenched methods of maintaining power and controlling populaces.

She closed her eyes. Maybe IST had been right. Perhaps man was born to die and try and die again, making way for the next, hopefully better, generations, purifying the stock of mankind. Was humanity ready for forever? If this was the end of evolution as the world had known it, was it coming too soon?

Unconsciously, Paige let out a tremulous sigh. She had to believe she'd done the right thing. She had to think so. There couldn't be any excuse for refusing salvation, no reason to consign generations to misery and death when redemption was possible. Paige had never been an egalitarian; she was a card-carrying member of a privileged class who used her education and her nepotistic clout to wring personal triumph and pleasure out of a world full of misery and death. IST had been the perfect home for her: everyone there, the cream of the technocratic elite, shared in a more perfect world built atop a pyramid at whose bottom were the Fourth Worlders such as Freedom Ayoub. You never saw them, you never touched them, you were never touched by their suffering except on the evening news or at the occasional fundraiser.

They were what they were because they were

uncivilized, unteachable, underprivileged and un-salvageable. They were the underclasses, and you found a use for them, because without their cheap labor and their primitive wars, your own world of mirrored towers and imported luxuries and mega-buck negotiations could never exist.

But Paige Barnett had gone out-system, because of an autonomic twitch of conscience that had caused her to object to IST's comportment on X-31A, and brought the Fourth World back with her: Freedom Ayoub and Allie Frickey, a piece of female white trash with prospects so dim in Earth's competitive structure that the best she could do was join the rangers and learn to kill.

In that moment, in that car, Paige would have undone it all if she could, staring at the back of Frickey's red-haired head instead of at IST's tower.

Frickey, that eerie creature of Cox's, stretched in the front seat and craned her neck at Paige: "Hey, Paige, don't get cold feet on us ...It's okay. You got nothin' to lose but life itself." The corporal grinned broadly. "And me and Freedom can fix that for you."

"Take it easy, Frickey," Cox said and then he raised his head enough to glance at Paige in the rearview mirror. "You want to leave this until an-other time, I'll live with it."

They had stopped at a sporting goods store and bought some army surplus fatigues for Ayoub, and coveralls for Cox and Frickey to wear over their suits. The coveralls weren't much of a disguise, and Cox had finally discarded Ross's advice alto-gether, saying, "I'm better off looking like what I am, no matter what Ross says. Intimidation's not just a word."

Now Cox inclined his head for a moment, then

got out of the car and walked around to open Paige's door, helmet under his arm. "Come on, IST lady. Let's finish this thing. Frickey says you can still have kids if you're resurrected, so we don't have anything to lose and a lot to gain."

Paige shrank from his touch. Had he really said that? Was he implying what she thought? She looked into Cox's eyes and saw only warm encouragement.

She found herself scrambling from the car and her lips said, "I have no intention of having 'kids,' Dennis Cox, not with you or anyone else." The huffiness there was from nervousness. At least she hadn't said, I thought you and Frickey were going back out-system to raise a brood of little killers.

But she thought it. Damn Cox, for distracting her.

And then, as Freedom came around the car and Frickey got out, putting on her helmet, Paige realized why Cox had said that to her now: he wasn't at all certain he was going to come through this alive, as he'd known life.

It was there in the set of his jaw and the distance in his eyes, even before he said, "I just wanted you to know—thought I'd offer. Everybody likes their slates clean before an action."

"Well, it's not going to be anything like what you're inferring, Dennis," she replied sharply. "Where do you think you are? Some primitive planet? I don't think Frickey needs that helmet, or those weapons, or that you do..."

He was already disappearing behind his visor. From the speaker pack in his suit came the words, "You let me decide how I want to risk my life, okay? You just go in there and shake your ass and stamp your feet and we'll be right behind you."

The four of them made their way up the broad steps and into the reception area of polished granite.

"Hiya, Phil," Paige waved insouciantly to the armed guard by the receptionist's desk. And to the girl: "Paula, long time no see. Is God up there?"

She was walking by, her two rangers and the big black man trailing in her wake, as if she were expected, as if it were nothing out of the ordinary that she'd show up after better than a year with such an outre escort.

And it worked: power is its own reward. The guard waved and smiled stiffly, questions he didn't dare ask in his eyes. The receptionist, who had blue-green checkerboard hair, said, "Let me check, ma'am," and consulted her roster before she added, "Well, he should be, but the top floor doesn't tend to sign in and out."

Paige knew that. That was how she was bluffing her way into the elevator without being forced to fumble for an up-to-date ID card she didn't have. Inside it, when the rosewood doors closed and the music tinkled down around her ears like a cool shower, she slumped against the wall and giggled hysterically. Cox's insect-visored head turned to her slowly and that made it seem more ludicrous. Here she was, with two rangers and a messiah in black, on her way to settle a score with the man who'd started it all.

By the time the elevator doors opened to reveal IST's top-floor elegance, she was wondering if this was really necessary. Now that she was here, she had no burning desire to wrest an apology from Raymond Godfrey.

She'd loved him once, an unrequited puppy love, an executive crush on a powerful superior, and he'd betrayed her. But oh, what he'd given her in return. And yet, she'd promised Kipling to deliver Godfrey, to help remove him from IST's top seat. And there were also the objective evils that had started all this: the debacle on X-31A, the obliteration of X-66B.

It was strange not to care now, when previously she'd cared so much, about settling up with God. She told herself she was frightened, that was all.

Cox hadn't allowed Paige time to find a lawyer; she hadn't gotten her legal means together, or thought about personal recourse. What if God denied it all?

What then?

Cox or Frickey shoved her gently, and she stumbled out onto the thick pink carpet and across it to the anteroom desk, flanked by six-foot palm trees shadowing rosewood walls hung with fine art.

She didn't know the moon-faced woman there, who was staring wide-eyed at the two rangers in their recon suits, and Freedom Ayoub in his new fatigues.

The woman said, "Yes, may I help you?"

There was a panic button under the desk, but the woman hadn't reached for it yet. Paige said, "I'm Paige Barnett, God's old exec assistant, back from an out-system tour. I need to see him."

"Ma'am, do you have an appointment?"

"No, but he'll see me."

"He's not in." The woman's hand, then her knee, shifted.

"Don't push that button. If you must, call Jill Ekberg out here. She'll get you off the hook." Paige smiled her barracuda smile, reserved for underlings in distress.

The woman moved to toggle Ekberg's line, but her knee came up at the same time. Paige shot a glance at Cox, a step behind her left shoulder, and warned under her breath, "The cavalry'll be right up."

Cox's helmeted head nodded and in a moment, Frickey and Ayoub backed away to flank the elevator.

Oh please, let's not have any violence here. The thing about Cox and his girl ranger was that they were trained for only certain types of responses.

Paige began praying that Jill would hurry.

The woman at the desk frowned, and toggled again, then said, "I'm sorry, ma'am, she must have stepped away from her desk."

Paige's skin was beginning to crawl. Maybe IST had been warned after all. Maybe Locke had gotten a message through. Maybe Cox was right to be so nervous... "Try God's lounge, maybe they're in there together."

This time, the woman did as she was told without quibbling. Paige watched closely and saw that she tried three times without result.

The elevator bell behind them pinged politely. Paige closed her eyes before she faced whatever was going to come out of there.

The woman at the desk let out a strangled cry before Paige looked to see why.

Frickey had her side arm out and two security men were holding very still, their arms well away from their bodies, inside the elevator.

Frickey was telling them to "Step out, back off: you haul out your papers, we'll show you ours, and nobody gets hurt."

Cox was sidling between Paige and the two men, and she hardly heard what he said to them. She was having visions of sprawled bodies and blood and Freedom Ayoub, like some manic angel, resurrecting every casualty on the spot.

None of it happened. Cox's speaker told the security men this was "Government business, fellas. You don't want to interfere. We've got a protected person here, and the rest of you don't fall in that category. You want to hug the wall, my corporal will check you out."

While that was going on, Paige found herself prattling at the receptionist to, "...just tell God and Jill I came by. I don't know where I'm staying yet. I'll call. I know they'll want to see me as much as I want to see them. And we'll just be going..."

"Can you tell me what this is in reference to, ma'am? I should take a more specific message." The receptionist was doing an admirable job of pretending to be calm, but her lips were blue and her face blotchy and when she unclasped her hands to take the message, they shook.

"No," Paige said, "I'd rather talk—"

"X-66B, tell him," Cox's harsh words came over his helmet speakers and seemed to reverberate off the paneled walls. "And tell him that next time, he better be here." And then, to Paige, "Okay, into the elevator. Move."

She wasn't sure how they ever got out of there, with Cox in some sort of combat overdrive, acting as if he expected the security men with their palms on the wall to explode into hostile activity, or more of their ilk to drop down from the elevator's ceiling.

She stood in the midst of her armed protectors and shook until the elevator reached the ground floor, when she demanded, "Before that door opens, put those weapons away. The guard down here is a friend of mine. He—"

"No way," Cox snapped.

The elevator opened. The lobby was absolutely empty: no receptionist, no armed guard; no one. Cox was walking backward, Frickey was dragging

Paige along, and Ayoub was trying to protect her with his big body.

It was all so ludicrous she wanted to cry.

She did, when she was pushed roughly into the sedan out front. She put her head in her arms and wept and refused to respond to any of Frickey's questions about what she thought had happened "up there."

She didn't answer Cox, either, when he suggested they get rooms and calm down and start looking for her lawyer. "You're not going to get to see those people. They were ready and waiting, that staff. Your Godfrey's probably beyond the two-hundred mile limit on some yacht, waiting this all out." His voice, unaugmented by speakers now that he'd taken off his helmet, let her know that seeing IST headquarters hadn't been without its effect.

But he'd seen her apartment, back at the beginning. He'd known what she was. She wasn't any different now. She just cried helplessly until Ayoub started to rub her back.

Then the tears stopped, but by then the sun was going down and they were driving south on Route 128.

She thanked Freedom, saying, "I'm much better now," and sniffled. She couldn't meet Cox's eyes. All this time, she'd managed to be brave, to perform creditably, and now she'd gone to pieces in front of everybody. She was miserable. "Where are you taking me?" she asked Cox querulously.

"Downtown, where we can get a good hotel, one that's too snotty to question a party like you comin' in with ranger escort. Want to pick one?"

She was just about to tell him that there wasn't a hotel on Earth where the kind of behavior he'd displayed at IST headquarters would go unremarked, or uncriticized, when Frickey said, "Crap, Det, I'm real sure those two cars there are on our tail."

And Cox floored the accelerator, pushing Paige back in her seat as if she were in a TAV taxiing for takeoff.

Before she'd recovered from the shock, she was thrown against Freedom as the car careened sideways. It seemed to go up on two wheels and teeter.

She screamed. The wheels came down with a jolt that banged her head against the window. Freedom grabbed her and held on. She screamed again, wordlessly.

Cox was executing some demented U-turn, one handed, across the meridian, groping for something on the seat with the other—a weapon, his helmet: she couldn't tell. She heard a crash, but it wasn't the car they were in; it was some car behind them.

Frickey was cursing and shouting in some ranger shorthand that didn't make any sense to Paige, waving her handgun, helping Cox with his helmet, and putting down the car's windows all at once.

Ayoub had Paige in a death-grip, one hand on her head, and was trying to wrestle her down between the seats. She knew she was screaming, "No, please God, no!" but nobody seemed to be listening.

There were more terrible sounds, and she realized that some of them were gunshots. They were so loud they deafened her. They were from this car! Frickey! That crazy Frickey was shooting at another car.

Then Paige and Ayoub were thrown forward as another car hit theirs from behind. She tried to get her head up, to see what was happening, to make

Freedom let her go, and then she realized that Frickey wasn't the only person who was shooting.

Metal squealed and shattered and a hole appeared right by her face, a hole in the back seat. A bullet hole. She screamed again, and the car seemed to buck. She had to get up. She had to see what was happening.

But Freedom was so heavy, so determined. Locked in his embrace, she was thrown around in the back of the car until she couldn't think of anything but the sounds of screeching tires and rending metal and the impossibly painful reports from the guns of the rangers in the front seat.

Then something hit her hard in the back of the head. For a split second she thought she'd banged her head against the door but then she knew that couldn't be: it hurt too much.

The car had banged her. Or part of the car had banged her. She couldn't see anything but white and red and pain and a sort of kaleidoscope of color. Then the pain was gone and she could hear distant shouting, and everything seemed to turn upside down.

She couldn't feel anything now. She was floating in a downy, warm space where nothing hurt at all and everything was preternaturally clear, but that everything wasn't composed of the reality her body had always known.

She could hear breathing and talking, but they were far away and they didn't make any sense. The noises came and went, and behind them was a bright light.

She wanted to swim toward the light. She was swimming as if she were at the beach, but she had no body to swim with.

She thought, Well, this is what it's like. Then she

wasn't thinking at all, in human terms. She was high above the car and she knew it was their car: it was overturned, its wheels spinning. One door was open. She could see herself, and Freedom Ayoub, sprawled on the meridian grass. But it was getting dark and it was hard to see exactly what was going on by the car. There were other people there, moving people, and other cars.

Everything was getting smaller, as if she were in a hot air balloon that was slowly rising. She felt like crying and she didn't have any tears. She wanted those bodies to move. She wanted her body to move. She didn't want to be dead. She didn't want to leave Cox, and Ayoub, and Frickey.

She didn't want to die. She was keening, wailing without a voice. Where was redemption, resurrection, the holy way? Where was Ayoub? Please, she thought, don't let me be dead.

And then she saw Freedom move, tiny so far below, and his body seemed to glow. It glowed brighter and brighter until it turned translucent and white and then it started to grow.

It grew larger and larger, like the white bright light up above the sky, the light she was floating toward.

Had been floating toward. Now she was floating back down, toward Ayoub, toward the hands that were white and so bright and seemed to touch her, even here. She floated down faster and faster, and as she descended she could see their car clearly, its upturned wheels, its crushed roof, the two rangers still inside.

She wanted to cry for all the pain and the waste and the cold around that place, but she still had no eyes to cry with.

Was she a ghost? Had something gone horribly

wrong? Was the holy way a trick; a horrid, awful trick? She wanted only to go back up higher, away from the cold and the pain—to go to the light above the sky.

But Ayoub was calling her back. His hands were touching her body and she could feel all the pain in him. She could smell the blood in him. She could smell the burned rubber and hot oil and expended powder from the rangers' firearms. She could smell through her own nose!

She was hungry for breath, suddenly. She was so hungry for breath that her lungs hurt. They hurt as if they'd burst because they had old air in them that must come out. She wanted to push that old air out and while she was trying to do so, she lost track of the car and the scene below.

Then her head hurt terribly. It hurt like fire and ice; it hurt like thunder and lightning. It hurt like the pulse in her veins because her heart was thudding so hard that the sound deafened her.

She took a deep, shuddering breath and inhaled clean, new air. Along with it, she inhaled something else: she inhaled the calm of the white hands touching her; she inhaled the wisdom of so many who'd died and taken this same breath and been reborn. She inhaled all of X-66B and even X-31A.

And she inhaled a joy such as she'd never known before in life. It was a joy composed of simply breathing, of feeling blood course and life renew itself. She inhaled a gift and that gift was God as she'd always known He would be—all forgiving and all encompassing and all powerful.

Then she exhaled that breath to take another, and most of what she called God went with it. She was Paige Barnett, and she hurt. There were hands on her face that were translucent at their fingertips and black everywhere else. There was blood

all around her on the cold grass and some of it was
hers.

Some of it was Freedom's too. His chest had a
hole in it and she knew just what she was supposed to do: the first movement she made was to
lift up her head and close her eyes and put her lips
to that wound and give the breath of life and heal-
ing to it.

She tasted blood and pain and metal and when
she lay back, she spit out a bullet.

Then she retched. And then she cried. She rolled
away from Ayoub and all the blood and buried her
head in the grass and her mouth in the soil beneath the grass and she cried and screamed into
the soil, because redemption was freely given, but
resurrection had its price.

She was not merely Paige Barnett any longer;
she could never be. She was part of something
much wiser, much older, much more demanding
than Paige Barnett.

And when she had finally come to terms with
that invasion of her mind by something so much
greater, so much more demanding, than her mind
or her conscience had ever been before, she felt
someone touching her.

It wasn't the electric touch of Freedom, and she
knew who it was by the way that flesh felt against
hers.

It was Cox, and he was injured.

She rolled over, her hands out to fix whatever
was wrong there, not out of choice, but out of duty,
and she saw Cox's blood- and sweat- and tear-
stained face, peering down at her. She saw his red-
rimmed eyes in the headlights of an ambulance
just pulling up, its flashers strobing.

Cox said, "Jesus, Paige, you scared the crap out
of me. I thought you were . . ." He brushed the back

of his hand over his eyes. He was scraped and bruised and he had a cracked rib he wasn't aware of yet.

But she was. She reached out to touch the place where he was hurt and she felt the contact singe her.

Ayoub's face swam into view. He frowned and his big lips said, "It's too early. Let me do that. You conserve your strength."

Ayoub helped Cox to his feet, an arm around the smaller man. Together they limped over to the men piling out of the ambulance, and Paige heard Ayoub saying in his deep voice, "The woman trapped in the car is unharmed, but we must get her out. And this man, he is somewhat bruised and battered, but in general, we are well."

We are well.

Paige tried to push herself up on her elbows, to call out to Cox. She wanted to hold Cox, who was unchanged, who was untouched by redemption, and feel normal. She wanted to hold him and be the same as she'd always been. She wanted to make Freedom promise not to tell Cox that she'd been dead. She didn't want anybody to know she'd been dead, especially Cox.

She put a hand to her forehead, lying there on the grass, terrified of the moment the paramedics would come running over to examine her. Would they know? Could they tell? But no, nobody had been able to tell with Frickey.

She was so frightened, now that it was over. So very frightened about how close it had been. She was telling herself that she hadn't really died, that she'd only almost died, when she moved her fingers and encountered the bullet she'd taken, somehow, out of Freedom's chest.

And then she could only lie there, telling herself not to be afraid, that you only died once, waiting for the paramedics to come and Freedom to come back so that she could grab his hand and never let go, as long as she lived.

CHAPTER 36

Report

———◆———

WHEN THE AMBULANCE had driven up, adding to his distress, Cox's ears were still ringing from shooting three clips of .500 magnums without the hearing protection of his helmet. He put it on.

Then came the state cops with their double-bubbles, and Cox found himself yelling through his speakers at the troopers, who yelled back and got nasty because it was such a goddamn mess out here. Cox was in no mood to be polite.

He had to get across the highway, to where the other car had crashed, and secure what prisoners and evidence he could before there wasn't anything left worth securing.

He had visions of his opponents from the mobile firefight torching their car and disappearing into the woods along the roadside, necessitating much more explaining than Cox was ready to go through.

So he yelled some more at the troopers and they yelled back at the armed man in government issue, and when they didn't fall in behind him like a recon team, he took his chances and sprinted through a break in the traffic, across the road, still armed and in as dangerous a mood as he'd ever been.

He didn't know whether he was more worried that those enemy bastards might be dead and Ayoub would get to them first, or that there wouldn't be anybody there when he reached the other car. Running across the pavement, he looked over his shoulder once and saw a third state police car pull up, three cops following him across the road, and the paramedics and Ayoub crouched down around the overturned car he'd crashed, the one that still had Frickey in it.

Frickey didn't need him, he told himself when guilt scolded him for leaving her. She was going to be okay, wasn't she? She was once-resurrected, wasn't she? And Ayoub was there with her. Like Ayoub had been there with Paige.

Cox didn't want to think about Paige. He wanted to think about the firefight, get it sorted out in his mind before he ran headlong into an ambush. But everything was hazy. That was why you ran your on-going recon log, because nobody's memory was good in life-or-death situations.

He wished to hell he'd managed to get his helmet on during the firefight, get his cameras up and running so he'd have some record of the proceedings to support his claims when those cops behind him got time to realize they'd better start asking questions.

But that was for later. Now he needed to collect what evidence he could, to satisfy Kipling in Washington and back up Paige. To do what they'd promised—pin Raymond Godfrey's butt to the wall, now that Godfrey had ordered something as stupid as a hit on Paige Barnett.

Cox had no doubt that the car with the shooters in it had been dispatched by IST. But when he got to their crash site, he saw two cars and he was damned if he could remember the second one.

He'd shot at it, though: there were nice big, armor-piercing magnum holes in both cars' bodies. Bless nonregulation firearms; all he'd had in his rifle was minimum-penetration ammo, left over from shipboard use, and plasma, which would have burned his evidence to shit.

As his feet hit the shoulder and then the grass and he slowed, handgun ready and his helmet recording with all sensors on maximum boost so that he could hear the bitching of the cops following behind, he suppressed an urge to hit the dirt and crawl forward on his elbows.

According to his infrared, there were living guys in at least one of those cars. He was grateful once again for the quality of his equipment. His recon suit hadn't just intimidated the local cops enough to keep them from disarming him out of hand, it was giving him the strategic edge without which Det Cox wasn't any better than the guys in jodhpurs behind him.

He stopped where he was, crouched down low to present as small a target as possible, and waved the men behind him forward like they were his. The signals he gave automatically brought the cops scuttling up to him through the grass. He didn't even think about whether they were going to take his orders, he just gave them quietly through his speakers:

"Two alive in the closer car; let's keep 'em that way. Infrared gives me weapons signatures, so keep low. On my mark, okay?"

One cop muttered, "Who the hell *is* this guy?"

Another replied, "Some friend of the one with the don't-fuck ID. Just do what he says. If he's bogus, we can arrest him later."

Cox gave the signal and moved out against the closer car, unconcerned with the police now that he was sure they weren't going to shoot him in the back.

He had at least two targets capable of shooting him in the front. But they didn't.

When he reached the first car, he realized why: Both combatants were alive, but one had a bad head wound and the other was unconscious. Cox already had the head-shot man's ID out when the cops came up behind him.

"IST," Cox said as if that was going to mean anything to the cops. He leaned down and got the second man's wallet out of his breast pocket. "Both IST, for the record. Get those medics over here. The last thing I want is any of these bastards to die before we can question them."

Now one of the cops said, "'We?' What the hell's going on here—sir?"

"Special op," Cox said vaguely. What would Kipling want him to say? "I gotta call this in to Washington as soon as we've got these prisoners secure. You guys have to help me keep 'em in custody long enough to see what DC wants to do—no quick bailouts, okay? Some way you can do that?"

"Not until we know what—"

A third state trooper interrupted, "Look, we'll shake out the collars later, guys. Let's see what's in the other car. You with the soldier suit—you want to use that surveillance stuff on the other car with us? Or are these two all you're interested in?"

"Right with you. All I need is these guys in holding. Give me that, and impound these vehicles so we can count the bullet holes, and I'll give you

everything I get: recon photos, collars, credit—
whatever."

"Deal," said the third cop quickly, and came forward, talking into his hand-held transceiver to the
radio-car across the road.

The other wrecked car held two more IST
players, and these shot at Cox, until they saw the
state cops. Then they started trying to talk their
way out of it. But the troopers had had to dodge
the bullets aimed at Cox, and they were now in a
much more certain frame of mind: Cox was a good
guy; the guys in the IST cars were bad guys who'd
just shot at state police.

Handcuffs and by-the-book procedures ensued,
none of which were any of Cox's business once his
helmet had recorded the hostiles firing at him.

He had everything he needed to get Godfrey, he
was sure. While the state cops were busy with the
prisoners, he took off his helmet and slipped away,
back across the three southbound lanes now barri-
caded by nose-to-nose police cars, and wandered
among the confusion of approaching tow trucks
and highway trucks with detour signs on trailers
and the paramedics running toward the IST crash
site.

There were more police to deal with on this side
of the road, but the officer he'd struck the deal
with must have called ahead. Nobody tried to disarm Cox or obstruct him in any way as he went
looking for his own people.

Frickey had been freed from their crumpled car,
and it was her use of the Special Science cards
Kipling had given them that had really cut
through the red tape. She was sitting stubbornly
on the ground beside a stretcher, loudly refusing to
get in the ambulance. Paige and Ayoub were
standing beside her, arm in arm.

"Hey, Frickey—thanks for the help with protocol," Cox said as he squatted down by her, helmet in hand, looking for harm.

She was scraped, like a regular human; there was blood clotting on her cheek. She brushed at her hair. "Det, I should have been with you, but it took them so damned long to get me out of that car—"

"It's okay." He craned his neck to glance at Paige, under Ayoub's arm. "You feelin' all right, IST lady?"

"I—yes, a little shaken up; a whopper of a headache. I'm sorry I panicked."

"Human nature," Cox shrugged, then regretted his choice of words. "Those guys across the road are wounded, and that's fine with me. They've got IST identification, Paige. We have to call Kipling right away. If he agrees, I'm going to shoot you right down to DC. No use waiting for more trouble."

He turned back to Frickey. "Sure you're fit to travel?"

"All I need is you to convince these paramedics."

"They can't take you against your will unless they're arresting you, which they better not be," Cox said, straightening up to go talk to whoever was in command of the state police.

Maybe if he'd had Paige with him to run political interference, it would have been cleaner. Cox didn't have the patience for finesse. He sure as hell had been driving to endanger and attempting vehicular homicide, you bet. But he'd been doing it on behalf of the US government and that was all he was willing to explain until he talked to Kipling.

He said, exasperated, "Look here, officer, you're not dealing with a civilian—best you can really do is hold me for MPs from Hanscom, if you want to try being a pain in the ass. I helped your guys over across the way, when the enemy started shooting ..."

"We don't have enemies in Massachusetts, soldier. All I'd like you to do is come back to my barracks and fill out a statement. You'll want to do that anyhow, right? To prosecute these IST people? Press charges?"

"Paige!" Cox hollered at the top of his lungs. "Get over here."

When she appeared, he told the cop, "This is Paige Barnett. She's the one those guys were trying to kill. Paige, get with this officer and explain what you want. Tell him you'll press charges for attempted murder and get through the paperwork as fast as you can. We're going to their station, where I expect to call Kipling. Until then, wing it, okay?"

She blinked like a cat caught in the headlights of an oncoming car. There was something wrong about her, and Cox didn't want to think about what it might be. She seemed too dazed, too shaken, even for somebody who'd just been shot at and crashed by a company she used to work for.

Cox left as soon as Paige had the state cop's attention, and found he didn't really want to go back to Ayoub and Frickey. He walked around to the far side of the ambulance and leaned against it. One of the paramedics was smoking and Cox bummed a cigarette.

Frickey found him there. "Det, they're bringin' the wounded IST prisoners over. We did great!" Her eyes were shining too brightly, like Ayoub's eyes shined.

Cox looked at his feet. "What happened with Paige? There was so much blood."

"You know what happened. Please, Det, don't be afraid of—"

"I'm not afraid, I'm fucking outnumbered. All by my lonesome down here with just you guys, whatever you—" His voice cracked and he clamped his mouth shut.

Frickey reached out to comfort him and he ducked away. "Det..."

"Don't 'Det' me. I needed you back there and where were you? Here with your goddamn freak—"

"Det, that's not fair. It's not true. You're just tired."

"Great, what are you, my mother? The ghost of my mother? Some zombie ranger who can't get dead no matter what—"

"Negative, Sergeant Cox," she said stiffly and one of the damned highway trucks pulled up just then, so he saw bright tears on her cheeks. "Don't feel this way, please. We love you. I—"

"Frickey, you're not even human anymore! Don't say shit like that to me. I want to finish up with you and your two zombie buddies and ship out for somewhere that the damned revolution isn't going to hit for the rest of my natural life. You copy, Corporal? I've had enough. Paige, too. Next it's gonna be me and let me tell you, I ain't ready."

Frickey's head bowed. She jammed her hands in her suit pockets and stared at the ground for a long time. When she looked up, she said, "For Paige's sake, don't talk to her like this, not yet. She's too shaky."

"Yeah, I bet." Cox threw his cigarette into the grass, ground it with his heel, and walked over to the state police cars to wait for his ride to the station.

They couldn't all ride together. He ended up beside Barnett in the back seat of one cruiser and she kept trying to take his hand. Eventually, he wedged his helmet between his knees and let her.

Her hand was cold as ice and shaking; she was shivering all over. He didn't want to look at her. He felt like she'd betrayed him. He'd done everything right, but it had all turned out wrong. He'd won the battle but lost the war. It wasn't the first time. He ought to be able to handle it.

But he couldn't. He kept thinking about Reynolds and Fritz Schultz, wondering whether they were happy living as cognizant chunks of rock or subatomic particles or whatever kind of life they had now. Not as humans, certainly—there wasn't enough left of either venue for that.

He wanted to wake up from this bitch of a dream and find out he was still in his Hanscom hotel room, in endless debrief that never resulted in a tour of X-66B.

That never resulted in him meeting Paige Barnett. Or thinking maybe it would matter that he had met her. She was further out of reach now than she'd been that first night he'd walked into her apartment and realized he hadn't earned enough to pay her yearly rent in his whole career as a ranger.

Now she was like Ayoub, like Frickey. And it was a barrier he didn't even want to try to cross.

They didn't talk on the way to the state trooper barracks. When they arrived, he bludgeoned his way through the confusion and got on the horn to Kipling in Washington, who was at home asleep and could be roused only when Cox declared to his aide, "This is a goddamned national security emergency, sonny. What's your name?"

Instead of the aide's name, he got Kipling's home number.

Kipling listened to what Cox had to say with only an occasional groan or grunt, and then sighed deeply. "That's the whole story, Sergeant? Nothing you've left out?"

"That's it, sir."

"All right, here's what you do: put me on with the ranking statie and I'll clear you to leave ASAP. That's after Paige Barnett has filled out an official complaint. Then you'll have a police escort out to Hanscom, where I'll get you a plane down here. Tell Barnett not to worry about a lawyer. We'll get one here in the District. That suit you?"

"Yeah, fine. I just want to get back in time for my physical—want to ship out again, soon, if you can manage it, sir."

"You and Frickey?"

"That's her decision. I don't want to be tied up in Washington procedurals, that's all. I'll give you one more deposition, the transcript from my suit, and I'm out of this, okay?"

"Okay, Cox, okay. Don't get nervous on me now. You did a wonderful job, especially by not killing those IST henchmen. We'll make sure we interrogate the truth out of them long before IST's lawyers can spring them."

"I couldn't have killed 'em if I tried," Cox muttered. He'd been so careful when he'd been shooting. He remembered now. He'd tried like hell not to give Ayoub another chance to do his stuff. And then Paige had gone and died on him, although she wasn't admitting it. He was getting so he could tell the resurrected ones . . .

"Excuse me, sir?"

"I just asked you what it was you said, Sergeant."

"Nothin'. Garbage. I'm just a little battle-fatigued, that's all, sir. I didn't expect anything like this down here, even though you told me that was what you wanted."

"Not what I wanted, Sergeant. What I expected. What I had reason to hope IST would feel pressed enough to try. Let's table this until you get down here. By the time the *Malibu* docks, we're going to have all the evidence we need to get not only IST and Raymond Godfrey, but probably Locke and Singer too, and maybe Wiley as well, for collusion. Now, put me on with that ranking trooper, and I'll smooth the way for you."

"Yes sir; thank you, sir," said Cox, and palmed the mouthpiece. "My boss wants to talk to yours," he told the trooper watching over him, and the man went running.

It was going to be all right, he told himself. It was going to be fine. Kipling hadn't said Cox *couldn't* get out-system right away. It was going to be just like it used to be, as soon as he delivered the three resurrected ones to Kipling in Washington.

Dennis Cox didn't want to be anywhere near Earth when the truth came out, and he especially didn't want to be close enough to Ayoub, Paige Barnett, and Frickey that he'd acquire any guilt by association.

He wanted to be in some nice clean ranger venue, like he'd told Frickey, where none of this resurrection stuff could ever find him.

He was feeling lots better by the time the cops were done with Paige, probably because his pharmakit got worried about him and somebody had brought him coffee and a pack of cigarettes.

He was feeling enough better that when Frickey came out and found him on the front steps, under the clear, starry sky, he didn't shy away from her.

"You okay, Det?" she said. She had coffee in one hand and a doughnut in the other.

"Yeah. Better. Sorry I got pumped up back there."

"I..." She moved closer, stopped. "I don't want to lose you, Det."

"Yeah, you said that before. Kipling says we can still make the physical and get a tour, next week. Be finished in DC by then." He met her eyes and held them. He wasn't scared of her. He wasn't scared of any of them; he couldn't have her thinking he was.

"That so?" she replied, and raised an eyebrow. "What about Paige?"

"Not my problem."

"So you're going back out?" She moved closer, throwing her doughnut into the bushes by the cement staircase. Their shoulders brushed.

"Soon as I can. I don't belong here. You should know that. You don't—didn't...Never mind."

"Not never mind. You want company, maybe I could get in your unit again." There was a wicked grin on her face, just like the old Frickey grin, and he wanted to put an arm around her.

She put hers around his waist and leaned her head on his shoulder for just a moment before she looked up at the stars. "Beautiful, huh?"

"Out there? Sure is. Look, about resur—"

Just then Paige and Ayoub came out, flanked by troopers. Paige was chatting with one officer gaily, as if nothing significant had happened tonight.

Frickey moved away from Cox and Cox unclipped his helmet from his left hip as he preceded Paige down the steps, taking them two at a time.

Frickey was right with him, pulling up her visor scans and checking the area for secreted hostiles. The cops weren't looking for any more trouble;

somebody had to watch out for Paige and Ayoub until they could be gotten safely to Washington.

Cox had given the police car in which his charges would ride a thorough once-over before it occurred to him that Paige didn't need protecting anymore. No more protecting than Freedom Ayoub did. Still, Kipling wouldn't like it if there was any more trouble.

But there wasn't, not all the way to Washington. Paige and Ayoub slept like babies throughout the whole flight in the little military jet Kipling had commandeered for them, and Frickey kept trying to convince Cox, any way she knew how, that she was just like she used to be, "but better, Det. Better."

Somehow, he kept trying to believe her.

CHAPTER 37

American Streets

———◆———

PAIGE SPENT FOUR days meeting with Kipling, four nights at a good hotel, four sunsets and sunrises walking American streets with Freedom Ayoub and the two rangers. It was good to be home, she kept telling herself.

When she would watch Ayoub on their long walks, his big soft eyes filled with wonder and his body radiating everything about the holy way that had made all she'd been through worthwhile, she was freed from doubt.

But when she was in the International Club

Building, in Kipling's office, alone and negotiating all their fates, she'd lose that feeling and fear would creep in to chill her.

I died. I died. I'm alive. I'm different, one part of her would mourn. And another would retort, *I'm stronger. I'm in receipt of something I don't yet understand, that's all.*

Kipling didn't understand it either. He asked Paige on the fifth day, "What if what Cox told me about Ayoub and Frickey is true?"

She said, "Surely you've thought about how it would sound if anyone in your position—or mine—tried to float such a notion publicly. " She felt like a thief in the night. She stared into Kipling's pale eyes, searching for some intimation that he knew, that he wanted confirmation because he realized the importance of the gift—that he wasn't afraid of her, or trying to trap her.

She was sure Cox knew. She was beginning to think that Kipling knew as well and would put her away for her whole precious eternity—and Ayoub with her. Put them away and hand the key to their cages over to the successive masters of the Oval Office every four years.

She felt like a criminal, withholding the truth of redemption, resurrection, and the holy way from Kipling, the most sympathetic representative of the American government she was likely to find.

As if reading her mind, Kipling said, "Now about Mister Ayoub—he's not, technically, an American citizen. We can give him temporary visas, of course, for as long as we need him—the proceedings against Godfrey and IST are going to take at least a year, what with continuances and appeals and the related actions against—"

Paige interrupted, "Just in case what Sergeant

Cox told you about Ayoub is true, you mean? Because if it is, we wouldn't want any other government to have him."

"Paige," said Kipling, leaning forward, his eyes full of cautionary flags, "I don't think this is the time or place to talk about hypotheticals. I'm offering political asylum; we've got Ayoub's dossier and we can do that—we can qualify him, given that he was shipped out-system from Chad for political crimes. We'll process him as a defector, then we can give him money and support—after all, we need him here for the trials."

It was a generous offer. She said so, even though both of them knew it was made for selfish reasons, and reasons no one wanted to discuss.

"Good, so you'll put it to him. I want you all in the Washington area for the forseeable."

"All?" She'd spoken to Frickey, who'd told her sadly that Cox was determined to get out-system as soon as possible. And she'd been there when Frickey told Ayoub that she wanted to go with Det.

Ayoub had bowed his head and spread his yellow-nailed hands and advised, "Follow your conscience, Corporal Frickey."

Now Kipling said, "All—you and Ayoub aren't exactly on IST's list of favorite persons. You'll need some protection. You get along well with those rangers, and they can do the job for you—did do it."

"Cox doesn't want—"

"Cox is a soldier. He'll obey the orders he gets. And we think he might have more to tell us, when he decompresses fully."

Paige's heart ached for Dennis Cox, who'd seen this trap before any of them, and risked so much in spite of it. She wanted to tell Kipling no, insist that Cox shouldn't be forced to stay. But she wanted him to. And she knew Freedom did too. They had to stay together, if they could.

Fear overswept her, sitting in a comfortable chair in Kipling's paneled office, as it did occasionally now when the holy way opened before her and she saw the world and everything in it from a perspective much deeper, and yet more lofty, than she'd had before. Cox would get out to his beloved stars eventually—they had eternity. And take Frickey with him, because those two were suited to spread resurrection among the far-flung children of the Earth, among the risk-takers and the peace-keepers and the explorers.

But now they were needed here. It was an imperative that came from the holy way, not from Kipling, who was a mere tool of fate. Inside her a voice whispered, "Courage," and with it came a joy that vanquished fear, and a certain knowledge that she had as much to learn as she had to do.

Redemption wasn't going to come easy, not to her, not to America, not to the world or the stars. But come it would. It got closer with every breath that she and Ayoub and Frickey took.

Ayoub had gone to Cox last night and tried to ease the ranger's distress. The black man had come back with a frown on his face, saying, "If Sergeant Det Cox can be taught to love life, then the world can learn it too."

Paige had known exactly what Freedom meant, because her new clarity brought her much more than the simple words Ayoub spoke: Freedom wanted Cox to learn not to fear the strangeness, or what he did not understand, or the changes ahead.

They all had to learn that. Paige had to, too. At first she'd been so disoriented, coming back into life from death and not being able even to mourn.

Cox had been trying to mourn for her, Freedom said. "But mourning is not appropriate in the face of such a gift." Freedom had said it to Cox's face, walking on the Mall at sunset. Cox had just looked at Paige and said, "Right. Sorry."

First must come the learning, then the doing. She'd looked at Ayoub, his face glowing with reflected sunset, and said, "We're going so fast." She recalled how tentative Ayoub had been, when first reborn; how angry Frickey had been, how confused.

Paige was doing only a little bit better than Frickey, and she'd had longer to come to terms with the holy way before she'd died. She'd looked at Cox, the last of them still unchanged—at Cox who was so defensive when he wanted to be protective, so frightened that the rest of them were somehow out of reach.

And under the blazing sunset sky of Washington, it had all made harmonious sense, suddenly—even Cox's pain.

Even Kipling, who sat now squinting at her in his office, waiting for a reply. She picked up her handbag and looked at her watch, "Well, they'll be downstairs waiting for me, Major Kipling. I'll ask the rangers if they'll stay on. I'd prefer them, of course, to strangers. But I don't want them ordered to stay against their will." It was a simple tenet of the new faith: you respected one another, inflicted no unnecessary hardship. You touched the hearts and minds of your fellows, and hurting them was like hurting yourself.

It would be a better world, someday. Someday in her lifetime. She shook Kipling's hand and promised she'd call him tomorrow, then brushed off his offer to walk her to the elevator.

In the taupe hallway, she waited calmly for the

elevator to take her down to the stone-and-cork lobby, beyond which K Street was busy at rush hour.

The rangers, in raincoats because it was drizzling outside, were waiting for her in the lobby. Det always looked naked without his recon suit. She smiled at the guard behind the directory board, and fell in between Cox and Frickey.

Not until they were out on the street did Paige ask, as casually as she could, "Where's Freedom?"

Cox grimaced, taking her by the elbow to lead her around the corner, down into the parking garage. "He'll be right where we left him, he promised. How'd it go today?"

"They want to know if you two will stay with me—with us, with Freedom and me—until the trials are over. Kipling thinks IST may try something; or Godfrey may. Godfrey's not without resources, simply without conscience." She bit her lip. She hadn't reached Freedom's level of generosity toward failings of the human spirit. She wasn't sure she ever would. But she'd seen the way Frickey was changing for the better, and she'd felt the deepening of emotions in herself. The holy way had to be felt; in words, it was too simple: the words were all short and very old, the way was one mankind had been trudging toward over centuries of struggle: life begets life; life loves life; life saves life and treasures each spark of it.

It was that spark that lit Frickey's eyes; Paige had begun to think she could see it in her own. Frickey touched Paige's arm as they got into the car and Paige felt strength come into her, and that deeper calm of the sort she'd learned to accept from Freedom.

Something was wrong, she knew from Cox's set jaw and Frickey's touch. Something more than

Cox's delayed reaction to Paige's proposition. But Frickey didn't want Paige to worry about it.

So Paige, in the front seat beside Cox, said, "Well, Det, will you stay for a while? On assignment to us? Kipling assures me it will all be by the book, and after the trial, you'll get your out-system trip."

Instead of answering, Cox wheeled out of the parking space and goosed the car up the ramp toward the kiosk and K Street beyond. "Now that you've had adventure, Dream Date, how did you like it? Was it worth it?"

She knew what he was asking, so she answered, "Dennis, it's worth even the ultimate price. Worth dying for."

Frickey put in from the back seat, "Worth living for."

Cox arched in the seat, took a bill from his hip-pocket wallet, and as he did, Paige saw the holstered side arm behind his hip. Cox couldn't go unarmed; his faith still rested only in his own ability.

"You'll be safer with me and Frickey than with anybody else," he said at last. "But I want to cut my own deal with Kipling—we might as well get Frickey her sergeant's stripes out of this."

Paige wanted to throw her arms around Cox and hug him, but he was collecting his receipt and pulling the car out into traffic.

Frickey, in the back seat, let out a noisy breath and said, "Fuckin'-A."

"Now that that's settled, maybe you can do somethin' with Ayoub, Paige. Me and Frickey been tryin' for three hours. He found a tent city with a bunch of bums in it and we can't get him out."

"Oh, no." It was too soon. They had to go cautiously.

When they reached the tent city, Ayoub wasn't there. But one of the homeless knew where he'd gone. Freedom Ayoub was all they could talk about. He'd been there when an indigent started coughing up blood, and now the man was eating soup and telling everybody how he'd died and been reborn.

It took them the rest of the afternoon to find Freedom. Paige had no idea which Washington slum they were in. There was mist in the streets, and dusk was coming on.

Freedom was wandering in an alley full of trash-cans and human refuse, and he had a dazed and stumbling old woman under his arm.

Cox stopped the car and ran toward him, cursing, "—scare me like that again, you black bastard, I'm gonna' leave your ass for IST."

Freedom looked at Cox, and at Paige and Frickey, coming up behind Cox, and nodded. "So you'll stay with us, Det Cox? Good. You cannot run from redemption, not from yourself, or what the holy way has taught you." Freedom smiled his bright, small-toothed smile and said to the tiny, filthy woman looking at Cox uncomprehendingly, "I want you to meet some friends of mine—Sergeant Det Cox, Corporal Allie Frickey, and Paige Barnett."

The woman who'd just been resurrected blinked at Cox and held out a fragile, trembling hand that the ranger took in his.

Reading—
For The
Fun Of It

Ask a teacher to define the most important skill for success and inevitably she will reply, "the ability to read."

But millions of young people never acquire that skill for the simple reason that they've never discovered the pleasures books bring.

That's why there's RIF—Reading is Fundamental. The nation's largest reading motivation program, RIF works with community groups to get youngsters into books and reading. RIF makes it possible for young people to have books that interest them, books they can choose and keep. And RIF involves young people in activities that make them want to read—**for the fun of it.**

The more children read, the more they learn, and the more they **want** to learn.

There are children in your community—maybe in your own home—who need RIF. For more information, write to:

RIF
Dept. BK-3
Box 23444
Washington, D.C.
20026

Founded in 1966, RIF is a national, nonprofit organization with local projects run by volunteers in every state of the union.

NEENA GATHERING

VALERIE NIEMAN COLANDER

It's the twenty-first century and America is no more. The U.S. has split into sections and destroyed itself with chemical warfare. A civilization based on technology, communications, mass transportation, factories, schools, culture, and medicine has ceased to exist. Forced to grow up quickly under such conditions, can Neena eke out a living while fighting off roving bands of survivors as well as the misguided attention of her uncle, Ted? Or will she choose to become the symbol of a reborn nation with the horribly scarred but loving Arden?

ISBN: 0-517-00643-X   Price: $2.95

LOOK FOR THIS ADVENTURE FROM PAGEANT BOOKS!

WINTER WORLD

C. J. Mills

Karne Halarek will inherit a planetary kingdom—if his enemies will allow him to come of age! This first book in the Starker IV series is a chilling account of the power-mad and evil men of the House Harlan, whose plotting against Karne knows no limits. Forced to dwell in vast underground complexes, the inhabitants of Starker IV are at the mercy of their severe winters and their captors—unless Karne Halarek can root out the traitors, quell a slave rebellion, and swear the sacred oath before his eighteenth birthday!

ISBN: 0-517-00065-2   Price: $2.95

EXPLORE A NEW DIMENSION IN SCIENCE FICTION!